CITY OF BLOK

By the same author

THE THERAPY OF AVRAM BLOK
THE DEATH OF MOISHE–GANEF

CITY OF BLOK

SIMON LOUVISH

[signature]

Well, whoduya know ? ?

COLLINS
8 Grafton Street, London W1
1988

William Collins Sons & Co. Ltd
London · Glasgow · Sydney · Auckland
Toronto · Johannesburg

BRITISH LIBRARY CATALOGUING IN PUBLICATION DATA

Louvish, Simon, *1947–*
    City of Blok.
    I. Title
    823[F]

ISBN 0-00-223395-9

First published 1988
Copyright © Simon Louvish 1988

Typeset in Linotron Bembo by
Rowland Phototypesetting Ltd, Bury St Edmunds, Suffolk
Made and printed in Great Britain by
Hartnolls Ltd, Bodmin, Cornwall

For Mairi and
for Tim O'Keeffe
above and beyond the call of duty

'You think you cute,
so you piss on the floor.
Be a hero
and shit on the ceiling.'

Address on Cleveland Greyhound
Bus station men's convenience

Instructor: What are ethics?
Student: Ummm . . . ethics is like when someone wants to
             kill you and you go to kill him first.

Classroom Vignettes, political
science seminar, recorded by
Professor Don Peretz

'History is a nightmare from which I am trying to awake.'

Stephen Dedalus,
in James Joyce's *Ulysses*

MORIAH

Where am I?
Who am I?
What am I?

Your name is Avram Blok. Your father is Baruch. Your mother, Shoshanah. Conception, Budapest, in the ruins of war. Birth, aboard the immigrant ship, *Irma Klein*, en route from Trieste to Palestine. Your first utterance, a strangled cry, as usual. (Do we have to labour the obvious?) Education: Jerusalem, kindergarten, primary, secondary. Army service, from 1965. Your army number: 958633. Your identity card number: 3425648. Your health insurance number: 876432. The size of your shoes: Nine. The size of your collar: 40. Inside leg: 78 centimetres. Colour of hair: Brown (or was until depilation due to natural causes in coma; no carcinogenic evidence). Colour of eyes: Brown. Present location: Bed 15, Ward 6, T—t State Mental Hospital. Present condition: wheelchair case. Distinguishing features: A long record of chronic malingering. GET ON YOUR FEET, SLACKER! We don't have to tell you all this, do we? You know the whole fucking schmeer. Faking innocence as usual, eh, Yul Brynner? Lying there quiet as a corpse, offering nothing, evading your responsibilities . . .

The Man With No Past.

A likely story.

WE KNOW HOW TO DEAL WITH YOUR KIND!

I know nothing.
I see nothing.
I remain in fog.
Gradually, shapes and patterns emerge.

11

Contours of the bed, line, white, metal bars, tubes entering the body, the left nostril, the nose, a linkage to the outside world, part of which can be wheeled down ruts of tiles, the walls of the corridors, dull blue-grey, plaster bulging like random braille symbols – Remember the Rorschach, brothers! clues for the moronity of science, the limits of organized imagination, order in the swirl, meaning in chaos, desire under the elms, teahouses in august moons, decembrist rebellions, armies on the march, Uzzymandias, remember the alarm-O, sirens in the night, blackouts at noon, the winter sun in the crosslights of barred windows, rumbling vehicles without, the sound of thunder, waterworks from the sky, laughter and tears, jam sandwiches, the old schoolhouse door, benches at dawn, wellington boots at mourning, fusillades over graves, cantankerous cantors, the bar mitzvah boy, the hand writing, the open Book, examinations failed, certificates passed, forms of progress, urine and faecal, the little jar of piss, the phial of crap, whitecoats to the rescue, prick of the needle, a tumescence renewed, shades of Nurse Nili, the philosopher stoned, the unknown soldier, absent friends, keening relatives, clerks from the ministry, army charlie chaplains, prick of the needle, the wheeled chair, comrades in misfortune, sunflower seeds underfoot, grinning nutcase faces, One of Us, Return to Sender, Address Unknown, tumescence again, rub-a-dub-dub, laxation certified, a self-expressed toilet graffito:

KILL THE DOCTORS!! FREE AVRAM BLOK!
A mere drop in the ocean . . .

Anybody there??

– Good morning. My name is Yakin. I am to try to help you to recover the hidden power of language. Speaking in tongues, ha, ha, ha. I believe it's all there, just reserved for better times. I teach deaf and dumb persons, but your case should be simpler. We are dealing with memory, which is like sex, no? heh, heh, heh. Once practised, never completely erased.
We shall begin with pictures:

12

— chicken

— sabbath
candlesticks

— armoured
command car

— Afternoon, *habibi*. My name is Kimchi. I am from the Department of Social Services. My aim here is to guide you back into the ambience of society, blah, blah, blah. For three years you have been, how shall we say, in orbit, in the stratosphere . . . But while you were up there, lo and behold, the State has been paying you five hundred shekels a month health insurance benefit! How about that? Now, mind you, if we were paying you in dollars, you'd be in clover, but you know how it is, in this climate, money rots, nothing's constant. Fiduciary corrosion. Very painful. Nevertheless, five hundred shekels a month, a total of eighteen thousand shekels; with tax deductions and all that goes with the empire, protecting us against our Enemies, Goddamn them, that leaves you with about ten grand. At the going rate, if you can get off your ass, comrade, you might clear eighteen hundred dollars. Am I the

13

bearer of Good News or am I not, Goddamit? Let's shake hands on it and remember: the State is not just a mountain of shit, boy – we look after our own! You don't understand? Well, no wonder. What you lack is a true sense of history . . .

HISTORY, MAN! Bend your ears: on May 17, 1977, Menachem Begin of the opposition Unity Party became the Prime Minister of the State of Israel. Born on August 16, 1913, in Brest Litovsk on the River Bug, then in Poland, he had been active in the 'Beitar' youth movement founded by one Vladimir Ze'ev Jabotinsky, a charismatic diaspora politician who believed the Jewish State would come about in Palestine not by wheeler-dealing in the back rooms of super-powers but by an act of rebellion and conquest, by fire and sword: 'In Blood and Fire Judaea Fell; In Blood and Fire Judaea Shall Rise Again,' his followers, and Menachem Volfovitch Begin among them, sang. Menachem Volfovitch wished to join the irregular soldiers of Jabotinsky's National Military Organization – the 'Irgun Tsva'i Le'umi' – in Palestine, which was fighting for Jewish sovereignty by means of violent retaliation against Arab acts of terror and violence in their own rebellion against the Jewish settlers and the British Mandate Government. However, now hear this, schmendrick – Menachem Volfovitch was delayed in his Palestinian anabasis by the German army's invasion of Poland in 1939, which precipitated him, as a Pole and a Jew, east, towards the Russians, who arrested the poor bugger and sentenced him to eight years in a Siberian labour camp as an 'agent of British Imperialism'.

Meanwhile, you son of a she dog's spittle, down south, in Egyptland, a number of young army officers were muttering ominously under their moustaches about the onerousness of British rule and eyeing, as the war progressed, the growing success of General Rommel in the Western deserts with more than a smidgin of favour. Among them were two firebrands, Captains Gamal Abd-el Nasser and Anwar el-Sadat, a quiet youth from a village in Upper Egypt. In February 1942 the British humiliated the Egyptian King, Farouk, who had grown so fat he could hardly waddle from one twelve-course beano to another, by forcing upon him at gunpoint a Prime Minister of their own choosing.

The young officers, despising the corrupt King, but despising the British even more, were inclined to welcome the approach of a Nazi agent, Herr Eppler, alias Hussein Jaafer, who had crossed the desert in a jeep cunningly daubed with British markings with a moneybelt of fake UK fivers. Ach, *Himmel!* he was rumbled, however, by an Egyptian dancer named Hikmat Fahmi, who shopped the lot to British Intelligence.

Meanwhile, in Siberia – are you still listening? – young Begin, who had exhausted both his Soviet interrogators and the common criminals in the Gulag with filibusters on the subject of Zionism, Blood and Fire and the Redemption of the Homeland he had as yet not laid one eye on, was released suddenly as a result of a treaty between Yosske Stalin and the exiled Polish General Sikorski. Menachem later described the aftermath thus: 'We proceeded on our way to freedom. On foot, in goods trains, in passenger trains, clinging to the sides. Southwards, southwards . . . The Caspian port of Krasnovodsk . . . the small Persian port of Pahlevi . . . We crossed the mighty mountains. Babylon. Bagdad . . . And here was Transjordan. Our heritage . . . The eastern bank of the Jordan – Eretz Israel. The military convoy stopped. We rested. I left the automobile, waded a little way into the grass, and drank in the odour of the fields of my Homeland . . .'

Jasmine. Honeysuckle. And myrrh. And frankincense. And saffron. And calamus. And cinnamon. And fresh dew. And pomegranates. And lemon trees. And other assorted Jaffa produce. And pine. And coniferous fir. And vineyards. And fields of barley. And wheat. And cornoil. And sunflower seeds. And cashew nuts. And *fistuk halabi*. And roast chestnuts. And salted peanuts. And fresh bagels. And ice cream on the bustle of Dizengoff Street. And falafel. And turkey schnitzel. And blintzes. And hamburgers in stale pitta. And kebabs. And *shawarma*. And grilled hearts. And grease spattering on whispering embers. And softened asphalt at the peak of summer. And rubber tyres burning during political turmoil. And the sweating armpits of men and women hanging on to straps in buses. And the diesel fumes, of buses, trucks, trains. And tar on the packed beach. And sulphur, from the pride of industry. And petrol, from an excess of napalm deposited upon our Enemies . . .

But Avram Blok was still engaged on his long day's journey out of night and fog . . . By day, wheeled about the dull grey corridors of the asylum by nurses or his fellow inmates, by night, the long march through the nuclear wasteland of the holocaust of his choice. The earth, fused perhaps into a flat grainy surface, the seas boiled away, skeletons of fish everywhere, starving fishmongers, stalls and kiosks of budding post-apocalypse entrepreneurs, piled with bric-à-brac of lost civilizations: bottle openers, swiss army knives, defunct walkmans, burnt-out dishwashers, fairy liquid, model aeroplanes from cornflake packets. Blok, crawling like a flea upon a formica tabletop. Naked, without even a pocket handkerchief to hide his dangling dong. A single lightbulb flickering above him, continually at the point of failure. 'Electrician! Electrician!' But only shadows came to answer his call . . .

–You hear me, lad? This is the second lesson: building a vocabulary. Pay attention to the following sample passage: 'Yossi goes to the post office to post a letter. The letter is addressed to his uncle, Benyamin, who lives in West Germany. Uncle Benyamin has a dry goods store in Hamburg. How happy he is to receive Yossi's letter. He shows it to his sister, Gertrude, who is Yossi's aunt. She is overjoyed. A letter from Yossi! she cries. We must frame it on the wall, along with your graduation certificate and the testimonial from the Israel National Fund. Uncle Benyamin goes down to the hardware store to look for a picture frame . . . Sit up straight, Mister Blok, I am beginning to suspect what they say about you is true. They are paying me to try and help you, not to jerk off by myself out here. I see I'm not getting through even one millimetre. OK, let's take it from the top . . .

HISTORY, DICKHEAD!

– Gamal Abd-el Nasser, leader of the Egyptian revolution of 1952, no less, died of a heart attack in 1970, three years after suffering the defeat of his people in the Six Day War of 1967. Remember? Those Were the Days, We All Were There, et cetera . . . Anwar el-Sadat, the peasant son of Upper Egypt, became the new President of Egypt. Within three years the bastard had launched a surprise attack against our Hallowed Homeland,

16

Israel, October 1973, resulting in the recovery by the Gypos, Goddamn them, of the western part of the Sinai peninsula occupied by Israel in that '67 War. But Anwar el-Sadat, give him his due, always said of himself: 'Each step I have taken over the years has been for the good of Egypt, and has been designed to serve the cause of right, liberty, and peace.' *Ach, so.* But the advent of Menachem Begin to power in Israel boded ill for Anwar's dreams. Severe shock waves rocked the Jewish State. Menachem's supporters rejoiced, freed, as they saw it, from the Shackles of Socialism. But the Left feared that the tyranny of the blackest clerical-reaction was at hand. Toothbrushes were packed at the first sign of the midnight knock at the door. But it was, as always, just the downstairs neighbour, desperate for a borrowed yoghourt. A deadly pall of apathy soon descended upon our land. Parliament failed to be dissolved, the tread of jackboots was tardy, the prophets of doom were confounded, for the moment, onerous currency laws were rescinded and MONEY, so long locked in the cage of Labour's national discipline, was LIBERATED! Huzzah! Bravo! Dollars gave song, deutschmarks took wing, francs, sterling and yen chirruped in the unexpected light of day, kronen skipped as deer, Jordanian dinars danced as rams – MONEY! like a rare, intoxicating liquor, flowing in hitherto parched wadis, gurgling into concealed wells dug by some in shrewd anticipation . . . and the river became a flood, and the flood a deluge, and inflation doubled, tripled, quadrupled, and not one fucking plank of a shitten Ark in sight, until, one cold November day, AD 1977, Anwar el-Sadat, deciding to materialize his long-cherished vision and throwing caution to the winds, suddenly descended upon the airport of Tel Aviv-Lod in his Egyptian presidential jet to offer PEACE to the Israeli people! Shock! Joy! Confusion! The Israel Army band played the Egyptian national anthem, Anwar el-Sadat and Menachem Volfovitch Begin embraced. The millennium has arrived!

But Avram Blok was unaware of this as he lay plugged into the intravenous drip at the T—t State Mental Hospital, undergoing a routine relapse. Teams of nurses turning him to prevent bedsores; he was like a barbecue that would never be done. Displaying no flicker of interest in history until that November night, one hour after Anwar el-Sadat's touchdown, when everyone was glued to their television sets observing the unbelievable new dawn – PEACE – the long yearned for, virtually abandoned dream, made reality by the motorcade of limousines flying the flags of Israel and Egypt, belting down the Lod-Jerusalem highway and entering the Holy City from the west, above the ruins of the old Palestinian village of Lifta, past the tall new buildings of the Apartotel and the Jerusalem Hilton, down the twisting turn of the century old lane of Jaffa Road, past the marketplace of Mahaneh Yehuda, the street now lined with people rushing out to view the miracle they had given up hope of witnessing, Jews weeping in their joy at a glimpse of a Pharaoh come to pay his respects to the descendants of Goshen, his brown hand waving in the snappy late autumn air, the flash of his white teeth, the beaming Begin beside him, hard-boiled citizens weeping before their TV screens, while Blok, waking alone in Bed Number 15, Ward 6, suddenly rose, scorning the vital prop of his wheelchair, slithered silently along corridors he could not remember, carrying his drip in his hand like the rod of Moses, closing unerringly in upon his target: the unguarded staff kitchen. Lo! Opening the fridge, emptying a half full pitcher of milk and devouring the cheese and tomato sandwiches the head nurse was keeping for the long night-shift hours. Gobble, gobble, gobble. He ransacked the frigidaire, tearing into cold chicken, spooning out a jar of pungent Telma mustard. Removing the drip carefully, he placed it in the freezer. And the stalactites of the new dawn . . .

★

– Hey, Avremel, don't you recognize your own father? I know, it takes some doing, doesn't it? I've thought of turning all the mirrors in the house to the wall, as they do in Dracula movies. Your mother wanted to come, but she's still not well enough, Avram. Life is a large, coarse toilet brush, just rubbing our substance away. We can soon visit you as ghosts, clanking our chains, ringing our bells – Unclean! Unclean! It's a problem putting it in words . . . Often as you're sitting there, or when you were stuck in the bed, I sat thinking at you . . . mental telepathy, they take these things seriously nowadays. What made you laugh

18

once now makes you cry. What can a father say? I tried my best. One always thinks – my son will be a better man than I. You look back at your own life and cringe. The errors! But despite it all . . . At least we shook ourselves out of our own graveyard. Europe, ruins, rubble, despair. A new country, we thought, new truths, new values. Not an ignoble thought, what do you say? Pass the orange juice? Na, take it, boy, they tell me you're suddenly eating everything. Excellent. Yes, we let you go your own way, didn't we, free of the umbilical cord . . . You went abroad, you saw the world outside. And still, you came back to us. You have to admit that. And what did we give you as a homecoming present? The October War. It nearly broke my heart. But now they say Peace is round the corner. Miracles and wonders in our time! Sadat and Begin kissing – that was a sight. It's been a long time coming . . . It's President Carter, apparently, who pulled the strings. He's the one who says he's born again. A chance you have too, eh, Avremel? From a new womb – zoom, afresh! . . .

Your old friend Avi still asks after you, all the time. He says he'll try to come next week. He has a new girl friend now, a social worker. Life does go on, outside these walls . . . New faces, as old ones drop out . . . Your old flame Nili, remember? No, perhaps not . . . she stopped coming about two years ago. Marriage, children, responsibilities. And your film making friend in Los Angeles, Yissachar, he hasn't written for some time . . . But Avi, Avram, that's solid gold – friends of your childhood don't just vanish . . . Still banging his political drum, out there, you know, Peace Now, et cetera. Mazel tov. They demonstrated, in support of Begin. I never thought I'd see the day. Perhaps, despite the wars, the conflicts, all the hatred, there's a healing process after all . . . It's working out with you, isn't it? We shall win through, asargelusha! The Blokkian Way! Survival, what do you say?

– All right, Avram, pretend you don't know me. Who the fuck cares anyway? Want me to jog your memory? This Is Your Life? – sexy dreams in the old schoolyard . . . the stagnant pool of old pirate ships . . . early erections . . . flaccid falls . . . Shall I warble your Bar Mitzvah portion? Never mind, the waggon rolls on. Me Avi, you Avram. Ug. Comprende? This red-headed lady on my right here is Esther. She is the new star in our firmament. Esther, meet Avram Blok, partner of my mishandled youth. The one that got away, almost. Ah, do I perceive a twinge? You're not fooling me, Avram, the old Blok stirs there: the old Adam seeks Eve. *Cherchez la femme fatale*, preferably with a fat dowry, villa and Volvo, first hand. We have none of those for you. But there is a spare mattress, in our apartment, when you decide to get out of here. Spring yourself from this cemetery, schmegegge! You've been here long enough. That bed has your outline, we could take a wax impression of it. Come on, you son of a bitch! Grab a ticket out of this dump! We need you out there – the Blokkian eye that sees all and takes no prisoners! Your time is up, schmendrick! Arise, Sir Avram! Ding, Ding, Ding! The fucking alarm clock is ringing!

. . . And Esther . . . the full moon face, crowned with flaming red hair, grey eyes, ivory smile . . . She presses her hand on his knee. He extracts a handkerchief and blows his nose. Both his visitors applaud.

DING, DING, DING!
    . . . Nevertheless, the continuation of his night journeys, slow advances, followed by regression . . . Genetic propulsion, struggles in the womb, the attempted abortion of nations . . . landscapes of snow, with burning barracks . . . gas chambers breached by the cannons of advancing Tartar forces . . . Blok, clambering desperately over mounds of corpses . . . brightly-coloured buses drawn up by the warehouses as tourists fire on all cameras . . . click, click, click, at Blok as he waddles, naked through the snow, teeth chattering, eyes bulging, desperately trying to conceal . . .

DING, DING, DING!
    In the morning, his frostbitten feet placed in a tub of boiling hot water by his room-mate and fellow patient, Tsimmes, an old Rumanian incarcerated for *folie de doute* and chronic aphasic dissonance. The old man, thin as a beanpole, twisted as a mismade pretzel, rubbing Blok's feet with a sponge as he nonchalantly whistles a defunct grapefruit commercial:

> If I were only a peeled grapefruit,
> If I were only a peeled grapefruit,
> A pretty girl would eat me up,
> If I were only a peeled grapefruit . . .

For the previous two years he had watched over Blok, wheeling him about the asylum, helping the ward nurses turn him over thrice daily in times of relapse, clipping his beard, toe and fingernails, occasionally rubbing Doctor Jochem's Hormone upon his bare scalp, in the vain hope of vegetation. He had also taken charge of Blok's singed scrapbook, saved miraculously from the fire which had gutted his previous haven, the Moses Klander Institute. Guarding it zealously from prying psychologists, updating it, with the help of other fellow patients, by the meticulous pasting in of blood, urine and faecal test forms, discarded cigarette packs, matchbox covers, bubble gum wrappers, bus tickets dropped by visitors, and available random cuttings from the local ethnic newspapers, *L'Information*, *Uj Kelet*, *Viata Nostra*, *Letzte Neues*, and from the main Hebrew press:

COCKROACH PLAGUE AT BEN GURION AIRPORT.

ZOO WORKERS HELD IN THEFT OF GORILLA'S TV.

PHILIPPINES ARMY SUCCESSFULLY EXPLODES
COCONUT BOMB.

SECURITY FORCES KILL DOG-CATCHER BY MISTAKE.

THE SURGEONS SAT ALL NIGHT BY
THE STRICKEN SHEEP'S BEDSIDE.

Heart Failure: An individual who receives a plastic heart forfeits his status as a human being, Chief Rabbi Goren said today. Anyone who kills an individual with a plastic heart, the Chief Rabbi ruled, could not be accused of homicide.

In the margins of which Tsimmes had written: 'Nobody is a peeled grapefruit.'

★

21

– But we tried, Avremel! We did our best! Escape to the Land of Milk and Honey! Jasmine and myrrh and mutant grapes big as watermelons borne on the shoulders of our spies . . . Ministries of Agriculture, Justice, Education, Defence, even Without Portfolio . . . Ministries of dreams and Historical Destiny . . . loyal followers of the Patriarchs . . . Abraham, Isaac, Jacob, Theodor Herzl, David Ben Gurion, Menachem Begin . . . saints and seers, prophets and loss . . . and people thought they were mad too . . . ! Theodor Herzl, Avram! There was a lunatic for you – the great obsessive, but what a Vision! Theodor Herzl, Avremel, Our Founding Father, the man who caused us all to be here . . . another Budapest boy made good too, isn't that a thought to conjure?

WHO AM I?
WHAT AM I?
HOW DID I GET HERE?
Theodor Herzl, schmegegge! Vienna, Schnitzler and Schriftsteller! The self-confessed ham who once wrote, at the apogee of his visions: 'If I think of it, I still remain the dramatist . . . picking poor people in rags off the streets, putting fine costumes on them, making them perform for the whole world a wonderful pageant of my own composition . . .' Our latter-day prophet, knocking on the doors of sultans, czars, chancellors, with that black beard, those mournful eyes . . . the anti-semites denounced him as the Prince of the Exile, the power behind the Elders of Zion, but it was all just bluff and bluster, magician's tricks, dramatist's wiles . . . although They called our bluff, pretty soon . . . The Jewish State, Avremel – who would have believed it! Who could have believed we'd come so far! It only shows you never know how thin the margin is between madness and sanity, success and failure, fame and derision, to be embraced by all, or spat out . . .

DING, DING, DING!
If you ill, it is no fairy tale . . .
The daily routine. Dawn reveille. Drugs and mush. The thin smile of day nurses. Avoidance of night floor vomit. Sopping rags wielded upon a hairless broom. Corridors of grey and peeling plaster. Bending of one's ear, by Bed Number 9: Don't believe

22

them, they'll rob you blind . . . I had it all, and now – nothing, you're left sucking your own banana . . . Offers of escape routes, through underground tunnels. The mystic and the occult, unveiled. Beware fucking by the ear! The five-year backgammon game in Ward 11. Look out for Saporta, he shits on God in the toilet! Repent! Book your seat in the next world! Discount tickets, the front row at the Resurrection! Guaranteed, or total refund! Eleven o'clock, drugs and mush again. Educational TV. Reams of silence. Incomprehensible monologues. TV and mush. Drugs and mush. Lights out. More night cries. Flatulence and disinfectant. Unattainable chemical slumber . . . The only break in the round: the Friday evening siren, ushering in the Holy Sabbath: The area air raid alarm, always used for the purpose, being situated on the hill above the hospital: Blasting out like the wail of God whose balls have been stepped on, at several hundred decibels, vibrating the walls, rattling the windows, sending the faint-hearted crashing into closets, careening under beds. Blok's Rumanian room-mate, Tsimmes, regular as clockwork, rushing everyone towards the bunker. 'Syrians at eight o'clock!' he cries, pulling the sleeves off idlers. Bulky minions of authority subdue him, as the pious melt away to prayer.

The old paratroopers' saying: You go up, you come down. You go up, you come down. Boring!
    There must be more to life than this.
    They released Blok from the asylum.

And now – the city. The dream of Herzl. The taboo of Moses. The agony of Abraham. The boy Isaac. The flourished knife. But where is the lamb for sacrifice? The hill of Moriah. The scattered seed. The Covenant. Commandments by the bucketful. Thou shalt not this, thou shalt not that, et cetera. The land defiled vomiteth out her inhabitants. Burnt offerings. Abominations. The shepherd king who smoteth the lame and the blind. New foundations: the Ark of the Lord. The House, built of stone made ready beforehand – the bowls, the snuffers, the basons, the spoons, the tongs of pure gold, the censers. The House of God! No backdoor hawkers, no riff-raff, no spitting, no smoking! Moneylenders by appointment only. No strangers. No schmutz. No perverts. No onanists, sodomites or women. None impure in either thought or deed.

Nevertheless – BLOK, trudging up from the junction of the Jaffa Road, the low stone fin-de-siècle houses, the honking vans, trucks, chuffing buses, the chafing crowds bent against March gusts, shuffling shoppers, trippers, idlers, soldiers on leave, soldiers on duty, weighed down by armaments and pouches, poking in waste bins, hassling Arabs for identity cards, proof of the legitimacy of strangers . . . Men of religion, women of the domestic hearth, perambulating the next generation, lawyers, accountants, itinerants, thieves, market analysts, civil servants, secretaries, shop assistants, pickpockets, brain surgeons, brush salesmen, tourists, jejune and japanese jews, jentiles, All Human Life Is Here. Thin Avi, loyal friend of Blok's childhood, by his side, ready to catch the elbow of the semi-invalid as he toils on rubbery legs up the unfinished pedestrian precinct of Ben Yehuda Street, past the early stake-outs at open air cafés, the sullen

24

American youths gnawing at ice cream and the intangible roots of their parents' neuroses, through the narrow alley of the vendor of foreign newspapers and magazines, *Le Monde*, *The Sunday Times*, *Herald Tribune*, *Newsweek*, *Paris Match*, *Der Stern*, the world outside, down into Shamai Street in the direction of the accommodation agency (eighteen hundred dollars from the State! and Papa Blok's sanction: 'You have a home with your mother and me, Avremel, but I know you'll want to stand on your own feet; live as you want to live.'): 'FLATS, FLATS, FLATS WITH ICARUS – WE GIVE WINGS TO THE HOPES OF THE HOMELESS.'

Buzzing, strobing neon lights upon silent young men and women sitting on stools too high for any but the tallest to rest their feet on the floor, glumly turning the pages of huge ledgers chained to an adjoining wall. Thin Avi, his ideals scraped raw both by History and Current Affairs, facing the stern-faced lady working her teeth through a cheese sandwich behind a wooden counter with non-negotiable demands:

'A two-room flat for my friend here. Centrally located. Under two hundred dollars. No bugs. No religious neighbours.'

'This is Jerusalem,' said the lady primly. 'You'll take what you can get.'

She dragged over the master ledger, reeling off the mod cons available. 'Two rooms Gilo, no bath. One room Tel Arza, no shower. Two in Rassco, supply your own heating. In Saint Simon, luxus, nine months deposit.' Thin Avi vetoing each location in turn: 'You don't want to live in the colonies . . . that street is far too orthodox . . . retired policemen live all over that one . . . a fascist stronghold . . . football fans . . . too many new Russian immigrants . . . a nest of Labour Party pensioners . . . Not that my friend, of course, is prejudiced. But where one lives, of course you understand.'

'Under two hundred dollars, you can forget paradise,' she said, giving them an address in Katamon D.

'We shall take the Number 18 bus,' said Avi. Blok nodded, as his friend took his elbow. The bus was packed to capacity with men and women heading home from the Mahaneh Yehuda market. Enormous shopping bags and baskets crammed with lettuces, cabbages, tomatoes, aubergines, potatoes, watermelons, carrots, marrows, turnips, oranges, grapes, plums, the fruits of the earth. Moved reluctantly as Blok and Avi pressed down the aisle of the bus and then replaced on their toes. At each stop another mass of humanity climbs aboard, pushing the luckless in the aisle further and further back amid loud demands and protests, until the interior of the vehicle is one pressed lump of flesh, cloth, textile fibres, sweaty hair. Women scream as heavy boots demolish their purchases, men trip over melons, onions, bananas squelch, crushing against knees, a pungent odour as of a glue factory on an indifferent day. As the driver presses his front door shut passengers cram illegally through the back door. A pregnant woman's fare is passed forward over people's heads, change reluctantly rendered and passed back the same way, small coins dropping down open collars. 'Thank you, thank you! God will bless you!' cries the blessed one. 'Next time . . .' the driver mumbles, his eyes baleful in his rearview mirror, the bus fending for itself down the Jaffa Road, his tone suggesting moral imperatives that cannot be sustained . . .

. . . Past the Generali building with its winged stone lion, the Street of Shlomzion the Queen, King David, the grand hotel overlooking the Valley and the walls of the Old City to one side, the stone tower of the YMCA on the other, landmark of a Jerusalem of a quieter and more tolerant age, they say, past the iconic diad of the Montefiore windmill and the Dormition Church on Mount Zion, skirting the Ottoman railway station, down Emek Refa'im – the Valley of the Ghosts Road, past the Semadar Cinema and Bank Discount and Ari's Pizza and the Rumanian Grill, the crush alleviated little by little along the way as the shoppers begin to disembark, until, the last hundredweight of carrots removed off Blok's feet, Thin Avi plucks him off the bus, pulling his tottering figure up a labyrinth of newly reasphalted roads, low houses whose patios have not quite decided yet to be gardens or garbage dumps, abandoned hoes and trowels everywhere, cement spilling from torn sacks lying by piles of bricks intended for unbuilt extensions, fat ladies on wicker chairs hidden by sagging laundry lines. An old man coughing in an open doorway. Ritual calls to small children to cease whatever they are at. Clothespegs underfoot. A young lady in a flyer's parka, holding a child of about two in her arms: Come in, yes, this is the right address, the self-contained flat is in the rear. A room large enough for a midget to swing a quail on Yom Kippur, and, through the connecting wall, the ominous thumpa-thumpa-thump of Seventies' hi-fidelity rock. Even here, modern times. 'Two hundred and fifty dollars a month.'

'No,' said Blok.

Exit, with Thin Avi, walking on, west, towards the Rabbi Herzog highway, cars, trucks and buses toiling by the brown sides of hills crowned with new apartment blocks: Jerusalem of new angular concrete, prosperity and the housing shortage. The clouds chasing a patch of blue sky towards the Monastery of the Cross. They took a Number 22 bus back into town, to Icarus.

'More wings,' Thin Avi ordered, curtly.

'Some people you can't satisfy,' the lady said. She scribbled on a torn-off note. 'Try this one. It's very central. The landlord is not the world's best charmer. But you have to look behind the face.'

Indeed. A picturesque old house in Ussishkin Street, red roofed and walled in well-worn stone. The third floor flat solid with congealed dust, old broken furniture and debris, cracked shoes, wooden clogs, hairless brooms, cardboard boxes inlaid with cockroach droppings. The landlord, a terribly decayed old man in a dressing gown, whose son, built as a retired sumo wrestler, sang the praises of the household. Neither Blok nor Avi wished to look behind the face.

'Three hundred dollars a month.'

A sigh, another exit, opposite the tall white building in which the Nazi mass murderer Adolf Eichmann had been tried and sentenced to death by hanging. Now it was a Cultural Centre with a fine theatre and a workshop studio where new immigrants and other lovers of Zion – or so they were assumed to be – could learn Hebrew in five months for a small fee and much sweat and dolour, unlocking, or so they hoped, the coded inner world of the Ingathered Exiles. For those not yet cognizant, adjacent billboards were covered with peeling posters in English, promoting a course of lectures by the learned Rabbi Levine, who had begun life as an agent for the FBI in America, but was now domiciled in the Holy Land, campaigning for the expulsion of the Arab population, the banning of marriage and sexual relations between Jews and non-Jews and the establishment of a theocratic state. His dark bright eyes gazed shrewdly upon Blok from xeroxed portraits, as on one yet far, far from enlightenment but still not beyond hope. VISIT THE MUSEUM OF THE FUTURE HOLOCAUST. The poster added, enticingly: FREE OF CHARGE. The picture of an eye, shedding a lone tear, was appended.

'We have moved on, since you locked yourself away from us,' said Avi. 'Even you can't stop the march of time.'

Time!

Hanging like lead weights on his buttocks, anchoring him to the only armchair in Esther and Avi's apartment, temporarily accommodated at the fourth floor of a Bak'a apartment block, amid rolled up sheets, cardboard boxes of old papers, documents and social service reports, defunct handbags, shoes, paintbrushes, half finished canvases propped against walls, the latest burst of her artistic endeavours. Esther's cat, Adolphe, named, she assured friends, after the French-Hollywood ladies' man, Menjou, scavenging among the gouache tubes and old nylons, sniffing about Blok's socks and feet, on those occasions he deigned to show. A huge ruffled black beast, scarred with a thousand combats, with one eye in a permanent squint; Esther informed Blok he was the terror of the neighbourhood, his stamping ground enclosing twenty garbage skips. 'He is my reminder that nature is wild,' she said. But Blok responded only with a raised eyebrow. He had maintained, since his release, a low verbal profile, restricting himself to a handful of key phrases: 'No.' 'Um.' 'Uh-huh?' 'Uh-huh.' 'Mmmm.' And a range of shrugs, nods of the head, drooping of eyelids, inclined eyebrows. Palm up, requesting an end of the matter. Forefinger and thumb, rubbing nose. Passage of the right or left hand over barren scalp, in the rare moments it is not hidden by the old 'sock' cap he had found in Avi's army kitbag: the old 'Palmah' commando icon, visage of an old lost age. Although Esther assured him: 'Bald is beautiful. There's nothing then between you and God.' A farrago of raised and wiggled eyebrows, as Blok pastes into the pages of his returned scrapbook an item lining one of Esther's junk drawers:

(Undated, *Yediot Rishonot*, probably early 1975):

WITHIN THREE YEARS THERE WILL BE TWO WARS, THEN – THE REDEMPTION –

– says Sh— Sh— (see picture), the man who prophesied the outbreak of the Yom Kippur War, based on verses from the Bible, the Zohar and the books of the Kabbalah. He says the enemy will conquer part of Jerusalem for a short while, and Israel will operate unconventional weapons – but there is no need to worry: the footsteps of the Messiah are near.

. . . In Zohar Bereshit (Zohar Genesis) these words appear: 'And all the nations will combine against the Daughter-of-Jacob to destroy her . . .' Pointing to the internal situation of the State, which also hints at the 'Time of the End', Sh— quotes the Zohar (Neso, page 125) relating that, at the approach of the End 'many and manifest will be the deeds of corruption in Israel, the people's leaders will take bribes, they will not support the pupils of the Wise and the rulers will be of the rabble'.

The main purpose of the rabble – writes the Gaon of Vilna – is to couple Esau with Ishmael and to separate between Messiah Son of David and Messiah Son of Joseph (his harbinger) whose joint task it is to bring Redemption to Israel. Therefore one must break the power of the rabble in Israel, which power lies mainly at the gates of Jerusalem and especially at *'iftecha de'karta'* – the Opening of the City – which lies on the western mid-line (perhaps a hint of the Government Offices District?) . . .

. . . 'For me this is not mysticism but physics,' declares Sh— . . . 'Empirical answers do not suffice when we are talking of the Jewish people or of Jewish problems . . .'

Rabbi Levine, secure upon his poster, smiled: 'My time will come!'

The late spring wind surged. Blok and Avi continued upon their long march: from the Sanhedria district to Emile Zola Street. From Maimonides Road to Lloyd George. Digressions to the little Latin America of Ir Ganim: Nicaragua Street, Costa Rica, Bolivia, Colombia Street, Dahomey (!?). An elderly couple of Russian new immigrants in Ramat Eshkol, renting their son's room, who had gone off to populate a new Jewish settlement on the Arab West Bank. His room was plastered with portraits of Jewish dissidents rotting in Soviet jails.

'One hundred and fifty dollars a month.'

'No.'

Out in an early April shower. Rushing clouds alternately darkening and lightening the patchwork of Jewish and Arab parts of the city, Nachlat Shimon, Sheikh Jarrah, Beit Yisrael, Zahira, the Old City.

'We'll find your promised land, Avram!'

And evenings, in the Bak'a ménage: Esther, telling a silent Blok tales of her youth; Avi, at a loose end due to a hiatus in the left-wing shoestring publishing business he was currently involved with, caused by a snapping of the shoestring, bending their ears on the perfidy of the Prime Minister, Menachem Begin, who had, Avi said, wasted the gains of his November meeting with Anwar el-Sadat. 'A flea in the ear of Peanut-Man Carter! He's just flushing the fucking peace down the drain . . .' The dangers that lurk at *iftecha de'karta* . . . Arguments that would often spill into the informal sessions Esther held with her clients and claimants of the Social Welfare Office. Tales of woe reverberating in the kitchen: 'I swear to God, I don't know how the television set got into my room, Esther!' A police sergeant, Tuvia, also made visits, representing the compassionate face of Authority. Quick, hide the dope! Avi scurries to the bathroom, till the man rolls his moustaches, sighing meaningfully: 'Ah! you don't happen to have a smidge of . . . you know what, around . . .?' He was especially fond of Adolphe – who instinctively avoided him – stating admiringly: 'That cat is a born criminal.'

Esther's story, as revealed to an apparently uninterested Blok, was a quotidian tale of the City: she had been born into a family of strict supporters of the Irgun and Menachem Begin. By puberty she stood in torchlit parades, in a black shirt and neckerchief, belting out into the brisk Jerusalem night of the Fifties the old songs of armed anti-British struggle:

Upon barricades we shall meet, we shall meet!
Upon barricades in blood and fire Freedom we'll greet!
Our rifles salute one another!
The bullets will sing to each other!
Upon barricades, upon barricades, we – shall – meet!

But the only person she eventually met on the barricades was Blok's old schoolfriend Thin Avi, representing another tradition entirely. For he, an ardent member of the Israeli New Left movement in the pre-Yom Kippur War, post-Dylan age, had been one of the Reserve soldiers caught on the Suez Canal on that fated Sabbath of Atonement, 1973, by the surprise attack of the Egyptian Army, escaping by the skin of his teeth to the status of war hero and embittered survivor. In the spring of '74, demobilized from the armed struggle, he had leapt into the public eye by means of a lone hunger strike against the Government of the October Blunder, a gesture which sparked off a mass popular movement, culminating in tens of thousands of fellow protestors standing daily in the sun, in front of the Prime Minister's Office, demanding and finally receiving the resignation of the key ministers of 'The Blunder'. The beginning of the end of the Labour Government, resulting in the rise of Menachem Begin . . . (So it was all your fault, Aviad Ben-Gur? Go away, man, I don't want to think of it . . .) But, out of the crowd, in his self-inflicted calvary, a young, flaming red haired girl brought the starving man cups of orange juice. 'Wow! A girl who brings me orange juice!' he thought. Though this arrangement did not last. Nevertheless, sparks flying, the hammer, the anvil, the molten steel, the passage of years, life together: the social worker and the hopeful publisher of left-wing books in translation – polemic, poetry, fiction, drama, in Hebrew and Arabic – the entrails of another vision –
  'We'll find your promised land, Avram!'

Barnstorming among the useless flats by day, the criminal classes and their keepers by night, or later, Adolphe out prowling his kingdoms of the garbage cans, the three masketeers, cross legged,

31

subdued, at home, throwing ersatz yarrow sticks on the floor. The I-Ching, selected from Esther's legacy of her 'theosophical' phase, her ongoing friendship with the Hermit of Ein Karem (of whom more later). The literary flotsam of other post-Dylan quests: Gurdjieff, Jung, Ouspensky, Hermann Hesse, the Mahabharatha, Khalil Jibran, Eckankar, the Astral Ray Theory, Near-Death Experiences (spurned by Blok). Gnosticism and Immortality. The *Book of Changes*, accompanying the Friday night joint, Blok, Avi, the cat Adolphe, and the sound of the TV weekend news, embalming them, from above, below, sideways, the neighbours' master's voice, the echoing shrine. Three terrorists fell in the valley of the shadow of death. The Lord did not walk by their side. The Prime Minister honoured a mother of twenty as a bastion of the nation. A pet monkey, Roger, in Kansas, can ride a bicycle. A poisonous spider, in Chile, is causing painful and permanent erections in the male victims of its mandibles. Esther read the lines of the hexagram:

'Nine in the second place:

Penetration under the bed.

Priests and magicians used in great number.

Good fortune. No blame.

The book says: At times one has to deal with hidden enemies, intangible influences in dark corners . . . When the elusive influences are brought into the light, they lose their power over people.'

Later still, Blok, lying on the spare mattress in the hallway, an aural witness to age-old clichés:

'Not now, Avi.'

'If not now, when?'

And if I am not for me, who is for me?

The next day Esther met, in the street, outside the Social Welfare Office, an aunt whom she had always tried to shun. The aunt wished to know if she knew, by the merest chance, an honest tenant for a flat she owned, which had just become vacant, in the district of Mekor Baruch . . .

'I'm sure you'll like this place. I wouldn't give it to just anybody. But to a friend of Esther . . . Look, you have everything here you could want. An armchair, a bookshelf, the cupboards, the bed, it's brand new. There was an old one, but would I cheat people? The walls were painted only last year. The cleaning things are right here, in the kitchen. Don't worry about the crack in the sink, the plumber swears it's just on the surface. Have you seen a fridge this size in a two-room apartment? I don't want anyone to think me a miser. There are anti-roach cans in here. Not that you should have cause, but in the summer, even on the fourth floor – better to be safe than sorry. An ironing board and some mops and brooms, this way, on the balcony. Note the table and the two chairs. The balcony door is sometimes a bit sticky, but don't use force, the whole house is delicate. The bedroom: in the summer the sun falls right across the bed. You wake up, I guarantee, to bird calls. And you have a view of the street, across a green yard, not somebody's garbage. It's a very quiet neighbourhood. This is a mixed block, religious and non-religious. Live and let live, that's always been my motto. There's a House Committee, which deals with any problems, garbage disposal, cleaning stairways, et cetera. Mr Kadurie, the House Chairman, is a really nice person. He's been here for thirty years, since they put the block up. I'm really glad that this apartment is going to someone Esther knows. You can't believe who's flat hunting nowadays. Some people are animals. You see it in their eyes. I'm not a prejudiced person, but this is my only spare property. I had a tenant who scribbled telephone numbers on the walls. There were guests who shat in the bath. You will throw out rubbish regularly, won't you? You can't believe the perversions of some people. The gas balloons are round the side of the house, I'll show you later. SuperGas. I've left the number to call. The man who left here said he would leave both balloons full. Maybe I should have checked that today . . . You have to assume that people are honest. Sometimes, though . . . You will take care of the place, I'm begging you, I'm letting it go for so much less than I could get, because my favourite niece recommends you. If I'd known earlier on you were looking . . . But one's relations don't stay in touch as they should, especially the young. It's not like the old days. In those times we needn't be so wary of strangers. But now, with my husband gone, bless his memory . . . You have to protect yourself, don't you? But don't worry about me being on your back – once we've signed the lease, I'll be invisible. I'm not one of those landladies who fret and bother and whine over every penny. I'm grateful for the little I can get. In the old days, before either of you were born – I still remember the hardships, the rationing . . . People smuggled meat in the boots of cars. My husband, bless his memory, and I were just married . . . We didn't have two pennies to rub together, but we were young, we felt part of something! Today . . . but you don't want to hear all this. The toilet's here. I got a new brush yesterday. There's a good place for that sort of stuff round the corner. Malachi's – he has everything – roach powder, soaps, shampoos, saucepans . . . God knows what my previous tenant did with the old brush . . . People frighten me sometimes. The ants might come through cracks in the tiles here. I showed you the ant powder in the kitchen . . . The window is a bit stiff, but with a little patience . . . The flush I had fixed last year. When you use the shower, the head tilts a bit this way. Maybe I'll call the plumber again . . . But those prima-donnas . . . And the charges! Some people have no shame . . . I've left you my phone number, in case, God forbid . . . And Esther knows where I am. I had a man here once who tore out all the electrics. He was fixing fancy lights round the bed. There were girls day and night . . . the House Committee was furious . . . But I can see you're not that type. I can always tell from the eyes. Also the way you walk, you don't mind me saying this – there's a tentativeness that's reassuring. You're a quiet person. You don't like flamboyance . . . Na! Enough! I should stop babbling. Any friend of Esther's is OK by me. I know you'll be happy here. Everything you might need is close by. The little grocery,

34

Eliyahu's – to the left, round the corner. But I understand you've lived in this area before? So I don't have to tell you anything. A man comes to whitewash the roof every six months. But the House Committee sees to all that. If he asks you for money don't give him anything. These Arabs try to take advantage. Don't think that I'm prejudiced. I'm just realistic. Don't we all have to live here, somehow?'

★

AYE, INDEED! The housing shortage, in the city where time stands still: barefoot prophets in white robes and staffs sipping coffee at Abu Moustache's café, Elazar the Zealot handing leaflets to tourists at the Jaffa Gate, Alexander the Macedonian window shopping up King George in search of platform shoes, Frederick I, Barbarossa, who drowned in the river, buying water wings at Sport-Hygiena, Sultan Suleiman is photographed against his own walls by Josephus the record keeper, while, under Moses Montefiore's windmill, on a public bench, Theodor Herzl sits, thrashing a fountainpen through notepaper –

SCRIBBLE, SCRIBBLE, SCRIBBLE: 'The idea which I have established in this pamphlet is an old one, the establishment of a State for the Jews . . .' But Herzl's own approach to the City had been un-Messianic, when he arrived by train – unlike Anwar el-Sadat in his limousine seventy-nine years later – upon Ottoman tracks (105 cm gauge), laid by the French firm Société Ottomane de Chemin de Fer de la Palestine in 1892 (a concession originally owned by one Yosef Navon, *grandpère* of a later State President) modern dreams become cast iron creeping, rivet by rivet, up on the slumbering Levant. For Theodor arrived at night, well into the Sabbath (Autumn, 1898) at the sleepy old-new railway station in the Bak'a district, and had to walk, cursing every step of the way, across the stark valley of Gehenna, Gei Ben-Hinnom, towards his hotel. He had come, oddly enough, to meet the German Kaiser Wilhelm, on tour in the Holy Land to pick up concessions of his own. But the temperature, rising to 106 Fahrenheit in the shade, frazzled the Kaiser's mood, and he gave the Jewish prophet a flea in his ear instead of his backing for the Zionist Cause. Poor Herzl had to turn tail and return to Jaffa, there to await passage back west. The

35

flea remained, in the bosom of its family. It had seen it all before. Prophets, Messiahs, Saviours, Crusaders: the true rabble at the western midline. Only the other day, Goddamit! all the riffraff of Modern Europe had been parked below the Old City walls: Robert of Flanders and his knights camped just by the taxi stand at the Damascus Gate, Robert of Normandy opposite Herod's Gate, by the Post Office, Geoffrey of Lorraine and Tancred besieging the Jaffa Gate while Raymond of Toulouse closed in on Mount Zion. June 1099 AD! And as the Frankish knights scribbled their first postcards home, the Saracen defenders poured boiling oil on their serfs . . . History, *ya shabab*! When the Franks finally breached the walls, on July 14 (Bastille Day), they massacred almost the entire population, Moslems in the mosques, Jews in their synagogues. The camp followers and tourists had to wade through blood and corpses to the Holy Places. A century later, when Yusuf Salah ed-Din, the Great Saladin, retook the City, he offered the Christians merciful terms of ransom, to the tune of twenty thousand dinars . . . Today this can buy a three-room flat in the suburbs, with kitchen, bathroom, shower, albeit no fittings. But the Christian nobles were too mean to ransom all their fellows, and over half were sold as slaves . . . The housing shortage, *toujours* the housing shortage . . . The Christian Holy Places were, however, saved from pillage. Jews were permitted to return . . .

★

Excellent news, as Blok is finally domiciled. Checked in for the duration, at 35 Hageffen Street. The 'Street of the Vine', in Mekor Baruch district – the 'Blessed Source' (no relation to Papa Blok, retired progenitor and philatelist). A neighbourhood of quiet old red-roofed houses between the buzz of the Mahaneh Yehuda market and the thoroughfare of the Kings of Israel Road. Quarried stone balconies with rusty iron railings and flapping laundry. Lazy clip-clop on asphalt. Winding alleyways, southwards, nowadays almost completely the habitat of the ultra-orthodox. Small boys in long black coats and homburgs, bearded men with resplendent hats of fur, women covered up against the devilry of lust. The ubiquitous notices upon walls:

36

WOE TO THE MEEK AND THE PUPILS OF
THE WISE WHOSE EYES WITNESS ABOMINATIONS!
STAND GUARD AGAINST THE FLOOD, O ISRAEL!

The terror of unchaste women in our midst . . . bare arms,
abundant thighs, a glimpse even of the pit of mammary glands, or
alien ideas:

PORNOGRAPHY AND SECULAR
AND CHRISTIAN LITERATURE ON SALE IN
OUR VERY STREETS!

Home is the atheist, home from the sea, and the punter home at the
tills . . . Chasing dreams, round the Porat Yosef Yeshiva, down a
few yards into the Geula district. The modern world played in
eighteenth-century dress. Kapotas, streimels, tight white stock-
ings, fringed tassels in the January wind. A cornucopia of whiskers, side curls. Shops selling wigs to women shorn for religion,
holy utensils of brass and silver. Souvenir mugs inscribed in
Yiddish. Fashion for the Religious Woman. Rabinowicz Pregnancy Clothes. The Light of Books and the Torah. The Elegant
Slaughter House. The Rose of Jacob Restaurant – *Kosher Leme-
hadrin Min Hamehadrin*. Shtisel's Self Service. Salon Shternsos –
Brassières and Corsets. Religious and Ethnic Cassettes and Records – 'Eli Lipsker And His Little Soldiers Singing: We'll Bring
Messiah Now', an Iwo Jima like portrait of skullcapped lads in
khaki, bearing FN rifles, raising the blue and white national flag.
The Messiah is nothing if not modern. On to the Geula Pickle
Shop, Under Supervision of the *Beit Din*, Pickled and Smoked
Fish, Preserves, Salads and Salamis. The Kfar Habad Nut Shop,
devotional magazines of the Habad Hassidim prominent in the
shop window, a fog of bustle and heavy breath within, the
pungent smell of roasting, mountains of almonds, chestnuts,
walnuts, peanuts, hazel, cashews, pistachios, shovelled by young
vendors, side locks flying, into little paper bags. 'Next! What will
it be for sir this fine day?' That's enough for the moment, thank
you. Outside, a street vendor, up against the traffic jam, calls the
crowd of hatted men, coiffed women, to witness his home-made
brand of washing powder. 'You see!' he waves black smudged

37

hands, painting a blue band on his forehead. 'I just dip this sponge in the material, and presto – wait a minute, it'll work better next time . . .'

★

FOR THERE WILL BE A NEXT TIME, Theodor Herzl vowed, as he walked the Old City's pestilential alleyways in the lingering autumnal heat of October 1898, much the same route as the lauded Anwar el-Sadat in a more clement November, eight decades later, but accompanied, not by the highest in the Land, but by his sweaty entourage of Central European Zionists and his gentile amanuensis . . . Clip-clopping on the old worn stones, solar topees jammed on their heads like so many tons of bricks, donkeys shitting on their shoes, beggar boys hanging on their trouser legs and braces, begging for European currency, professional vagrants thrusting forth club feet, severed torsos, three, two, one or no fingered hands. Bearded, black-coated touts waving books of tickets at them, demanding cash for real or fake Yeshivas. Gaberdine coats, *abbayehs*, kefiyahs, brushing against their suits. Lice, nits and fleas leaping aboard. At the Wailing Wall they watched bedraggled figures twisting, knocking their brows upon the stones. The sound of lamentation merging with the buzz of flies and the nasal cries of tamarindi vendors. The Mittel-European prophet was appalled. He determined that all this should be transformed, utterly, and the sooner the better, into a suburb of Vienna, filled with art galleries, opera houses, museums, pastry shops and strudel parlours.

Having been rebuffed by the Kaiser at the Imperial camp just outside the City, Theodor returned for his last night at the Hotel F—, to be plunged into a venture wholly unrecorded by official hagiography. Disappointed, he faced the trip back to Jaffa, after a mere five days in the City. He lay, half asleep, in his room lulled by the rustling of the hotel roaches, attempting to assimilate the frustrations of reality to the purity of his dreams, when, a little after midnight, a light rapping at his window jerked him fully awake, introducing the intrusion of his fellow pilgrim, the Christian Zionist William Hechler.

The Reverend Hechler, an Anglican clergyman born in

38

Benares, India, to a German evangelical missionary and his English wife, had nurtured ambitions to become the Anglican Bishop of Jerusalem but instead had been appointed by his church as a chaplain in Vienna, where he was attracted to the cause of Herzl's Zionist Enterprise by calculations, based on the Book of Revelations, which revealed the date of the commencement of the Jewish Redemption to be 1897, only one year following the publication of Theodor Herzl's pamphlet *Der Judenstaat – The State of the Jews*. It was Hechler who had introduced Herzl to the Kaiser, as he had once tutored the Emperor's uncle's children. But Hechler was known to have a personal, as well as an evangelical quest, to wit: his researches had lead him to believe the original Ark of the Covenant was hidden intact on Mount Nevo, east of the River Jordan, and that it contained not only the two tablets of Moses, inscribed with the Ten Commandments in God's hand, but also the manuscript of the Five Books of the Torah, in old Moish's own scrawl . . .

'Wake up, Theodor!' the Reverend hissed, urgently. 'I believe I have made a breakthrough!' Herzl reluctantly donned his dressing gown. In his half slumber he had distinctly imagined the hotel roaches practising a sibilant conversation in the international language recently invented by a Polish oculist, Dr L. L. Zamenhof, and named by him 'Esperanto'. The speakers, who seemed to have formed their tutorial circle under his bed, were not at an advanced stage. '*Mia hundo estas pli bona ol via.*'*said one. '*Cu ni dancu?*'** said another. '*Cu vi povus prunti al mi du dinarojn a pagtage?*'*** commented a third. He was glad to leave the room, assuring himself by the snores from the adjacent chambers that his three other travelling companions, the Jews Wolfson, Schnirer and Bodenheimer, were happily out for the count.

'Come, come!' the Reverend gesticulated wildly. Donning his solar topee and cloak over his striped pyjamas (blue and white) the Prophet stepped over the ground-floor windowsill. William Hechler was clad in a black cape and topper over maroon knicker-bockers. Venturing out in the harsh Jerusalem moonlight, the two

---

*   'My dog is better than yours.'
**   'Shall we dance?'
*** 'Can you lend me a couple of bucks till payday?'

visionaries made their way down the narrow alleys, the Suq-el Bazaar, past Muristan, al-Khawajat, al-Lahamin, the heart of the Old City, into the Street of the Chain. Unknown to them, however, one of their companions, Max Bodenheimer, had been awakened by their exit and, unwilling to listen to the roach rapping, followed, at a judicious distance, flitting under arches, flattening against walls, crouching in rubbish-filled niches. Unseen eyes watched behind Judas windows. Scrawny cats hissed. Mosquitoes gathered in hordes. Turds lurked everywhere for the unwary . . .

But Bodenheimer soon lost his quarry. For in the maze of alleyways he took the wrong turning, and found himself confronted by a mentally disturbed pariah dog in a small, closed-off courtyard. Managing to scramble over walls and cupolas he escaped serious injury, while irate householders soaked his ankles with slops. He had to return to the Hotel F— empty handed and, waking in the morning, found the night owls returned too, though neither would say a word. The entire group then decamped for the port of Jaffa, and soon sailed forth upon the citrus packet for Alexandria. One year after their departure, the nineteenth century ended and the twentieth century began. Theodor Herzl, history relates, continued his efforts to sell the Jewish State, door to door, until his death in 1904. The Reverend Hechler, devoted to the end, recorded himself as the witness of his last words, which he claimed to be: 'Tell them all I have given my life's blood for my people', though the *Jewish Chronicle* on the other hand, reported the last phrase as: 'How I wish to rest.' The Reverend himself, the official historians say, never found the Lord's Ark. It did not seem to be anywhere near Mount Nevo, which today sports a minor ruined church with a souvenir stall, an iron cross with lightbulbs and a listening post of the Jordanian Armed Forces, and from its summit, on a clear day, one can look out over the Judaean Desert and glimpse the City of Jerusalem – its environs and petrol stations gleaming in the desert sun . . . But legends, and highly classified files, rumours have it, tell a somewhat different story, leading us back, in the shimmering waves of half slumber, half consciousness, tinkling with non-Esperanto roaches, floating down upon the early spring haze, to –

★

– BLOK, waking to find the youthful Arab handyman, Omar, nonchalantly whitewashing the roof, his heavy boots clomping the sky side of the ceiling, his bucket scraping the hardened tar as his voice tunelessly rendered the Palestinian anthem: '*Biladi, Biladi*', – 'My Village, My Village' . . . Perhaps he was painting a large red cross up there, as a target for kamikaze buzz bombers of the Liberation Armies, as reported only the day before in the press:

> A report claiming Palestinians are training to pilot 'flying bombs' to attack Israel has been published in a Kuwaiti newspaper. This follows the recent revelation of the failure of a terrorist attack by hot air balloon . . . [But if only he would just once lift that bucket!] The balloon, with four terrorists, ammunition and explosives on board, was about to cross the border from South Lebanon when it developed a fault and fell from the skies near the village of Tabnin. All the terrorists were killed. It is thought the attempt was based on the element of surprise, as the Israeli authorities, so the terrorists surmised, would not be on the lookout for an attack of this kind, and it would also enable them to surmount such border obstacles as booby traps and electronic fences.

Clump! Clump! Clump!

He turned over, idly brushing the torn-open envelope of his first postal delivery at Hageffen Street. A letter from a place apparently called Los Angeles, forwarded by Papa Blok after a mournful phone call:

– Hey, Avremel – happy now? Your own place – no doctors, no psychiatrists, no parents. What is it young people say? – time to collect your head, or whatever . . . But remember, you have a home here too. We have a letter for you – remember I mentioned Yissachar, your old friend in the movie business? Holyland Films in Ein Karem? Any memory? No? Well, take my word for it – and this letter, all the way from Hollywood! You won't mind if I keep the stamp? Not that I can afford to update the old collection any more . . . but it keeps your mother at bay . . . OK, let me put your mother herself on now . . . Rosa . . . just try to have patience, Avremel . . .

– AVREMEL, HAVE YOU FORGOTTEN YOUR MOTHER?—!—?

He re-read the short letter, from a perfect stranger:

Dear Avram!

Out of the nuthouse, eh, comrade? It's about time, soldier! Your old friend Yissachar *hier sprechen* – though they tell me you don't remember anything. So how's the 'real world'? What shit, eh? Not that I can complain! sitting here, at the edge of a private pool, with Mexican servants rolling the lawn. Palm trees and rum daiquiris. Boring! I've had my fill of it. Go East, Young Man – I am about to join you in the pit down your way . . . Wait till I tell you of all my twists of fortune! Just a preliminary fair warning of my new partner/ boss – for I have hitched my waggon to the great Adir Kokashvili, one time shoeshine boy, and today our biggest home-grown film mogul! You have seen 'Sin City Sodom'? 'The Singing Commando'? 'The Little Beggar Girl From Tabriz'? No? Fuck you, Avram! We'll soon let you know what's what in the world! So stand by for my Triumphal Re-Entry into the Land of Milk and Money! Man the barricades! Don't spare the bread and salt!

Your Franchiser of Manna,

Yissachar (the Returning Exile)

PS: Awake! Awake!

But Blok was fighting daily to retain his slumber, unaware that his arrival at 35 Hageffen Street was being debated within the House Committee . . . Battling, in the pre-conscious sphere, to remain undercover while the new dawn unfolded: four thirty in the morning, the daily newspaper delivery of the religious organ *Hamodia* by Vespa motorbike to Elrom, his neighbour one floor down. The delivery boy always left his motor running while he schmoozed down the path and back. But Elrom never got up before twelve noon to collect the fucking rag! Five thirty, the Revenge of the Natives, the Arab woman carrying a crate on her head, perambulating the courtyard, yelling: 'FRUITS! FRESH FRUITS!' Then a merciful hiatus. But, *punkt* at seven, the foghorn voice of Mrs Almoshnino, the neighbour from the adjacent floor of Entrance B, emerging like a ton of lard dressed in an old bedcover on to her balcony to converse, without fail, with Mrs Weiss, in Entrance C. Nought avails against the blast, windows shut, shutters drawn, bolted, cottonwool in the ears, head drowned in the pillow, earplugs, earphones, maximum volume turned up on the News: 'The President of the Republic of Egypt, Little Eli, rejecting the proposals, passed the night very well . . . He only had to go three times, Party Chairman Brezhnev said . . . Do you have Sanatokleen? A Parliamentary Committee has been formed. I'm getting the ants again! The little red ones, who issued a prompt denial. I know, I found them in my drawers . . .'

Indeed. Issues of moment which would have to wait their turn in the House Committee's conclave. The Chairman, Yehezkel Kadurie (Flat 3, Entrance C), as usual moving the agenda. Item A: water sprinkler rotation; complaints by Kimchi of Entrance C that they ought to patriotically rotate to the right instead of the left were dismissed, by majority vote. Item B: The Case of Cohen-Deshen of Flat 2, Entrance D: a regular listener, as is his right, to Jordan's Hebrew TV News. Anyone may listen to what they damn well like, it's a Free Country isn't it? but does the volume have to be so damned loud? The entire street lies open to the enemy every night at seven thirty, said Zilber of Entrance B, Flat 2. Well, they have the best coverage of the English football league, suggested Kishonski of Entrance C, Flat 5. I shall call again and request volume reduction, said Kadurie, ever reconciling. There was a short recess for mint tea.

Apropos the Enemy, Kimchi resumed, remorseless, did the Arab dustbin collectors, whose work he had been watching, have to drop so much trash in their trail? The house garbage containers were the very latest scream – wheeled skips that clipped directly on to the truck's automatic load. Why then is so much rubbish strewn in the yard? The police should be called. Kishonski (obviously a Labour Party voter) said: 'I see the dustmen at their work often, and I haven't seen them spill a chicken bone. Someone else might be playing with the rubbish, kids, hooligans, juvenile delinquents.' Kadurie noted this for investigation and turned, as ever in such cases, to the fifth attending member of the House Committee – Tolstoy of Entrance D, Flat 3. It was known, though never acknowledged openly, that Tolstoy was employed in some un-

43

clear capacity by one of the Internal Security Services. A small, nondescript man with the face of a dachshund, he always sat in his chair uneasily as if nesting upon haemorrhoidal secrets. (An impression close to the truth, for Tolstoy's private secret, which was, unknown to him, common knowledge throughout the building, was this: he had only one testicle, the other having mysteriously vanished into his body, without trace, some time in 1960. The medical profession had declared itself baffled, and experts in Bern, Paris and San Francisco had examined him keenly, over the years, to absolutely no avail. But more of this later . . .)

I shall look into the rubbish spillage, he promised morosely, tugging at his flapping right ear. Let us get on to Item C – Blok, Avram, the new tenant in Entrance A. Tolstoy had printed out his file from the Central Databank, and he now unconcertinaed the sheets all over the table, over the glasses of tea, ringed stains, stubs of pencils, morsels of tomato and cucumber sandwiches. Everything down in dot matrix grey: Blok's arrest for peeping in 1967, his first, subsequent, committal for observation at the Klander asylum, his return there after the '73 War, due to chronic malingering and military insubordination. His third sojourn at Klander, end of '74, which led, due to the fire which gutted the asylum during the ill-fated film therapy project, to his three-year trauma at the T—t Hospital. Even his involvement, with his old pal Yissachar, in the porno film trade in New York, during the halcyon years of 1971–2, was chronicled, as well as his acquaintance and recent reacquaintance with Aviad Ben-Gur, left-wing publisher, pro-PLO and so-called 'Peace' activist. No need to remind the House Committee, Tolstoy reminded them, of the presence already in our building of the known ultra-leftist and subversive activist, Basuto of Entrance D, Flat 5, who has for years been holding meetings of his shadowy 'Situationist Fractlet' under the guise of a 'Guy Debord Study Group' under the Committee's very nose. Some sinister preconceived plan might be unfolding here, said Tolstoy. We Are a Free Country, protested Kishonski. Everyone agreed with that. But What About Them Arabs? Kimchi, banging his fist on the table, returned to the issue of the garbage. The tea glasses jumping, the computer sheets unfolding on to the floor, Tolstoy leaping to reclaim them. What

About Them Rubbish Spilling Arabs?! The meeting broke up in disarray, with a vague agreement to reconvene at Kishonski's, next Monday. The issue of Menachem Chang, the Vietnamese boat person (Entrance C, Flat 8), who emitted atonal Buddhist chants, well after midnight, had to be left to another occasion.

Following is a complete list of the tenants of 35 Hageffen Street:

Entrance A: Flat 1: Mr & Mrs C. Vardi. Haberdasher. Housewife. 1 m. child. 2 f.

Flat 2: Mr & Mrs Dinar. Bank clerk. Hairdresser.
1 m. child, Air Force, ground crew.

Flat 3: Mrs Cohen-Kerem. Ret. Widow. 1
daughter, in Petah-Tikva.

Flat 4: Mr Farajoul. Orthodox. Very private.
'Financial consultant' in religious trust.

Flat 5: Mr & Mrs Elrom. Orthodox. She –
teacher. He – reader of *Hamodia*.

Flat 6: Sirkin. Ret. merchant seaman. Eccentric.
Exercises on roof.

Flat 7: Mrs Bejerano. Ret. Ex-dressmaker.
Offspring scattered, some abroad.

Flat 8: A. Blok. New boy. Ex-lunatic. Potential
trouble.

Entrance B: Flat 1: Mr & Mrs Teherani. New Iranian immigrants. 1 m. child.

Flat 2: Mr & Mrs Zilber. Both ret. Son in West
Bank settlement.

Flat 3: Mr & Mrs Sh'chori. Hospital cleaner.
Housewife. No c.

Flat 4: Ms Preminger. Secretary. Dubious visitors. Much furniture moving. Complaints. Due final warning.

Flat 5: Dardak & Tarablus. Orthodox yeshiva
students.

Flat 6: Mr & Mrs & Grandma Levy. 1 m. child,
shits on staircase.

Flat 7: Mr & Mrs Almoshnino, Electrician. Kokhelefel. 2 m. child, 1 f.

Flat 8: Mr & Mrs Ben-Bagdadi. Both Ret. Both deaf.

Entrance C: Flat 1: Ella Weiss & Son. Sociologist. He un-employed. Rock music. Seventy-four complaints. Criminal record – theft of hi-fi.

Flat 2: Kimchi. Carpenter. Activist of right-wing 'Tehiya' Party. Protests lawn sprinklers fixed by 'leftists'. Repaints neighbours' red post boxes. Number One complainer. Arsehole.

Flat 3: Mr & Mrs Kadurie. Electrician and House Committee Chairman. Housewife. 2 m. (1 in army), 1 f., married to dermatologist.

Flat 4: Professor Malpaso. Retired mathematics lecturer.

Flat 5: Mr & Mrs Kishonski. Municipal Clerk. Shop assistant. 1 m. House liberals.

Flat 6: Tishbi. Widow. Many sons & d. visiting. Loud singing. Parties.

Flat 7: Vacant. Owned by Mrs Transvisotski, Tel Aviv.

Flat 8: Menachem Chang. Vietnamese Boat Person. Door daubed: 'Out with the Idolator' by person or persons unknown.

Entrance D: Flat 1: Mr & Mrs Shemesh. Clerk. Housewife. 1 m. 1 f.

Flat 2: Cohen-Deshen. Garage mechanic. Jordan TV fan.

Flat 3: Tolstoy, the Secret Policeman with One Testicle.

Flat 4: Kushnir. Journalist. Writer. Discharged bankrupt.

Flat 5: E. Basuto. Student. Leftist. Rock music.

Flat 6: Baruch & Dina Manilov. New US immi-grants. Young, quiet, orthodox, boring.

Flat 7: Arkadi. Russian immigrant. Interpreter
and Translator. Very quiet.
Flat 8: Mr & Mrs Almaliah. Vegetable vendors.

★

Elyakim Moshe Tolstoy's precise metier was this: he was a senior
Research Officer of the Ministry of Religion's secret Department
of Apocalyptic Affairs. Every working day (when he was not on
field-duties) he would rise from his meagre and lonely single bed,
perform the instinctive finger quest for his long vanished member,
sigh, piss, shit, wash, dress, percolate the coffee, check the
functioning of the bugging devices he had affixed to Basuto's
apartment, just above, make the bed, take down the net shopping
bag from its hook on the kitchen door, exit the flat, carefully triple
locking the front door, traverse the block yard by the mangy
azalea bushes and half-height palm tree, nodding good morning to
whoever else might be on the path, amble down Hageffen, round
the corner of Haturim Street to queue at Mordechai's hole-in-the-
wall grocery, watching the gruff unshaven proprietor, with octo-
poid grace, rushing tins off shelves, bottles into baskets, cutting
loaves of bread, extracting eggs, yoghourts, plastic bags of milk
from the cooler, writing down the items on grimy bits of paper,
checking the day's inflation price-rise, fending off cries of protest
at same, shouting out to the boy behind the basement door
eternally rattling bottles, crates and God-knows what else: 'Yosske! Five more Goldsun! Three olive oil! Four potato flour! What's
up with you down there? Stop wrecking the joint! It's a hard life,
Madam, you said it. They can deliver Sam missiles to the Arabs,
but I have to wait five months for tuna. Speak!' his normal
admonition to the next in line. 'The usual, Mister Tolstoy?' Two
light yoghourt, half a loaf, a hundred gramme olives; back to the
apartment for the frugal meal, the second coffee, rechecking the
bugging devices; exit again round the corner, towards the Kings
of Israel Road and the Number 15 bus stop, jostling to board with
the crowd; mind shutting out the cries of his squeezed brethren,
body swaying with the motor; climbing off the bus gratefully at
Beit Yoel, just past Jaffa Road's Zion Square, down the steps
below the new tall white building, with its bank branches and

foreign airline offices, past the incongruously sited Sephardi Syna-gogue, two souvenir shops, and Mittag's Café, following the arrows and signs pointing 'TO THE TAILOR', 'YUSIPOV RUBBER STAMPS AND SEALS', passing through the open doorway of the latter, nodding to old skullcapped Yusipov on his wicker stool tending the pungent pressing machines, the rows of polished handles, smooth rubber plates waiting for inscriptions, continuing down the stairs at the back to the door marked 'Ladies, Out of Order', opening the apparently rusty lock with his key, pulling the flush the usual three times, waiting for the sliding panel to open, entering the secure booth, punching the regulation code on the keyboard, waiting for palmprint and voiceprint verifi-cation, entering the lift, adjusting his thought processes to the Departmental ambience: sleek hi-tech, rows of visual display units searching eternally through buried databanks; men and women in white coats, with clipboards, soft homeland tunes from hidden speakers. Taking his seat, he unpacked his lunch bag (two sand-wiches, marmalade and cottage cheese) and, typing the access code into his console, entered the maze of the arcane . . .

ACCESS!
  ACCESS!
  ACCESS! Bring out your undead megabytes!
– All parahuman life is here, a wealth of electronic ectoplasm: alleged, reported, sworn and unsworn sightings of a wide range of paranormal events, ghosts, apparitions, visions, visitations, in-cubii, (within State Jurisdiction, Occupied Territories included), including: the Holy Virgin, the Prophet Elijah, the Imam Hussein, Jesus the Nazarene, Haj Harun, Elyakim Haetsni, Judah Macca-baeus, Ishtar, Beelzebub, Hermes Trismegistus, Edward Whitte-more, Queen Melisande, Theodor Herzl, Salah ed-Din the Merci-ful. No rumour too obscure or elusive to escape record on hard disk or tape streamer: Stalin, identified in broad daylight in Ben Yehuda Street, Frederick Barbarossa, seen in snorkeling gear by a man saved from drowning off Ashkelon, Olaf Tryggvason, first Christian King of Norway (last seen in Palestine, AD 1000, wearing a wool undershirt, Marks & Spencer's chain-mail and two upside down shofars perched on a tin yarmulka), reported in a brawl at a Beersheba shebeen. Herzl, seen by the Jerusalem

windmill, with a takeaway Chinese in a paper bag. Along with the more mundane arcana: UFO sightings, in the Sinai and the Negev. Levitation in Hadera. Occult cells in Tel Aviv. Cults of the Astral Ray, the Human Aura, the Code of Adonis, Pythagoras. Reported quests for the Philosopher's Stone. Feminist-mystic adoration of Ashtoreth (very widespread throughout the country), Yeti worship. Raising of the Baal in Jaffa. Alchemy, necromancy. Spontaneous Combustion in almost every sector. Not to speak of the more overt pains-in-the-neck – Freemasons, Hare Krishna, Moonies, advocates of the Living Ek, Jews for Jesus, Sufists, Baptists, Mormons, Temple Mount Plotters, Christian fundamentalists, advocates of the Rapture, prophesiers of the War of Gog and Magog. All manner of fans of Second Comings, Nazarene, Shi'ite, Druse, Buddhist. Not to speak of the Jewish mystagogues and messianists, State approved or paralegal (the one transmutes so swiftly into the other): the Block of the Faithful, Repentants, Sons of Judah, the Zealots of Bratslav, the followers of Rabbi Levine. Linking databanks here with other para-services, of the Ministries of Defence, the Interior, Foreign, Tourism, the PM's Office, SHABAK, MOSSAD, Military Intelligence. For the Department's remit was the core, the Theological Basis of National State Strategy. The decoded data streams before Tolstoy's eyes as his fingers dance on the keyboard, allowing the passage of the Secret of the Great Pyramid, the unexplained and escalating affair of the Rabid Sheep, the ominous recurrence of Time-slips, the file on the Reverend William Hechler, the Herzl affair, a thousand and one ramifications. Not for Elyakim Tolstoy the high affairs of State which were, in fact, wisps of the moment: the transience of President Carter of the USA, beckoning the reluctant Menachem Begin towards his political orgasm with the last Pharaoh of Egypt . . . the born-again Christian grabbing Isaac and Ishmael, tying them to the log cabins of Camp David . . . mayflys, in Maryland, meeting and mating after two weeks of intensive head banging . . . Anwar and Menachem embracing again in full view of the world's press on the White House lawn, while Palestinian Arab demonstrators waved banners outside the fence:

'HAVE YOU NOT FORGOTTEN SOMEONE???'

Tolstoy's databanks never forgot anything. Elijah's disappear-

ance, the sins of Amalek, Ezekiel's bone surgery, the name of
Jonah's whale, Job's answers to God's questions, the aerosol
sprays of Babylon, the shape of Adam's rib, the genealogy of
the fourteenth tribe, the true fate of the missing leper messiah,
the origin of the sephiroth, the limits of the *tsimtsum*, Haroun
al-Raschid's Cookbook, the address of the hidden Imam, the
hundred and sixty-nine deposit box numbers of the keys of the
kingdom, the ninety thousand forbidden names of Christ, the text
of the Scroll of Thoth, the fourth and final alias of T. E. Lawrence
and the fate of the Judas Pig. But there were some holes in the
databanks' provenance, matters left unresolved, bytes of the apple
that might just conceivably be hiding in the works, to be retrieved
by diligent search. Tolstoy leaned back in his seat, allowing the
pixels to dance on the VDU screen, calling up his random choice
of the morning, the file of –

★

The Legend of the Reverend Hechler (Christian Zionist to the Gentry)

Official history, which we should never believe, tells us the
Reverend William Hechler spun out the long years remaining to
him after the death of Herzl (1904) in quiet contemplation and
dedication to the Zionist cause, gently penning his memoirs,
debating philosophy and theology with weighty scholars and
preserving artifacts of the Jewish renascence in Palestine in his
London house. But in 1913 (the hidden file tells us), the gentile
Zionist visited an old Coptic fortune teller by the bustling Bab
Es-Shariyah in Cairo, who foretold the date of his death to be June
the 6th of the immediately following year. Stunned by this chilling
threat to his continued stubborn search for the Lord's Ark and the
First Editions of Moses, Hechler conceived a daring plan suggested
to him by a certain ancient manuscript among the many he had
collected in the course of his occult researches. These lead him, to
telescope a lengthy anabasis, to a crumbling tenement in the Old
City of Amsterdam, to knock tentatively at the door of the
renowned Dutch mesmerist, Cornelius Onderdonk, who ushered
him effusively into his laboratory, brim full with the obligatory
test tubes, beakers, phials and crucibles, but dominated by a great

alchemical vas, or vessel, emitting unbelievably foul-smelling droplets of an unknown liquid, floating in the general miasma.

'De mercurial sperm,' explained de Dutchman.

'Quite so,' murmured the distressed Reverend.

Onderdonk's assistant entered. The pixels shudder, describing her as a maiden of astonishing beauty, with golden locks and a skin of ivory, holding in her perfect hands a large ball of twine, with which she proceeded to secure the Reverend to a mahogany rocking chair in the room's centre.

'For de convulsions,' de Dutchman reassured him. 'Trost me.' He cuffed Hechler's hands behind him, and began attaching wires, while the gold lady, the *regina* or *filia mystica*, sat back on a small stool, holding the end of the twine. (There should, according to most authorities, be a dog in this process, but Onderdonk was a charlatan.) He did, on the other hand, have the requisite worms, virgin's faeces, the pubic hairs of a red-haired man hanged on the gallows, and the severed ear of a failed artist. 'Perhaps,' ventured Hechler, 'we might postpone till tomorrow. I only came to make an appointment.' But de Dutchman laughed, and began reading out from an ancient Egyptian papyrus:

> To whom can I speak today?
> Brothers are evil,
> The friends of today do not love.
> To whom can I speak today?
> The gentle hath perished,
> The bold faced goes everywhere.
> To whom can I speak today?
> Laden with wretchedness,
> I have not one friend of good faith.
> To whom can I speak today?
> Wickedness smites the land,
> Wickedness which hath no end.

An ancient pharaonic amulet dangled before Hechler's face. De Dutchman's eyes grew large as saucers, then as brass gongs, then as radar dishes. The woman behind the mesmerist, growing soft in focus, began to metamorphose, becoming, in quick succession, a large pig, a hairy Breton goat, then a small Imperial snuffbox, out of which clouds of ash emerged. The twine enfolding him seemed to cut like a steel hawser, then, with a sharp twang, it parted. He found himself lying on his back (the file relates, excitedly, trembling before Tolstoy's eyes), on a creaking sofa, in the Petra Hotel, just inside the Jaffa Gate in Jerusalem. His bill had been unpaid for three months. The date of his foretold death had long passed. He prevailed upon the kindly hotelier, Sheikh Anton, to lend him a few Austrian kreutzer, with which he despatched an urgent telegram to the British Embassy at Vienna, soon receiving a chilling reply: The Reverend Hechler was living, quite happily, and in good health, at home in London, in the bosom of his manuscripts. Attempts by an impostor to importune friends for cash would be rigorously opposed. The Reverend Hechler had no intention of returning to Palestine. Further approaches would be ignored.

Hechler staggered out of the Petra Hotel and wandered, in a deep fever, in the Judean Desert. The file suggests he passed the following twenty years in a cell in the Mar Saba monastery. The English Hechler died in 1931. But the Palestinian Hechler, holding on under the mesmeric power of de Dutchman, persevered, resuming his occult researches in the eye of the storm, prospering by the sale of ancient scrolls he dug up in hidden desert gorges. In 1945 he was a hundred years old, and his bodily functions began to decay. He engaged servants to carry him about in a sedan chair, but later on, as his physical deterioration increased, he had to be ferried about in a sealed box, with a mouthpiece to instruct his bearers. And thus, the legend goes, and the recorded sightings indicate, he is abroad to this day, one hundred and thirty odd years after his birth, kept alive like Edgar Allan Poe's Monsieur Valdemar, rich enough by his endeavours to buy silent serfs, but still as determined as on that Herzlian night in Jerusalem to locate his heart's burning desire . . .

The telephone rang. It was thin Avi.

'Avram, you bastard! Are you alive?'

'Uh-huh,' answered Blok.

'Come and meet me in town, shithead!'

Blok ambled towards the point of the rendezvous, the corrugated iron passageway of the Orion Cinema. The prevailing feature was a Clint Eastwood picture, co-starring an orangutan. Avi was puffing zealously on a cigarette under the Coming Attractions: *1941*, *War God Beach*, *The Land That Time Forgot*. It was a hot autumn day, closing in on the Hebrew New Year, but no balm yet from a harsh August. A newspaper vendor cried the latest cry on the unrest in Iran, 'Shah Declares: I Am In Full Control', and the Camp David talks: 'Peace With Egypt – In the Oven!'

'Hopes, hopes, hopes,' said Avi. 'I have to have a quick lunch.' He took Blok to the quick-service restaurant, 'Ma'adan', run by the ebullient Ezra D., who often disconcerted patrons in his densely packed cubbyhole by standing over the tables, encouraging a rapid turnover by the raucous cry of 'SWALLOW, DON'T CHEW!' Shocked newcomers gobbled in panic, soup dribbling down their chins, Ezra waving his arms over their heads: 'HURRY! HURRY! YOU THINK YOU'RE AT HOME HERE? I SHOULD SLAP ON A COVER CHARGE!' He also refused to serve tea or coffee, as either would take too long to prepare. Unfortunately, it was the cheapest lunch in town. Some patrons had been coming for decades.

'They've called me up for Reserves duty,' Avi said, angrily. He had ordered two humus and fuls. Tea? Not a chance. Two orangeades then. 'The fucking Israel Defence Forces.'

53

'A problem,' said Blok. He had been building up his vocabulary.

'Not a problem,' said Avi, 'a fucking scandal. By their timing, I'm sure they know all my moves.'

'Uhm-huhm.'

'I'm due to go on Sunday. Manoeuvres in Sinai. Captain Sucker, at their service. But if I don't turn up my poor platoon will be at the mercy of Captain Karish, my alternate. He will lecture them about God's Plan for the Nation, and get them completely lost in the *jebels*. Ezra! Bring us some pickles, will you?'

'THEY DIDN'T BRING YOU PICKLES?! WHAT'S GOING ON HERE? MY OWN STAFF ARE SABOTEURS!'

'I bequeath you the charge of my humble household,' said Avi, 'Esther does ask after you, you know. But don't allow her to bully you. I know you. You are a sucker for powerful women, Avram. I suppose that's something we share. But you have to realize Esther can't avoid seeing you as a guinea pig for her hobby-horses. The Paranormal. Near-Death Experiences. New Models of the Universe. Esther clings to some of those old Sixties' relics. She'll probably drag you off to Ein Karem, to see her eminence grise, Armand, the Happy Hermit of the Hills. From the New World via California and ashrams to the Old. But he's just another Jewboy like us, pretending to be someone else. It's one way of surviving here, I guess. Esther is into the "meaning" behind the apparent. Levitation for Terrestrials. Guru shadows. Not to speak of all the welfare clients. Give us your poor, your huddled masses, yearning for their monthly allowance. Even the fucking cat is eligible. That evil beast. Always prying and watching, like a tax inspector. But you seemed to get on with the critter. I remember you two, tête-à-tête, in the kitchen. What were you discussing with Adolphe, Avram?'

'This, that.'

'Is it in favour of Peres or Rabin?'

Blok lifted a neutral palm.

'The cinema, maybe. Fuck! With all this I'll miss the Cinematheque's Fassbinder season. Is there no limit to their perfidy? Apropos – your old friend Yissachar – you showed me a letter a few weeks ago . . . time just moves, fuck it . . . I should have

54

called you much earlier, but the book business . . . Anyway, I heard he's now in Tel Aviv . . .'

'STILL TALKING!' Ezra D. leaned over their table, dangling his wristwatch suggestively, 'WHAT DO YOU THINK THIS IS, THE PARLIAMENT? WHO TAUGHT YOUR FRIEND TO CHEW THIRTY-SEVEN TIMES? HIS MOTHER? YOU TWO TRYING TO DRIVE ME OUT OF BUSINESS?'

'Ah, Yissachar,' said Blok, non-committally.

'The fellow is into all sorts of scams, I hear,' Avi said. 'The movie business, leisure centres, the empire of dreck of Adir Kokashvili, our new home-grown Golem. We all move one, take on new flesh. Success, failure, the fucking treadmill. Only you seem immune, old friend. Time knows you not. So what's your fucking secret?'

Tick-tock, tick-tock, Ezra D.'s wristwatch. Avi masticated slow mouthfuls. 'Shall we call for seconds?' he asked Blok. Ezra's eyes widened. A shocked silence fell upon the adjacent tables. Spoons paused in soup, knives poised, quivering, forks frozen half way to mouths.

'No, thank you,' said Blok.

Business resumed, in some relief. Ezra D. scribbled out the bill. Avi paid. They proceeded down, towards the Jaffa Road, past the toy and clothes shops, the PazGaz Agency, Chez Simon and the Habira Cinema, now showing *Twenty-One Hours At Munich*. The cry of the traffic, the mumbling crowd, the hoot of the newsvendor: 'FIRST MOSLEM IN SPACE! ONE HUNDRED MILLION TO GO!'

'The world's becoming stranger and stranger,' said Avi, guiding Blok by the arm. 'Ethnic bombs, gene warfare . . . Most of the world's leaders are either drugged or senile. They say Sadat and Begin were both doped up in Camp David with euphoria-inducing heart drugs on Jimmy Carter's own orders. Do you know that Haiti has the world's lowest standard of living but makes eighty per cent of the world's baseballs? I'll bet that's mint news to you. The spirit of dislocation moves across the waters. Entropy at every turn. Beautiful girls, in our own city, are getting dumber by the minute. All the statistical surveys bear this out. For quality these days one has to import women across vast distances, from far off cafés.'

55

They paused by Gertwagen's bookshop. Paperbacks in the English language, many at vastly reduced prices. New titles sold at a loss.

'I don't want you to get me wrong about Esther,' Avi said. 'I love her like a lover. But I never thought I'd go for redheads. It's sometimes difficult to avoid clichés. They burn, you know, but are never consumed. One's soul gets blisters, being too close. There is this thing with independent women. I always knew I'd only go for someone who had willpower and brains, like the old pioneer women who lived in mud huts and carried about sacks of manure. But somehow in my callow youth it never occurred to me that they would have DESIRES! You know what I mean, these unshakable views on exactly where to put the hi-fi. Modern life is not what it used to be. It's a hard life, breaking up status quos.'

They had reached Zion Square, and were set upon by a skull-capped youth and a headscarved young woman, tending a table draped in the national flag by the frontage of the long dead Zion cinema.

'Sign a petition to the Parliament! Say No to the Camp David Agreements!'

'A deception practised upon the People of Israel!' cried the youth. 'No to Carter and Sadat! No withdrawal from the Land of Israel! Support the Death Penalty for Terrorists!'

They flourished pens in Blok and Avi's faces. Fire belched from Avi's nose and ears. 'A Curse upon ye and all like ye!' he cried. 'Neo-fascism to the gallows!'

A crowd began to gather, encircling the combatants. Heads bobbed up from the back rows. A clean-shaven man in suit and tie enquired of the petitioners if they were criticising Prime Minister Menachem Begin.

'Heaven forbid!'

'Begin is a Great Man!' said the girl.

'He is our saviour!' cried an invisible woman.

'He was deceived by Dayan and Ezer Weizman, his so-called advisers!' the girl explained.

'They are all Heroes of Israel!' cried the woman.

'God didn't take us out of Egypt in order to return the Sinai,' said the youth.

'You're a complete imbecile,' Avi informed him.

The crowd grew, drawn by the smell of conflict. 'Where do I sign?' The invisible woman elbowed her way through, becoming flesh, cartilage and shopping bags. 'I want the Death Penalty for Terrorists, but nothing against Menachem Begin!' A group of men, triggered by the name of the saviour, began singing 'BEGIN, KING OF ISRAEL!' A policeman with an injured look materialized, palms spread out in supplication. 'Ladies and gentlemen, you are blocking the way.' 'BEGIN, KING OF ISRAEL!' the crowd sang. 'Very true, very true,' said the policeman. 'Move on.' He looked in Avi's eyes. Avi shrugged, turned to Blok. 'Let us obey the Law,' he said. They proceeded, across the old alleyway of Yoel Moshe Salomon, past the Arieh taxi stand.

'You see what I mean?' said Avi, as they ignored Steimatsky's. 'The deification of the irrational. War is Peace. Love is Hate. Truth is Lies. And here am I, preparing to put on the uniform again, to serve this whole can of worms. I tell you, Avram, it's me, not you, that's crazy. Is your bed at T—t still free?'

They passed Tamar's Gifts and Souvenirs (forty cards of Jewish Happy Families, giant blue-and-white pens), crossed the road, ambling past the Jordan Bookshop, the Alba Pharmacy, The King of Humus and Mekor HaCafé, to an old Thirties office building whose dilapidated entrance sported a phalanx of faded plaques and arrows pointing up a winding cracked stairway; gloomy corridors barely admitting the sun, doors with chipped signs on frosted glass. A burst of loud abuse came from behind a half-open door labelled, 'KASTORAK – PRESS DISTRIBUTOR'. Avi poked his head through the doorway. An immense blue-jowled head extruded from the other side of a desk piled high with magazines and newspapers, other piles, many reaching the ceiling, covering almost the entire floor space: not only the full range of the daily rags, but a cornucopia of special-interest journals, motorcycle reviews, popular engineering, farming news, the *Plumbers' Weekly*, the *Police News*, the *Safe Crackers' Magazine*, *Horseflesh Monthly*, the *Religious Fashion Flyer*, the *Orthodox Oasis*, the *New Woman*, the *World of Cinema*, the *Ballet Bullet*, *Books and Boozers*, *Weapons and War*, *Dishwashing Daily*, the *Nippon Nebesch*, the *Hassidic Hawk*, the *Ku Klutz Klan*, *Brides and Brideswear*, *Kitchens and Kitsch*, *Brats and Brasso*, *1001 Football Failures* and many many more. In the midst of these a brown-faced, bearded dwarf, clutching a sheaf of magazines, at whom the proprietor was firing multilingual verbal fusillades:

'*Vai funculu! Bazom Kristus Mariat! Yebenti Boga! Stronzo! Tschorta mati! strungul! mboro! tizz al nabi!* You told me the last time, you little bag of pustules, you only needed four *World of Puzzles*!' He had switched to Hebrew for the audience.

'Ah! Last time!' the dwarf raised his eyebrows and arms, rolling his eyes. The vendor fired another salvo.

'Our Kastorak is fluent in sixty-seven languages and dialects,' Avi explained to Blok, waving to the combatants, who waved back, and guiding Blok past the tableau. 'Yes, all human and demi-human life is here,' he said cheerfully. 'Upstairs, a man who makes false beards for joke shops. Downstairs the King of Lavatory Brushes. Top floor, a man who writes sex manuals for the Orthodox and Dr Fish, our Veterinary Surgeon. But this is our very own Den of Iniquity.' He stopped at a closed door marked 'Bridge Publications' in small letters in Hebrew, English and Arabic and, knocking on the door, called out: 'Amnon? Avi. *Iftah el bab, habibi.*' The door was unlocked from within, allowing them to step into a small room with a wooden table, four folding chairs, a few dozen books on bookshelves, and a number of posters pinned up on peeling cream walls, thus:

– A dove fluttering over a map of Mandate Palestine.

– A jigsaw mass of Jews and Arabs.

– A porter bent under the weight of the city of Jerusalem crowned by the golden Dome of the Rock, which he was carrying as his load, secured by a red band round his forehead.

– A black bordered black and white portrait of a sad eyed, thick lipped man –

'Kamal Nasser,' explained the dark long-haired youth who had let them in, at whom Avi waved a hand. 'A Palestinian poet. Our army killed him in Beirut in '73. The soldier fired a round into his mouth. We're having some of his poems translated. Kill and resurrect, that's our national motto.' The youth was wearing a white T-shirt with a portrait of President Amin of Uganda announcing in a Hebrew speech balloon: 'I am a Zionist.'

'Amnon – Avram Blok. Avram Blok – Amnon, my partner in this doomed enterprise,' said Avi, picking up a thin stack of letters. 'Culture Across the Chasm.'

'Ghassan Kanafani,' Amnon added, still under the portrait, 'another fine Palestinian writer and patriot. We published some of his short stories. The Secret Service got him with a car bomb in 1972.'

'A writer's life is not all literary prizes and fucking,' said Avi.

'What a pity,' said Blok.

'That picture is there just to remind us,' said Amnon. Blok nodded in silent approval.

'To the point, Avram,' Avi laid down his letters, waving Blok to a rickety chair. 'I brought you here to make you an offer you probably can't accept. Esther would kill me if she knew. Everyone thinks you need rest and recuperation. But I think I know my old Avram. You don't really want to bury yourself for ever in Hageffen Street, munching through your Welfare nest egg, lulled every weekend by Shabbes prayers, driven crazy by neighbours beating carpets, waiting for the postman to bring you the final licence demand for the TV set you don't own. No, what you really want is a kick up the arse, if you'll forgive the bluntness. Something to get the old adrenalin flowing, however bizarre it may seem. After all, are you not Blok, Avram, connoisseur of the unexpected? I rest my case. So sit down, old friend, rest your feet, polish your eyeballs, relax the oesophagus, uncoil the intestines, and hearken to my proposition —'

The wind, such as it might be in mid-September, died down. The midday sun quietly baked the city. A bead of sweat gathered on the brow of the porter in the poster, carrying the Dome of the Rock. Down the corridor, the magazine distributor Kastorak still fulminated in a dozen tongues. House cockroaches, who had long given up on Esperanto, exchanged Prison Six slang. The dwarf vendor, retreating, exiting the building, resumed position at his stall just on the street corner, proudly adding to his display six new copies of the *World of Puzzles*. The Brain Teaser, the National Rebus, the Talmudic Crossword, the Junior and the Senior Acrostic, the Gimatric Enigma, the Astrological Cipher, the Ruse of Rabbi Nachman, the Political Labyrinth, the Incomplete Cartoon. 'Puzzles! *Yediot! Ma'ariv! Jerusalem Post! Astrology Weekly!*' he offered, in a buzzsaw cry. 'See the End of the World and Its Beginning in your stars! Everything you can't afford not to know!'

★

Just across the road, and several levels below ground, Elyakim Moshe Tolstoy of Hageffen Street was consuming his cottage cheese and marmalade sandwiches in the company of two of his Departmental colleagues, Pinhas Peterkin, alias 'Lermontov', and Nehemiah Buzaglo, otherwise known as Rashi, as his field reports were often presented in an indecipherable script not unlike that of the famous sage of that name. It was a hurried lunch, as the mainframe was crunching through one of the central databanks, trying to find correlations and reciprocities between the mass of its mystagogic data, its reborn crusaders, transubstantiated prophets, avatars, sylphs, seraphim and so on, and the Department's latest can of worms . . .

'I don't see how they expect us to take on the extra case load in these conditions,' Lermontov said. 'At least in the old building we had the cafeteria.'

'I disagree,' said Tolstoy, carefully trapping a crumb in a Kleenex tissue. 'You want to go back to the old days? The kilometres of paper files? The dust? The lead poisoning? Those days you really earned your salary.'

'Ah, but money was money then.'

'Istiqlal put me on to a good wheeze,' said Rashi. 'Put the lot in Jordanian dinars. While our shekels go down the drain like water, the dinar actually picks up against the dollar. You can't believe it till you see it.'

'You can play Istiqlal's shady games,' warned Tolstoy. 'I wouldn't have any truck with that lot. I'm for keeping the Department clean.'

'Cash is neutral. It flies no flag.'

'We heard you. Is anyone impressed?'

'Hey, you guys,' said Lermontov, diverting the conversation. 'Did you hear the latest from the bargain basement – Young Kazha's Hechler sighting? The famous box has been seen, in the Armenian Quarter. A museum guard signed a chit for it.'

'Museum guards!' scoffed Rashi. 'They are like Abbott and

Costello. Next they'll sell you the original Scroll of Thoth, or the skeleton of Haroun al-Raschid.'

'I saw the chit.'

'How did you get to work here? I used to have boxfuls of those.'

'I'm getting back to work,' said Tolstoy, 'never mind you layabouts. Some people actually believe in State Security and dealing with the problem to hand . . .' He stepped away towards the consoles. The other two watched his departure cheerfully, whistling in unison the theme tune from *The Bridge on the River Kwai*. Banks of tapes, behind them, revolved inexorably, recording, and transmitting to thirteen other Departments a multitude of regular voices, confabulations, drones, whispers, gasps, stutters and moans, telephone calls, taxi drivers' flim-flam, children's street cries, hagglers in bazaars, the whispers of lovers coupling, trade union negotiations, prayers to the Almighty, terrorist conspiracies, cheaters in exams, the agonies of constipation on toilets, cries of newspaper vendors, the curses of Kastorak, the quiet conversation in Avi's office, the wheezing of the porter on the wall, the uneasy gyrations of the thwarted dead in tombs, the jabberings of lunatics and television presenters, the chatter of politicians' teeth, the slow bubbling of intellectual minds poised over a tub of Eshed yoghourt, and so on. Tolstoy reaccessed his screen, ready to wrestle again with the knotty problem of the latest mystery thrown up by the City, the ongoing affair of –

The Saga of The Rabid Sheep
[Dept. Ap. Aff./06/J/(mamm.)
AHF/MR/KJ2/KD/01/02/05
JHB/(all sections)/GBH/335/d]

1st Report, Yediot Rishonot, *12.2.78:*

INCIDENT AT THE BIBLICAL ZOO
A strange and unexplained event took place during the previous night at Jerusalem's Biblical Zoo. The night shift guard, Ali Ibn Shaaban, was roused at about three thirty a.m. by a loud ruckus from the direction of the Zoo's lower perimeter, near the wolves' and jackals' enclosure. Proceeding cautiously down the hill he found the grey wolves leaping

against the mesh of their cages in a state of great excitement, but a complete lack of movement in the jackals' cage. His fears appeared confirmed when he noticed a gaping hole in the side of that cage. His torch also revealed torn bushes, patches of wet blood on the path, and a corresponding gash in the outer perimeter fence, opening up on B. Z. Yakobson Road. However, on unlocking and entering the jackals' enclosure he was astounded to find all five of the animals lying lifeless, with their throats savagely torn. Zoo officials and police, alerted immediately, combed the surrounding area. But in the morning the mystery only deepened when tufts of sheep's wool were discovered clinging to the torn cage mesh and scattered over the adjacent ground. And yet there were no sheep's bodies, nor any indication that any other animal had escaped from the Zoo. All carnivores were definitely accounted for. Now police forensic laboratories have reported traces of rabies in the blood found. The jackals, however, were found to be free of the disease. The police have warned the public to be wary of stray dogs, and keep their domestic pets indoors . . .

Report 2, A-Sha'ab, East Jerusalem, 25.2.78; (Items in Brief):

Verily our country is full of wonders! A shepherd of Ras Shihadeh reports the unique behaviour of one of his own rams. It appears that while trying to round up his flock one evening the animal turned and attacked his dog! The dog turned tail and fled up the mountainside, with the ram in hot pursuit! It had actually been bitten on the neck and rump and was bleeding quite heavily. The shepherd ran to get his gun, but when he returned night had already fallen and he was unable to identify the recalcitrant ram. The next day all his animals behaved normally, except the dog, which refused to proceed with its herding duties, and had to be destroyed and replaced.

Report 3, SECRET: Police Intelligence Unit, J'lem Div., 2.3.78:

For limited distribution: general health & security alert: It has been established that blood infected with rabies found in the vicinity of Biblical Zoo incident (see attached) is definitely that of a mammal of the Ovis family, i.e. a sheep or goat. Veterinary opinion is divided on the circumstances of the infection or its consequences (see attached). In light of the attached press item from *A-Sha'ab*, investigations have been carried out among the farmers of the northern and northeastern suburbs. Under interrogation the said subject of the item, Mahmud Nagif al-Shazli, confirmed the incident and also admitted he had subsequently missed one ram, but did not reveal this, as he thought his animals might be destroyed. This indeed had to be resorted to under the Health and Safety Compensation Act (Amend., 1971), but no trace of disease was found in any of the animals dispatched. The body of the dog in question, however, was exhumed and found to be infected. All police and army units should be warned to look out for any stray or individual ram acting in any way out of character and take immediate and appropriate action. The relevant sections are inquiring into the possibility that enemy saboteur activity might account for this unusual medical condition in domestic bovid stock.

Report 4, Army Central Command, Rammallah Distr., 10.6.78:

Private Michah T.: Well, there we were, going along, minding our own business, patrolling in the Wadi Simniyah area, not far from Ein El-Oujah, not a worry in our head apart from the thought of terrorists in the escarpment caves, when suddenly we hear a sound somewhere from a rocky cleft . . . I find it difficult to describe . . . It seemed almost semi-human . . . Sergeant Eli B. immediately ordered us to take cover, and we cocked our weapons, ready for any eventuality, but then, just above the Sergeant's head, this . . . sheep, or ram, that should have been perfectly normal, hurled itself on top of him . . . ! None of us could believe our eyes . . . We just squatted there, rooted to the spot, while the animal snarled and growled . . . He cried out – 'Almighty God! Help me!' I unfroze and rushed over. But the beast had leapt beyond the cleft again. Doron and Shuki opened fire, with automatic bursts, in vain . . . I sat there cradling the

Sergeant's head . . . His throat was torn bad . . . But I didn't think he'd die! In God's Name, by my mother, it's the total truth I'm telling you! You just have to believe me! I'm not telling a lie! you've got to believe me! (*repeated*) Nyaaahhhhh . . . (*remainder unintelligible*). [Classified Intel., Med.Intel., ABC Research (Bio.), Dept.Ap.Aff.] [Update: 16.9.78: Twenty-one further confirmed encounters, no further human casualties; six domestic bovines; five assorted poultry; four feral cats; three stray dogs; two household cats; and a partridge in a pine tree.]

Beads of sweat gathered on the brow of the porter pinned to the wall of 'Bridge Publications'. The sweat ran down the length of the coloured poster, staining the cream wall beneath. The porter climbed off the poster, laid down his burden of the City on the floor. He cadged a smoke off Avi, who lit his cigarette. The porter said, '*Shukran*' – Thank you. The Domes of the Rock, El Aqsa and the Holy Sepulchre, along with spires and turrets, cluttered the room. Amnon perched on the desk, and Blok had to move his feet to avoid being crushed by the Citadel. Kamal Nasser, in his black border, closed his eyes, pursing his lips and softly humming the Palestine anthem, '*Biladi, Biladi . . .*' After a few puffs the porter returned the cigarette, nodded his thanks and climbed back on the wall.

'There is a theatrical group in the Old City,' said Avi, 'who have been doing radical work for some time. You know the sort of thing: allegorical drama, adaptations of Brecht, poetry reading, ethnic dancing. As much as the censor will allow to be presented of critical thought and Palestinian culture. This group is one of several active in the West Bank – they call themselves the *Zurafa* – that's an old tenth-century concept of gentlemen of cultured wit, people who ridicule the pretensions and lies of the day . . . Anyway, one of the actors, Latif, has written a play which they now have permission to perform. It's a satirical piece. This is the story: Abd-el-Salaam Mishraqi, the only son of a well-off small town vintner, is hit on the head one day by a cask of wine and falls into a deep slumber from which he doesn't wake for three years.

64

His father dies of grief, the family's wine goes stale and rival families foreclose their business. The sleeper is laid down in a dusty warehouse while his surviving relatives await his awakening. Various doctors, lawyers, and soothsayers try to bring him back to life, in vain. However, one day he does wake up to find he has been miraculously turned into a Jew. Here, in the original text, he took immediate charge of everything and evicted his relatives from their house. But the censor would not allow that. Praise Him! So instead the Sleeper just sits in a chair, sipping orange juice, speaking nothing but Hebrew, and reading the Israeli newspapers. He becomes a centre around which the soothsayers revolve again, trying to change him back into his former self. Songs of the Homeland (the few the censor allowed) are sung to him, prose and poetry read. It's all a bit of an excuse for a nationalist lesson, dressed up with a lot of hooh-hah. The problem is, they would prefer, despite all the difficulties involved, to have an Israeli play the role. Someone not too eastern looking – a pale Ashkenazi, a typical European Jew. The parallels with your own life, Avram, struck me immediately! Your pudgy face rose in my mind. True, the military authorities will bust a gut. They'll strew obstacles along the road. They might even ban you from the Areas. And the stuffed shirt Arabs won't like it either. But it would be a bold experiment. A real breakthrough for joint activities. I know, you never gave a fart for politics. But Fate, Avram – the tendrils of Destiny! The whole matrix seems too perfect to pass up! You wouldn't need to learn much text, the hero says very little. Most of the time he's just lounging on stage. A familiar situation, eh, Avram? What d'you think, what d'you say?'

★

'Biladi . . . , Biladi . . .' the porter on the wall tunelessly joined in with the adjacent poster of Kamal Nasser. Deep below ground, recording tapes revolved; Tolstoy, at his VDU, searching desperately for clues. In the street outside, four men, carrying a large sealed box, which nevertheless emitted a putrid smell, paused by the dwarf vendor's news stall. They bought a *World of Puzzles* and a *Jerusalem Post* and moved on, carrying their load, up Helen the

65

Queen Street, towards the Russian Compound, followed by a pack of drooling alleycats. The midday traffic continued to pour down the main Jaffa Road, snorting, snarling, braying, scratching, clamouring for the right of way . . .

AL-QUDS

In the Name of Allah,
The Merciful, the Compassionate!
Praise be to Allah, master of the Universe! And prayer and
peace upon the Prince of Messengers, Muhammad, our lord
paramount! And upon all his people prayer and peace
together for ever until the judgement day!

★

On September 26, 1187, 21 Rajab, 585 by the Moslem
calendar, the armies of the great general, Yusuf Salah ed-Din,
Saladin, encamped on the Mount of Olives, between Abu
Sneima's kiosk and the Intercontinental Hotel, on the site of the
alleged Ascension of the Nazarene to heaven. A small detachment
of sappers was already mining the City walls, by the Damascus
Gate, right under the all-night taxi stand. On the 24th of Rajab a
breach was made in the wall, and the Saracen and Crusader armies
prepared for the final showdown. The end of the Christian
Kingdom of Jerusalem, which had lasted for exactly eighty-eight
years, two months and twelve days, was at hand. That night in his
tent, in the brisk Jerusalem autumn, his loyal retainers watching
over their general's slumbers, the great Saladin had a singular
dream –

Saladin's Dream
He dreamed he was on the threshold of a vast plain, strewn with
countless putrefying dead bodies, slaughtered multitudes as far as
the eye could see: white bones thrust like a billion markers out of
an ocean of rotted flesh. Scooped-out eyeballs and internal organs

69

glistened under the deep blue sky. Bared and severed hearts palpitated, fingers writhed, intestines slithered like giant worms. Over this unimaginable sea of horror a figure approached from the horizon. Floating, with effortless grace, over the field of carnage, the figure resolved itself into a graceful maiden, her slim body clad in a blue bathrobe, her blonde hair bobbed, her pale blue eyes piercing his valiant Kurdish heart as she held out a ball of twine. He caught the edge of the twine, and she led him across the field, the ball unravelling slowly but steadily as he failed to keep pace, his mailed feet sinking and squelching in the carpet of decaying carrion. Skeleton hands snatched at his ankles. The remains of barely familiar faces gibbered at him from the gloop. There was the head of Shawar, treacherous vizier of Egypt, which he had severed with his own hand. The Nubian eunuch al-Mutamen, Confidential Adviser of the Fatimid Caliph, similarly dispatched. Hideously disfigured features of the Armenian guards he had burnt to death in their barracks in the same purge of Cairo, summer of '69. Slain Assassins, Hashasheen sent by Sheikh Sinan, the Old Man of the Mountains, on behalf of King Amalric of the Franks, creeping, knives clamped in their mouths, over the corpses, eager to resume their task. The head of the latest victim of his sword, Reynald of Chatillon, decapitated at the Horns of Hittin, gnashing at his toes. Not to speak of the acres of freshly slain Frankish knights, delayed, in their inevitable journey to hell, by the drama of Jerusalem . . .

'But I am a reknowned man of mercy!' he cried. The blonde lady paused on the horizon. She beckoned to him and then fell below the skyline. He thrashed on, holding on to the twine. The corruption reached his thighs, his genitals, his chest. But suddenly he stood facing a clear escarpment, rearing out of sea of dead. An immense billboard was affixed to the rocks, proclaiming in blood-red letters, each fifteen feet high:

DOST THOU SUFFER FROM CORPORAL MALODOUR? DO THY BEST FRIENDS ALWAYS SHUN THY COMPANY? DOST THOU HAVE TO WEAR CHAIN MAIL EVEN WITH THY LOVED ONES? DO THY PRESS HANDOUTS ALWAYS REVEAL THE SECRET CORNERS OF THY HEART?

He awoke. The city of Jerusalem stretched before him. The eastern wall was etched in golden dawn. Buses and trucks rumbled tiredly up and down the road to Jericho. An early-bird party of Belgian tourists force marched towards the pillar of Absalom. And, charging up the hill to his tent, came a full union-approved camera team of Israel Television, closely followed by a platoon of Military Police in full battle gear, wielding signed banning orders and blindfolds.

★

Unburdened, at first sight, by such scrutiny, Theodor Herzl and the Reverend Hechler continued their post-midnight creep down the labyrinth of the Old City, pursued furtively by the hotel roaches heroically paraphrasing Professor Zamenhof's international language:

'*Kiu estas la viro kun la grandioz barbo?*'
'*Estas pretenzo reg las Judoj.*'
'*Kiu estas la viro accompanes li?*'
'*Estas un imbesil.*'

Nevertheless, the two wanderers rendezvoused with their contact by the Church of Our Lady of the Spasm, to wit, one Baraq al-Zahr, 'Lightning Dice', a name gained by his dubious talents in the shebeens of the City. 'This way, gentlemen,' he rasped in broken German, sweeping the muck and debris of the streets ahead of him by means of a large broom. Now there were three figures loping deep into the Moslem Quarter, hidden eyes peering at them from behind grilles, grids, gratings, peepholes, cataracts. Eventually they fetched up at the Bab-el-Ghawanimeh, just below the Dervish Monastery. A portly turbanned figure sat in an arched niche toplit by an Ottoman Army oil lamp.

'Baksheesh,' whispered Lightning Dice to Hechler. The guard bit each coin and examined it by the light of the oil lamp and then threw a towel over his head. The intruders passed by him, climbing a short flight of stone steps to emerge through the ancient north-western portal on to the Haram Es-Sherif, the forbidden precinct of the two great mosques, the third holiest place of Islam. The great golden Dome of the Rock shone in the moonlight. The

71

smaller silver dome of Al-Aqsa glimmered like a timid firefly at the further end of the court.

'In the year 638 of the Christians,' intoned Lightning Dice, nasally, 'the victorious Caliph Omar entered Al-Quds, the Holy City, upon a white camel. He asked the Christian Patriarch, Sophronius, to show him the site of the *isra*, the night flight of the Prophet, Blessed Be His Name, from the Black Stone of the Ka'aba to the Holy Rock of Our Father Ibrahim, Blessed Be His Memory, from whence the Prophet embarked on his ascent to the Seven Heavens to meet the holy angel Gabriel and the Prophets Adam, Joseph, Jesus, Enoch, Aaron, Moses and Ibrahim, Blessed Be Their Names, to feast his eyes on the tree of life and the vessels of wine, milk and honey and receive the obligation of prayer . . . But the Caliph Omar found the Holy Site covered with rubbish the Christians had thrown there in their contempt for the Temple of the Jews, which the Roman barbarians had destroyed. Therefore the great Caliph marked this spot, upon which, in the year of the Hegirah 69, 691 in the count of the Christians, the Caliph Abd el-Malik built the glorious Sixth Wonder of the World known as the Kubbet es-Sakhrah, known in modern German and High Dutch as the Dome of the Rock and wrongly called by the Jews the Mosque of Omar. The Dome is 97 feet high and 65 feet in diameter, and is covered, upon a wooden framework, with . . .'

Herzl passed him a twenty Heller nickel, and the varlet ceased his natter forthwith. 'Come with me,' he said, leading them, not to the glorious Sixth Wonder of the World but to a solidly bricked-up alcove which appeared a complete dead end. But, setting his hand in a groove in one of the stones, he activated a concealed mechanism which caused the wall of the alcove to swivel open. Taking an oil lamp conveniently slung on a hook inside, the rogue deftly struck a flint against the wall, lighting it, and motioned the two seekers inside. Down, down they spiralled, round an immense central stone pillar that seemed to stretch far below into the centre of the earth, their footsteps echoing on the dank, crumbling stone steps, the lamp casting great distorting shadows on the oozing walls of the shaft, and no sound except the stentorian breathing of the three human moles and the slow, dirgeful fall of adjectives into a bottomless pit . . .

Finally the steps ceased and a long corridor stretched ahead, opening after a short while into a vestibule fetid with vermin droppings. Not a syllable of Esperanto could be heard, but the resonant rush of a stream or river somewhere beneath their feet.

Al-Zahr's lamp went out.

'Oh, shit,' said Herzl.

Someone had grabbed hold of his beard.

It was Hechler. 'We are underneath the Holy Rock itself,' he whispered, 'the sacrificial stone on which Abraham offered his only son to the Lord, on the underside of which is inscribed the *"shem hamephorash"*, the forbidden name of God. It is another site where, according to some legends, the Ark of the Lord lies hidden. The running waters we hear are the headwaters of the magical Sambation River, leading, according to the best of sources, to the Other World, being that known by the Greeks as Styx. Once crossed, there is no return.'

'I think I left my Andrew's Salts at the hotel,' said Herzl. 'I knew I shouldn't have eaten those kebabs . . .'

'*Courage, mon vieux!*' said Hechler. 'Can't you relight that lamp, varlet?' There was no response from al-Zahr, but a sombre glow from no apparent light source began to permeate the vestibule. The further wall, which had appeared as solid as the pound sterling, slid smoothly aside, revealing a dimly-lit chamber beyond. The three voyagers gingerly stepped within, and the lobby wall closed behind them. The room in which they now stood had been hewn out of the solid rock, and was lit by thirty-six flickering torches. It was occupied by sixteen men ranged in two rows of eight at either side of a long stone table. Between each pair was a backgammon board with simple counters, red and black, made out of polished wood. Some of the men were turbanned, others wore the tarbush or fez, others the burnoose hood of the warrior, one or two a large black cap. Above the players, chiselled into the rock, was the ubiquitous inscription which was total Greek to Herzl, but which the learned Hechler could recognize:

'*LA ILLAHA ILLALLAH
MUHAMADUN RASULLULLAH* –
THERE IS NO GOD BUT GOD,
MUHAMAD IS THE MESSENGER OF GOD.'

73

There was no other ornament. Lightning Dice appeared caught between an awed terror and a compulsion to kibitz upon the position of each game. The eight players with their backs to the intrusion paid it no attention. The man centrally placed, facing, and directly under the formula, looked up into Herzl's eyes. He wore a green turban, indicative of a direct descendant of the Prophet, a Sherif.

'You are Herr Herzl, the one they call King of the Jews, are you not?' he asked politely, continuing, in impeccable German: 'I saw your play, *Das Neue Ghetto*, three years ago in Vienna. The production was a little on the flamboyant side, but the character of Jacob intrigued me. You were suggesting that salvation for the Jews implies their recognition and rejection of their own "ghetto" qualities. This savours a bit of Marx, does it not?'

'I am opposed to Socialism in all its forms,' said Herzl.

'*Bitte*,' said the Sherif. He motioned Herzl to the seat opposite him, whose occupant smoothly made way. Lightning Dice shook his head sadly as he saw the game Herzl inherited. He was playing black, and half the red counters had been advanced off the board. Still, al-Zahr thought, there was one chance. The other seven games proceeded, ivory dice clicking on stone, the scrape of wooden counters, as if no interruption had occurred.

'Let us play for high stakes,' said the Sherif. 'A dangerous idea against a sacred memory. It is your friend who seeks the Jews' Ark, is it not?'

'You know its whereabouts?' Hechler leapt forward.

The Sherif threw his dice, obtaining 'six trois'. He carefully advanced his counters and passed the dice to Herzl.

'The Jewish State,' the Sherif stated. '*Der Judenstaat*. The Chartered Company. The Colonization Project. We don't like it. It will bring nothing but trouble, and it will end in tears.'

'Your people will derive great benefits,' said Herzl. 'Wealth begets wealth. Progress, progress. We will bring electrification, industry, the telephone, the march of profit. I intend to write a more comprehensive study of the subject.' He held the dice in his hand.

'Man lives not by bread alone,' said the Sherif.

'I cannot argue with your religion,' said Herzl, 'but I believe

74

both Jews and Mussulmans can derive benefits from an Independent Hebrew Nation.'

But he laid the dice, unplayed, on the table. The other games, surrounding them, continued. Farts and burps filled the dank air with even danker bubbles. Al-Zahr picked his nose nervously. Hechler wheezed and snorted with impatience.

'I will not play dice for my people's fate,' said Herzl. 'Historical destiny rests in the hands of men, not upon the whim of chance.'

'It is God who holds us all in His hand,' said the Sherif. 'Are you a better Judge than Him?'

'Play the game, Theodor, for God's sake!' cried Hechler.

The rush of the river below could be heard. The atmosphere became as leaden as dumplings. A row of massive farts ran round the chamber as the other seven games ceased, counters halted in the air and floated like miniature flying saucers.

Baraq al-Zahr fainted.

The cursor winked blandly on the end of the display.

'This is the nub of the Herzl file,' said Tolstoy. He was instructing a rookie, Nehemiah Kimmerling, in the retrieval of basic data. 'The report is based solely on the sworn affidavit tendered by al-Zahr to the Ottoman Secret Service. He awoke in his dingy attic in el-Wad Street with a smell of graveyards in his nostrils and a pair of ivory dice in his shoes. Theodor Herzl and Hechler had already left the City. The Hechler file shows the Ark remained hidden. Did Herzl play the game or not? We cannot form an opinion. True, we have the Jewish State, but if Herzl had not died in 1904 might we not have had it sooner? Might we not have been spared the millions of dead of the Holocaust? Can we rule out foul play? After all, the man died aged forty-four. Shady rumours of VD. Myocarditis chronica, said the doctors. But what did those fin-de-siècle quacks know? Gaps in secret knowledge are quite galling, both in substance and in principle. Hechler might have the answer, if we could reach him before his total decomposition. You will come to learn, young man, that in our Department there is no such thing as trivial knowledge. Every thought, every event, every thing is interwoven, absolutely intermeshed. Modern physics teaches this most strongly. Cause and effect can be reversed. Scientists have discovered what the police have known all along – one thing leads to another. Out with Descartes. In with the Rabbi of Breslau. Just follow the unwinding string, Goddamit, of that fucking ball of twine!'

★

Unwinding, as Esther drives Blok down the twisting hillside road towards Ein Karem, the olde preserved village in the crook of Jerusalem hills, alleged birthplace of Saint John the Baptist. He had visited her for the first time since Thin Avi's departure to serve the Nation, after telling her of Blok's agreement to have a go at acting in the *Zurafa*'s play.

'You lunatic,' she said sadly, hefting Ouspensky's *In Search of the Miraculous*, a potentially lethal weapon. Adolphe, sensing the potential of violence, scuttled safely to the top of the fridge, watching eagerly for developments. 'Why did you listen to that donkey?'

'Why not?' Blok inquired succinctly. He had been advancing his vocabulary, humming to himself as he trajected the route between Hageffen Street and the Bak'a apartment, a long pedestrian crawl, it being the transportless Saturday, down the Kings of Israel Road, avoiding the ultra-orthodox district of Mea Shearim, round the back of the Russian Compound, down the Tribes of Israel Road, past the north-west corner of the Old City walls, down into the Valley of Hinnom, below the windmill, skirting Abu Tor and the Ottoman railway station, down the Bethlehem Road past the Paz petrol station, across the trainless tracks, by shady red-roofed houses, peeling billboards, the football tote kiosk and glazier, the Orgil laundry, Vaknin the Grocer and the falafel hut, up the path to her gritty concrete apartment block, dodging the kids hurling balls against stone fences, climbing the four flights of stairs.

She placed the *Search for the Miraculous* back on her bookshelf and sighed, ignoring the vibrations of conflict shot at them by Adolphe on the fridge. 'I was planning to visit my friend, Armand, in Ein Karem,' she said, 'the guru of the hills . . . You want to come? You might have something in common – you're both stubborn, and live in your own worlds.'

'Why not?' Blok said. Adolphe was tipped unceremoniously out of the front door, vowing vengeance.

Esther drove a battered red Volkswagen beetle, which rattled and yawed over the roads. It was her unspoken thesis that other drivers ought automatically to give way, and as each of the other drivers thought likewise, this made for an exciting ride, even in the light Sabbath traffic. But Blok sat impassively at her side as she slewed single-mindedly round corners, reluctantly allowing a truck to pass, swivelling constantly to face him as she expounded:

'Don't think I want to dissuade you from doing anything you really want to do. But if you're doing this just to do Avi a favour, you ought to know him just as well as I do. Avi expects people to follow his big gestures of defiance and rebellion. You know he's tried for years to get court-martialled for refusing to serve in the Occupied Areas. But they just shunt him off quietly to the Negev and trap him by his own sense of duty. It's always the same with heroes. They want to get the Medal of Peace as well as the Medal of War. Martyrdom, it's an old Jewish hang-up. Don't think I don't respect him for it. And he's always gushing with new ideas. It's wonderful. Just, sometimes, you have to put on the leash, you know – good doggie, sit down? It may not be the best idea for you to dive right away into the political deep end. I mean, what do you know about this Arab theatre business? But I don't know why I'm lecturing you, really. You have it all figured out in there, don't you? You're not as innocent as you seem.'

'A sheep crossing the road, there,' said Blok.

'I saw him,' said Esther. 'The poor thing must have lost its flock.' She honked at the beast, which gave her a malicious look and hurried off into the undergrowth. They had turned off Theodor Herzl Boulevard and were clattering down the narrow, winding Ein Karem Road, past the Yad Vashem Holocaust Memorial and the brown-green terraced slopes leading off towards the Jerusalem Forest. The low newly-renovated stone village houses, previously of Arabs, now of artists, sculptors and interior decorators, preceded by the bell tower of the Church of Saint John the Baptist, in the nook of one hill, and the spire of the Church of the Visitation (Franciscan), high up on the other. The embalmed enclosure of the Russian Convent shyly hid behind a cypress grove.

'You once worked in this area, didn't you?' Esther prodded him.

'Could be,' Blok said. Can there be a flicker of sweet and sour memories? Halcyon days of the late Sixties, Holyland Films, with young Yissachar Pri-On . . . but the studio's gone now, replaced by an art gallery and a health food restaurant . . . advertisements for bran and muesli and honey from pampered bees. Not only antiquity is ploughed over. Yesterday morning has bit the dust.

Esther's friend's house was buried in the wrinkles of a hill curving back towards the suburbs of the city, amid the lush growths of recent spring, thornbushes, hedges, stubborn wild flowers, narcissi, daisies, cyclamens, squill. Bees. Sparrows. Crows commuting between cypresses and pines. A hare even darted ahead of them. 'It is possible to find a private paradise,' said Esther. Blok wiped a flying ant off his skull.

The main gate was unmarked, but a door at the end of a pathway bore a sign saying simply: '*ARMON*' – 'Palace' in Hebrew. 'Just one of his little jokes,' said Esther. 'You'll like him. He's such a strange man.' She deployed the old-fashioned door knocker. A small, sad-eyed man opened the door, dressed in a T-shirt and dungarees, his face like that of a bewildered, wizened baby, grey eyes, pale complexion, thinning brown hair. He put his finger to his lips, motioned them in, and handed Esther a piece of paper. She read it aloud.

'DEAREST ESTHER. I HAVE MADE A THIRTEEN DAY VOW OF SILENCE. YOU MAY SPEAK AS YOU PLEASE. I WOULD HAVE PHONED TO CANCEL OUR LONG ARRANGED APPOINTMENT, BUT, ALAS, THIS COULD NOT BE. *MEA MAXIMA CULPA*. SINCERE APOLOGIES FOR INCONVENIENCE.'

'Well, isn't this a wonder!' said Esther. 'Please meet my friend, Avram Blok. He doesn't say anything much either.'

Armand nodded graciously, putting his arm around Blok's shoulders, propelling him into the house. The interior of the house was almost entirely one room, apart from a kitchen alcove and bathroom, the main space split into three parts by arches cut in the dividing walls. Bookshelves everywhere, neatly stacked, cushions spread all over the floor. A great deal of bric-à-brac, pots, figurines, ornamental brass arabesques.

Armand rapidly scribbled another document, with a red china-graph pen: 'HUMUS? PITTAS? PICKLES? COFFEE? TEA?'

'Yes. Yes. Yes. No. Yes.'

'Just coffee,' said Blok. The silent man bustled in the kitchen while Blok and Esther roamed the bookshelves. Thirteen different Bibles, Gospels, Apocrypha. Talmud, Mishnah and commentaries. Shulkhan Aruch. Pardes Rimmonim. Tikkunim. Zohar. *Guide for the Perplexed* by Maimonides. Christian Kabbalah: Blau, Von Rosenroth, Papus, MacGregor Mathers. Esoterica, Magic: Eliphas Levi, Sepharial, Crowley. Theosophy: Gurdjieff, in toto. Ouspensky, Lobsang Rampa, Krishnamurti, Idries Shah. Christian Theology: Kung. Niebuhr . . . More Jewish studies: Scholem, Buber . . . Mythology, Classics, Aeschylus to Zarathustra. Buddhism, Hinduism, the Arabian Nights. Zen and the Art of Library Maintenance. Jung, Freud, *et al.* Reich, Klein, Bion, Szasz, Sacks.

'How would you sum all this up in one line?' Esther called out to the kitchen.

Armand flicked a page off a pad and scribbled, folded it into a paper plane and threw it, turning back to the fridge. She caught and unfolded the message: 'IN THE KINGDOM OF THE BLIND, THE ONE-EYED MAN IS HALF BLIND.'

He threw four pittas in a gas oven, then rolled up a trolley laden with the pickles and dips. The pad of paper and chinagraphs displayed like an ominous restaurant bill.

'Ah, this is so nice,' said Esther. 'It's like an outing to the deaf and dumb ward. How are you, Esther? I'm well, thank you. The welfare job? Fair to middling. I have the son of the famous miracle worker, the Dayan Ezuz, among my clients. His father is the spiritual head of his people. The son steals cars and motorbicycles. Still, he swears he'll go straight from now on. My boy friend has just gone off to Reserve duties, cursing and yelling as usual. My friend Avram here is about to involve himself in Arab politics and culture, just for the hell of it, it seems. Should I believe in fate, or free will?'

Armand scribbled: 'MAN IS BORN FREE, BUT EVERY-WHERE IS MERELY CHEAP.'

'Why do I get myself into this?' she moaned. 'Life is tough enough, God knows.'

Armand poured olive oil on the humus and scribbled: 'WHEN THE GOING GETS TOUGH, THE TOUGH FALL ASLEEP.'

Blok seized the note pad. 'THIS HUMUS IS VERY GOOD,' he wrote.

'THANK YOU. IT IS HOME MADE,' Armand scribbled back.

'PERHAPS A TOUCH MORE HOT SAUCE,' wrote Blok.

'THANK YOU FOR REMINDING ME. I SHALL GET IT FROM THE FRIDGE.'

'DON'T MENTION IT,' scribbled Blok.

'My God,' said Esther, 'they're conspiring against me. I knew I shouldn't have brought you two together.'

Armand brought the hot sauce, then scribbled rapidly: 'WE BOTH LOVE YOU, ESTHER. YOU BRING WARMTH TO OUR HEARTS. NEITHER OF US CAN LIVE WITHOUT YOU. YOU ARE A LANTERN UPON THE SHINING PATH. THE FORCE OF OUR LOVE PRESERVES YOUR AVI FROM ALL EVILS IN THE SIGHT OF GOD.' He signed his name, and passed it to Blok, who signed too. Armand sealed it with a dash of hot sauce.

Esther sighed, shaking her head, nibbling on a pitta, as Armand continued to inscribe: 'THE MEANING OF LIFE. HAVING ONE'S CAKE AND EATING IT. CLARITY IN OBFUS-CATION. THE ALCHEMISTS HAD A MOTTO: THE OBSCURE BY THE MORE OBSCURE, THE UNKNOWN BY THE MORE UNKNOWN. TRUTH IS AN ONION. THERE ARE MONKS LIVING HERE WHO DO NOT ACKNOWLEDGE THE TWENTIETH CENTURY. WHY SHOULD I? IN THE AMNIOTIC FLUID OF LOVE, TIME DOES NOT EXIST.'

Blok held up his ticking watch.

'I HEAR WHAT I WANT TO HEAR. THERE IS FAR TOO MUCH NEEDLESS NOISE. HAVE YOU EVER LISTENED TO A CHICKEN SNORING?'

'NO,' wrote Blok.

'WHAT CAN WE PLUCK OUT FROM OUR EXPERI-ENCE, TO LIGHT A PATH FOR OTHERS? HOW CAN WE RECONCILE FAITH WITH CHAOS? VOLTAIRE: FAITH CONSISTS NOT IN BELIEVING WHAT SEEMS TO US TO BE TRUE, BUT WHAT SEEMS TO US TO BE FALSE. AND ALL THESE BOOKS, THE WORDS OF WISE MEN: WITH-

OUT BURNING, THERE ARE NO ASHES. TRUTH IS
THAT FROM WHICH CONSCIENCE CAN BE AT PEACE
– GURDJIEFF. IN SHORT: IT'S ALL IN THE MIND.'

Blok wrote: 'IS THERE ANY MORE HUMUS?'

Armand lumbered to and from the kitchen.

'RABBI NACHMAN: MY ENTIRE TORAH IS PRE-
FACES. WE HAVE NOT EVEN SCRATCHED THE SUR-
FACE. NO NEARER GNOSIS THAN AN AARDVARK.
OR DO ANIMALS HAVE THE EDGE? IS EVOLUTION
REGRESSION?'

'The amoeba is God,' said Esther.

Armand nodded, very thoughtfully. Blok dipped pitta, raised
it, chewed. They sat, quietly, over falling humus levels, as the
angle of the sunlight sharpened. A golden glow falling across their
faces. A bee entering through the open window. It settled determinedly on the humus remnants, manoeuvring to avoid the olive
oil. All three watched it in sombre concentration. It preened and
fluttered in their gaze, then flew back out of the window, buzzing
in appreciation. Yellow gold deepening into red. The sonic double
boom of a jet aircraft in the afterglow shattered the early evening
silence. From the road, a car horn beeped. But the congregants sat,
as the sunlight faded, until the Sabbath siren blasted to mark the
end of the Almighty's weekly air raid.

★

Meanwhile, Adolphe wandered, pissed off, through the backyards of Bak'a, hating the brightness of day but resigned to it,
pausing to eavesdrop on the conversation of two housewives
pushing heavy prams before them. One never knows what nugget
of information might lie in the most apparently innocuous dialogue. But this was total dross. Win some, lose some. He drooled
on to a pram wheel and moved on, unnoticed by anyone of
consequence or authority . . .

At the same time, somewhere in the upper reaches of Wadi
el-Arish, not too far from Bir Umm Said, Thin Avi, caked with
sand, wrapped up warm against the autumn evening snap, was
breaking open an army issue tin of corned beef. Captain Karish,

his fellow officer, otherwise known as Krishna because of his wild eyes, predilection for atonal humming and wearing sandals even on the coarsest manoeuvres, was bending his ear about the latest misdeeds of their Brigade Commander, the baby-faced Colonel Adashim, otherwise known as The Sorrows of Young Werther.

'Laxity in command,' he burbled, 'verging on apathy. You'd think the man was sixty years old. You might have run the Palmach cavalry on those lines, back in '48. But men these days need the whiplash.'

'They've got you,' said Avi, 'isn't that enough?'

'We're not going to win the war with milksops. The man called three halts in a forty-kilo march. We might as well hand the State to Arafat.'

'It's General Headquarters Regulations,' said Avi.

'What do you expect?' Karish threw his hands in the air. 'The whole High Command is riddled with traitors.'

'Vote for Rabbi Levine,' said Avi. The corned beef was like fresh ashes . . .

Only four days before, on an autumn balm Wednesday, he had been conducting Avram Blok towards his first rendezvous with his *Zurafa* contact in the heart of the Old City: passing through the Damascus Gate, past the moneylenders' booths, the vendors of Arab, Hebrew and English newspapers, down the stone steps, by the eternal cafés and souvenir stalls with gaudy nationalist posters – the Palestine dove flying through prison bars, the jailed woman, the porter with the City on his back, et cetera, skirting piled crates of orange squash and Cola, on into the Khan el-Zeit market, with its fake antiques, stamp and coin collections, sweets and savouries, halva, baklava, kunafa, thyme and onion bread, dead chickens and sides of meat hung on hooks, ironmongers and carpenters in cave-like workshops, men, young and old, sitting on stools, ogling Jewish American Princesses. A cat may look at a Queen. No further. Porters trundling iron trolleys, crying warnings, covered women with bags on their heads, old men with canes, obstructing passage. Life just goes on.

Round the corner to Zaroubi's Café, a hole in the wall in Bab el-Habs Street. 'Latif here?' Avi asked. Negative motions. Waiting, with coffee, brought in studied silence, but on squeaky shoes, the battered brass tray, the small white cups, a couple of pittas and *za'atar*. Within the cubbyhole, an eternal backgammon game, click, click, click, since Lamentations. An androgynous young man, joining the two Jews, cheerfully exposed his philosophy:

'I believe the world we are living in now is the real hell of the Scriptures. The eternal punishment. If we try hard we can remember the life before. This was what we now call paradise.'

'It's an old gnostic heresy,' Avi informed him. 'Schopenhauer also adopted something like it.'

'Ah, Schopenhauer!' the youth threw the name in the air and caught it, with an old familiarity. 'You Jews think of everything, but you have lost the talent to FEEL. One has to sense the Absence of God. He spends all this time now in the Other Place.'

'That would account for a lot,' said Avi, mopping up *za'atar*.

'There is no use,' said the youth, 'in nailing up the Son when the Father is allowed to go free. Don't you think?'

'Absolutely,' said Avi. 'Get the bastard who's really responsible.'

They were rescued by the arrival of Avi's contact, a stocky, well-built character, with a beaked nose and an air of walking on stilts, accompanied by Avi's colleague, Amnon.

'Latif Sa'adi – Avram Blok.'

'A pleasure,' said Latif. 'Let's go.'

'Humanity is a failure!' cried the androgynous youth as they paid the bill and walked off.

'A sad case,' said Latif. 'The City is always full of them.'

They turned down an alley marked with stumbling children and running sewage, zig-zagging past high walls, out into the Via Dolorosa, past the Prison of Christ and Ecce Homo, in, through a maze of further courtyards, to the premises of the Khalidiyah High School. The school assembly hall, a large arched basement full of wooden folding chairs leading to a stage of rude planks. Six young men and three young women, on the stage. A rehearsal evidently under way. Several more young men and women, in the front seats, with stencil copy scripts. A cosy air of non-expertise. The entrance of a bald Jew in a sock cap raises no hackles. The newcomers settled down in the back. Later, they sat on cushions in a living room decorated with local fabrics, bedouin saddlebags, assorted needlework, a portrait of Yassir Arafat and framed reviews and features about the group from the *Christian Science Monitor*, the *Middle East* and the *Beirut Daily News* and assorted Arabic cuttings, while Latif, speaking in English, completed the introduction of Blok to the eleven other members of the group, and vice versa:

'Majid Nouri, Salah the Nose, Lena Khalili, Marilyn "Monroe", Salim Abu Ghallallah, "Zeppelin" Khalid, Yassir Not Arafat, Mouna and Rasha Elias, Muhammad "Nightingale" Abu Abbas, Ali Fitzpatrick. His grandfather came with the British Army, but we swallowed him up whole.'

'We were twelve,' said Ali Fitzpatrick, 'and now thirteen.'

'It's lucky,' said Mouna Elias, with some sarcasm, 'that no one here is superstitious.'

'Zeppelin' Khalid, who was spread over three cushions, threw a salt cellar at the wall.

There appeared to be two factions in the room. A reluctant, or Anti-Blok, faction, keeping a silent distance, consisting of Majid Nouri, Salah, Salim, Mouna Elias and Marilyn the peroxide blonde. But a majority group, sitting close to the three Jews, was composed of fat Khalid, Yassir Not Arafat, the other Elias sister – Rasha, Muhammad 'Nightingale' Abbas, Lena Khalili, Grandson Ali and Latif. They fired questions at Blok in English: Have you been on the stage before? Do you know what is involved in this project? Are you aware of the situation in the Arab sector? What do you think of the Camp David treaty? Do you have access to any private transport?

'I don't see any problems,' said Blok. A cautious silence fell on both factions. Avi looked up from the bar of sesame halva he was munching.

'Well,' he said. 'It's an experiment, as the Americans told Hiroshima.'

'What did they tell Nagasaki?' asked Salah.

'TWO HEADS ARE BETTER THAN ONE,' suggested Khalid.

'YOU CAN'T HAVE TOO MUCH OF A GOOD THING,' said Yassir.

Avi said: 'EVERY CLOUD HAS A SILVER LINING.'

★

'But do you really believe that by means of "human rights" you will bring Arabs and Jews together?' asked Karish, carefully unwrapping the crumbling silver paper from the army issue bar of halva. It was difficult to tell, in the Sinai gloaming, where the sand stopped and the halva began. Sleeping soldiers were dotted about everywhere, in blankets, like little dry camel turds.

'I haven't the foggiest idea,' said Avi, 'I just don't want us to turn into Nazis.'

'And if we have to to survive?' Karish insisted.

Avi inclined his thumb downwards.

'You are the first on my list,' Karish said, firmly, rolling over in his sleeping bag. 'Wake me at four thirty prompt,' he added, 'unless your Russian friends come sooner.' He called out a warning to the adjacent heaps: 'Make sure this man doesn't broadcast to Moscow. He's already brought down one government!'

The stars winked on, one by one, the night continuing to deepen, into the hours of anything goes. Back in Jerusalem, Adolphe lurked by the most prestigious location in town, the garbage skip of the Prime Minister's private residence. He was far from his territory, but this gave him no pause. Only the bold progress. Who dares wins. Another milestone on the winding path to power and the objective of every presumptive feline in town, to wit: control over the great communal rubbish skips of the Mahaneh Yehuda street market. The lush pickings of daily mass consumption and conspicuous wastage – discarded vegetables, rotted fruit and fish, rejected carcasses of fowl. The skips were emptied each night, but the enterprising could remove vast portions to storage in private nooks and crannies. For the time being this manna was in the paws of the infamous Agrippas Street Gang, a pack of verminous, flea-bitten, moth-eaten beasts of unparallelled ferocity, who sharpened their teeth and claws against street lamps, and the treads of armoured police cars. But while they relied entirely on brute force, Adolphe planned to move with the times, and use the old fish-fed kop. Information, he knew, was the root of power, the movement of goods, the ebb and flow of commerce, the National Economic Plan. He had spent long nights pressed against the portholes of Ministries and municipal offices. But this was his first try for the core: Number One, the vaulting summit. He perched on the security wall, facing down the swivelling video cameras which recorded his every move. Squeak, squeak, they cranked uneasily, as he bounded across the back lawn, gaining purchase on the unwise but convenient climbing ivy, leaping from ledge to ledge. Arriving finally at a lighted window, closed, with heavy curtains drawn, but a chink, enabling him to peek into the room beyond, at the seven solemn persons seated round a table, their faces pinched and tiredly serious, cigarette smoke curling sheaves of blue, papers messed upon the tabletop, jackets rumpled, ties askew, fingers wagging. Adolphe could not lipread, but his audial reflexes, honed in months of listening, even in the midst of slumber, to Esther and Avi's night gyrations, often followed by whispered exchanges of great importance, for example, the ominous question: 'Honey, When Are You Getting Rid Of That Fucking Animal?' et cetera, were acute enough for him to absorb the nub of the fierce debate. His ears pricked, then reddened, then grew a deep blue, as he eavesdropped on the sinister discourse of the inner Kitchen Cabinet . . .

The night snap of the desert, long fallen. Rocks, spontaneously combusting, kept Avi awake, living in memories, reflecting on the truth of Karish's parting shot, recalling his days of glory: Aviad Ben-Gur, the Giant Slayer, Don Quixote who slew his windmill . . . Spring of 1974. Crouched in a tent by the gate of the Prime Minister's Office, a lone Lieutenant returned from the fog of war, surrounded by banner-wielding multitudes – 'OUT WITH THE BLUNDERERS OF YOM KIPPUR!' 'GOLDA MEIR, DAYAN, RESIGN!' Well, someone had to make waves. And out of the crowds, that fiery redhead, the self-appointed one-woman Catering Corps to the Heroic Hunger Striker (wasn't there a tale by Kafka of the Artist of Starvation?). The foghorn voice willing him vitality, keeping the more emotional of his supporters from requisitioning his bootlaces, or tearing locks off his hair. Good training for her current crop of Welfare clients, the Dayan Ezuz's larcenous heir . . . The future, and past victories: 'The bastards have resigned!' But what followed? Menachem Begin in power!

I am to blame for it all, thought Avi. But does anyone care these days? A small band of piss-artist lost causers scratching on, against a solid wall. At least right wingers like Karish remember us enough to spit on our name. Or is this just some awful symbiosis we've found with our worst enemies? Keeping the tattered flag of any sort of ideal flying, while the masses worship at the flickering screens of television and the bourse . . . The final delusion, brothers and sisters, our true sheepness in a wolf's mask . . . ?

★

Long after Blok had left the Old City apartment, arguments raged between the factions over his acceptance by the *Zurafa*. Lofty ideals of Solidarity are fine, in theory, but in practice, can we afford the risk? The entry of an Enemy into our counsels, never mind the *hantarish*. With all our vulnerability to the Authorities, the on-off switch of the Censorship Committee. Look at Ali Fitzpatrick, he's as pale as a Jew, with his ginger spots he'll pass for one any day. We don't need to make this statement at this point of the Struggle. What do we know about this Avram Blok, anyway? At least Ben-Gur is a known quantity. The man barely says anything. Ah! say the Acceptors, that's the best thing about him, thank God! He doesn't gush with liberal platitudes! All that false, self-serving identification with 'the Oppressed', in order to smoothe a guilty conscience. This Blok is neither for us nor against us. The perfect casting for our play! A madman, scoffed Marilyn, straight out of the asylum! Wonderful! said 'Zeppelin' Khalid. I wonder where I have seen him before? Salim muttered, tugging at his moustache – That face, it seems terribly familiar . . .

But Blok had recognized Salim from the start: For he had seen him clear as daylight, not so very long before, as 'Omar', the young Arab handyman who had whitewashed his roof at 35 Hageffen Street. Man does not live by theatre alone. And a Palestinian always needs at least three identities. Even if he does sing '*Biladi, Biladi*' while waiting for the Fatah's hot-air balloons. At the best of times it is difficult to tell, Jew or Arab, just who one is supposed to be . . .

★

As Esther drove Blok home from Ein Karem, she shook her head over Armand. 'What to make of the man? Sometimes he drives me crazy. Sometimes I think he's the only sane person alive. Sometimes I think he's just going to fade away one day, like the Cheshire Cat, leaving only a smile . . . But I remember him when he was all fire and passion . . . a real demagogue of New Ways. I suppose it ran in the family . . . We haven't told you the great Armand family secret, have we, Avi or me?'

Blok held up a scribbled note: 'NO.'

'He is not French, of course. He's a good Brooklyn Jew, whose father was the Rabbi of his community. Armand was his escape name, when he ran off to California, twenty years ago . . . His real name is Zev Levine. Our own home-grown fanatic, Rabbi Levine, who wants to kick all the Arabs out of the country and bring about the rule of the religious *Halacha*, is in fact Armand's brother.'

Blok scribbled furiously. 'WHAT DOES HE INTEND TO DO ABOUT IT?'

'Nothing,' said Esther. 'He said to me once: "If I were only Cain, and he were Abel. But unfortunately, it's the other way around . . ."'

She dropped Blok at 35 Hageffen Street and drove off to Bak'a alone. Climbing up to his apartment he found, pinned to his door, a postcard forwarded by Papa Blok but presumably received on Friday by his downstairs neighbours, Elrom (recipients of *Hamodia*), and only just delivered, smudged by their fingerprints. A colour portrait of a distant city stirring vague recollections and a strong smell of cabbage. A stamp with the silhouette of the Queen of England, stirring vague recollections. The scrawl on the obverse side was signed by the elusive Yissachar, self-appointed movie mogul's minion:

Hey, Avram!

Made Landfall, tried to reach you but had to leave town pronto on KOKASHVILI business! Remember the new Lord of Celluloid? I am now in swinging London. *Ici Londres!* Remember? Sects and dregs and rotten rolls? Arranging post-production of latest Kok epic: *She Wore Sandals, He Had Club Feet*. It's a harsh age, Avram! We are all swallowed

88

by our own spew! But back soon, with kitbag! So keep the flag flying! Your re-exiled, but still returning –

Yissachar!!

He put this flash in his jacket pocket and walked out into the autumnal end of Sabbath evening. Taking the dank air of the empty street market of Mahaneh Yehuda. Splintered memories of his delight in its bustle and clamour in pre-T—t days, though the corrugated iron shutters were closed at this time on the fish-mongers', greengrocers', butchers' shops, the biscuit, sweet and halva palace, the feta cheese and olive stalls. The faint cluck, cluck, cluck of tomorrow's doomed chickens from behind locked grilles. Out into Agrippas Street, to stand in the short queue before the open falafel shop. Patrons discussing the rare new peace with Egypt. 'Are you going home, to visit, Menashe?' 'I crawled out of there on my belly, in '56. Let the Ashkenazim go.' The smell of frying chickpea balls punching through the October night. The great garbage skips lying empty on either side of the road, ready for the new week's waste, furry figures with flashing teeth scrambling around them, jealous of any usurpers. For a fleeting moment Blok thought he recognized a tubby feline shape peeping from the shadows left by street lights on the stone walls. Another lost soul. He bought a whole portion of falafel, with no hot sauce, dropping bits of cabbage, cucumber, tomato, all the way home.

Night, the City, autumn timbre, the shifting sounds of wolf hours: static of taxi-drivers' CBs, jingle-jangle of late show army radio, grunts, farts, groans and moans of the sleepless, the scratch-ing of dogs digging up bones, manic laughter from the hyena cage of the Biblical Zoo, the stentorian breathing of killer sheep, unstifled cries of outrage from the Old City, the agonies of defective plumbing, skeletons rattling in closets, beeps, trills and bloops from round-the-clock databanks in underground depart-ments, ants marching through spilled oatmeal, cats squabbling in distant garbage skips for the leftovers of power . . .

. . . while, In The Prime Minister's Kitchen Cabinet –
– in amongst the tins of tomato purée, the jars of salt, pepper, oregano, tarragon, cumin and mixed herbs, the tins of rice and

imported Maxwell House coffee and Earl Grey tea and marmalade and jam, behind the Telma mustard, the Osem Quick Jelly, Tropical Fruit Segments and vinegar, bags of sugar and flour and soup mixes and matzoh meal and bran, free (it is hoped) from the scrutiny of foreign spies, the press, the wakeful vibes of released mental patients, and cats on window ledges –

– the Inner Circle of the Government of the Promised Land deliberates – ('I want that incident investigated,' the PM had said. 'We have all heard how the Americans train dogs and dolphins to attach limpet mines to ships, submarines, taxicabs, ballistic missile convoys.')

Present are: the PM himself, the DM, chewing on a hambone, Perpetuumobile the Minister for Internal Affairs, Ganef and Messting from Finance and trade, Shapikhes, the bald Minister of Religion, Fouche of Labour and Police. (Missing is the eighth member, Shvester-Zelma, the 'Old Lady' of the Opposition Party, who was maliciously informed the meeting place was to be the men's toilet of the Shrine Of The Book.) On the agenda are seven items:

a) The escalating affair of the Rabid Sheep, its general effect on the zeitgeist.
b) The disturbing reports of groundshift under the Tomb of Our Founder, Theodor Herzl, on the Mount bearing his name.
c) The relating increase in Time-Slips (Report of Min.Reg. Dep.Ap.Aff./Sept. '78/b/c).
d) The catastrophic drop in the imports of pistachio nuts, due to the troubles in Iran and the imminent overthrow of our stalwart ally, the Shahinshah, Pehlavi.
e) Preparing the sale of the country to a Shabbes-goy, in the event of Apocalypse.
f) The replacement of the Cabinet barber.
g) Members' Portfolios, Revenues, Dues, Investments, Assets, Goods and Chattels, Real Estate, Substance, Dowries, Kine, declaration and protection of. I myself, the PM reminded them, own nothing but the shirt on my back, biting deep on a spring onion. But his droning voice, combined with the lack of air in the Cabinet, had already

90

made the other Ministers drowsy. Unable to open the windows for fear of feline intrusion, Pentagon trained or not. The close, dank air takes its toll. One by one the Kitchen Cabinet members drop off, falling behind the salt cellar, steak seasoning and Osem Oven Farfel. The DM's teeth grinding leftover matzohs. Messting fallen into a jar of raisins. Only Perpetuumobile, loyal to the last to his Leader, with whom he had served throughout the years of the underground, sharing his hiding place in a Beit Hakerem broom cupboard for six months in 1946, in a temperature of 36 degrees Celsius, struggles to remain in equilibris, using toothpicks to prop up his eyelids. But even he succumbs to the nasal drip dry, and lies, unseeing eyes bulging, in a pile of spilled peppercorns . . .

(Does Time exist?)
(Is the entire Torah prefaces?)
(Is Truth an onion?)

                    Z
                     Z
                      Z
                       z
                     z
                    z
                   z
                  z
                 z
                z
                 z
                  z
                   z
                    z
                     z
                      z
                       z
                      z
                     z
                    z
                   z
                  z
                 z
                z

Z
  Z
    z
      z
        z
          z
            z
              z
              z
            z
          z
        z
      z
    Z
  Z
Z

For thirteen weeks, in the winter of '78–9, Blok played the part of Abd-el-Salaam, The Sleeper, in the Khalidiyah School in the Old City of Jerusalem, as well as several performances in towns all over the Occupied West Bank. He appeared in school halls, open-air cafés, hospital wards and churches, in Rammallah, Hebron, Bethlehem, Halhoul, Beit Jalah, Kalkiliah, Tulkarm, Tubas, Jericho and Jenin, and finally, the fated show – in Nablus . . . In Halhoul the stage collapsed under the actors, and the play was resumed in an orchard. In Jericho Moslem Fundamentalists invaded the hall and declared an impromptu prayer meeting. Blok was hustled out, hidden in a blanket, through a toilet vent to a haulage van marked 'Best Olive Oil – Abu Usman'. In Tubas the electricity was cut off, and the entire performance took place in pitch darkness. In Beit Jalah the army stopped the performance well before the transformation scene. They surrounded the café in which it was taking place, but Blok was lowered through a loading trapdoor into a basement piled with cartons of smuggled American cigarettes and pirated video cassettes, many, oddly enough, of Adir Kokashvili productions (*The Blind Beggar Girl of Tabriz, The Deadly Dolphin, I Kill My Friends For Nothing*). Finally, in Nablus, the most nationalist town in Occupied Palestine –

But, before all this . . .

The Rejectionist: Salim's Story

Although Blok had recognized the rejectionist Salim instantly as 'Omar', the Arab whitewash man, it took a little while for Salim to connect the pudgy face of Blok and Hageffen Street. All Jewish roofs looked the same to Salim, and the tenants of their buildings equally diminished insects grubbing about below. To Salim the Israelis were the termites of the Levant, little white ants gnawing at the foundations of the renascent Arab world. The Arab East had, for centuries, been flat on its back, a plodding tortoise flipped over by the effete and corrupt Turks, the curse of feudal barons, and the vaulting greed of Western Imperialism, waving its legs pitiably in the air until it realized its time hardened carapace could be a weapon as well as a bane. Meanwhile, one took one's pleasures as one could, clumping up and down in heavy boots over the Jews' heads in the early morning, charging the most exorbitant rates one could get away with, spilling the lime occasionally over their pot plants by mistake, singing the Palestinian National Anthem while beating time on their balustrades with a trowel. In Tel Aviv, working in restaurants in the mid-Seventies, he had pretended to be a Jew named Eliyahu. But he became tired of this fakery and decided to be a pain in the Jews' neck in his home town. When the *Zurafa* had been formed in the University of B— he had joined, to help express the National Culture. He had studied Civil Engineering for four years and had a Bachelor of Arts certificate. But in the reality of the Occupation he had little hope of plying this trade unless he emigrated to the desert, the Gulf States, Kuwait or Saudi Arabia, so he remained in the homeland, as one of the Steadfast – the *tsamidin*, the people literally stuck to the Land, shlip-shlopping with his lime-dipped paintbrush, dreaming, too, of turning tides.

Salim's father, oddly enough, had been a housepainter by trade and choice, who claimed to have enjoyed painting the houses of all the City's denominations and creeds. While his mother remained at home embroidering a vast tapestry of Historic Palestine and tending their first son and daughter, Salim's father, Yusuf, wandered the length and breadth of the City, carrying brushes and two pails in one hand and a paint-stained folding ladder held over his shoulder by the other, calling out, '*Wishshak, ya sheikh!*' '*dahrik, ya sitt!*' – 'Watch your face, man, look out for your back, o lady!' as he scattered the pedestrian traffic. 'We all lived together under the British,' he always told his son, 'God rot their souls.' But his downfall came at the moment of his greatest triumph, the contract to paint the Commandant's wing in the King David Hotel. The building housed the main offices of the British administration in Jerusalem, military and civilian. On July 22, 1946, half an hour past noon, while Yusuf Abu Ghallallah was slopping away in the Commandant's private office, the Irgun hit men of Menachem Begin detonated 350 kilos of TNT in empty milk churns on the ground floor. 'I had just about finished the ceiling,' Yusuf later related, 'I had just one tiny patch left in the south-west corner when the Jews blew me up.' Twenty-eight British men and women, forty-one Arabs, seventeen Jews and a smattering of other minorities were killed. But Salim's father was lucky, being thrown through an adjacent open window into a casuarina tree outside, surviving to father five more children, Salim, the youngest, bouncing forth five years later. By that time the Catastrophe of 1948 had struck, splitting the country and the City in two halves, blighting the hopes of the Palestinian Arabs and casting hundreds of thousands to exile. Yusuf, his wife, the children, and the unfinished embroidery, became subjects of the Hashemite Kingdom of Jordan. The Jewish customers were barricaded behind concrete walls, with their single-coated bathrooms. Twenty years would pass before an Abu Ghallallah again touched paint to their plaster. On his deathbed, in April '67, Yusuf said: 'And there was just that little patch left, in the corner . . .' He pointed up, towards the seventh heaven, and expired. Two months later the war broke out again. Jewish paratroops crashed through Saint Mary's Gate, into the Old City, and took over the holy Haram. Uncomprehending eyes gazed on the Rock of Abraham and Isaac, at the footprint of Muhammad. Beneath the rock is the 'well of souls', the *bir el-arwah*, where the dead gather to pray twice weekly. On the Day of Judgement the Black Stone of the Ka'ba in Mecca will thrust its way here to the surface, forming the throne of God as the Last Trump sounds. But many Palestinians, Salim among them, were not prepared to wait that long.

'And there was just that little patch left, in the corner . . .'

The tapestry was never completed, either. But over the years it became a communal affair, with the Widow Sharabi, Mrs Antonius and the professional seamstress, Umm Hamadiyeh, neighbours of Umm Salim, Salim's mother, in their Sheikh Jarrah home, joining in the stubborn needlework. Stitch, stitch, stitch, yatter, yatter, yatter, for over twenty years. This was the emerging pattern: in the upper right-hand corner, a discreet portrayal of the *isra*, the Prophet's night flight from Mecca to Jerusalem. The crescent moon, shadowed cupolas, the left foot only of the Messenger gliding in at extremis, the *Buraq*, the Prophet's mystery steed, winged and peacock tailed, at the foot of the Hebrews' Western Wall. Below this, the silvery thread of Yarmuk, tributary of the River Jordan, the white burnoosed armies of the Khalifa Omar poised to win the decisive battle which gave the Levant to Islam. (AD 636, 20 August.) Further in, the Khalifa, in the desolation of the Temple, from which, in a glorious symphony of turquoise and gold, the magnificent Dome of the Rock of Abd el-Malik dominates the entire composition, looming over Al Aqsa, the Christian Sepulchre and many minor mosques and spires. Abd el-Malik and Omar lead the throng of khalifas, sultans, scholars, generals, dotting the matrix, submerged in a sea of figures, men, women, children of the general public, kefiyaed bedouins on horseback, peasants with their hoes, artisans, tamarindi vendors, shitkickers in wide trousers, red pointed shoes and many-coloured turbans, veiled women in markets, leaning on battlements, writing poetry, inflaming the senses. Down the left flank of the work: the Crusader era: blonde giants in armour, with rotting teeth, battle-axes, siege towers, mangonels. Fire licks at the outer walls of the Dome. Battle lines march in a great arc, left to right, across the entire fabric: Jerusalem, Ramleh, Tyre, Ashkelon, Kerak, Hittin, Ain Jalut. Saladin, sad eyed though triumphant, looks inward, reflecting on his dream. The cruel but effective visage of Baibars, the slave-sultan, pushes back invading hordes. But even within the fires, the waves of red, mounds of corpses, severed limbs and heads with wide staring dead eyes, cleverly enfolded between gobs of flame and ruin, patches of green and cultivated fields peek through, with tiny peasants, stubbornly tilling the soil, building terraces, shepherding sheep, tending

95

orchards, picking plums off trees into baskets, sitting under trees with nargilehs, playing dominoes and backgammon, generally shooting the breeze, and everywhere, little groups of women still stitching, stitching away in every nook and cranny of the design, through the Ottoman incursion, Napoleon at Acre, Egyptian, French, and British cannon, General Allenby and the Turks at Megido/Armageddon, the New Crusaders and the Great Disaster of 1948, the *nakba*, the victory of the Jews. By this time space was at a premium in the work – not even a little patch left in the corner – and new additions had to become more and more minute, Lilliputian miracles, so that heroes of the current Palestinian Struggle had to be made out with a magnifying glass, a miniature Arafat, a diminutive George Habash, a barely visible Naif Hawatmeh and the merest wisp of Ahmed Jibril. 'This will not do at all,' said Mrs Antonius, who was a member of the National Women's Council. But Umm Hamadiyeh said: 'It's either this or leave the whole lot out.' As she bent, picking away with the thinnest thread and needle at a minuscule Farouk Kaddumi. The entire PLO Executive Committee would soon be apparent under an electron microscope.

But Salim had a different view of National Priorities, and Art figured in it as a mere mask. For Salim had a third, concealed identity, apart from the Actor and Tar Baby: he was also known, he hoped not too widely, as Abu Kerim, member of a three-man cell of the Popular Democratic Front for the Liberation of Palestine. Recruited by a cousin, who had left the country for Lebanon in 1969, and returned clandestinely for a short while in 1976, he was designated, with his two companions, to sit tight undercover until further notice, waiting for the call to action, living as 'normal' as possible a life the while, arousing minimum suspicion. The radical actor's role, he thought, would be a neat double bluff, though a slight risk for his colleagues. But one could not remain a menial labourer for ever . . . Thus he navigated his one-man nuclear submarine through the Occupation's muddy ocean, venturing out with his bicycle laden with bags of whitewash and pails into Enemy territory, gazing daggers from rooftops into the dandruff-ridden craniums of the Usurping Hebrews, and having to swallow his ire at evening rehearsals before the throne of Blok, The Sleeper, accepted as a bona fide member of the *Zurafa* by majority decision. The play ready for its opening night, the last excisions made by the Censorship Committee, every last letter of the municipal licence to perform observed in fanatic, cautious detail, the policemen paid off, the posters pasted on billboards, café walls and outside toilets, the costumes prepared, the electricians briefed, greasepaint procured, all and sundry given notice of the innovation/provocation to come, the last butterflies calmed down, the improvised curtain, poised –

– while Thin Avi, released at last from his onerous thirty-one days of military powerlessness, was bowling up the narrow road leading from El Arish to the 'mainland' in a bright blue and yellow Egged bus, dozing off, along with forty other demobilees, who had done their stint of leaping and crawling over sand and gravel, boiled alive in khaki fatigues, loaded down by rifles, pouches and what have you, fed on tinned garbage, and forced to listen to Captain Karish's patriotic babbling in the frozen dead of night (no one could escape that nasal grind): 'So what is our real claim to The Land? It is this – that we were always the best Guardians of its Heritage. Say you had built a wonderful house, and decorated it, and put tapestries all over the walls, and really sunk your heart and liver in it, and then a foreign invader came and took it by force and exiled you, and someone else came and lived in it, turning it into a pigsty, shitting on the floors and ripping up the tapestries to wipe his bum, and when you finally came back from exile to claim your house he said to you – Keep Out, this is mine! You wouldn't stand for that, would you? You'd kick him out good and proper and restore the apple of your eye. To what is this parable analogous?' 'To your asshole.' Avi suggested. 'His wife's cunt,' his colleague, Captain Yasu (né Pandis) offered, trying to stuff his blanket in his ears. 'Give it a rest, *hevreh!*' mumbled their commander, the mournful Colonel Adashim, alias the Sorrows of Young Werther. 'What d'you think this is here, Parliament?'

Free at last! Hurtling, for time if not safety's sake, at twenty kilometres past the speed limit through the Gaza Strip, the ominous orange groves, the refugee camps, the silent 'natives', the barbed wire fences of the new settlements, disembarking at Ashkelon to take the civilian schedule north-east, home – the unarmed citizenry, God bless 'em, with shopping bags, brown paper parcels and live chickens, the cackle of small town gossip. Eucalyptus trees, sleepy villages, decaying porches, old men on chairs. A dreamlike entrance to the City, the bloodshot sky of brief twilight, a somnambulant ride on the Number 7 bus to Bak'a, to find a scribbled note from Esther: 'GONE TO AVRAM'S ZURAFA PREMIER. WEREN'T YOU COMING? THINGS IN THE FRIDGE. THE LAUNDRYMAN, THE SCHMUCK, DIDN'T DELIVER.'

What the hell! He undressed, bathed, changed, flushed Karish, Yasu, Werther and the entire Israel Defence Forces down the drain and tottered out, took the Number 6 back to the top of the wall and walked down into the Arab City, the evening closures of the Damascus Gate stalls, the quiet of El-Wad and the narrow twists of the Via Dolorosa, arriving at the Khalidiyah school just in time to locate and squeeze Esther, to be shouted at in Arabic by young and old, lean and fat alike, to Sit down for God's sake, *habibi*, and to see the curtains part, upon –

★

The Sleeper (A Prologue Without an Epilogue)

A Play in Three Acts. (As seen by Thin Avi, who hadn't slept for ten days, and could barely keep his eyelids apart, and who had not enough Arabic to take in the whole text, which had in any case undergone several levels of censorship, first by the actors themselves, then by the civilian Censorship Committee, then by the Military Censor, Major Albaz, who had to pass it for the West Bank performances, and had done his piece and passed it on to his four-year-old son, Yoni, who passed it to the family dog, Benjie, who passed it round his friends at the municipal trash dump, who peed on the manuscript, and passed it on to the household roaches, who ate every third letter of several key passages and thus, having rendered the whole suitably safe and allegorical, the work was fully ratified, and handed back, the day of Free Speech cleared to dawn . . .)

ACT 1

The bedroom of an Arab petit-bourgeois. Tasteful western furniture: plastic chairs, a little table with a lace tablecloth and a bowl of fruit, some ethnic artifacts hanging on the walls – a bedou saddlebag, a water pitcher, a nineteenth-century print of rolling hills with olive trees. A cluster of framed family photographs, several sepia generations. But in the centre of the stage, a great four poster bed facing front, upon which Our Hero, swathed in the bedclothes, is down and out, but not completely silent –

THE SLEEPER [*Avram Blok*]:
   ZZZZZZZZZZZZZZZZZZZZZZZZZZZZZZZZZZ . . .

[*A Doctor (Salah the Nose) enters, with stethoscope and bag.*]

THE DOCTOR: Good morning, good morning everyone. As you might have guessed, ladies and gentlemen, you all being persons of discernment and understanding of the little nuances of life, the subtleties that differentiate between the Heavens and the Earth, that separate Enlightenment from the Abyss of Ignorance, I, Khalil al-Azm, am a humble practitioner of the Medical Profession. Nervous strain and Occupational stress a speciality, as well as irregularity of the bowels and all that stuff. But never, in all my long years of medical experience, traversing the length and breadth of our fair land, bleeding the plague ridden, comforting the flatulent, dispensing the little pills of happiness and tranquillity, have I come across as sad and baffling a case as this. [*Moves round to gaze with pursed lips at The Sleeper.*] Behold, Abd-el-Salaam, son of that pillar of Our Community, Haj Amin Ibn-Umar, benign master of vineyards, plantations and orchards, friend of the great, benefactor of the poor, a man whose name was a byword for piety and steadfastness, dispenser of justice, sword of the faith . . .

ADILA [*entering stage left, played by Lena Khalili*]: Get on with it for God's sake, how long do we have to get the same runaround? [*Some applause from the back seats, held by the Marxist-Leninists, sullen shuffling in the more affluent front rows.*]

THE DOCTOR [*giving way*]: Ah! the fair daughter of the unfortunate

Haj Amin,* Adila, sister of this poor somnambulant mountain who is the subject of our story. [*Adila sits by the Sleeper,
taking his hand.*]

BLOK [*continuing his pretence*]:
ZZZZZZZZZZZZzzzzzzzzzzzzzzzz. . . . .

THE DOCTOR: You are right, fair daughter of our unhappy land.
What we are after, in this day and age, are plain facts. Facts are
the centre of our existence. Without facts where would we
be? Facts create facts, which create other facts, in an unbroken
chain. Well, the plain facts of the matter are these: Three years
ago this same Abd-el-Salaam, whom you see lying here, as if
bereft of life and yet undoubtedly still present in the land of
the living, fell into the deep sleep to which you are all witness.
Nothing his great and distinguished family could do sufficed
to rouse him from this torpor: no chanting from the Holy
Quran, no magic charms or medical potions. No camphor,
cod liver oil, ammonia, the recitation of editorials from the
village press, the banging of cymbals, the waving of flags, the
fragrance of his own family's wine, their figs, their plums,
their citrus fruits. Nothing availed. They called in a famous
Doctor, from Tel Aviv, but he said: Let the man sleep, he's
better off. Six months later Haj Amin, stricken with grief,
suffered a savage and fatal heart attack. It was discovered he
was in fact deeply in debt to moneylenders and the powerful
Bank of the Steadfast Friends of the Arab Nation. The
vineyards and plantations were attached, the family's fortune
placed in escrow. Over the next two years the sons and
daughters were reduced to the penury you see them suffering
now. And still the inheritor, the new head of the family, lies
there, completely inactive, like a great sack of cabbage.

---

*Haj Amin al-Husseini, mufti of Jerusalem and religious leader of
Palestinian Moslems from the 1920s to the 40s, led the resistance against
British rule and the Zionist settlement by a combination of nationalist and
religious fervor and assassination of Arab opponents. During World War II
he sought support from Hitler, and was banned by the British from
returning to Palestine. Many Palestinians regard him with mixed feelings, as
a legitimate patriot and at the same time as a feudal representative of a corrupt
old guard.

[Enter Rashed and Ali, two youths dressed in shabby casuals, dusty from toil, with spots of whitewash and paint, tossing shopping bags on the table. (Played by Majid Nouri and Brahim.)]

RASHED: God! What a piss of a day! I sat waiting for hours at the junction.* Finally two gentlemen in a Mercedes picked me up, about nine thirty. Do you do gardening? one asks me. I do anything, I say. I dig latrines. I move mountains. Yallah, he says, get in. We drive across town, to Rehavia. There's a woman waiting there, with a dog in her hands, a poodle, looking very anguished. The woman, I mean, not the dog. Listen, she says, this is the problem: My dog has buried a bracelet of mine, somewhere in the garden, and I can't get him to dig it up again. We've had the lawn up, so it's all fresh earth, I can't tell where it could be. It's very precious to me, of sentimental value. My husband gave it me on our divorce. And while you're at it, you might also straighten out the fence. Too many people can look over. Can you imagine? I dug there all day. And it wasn't a large garden either. The fucking dog looked on with the devil's eye at me, barking all the time. I dug and dug and couldn't find the bracelet. I'm sorry, madam, I said, he probably buried it somewhere else. Oh my God, she said. You must have stolen it! Her two beefy brothers came, the ones who'd fetched me, and forced me to undress in front of them. The fucking poodle was jumping up and down, reaching for the keys of my kingdom . . . I'm lucky I escaped intact . . .

ALI: What the hell are you complaining? You had a breeze of a time. I got up at three in the morning to catch the early service bus. We were told we were going to build new houses for pioneers in the desert valley. We drove there, on roads that were not roads, shaking and rattling all our bones. Uphill, downhill, around the mountain, looking for those promised lands. The coming of the dawn lifted our spirits, touching the crests of hills with gold. Ah! We felt so proud to be part of such an edifying and progressive venture . . .

*Many Arabs in East Jerusalem live by casual labour and odd jobs for Jewish employers. The cafés opposite the Damascus Gate are a common pick-up site for Israeli Jews looking for Arab daily workers.

101

RASHED: And what happened?

ALI: The bus broke down, half way up the *jebel*. We had to walk all
the way back, twenty-five fucking kilometres.＊

RASHED: Ah! But you were so close to the Land!

[*The beat of the* tambur *sounds offstage. The strains of the* oud. *The
dulcet tones of Muhammad 'Nightingale' Abbas, singing his own tune to
the words of the poet Samih el-Kasim*]:

> Who built the stone barriers at the mountain foot?
> Who taught the breeze to be kind to the trees?
> Who but my good-natured grandfather?
> Who taught the plain to give generous crops?
> Who but my father and his elder brother?
> Who carved the names of relatives, one by one, on every tree
> trunk in our groves?
> Who, but this adorer and worshipper?'

[*As the song unfolds, the other members of the Ibn-Umar family gather
around the Sleeper's bed; the remainder of the cast: the Elias sisters, Yassir
Not Arafat, 'Zeppelin' Khalid, Marilyn and Ali Fitzpatrick, with
Muhammad 'Nightingale' following, to applause from the audience.*]

OLD MOTHER AMINA [*played by Mouna Elias*]: These sweet sentiments are pleasant to the ear, but someone has to load the
donkey. Uncle Banias, what have you been doing at the bank
to get back the deeds to our vines?

'ZEPPELIN' KHALID: Well, I had thirteen cups of tea.

YASSIR: By now you've got off them thirteen hundred. And what
have we got? Nothing.

'ZEPPELIN' KHALID: Allow me to contradict you. [*Begins pulling out
of his waistcoat pile after pile of teabags.*]

＊The original passage, censored by Major Albaz, ran:
RASHED: And what happened?
ALI: When we got there, the army had arrested all the pioneers, for settling
without a government licence. We were all arrested as accomplices, and
spent the whole day in jail. We had to listen to their songs from the next
cell: 'David King of Israel'; 'I Believe in the Messiah'; 'The Sound of
Mirth and Merriment' . . .

AUNT AISHA [*Rasha Elias*]: This can't go on. I'll commit suicide and burn this whole accursed house down! [*All rush to console her.*]

ADILA: Mother! Brothers!

MARILYN: What is it, Adila?

ADILA: His hand! It moved! Abd-el-Salaam's hand moved!

AMINA: Praise be to God! A miracle!

'ZEPPELIN' KHALID: What? What?

RASHED: Abd-el-Salaam is waking!

THE DOCTOR: Move back! Give him air! [*He pushes them away from the bed.*]

[*Muhammad 'Nightingale' strikes chords on his oud. The old women fall on their knees. Muhammad quotes two lines of Fadwa Tuqan*]:

> 'I stood by the cracked balcony,
> dreaming of creation . . .'

AMINA: Abd-el-Salaam! My son! My son!

ALI FITZPATRICK: The vineyards! The vineyards!

RASHED: No more wretched poodles!

'ZEPPELIN' KHALID [*scrabbling on the floor*]: Give me back those teabags!

THE DOCTOR: An historic moment! [*Strikes a heroic pose.*]

[*The Sleeper sits up, yawns, looks around, blinking in some surprise, then speaks, in Hebrew*]:

BLOK: What's going on, *hevreh*?

In the silence that followed, one could have heard a grenade pin drop. Luckily, this did not occur. But Avi, in the third row, could no longer keep his eyes open, and dropped off, dreaming of green pastures and the brown terraced hills where he and prepubertal Avram Blok wandered about in search of Martian aliens, buried treasure and an escape from the iron hand of parental-national destiny. Ho, ho, ho. A sharp elbow nudge from Esther jerked him awake to catch the piece quite far advanced along its winding path, with Abd-el-Salaam reclining, like a Passover patriarch, on a pile of cushions on a huge tattered armchair resembling a stuffed labrador with elephantiasis, his head encased in the old Palmach sock cap, perusing a month old copy of the Hebrew newspaper *Yediot Rishonot*, whose main headline, turned towards the audience, read, 'KATYUSHAS FIRED IN THE NORTH: SABOTEURS TRYING AGAIN TO ORGANIZE IN SOUTHERN LEBANON', while the *Zurafa* sat about him in traditional costumes,* in a timeless café set, re-enacting selected scenes from history in the hope of dislodging The Sleeper's new alien persona and uncovering the old and true:

LATIF SA'ADI [*as the café owner, serving tea in tiny glasses*]: God will have mercy, they say the Mongols have sacked Baghdad. General Hulagu and his evil minion, Kitbag, are marching west towards Damascus!

'ZEPPELIN' KHALID [*as 1st Notable, ensconced with nargileh*]: It is a storm in a teacup, brothers. Have we not seen off the Seljuks, the Greeks and the Franks? Have we not slept through the death of leper-kings? Mark my words, they will just pass through like everyone else, kill a few peasants and move on.

YASSIR NOT ARAFAT [*as 2nd Notable*]: And even if they stay, I hear they are quite an efficient people. They have an excellent postal service.

SALAH THE NOSE [*3rd Notable*]: It would do us good to have a little progress. Let's face it, we have always been a backwater.**

---

*Traditional costume: the *kumis*, or inner shirt, of cotton, silk or linen; the *libas*, or inner cotton drawers; *sherwal* – large loose pantaloons; the *suderiyeh*, or inner sleeveless waistcoat; *mintian*, or outer jacket; *kuftan* or long, open gown, girded by the belt, or *zunnar*; the *abayeh* or outer cloak, often richly ornamented, turban wound round a *tarbush*, with a long tassel. For women, the *jillayeh* and headdress (*smadeh*); the dresses often richly embroidered in distinctive local styles.

**The pre-censored text runs on as follows:

CAFÉ OWNER: But in Baghdad they say they killed every Moslem they could find, eighty thousand souls! They slaughtered women, children, new-born babes, they waded in blood up to their eyes!

1st NOTABLE: I am sure these reports are exaggerations. We should not take notice of propaganda. After all, this is the thirteenth century. The Mongols, surely, are just people, like anyone else, looking for a little living space.

MOUNA ELIAS [*in her usual Old Woman costume runs on*]: Praise be to God and his Prophet! The Mamelukes have defeated the Mongol army at Ain Jalut! Their evil general, Kitbag, is dead! His head is cut off! Long live the Sultan Kutuz and his brave Lieutenant, Baibars! (Runs out. Whooping and ululating breaks out offstage.)

1st NOTABLE: These women get so excitable about everything. Didn't I tell you there was no problem?

2nd NOTABLE: God looks after his own.

3rd NOTABLE: Ahmed! Bring three more mint teas!

CAFÉ OWNER: I am yours to command, O effendis . . . (*to audience*): What a pathetic bunch of arseholes!

Muhammad Abu Abbas (*in minstrel costume, strolls on stage, strumming up another of his own tunes to the well-known lament of Al-Bayati*):

In the cafés of the East we have been ground by the
    War of words,
by wooden swords and lies and Quixotic knights . . .
In the cafés of the East we pass the time in swatting flies,
wearing the masks of the living.
We are placed in the dunghill of history,
mere shadows of men . . .*

---

*'Very well put,' approved Major Albaz. 'I couldn't have said it better myself . . .'

** *footnote continued*

('No! No! No!' said Major Albaz. 'Nobody appreciates a joke more than I do, but there is good and bad taste, don't you think?')

Other historical events completely disallowed by Albaz: The victory of Saladin over the Crusaders (on grounds of causing offence to Christians); Arab-Jewish co-operation ditto; the entry of Caliph Omar into Jerusalem; the battle of the Yarmuk (AD 636); Napoleon's defeat at Acre (1799) at the hands of Ahmad al-Jazzar, escaped Bosnian sex-criminal and former slave of a Jew, later become viceroy of Damascus. And so on. But the Mamelukes were allowed through – 'everyone knows what a load of swine they were'. Wilful ignorance of Baibars' standing as the greatest liberator of Islam . . .

Loud Voice Offstage: BUT THE LAND! THE LAND! [*Audience applause. Thud of tamburs up. Lena Khalili enters as The Sleeper's sister Adila*]:

ADILA: Why tell our brother only of the falling leaves? Tell him about the trunk of the oak tree! [*More applause. The players strike up on all instruments.*]
CRIES: Our olives! Our plums! Our fig trees! Our pomegranates! Our vines!

[*Peasant song and dance. Much rhythmic stamping of feet on boards. THE LAND! THE LAND! Even Avi is unable to drift off again, but neither he nor Esther feel able to join in the communal clapping. The Sleeper, in the centre background of the stage, takes no notice of the whole schmeer. Turning the pages of his Hebrew newspaper he has reached the small ads*]:

'BUY ZIP BY ELITE –
THE READY MADE REFRESHMENT! –

I TOLD MY BOY FRIEND: IF YOU'RE ONLY
VISITING ME FOR THE ZIP YOU CAN
GO AND GET ONE YOURSELF!' . . .

'Dear Citizen –
You have a problem? You have a request?
Send a message to the Western (Wailing) Wall!!

Write your own prayer on a slip of paper, fold it and send it to us! We will add a prayer for you and your entire family, the message to be placed between the stones of the Wall on the day of Hoshanah Raba.

If you wish to remember the names of your loved ones on the day of Shmini Atseret, please enter their names and the names of their parents in the spaces below:
    To: Organization of Loyalists of The Wall,
    —— Street, Jerusalem.

Please mention my name and that of my loved ones in the Memorial Prayer of Shmini Atseret, the Festival of Simhat Torah:

Private Name: _____
Family Name: _____
Father's Name: _____
Mother's Name: _____ (Etc . . .)

I enclose my contribution, to be divided among recognized Institutions of Education, Charity and Public Health. (Contributors will receive by return of post receipts for tax deduction purposes.)

EROS!!

FOR THIRTEEN YEARS LEADING THE WAY IN THE VARIETY AND EXPANSION OF SEXUAL SATISFACTION FOR ALL TASTES AND ADULT AGES – NOW FOR THE FIRST TIME IN JERUSALEM! Send NOW for these assorted items (Discretion Guaranteed, Visa Accepted):

Sex Games Manual: 154 Erotic positions in stunning colour, text in Hebrew/Russian or English/Arabic .... 670 Shekel
Black Cat Vibrator: Made of wet rubber for stunning penetration with spiral movements, vibration & remote control, Exclusive! .... Only 5900 Shekel

For the Man who Finishes Quickly:
Do you Finish Quickly? Whether from excitement or fatigue – Use TIMER, the fantastic condom with Special Retarding Cream for a long and satisfying sex act .... 850 Shekel

Plus Videos, Films, Magazines.
Free Pocket Vibrator With Every Purchase!!
BUY NOW! DON'T BE AMONG THE LATECOMERS AND THE DISAPPOINTED! ! ! !

107

And, on page 6:

JEWS! RETURN!

Only a cruel and bitter Enemy could have sucked the strength out of the House of Israel, first preventing its return to its Land, then cutting into the living flesh, causing Enemies to present themselves as false friends, distancing the people from their Faith which alone keeps them from disaster, abandoning them to corruption, prostitution and bloodshed, unto the very Brink of Destruction!

JEWS! BROTHERS! SAVE YOURSELVES! Return to the ways of the Torah and her Commandments THIS VERY DAY, before it is too late! Return to prayer, to charity, to the Holy Sacraments of Our nation! Let each man and woman, each youth and each adult, each student and each soldier, each boy and girl, take unto themselves to carry out TODAY just ONE Commandment of the Torah. For One Commandment leads to Another, and the HOLY ONE BLESSED BE HE, Creator of the World, will fulfil every hope of our hearts . . .

BUT THE LAND! THE LAND!
The audience are on their feet. They care no more about The Sleeper, they have been awakened themselves. Not for them, at least for this brief moment, the confusion and frustrations of overlapping claims, rival truths snapping at each other's ankles, the cock fights of ideology, the life and death of family life and death, the pails of whitewash and the brushes, that tiny patch left undone in the corner, the tapestry that has no more room, backgammon games that go on for ever, stalemates that sap the soul. All forgotten, yea! in a moment of high passion, the lure of the mud, the tadpole hour, the collective conscious, the eternal flames lit by the pilot light of words and music, the struck geyser

of Hope, brothers and sisters, all the stronger for the pressure capping it –

So many hot air balloons, drifting over Maginot lines.

Esther and Avi, uneasy at the hub of an ardour not their own. Raised mirror-memories of past enthusiasms, campfire songs of dead dreams – Oh Oh the Clods of Earth, We'll Build Our Country, Our Homeland, the Plough in One Hand, the Gun in the Other, Oh Oh Oh. One side ought to charge the other royalties, but which? The old argument of who came first, the egg battering the chicken . . . The Nightingale's chords soaring to the words of Mahmud Darwish:

> My homeland is not a travelling bag,
> Nor am I a passing traveller.
> It is I who am the lover and the land
> is my beloved.

Selah.

In these conditions Act 3 is virtually superfluous: the entry into the twentieth century. The bombardment of The Sleeper with whatever ragged remnants the censors allowed through to hint of current Arab history. Colonialists, sipping whisky on the terrace, drawing maps of the Levant. No direct mention passed of Arab Independence, popular struggles, insurrections. No Syrian war against the French. No Palestinian rebellion and general strike against the British Mandate. No Egyptian Revolution, no Gamal Abd-el Nasser, no sneering at poor Anwar Sadat and his alleged hashish habit. No Fatah. No Popular Front. No Ba'ath. No Communist Party. 'What do you want with politics,' asked Major Albaz. 'It's all so depressing, don't you think? Just tell your story, entertain your audience, and hooplah, to bed.' 'But what of the Truth?' asked Latif. 'The Truth?' said Albaz, eyes widening. 'You must be out of your mind! If we all told each other the Truth in this part of the world, we would all be hot ash in no time! Mark my words, young man,' he leaned across his desk solicitously, as if sharing a secret with the appellant, who was in fact two years his senior, 'the name of the game for both of us is Survival, and for that a little reticence, a few drops of self-restraint, will go a long way.'

For this reason, too, Albaz and the Committee excised the entirety of the following speech, placed in the mouth of Salah the Nose as a café intellectual:

But who are these Palestinians, these midnight ghosts, whom some scholars say do not exist? Whom some claim are mere figments of the paid imagination of propagandists . . . while others say they have been sighted, disguised as Jews, as extras in television programmes depicting the ancient Hebrew tribes, et cetera . . . And still others have seen them in their nightmares, knives in mouths, slavering blood . . . Can they really substantiate their own existence, de jure, in a court of law? Can they dredge up their manifold alleged ancestors, that Caananite seed core of Akkad and Sumer, Nineveh and Babylonia, the so-called real Hebrews, hiding in cellars from the sword of Nebuchadnezzar, all the acorns blown by the great winds which swept across this fertile, infertile swathe: Chaldeans, Assyrians, Privites, Hittites, Nabateans, Persians, Macedonians, Medes, Greeks, Romans, Egyptians, Hijazis, Yamanis, sons of Ghassan and Kuraish, Jacobites, Armenians, Nestorians, Maronites, Circassians, Samaritans, Druse, what have you, stalwarts of the Sunnah, Shafi'ites of the Golden Mean, survivors of Ummayads, Abbassids, Fatimids, sons and daughters of Ayub, touched even with a dab of the blonde Frankish brush, husbanders of the ancestral soil for more than four and forty generations, the Steadfast, the *tsamidin*, the rock of ages, vanguard of the Arab East's working class – IS THAT WHO THEY REALLY THINK THEY ARE? What ridiculous effrontery! For we know the facts, the true measure of these people: this rag-tag of runaways, orphans of storms, the wretched of the earth, God help us – hewers of wood, drawers of water, waiters, dishwashers, lavatory cleaners, unskilled farmhands who should know better than to have dreams far above their station. After all, somebody has to do the dirty work! Who else would you suggest?

'You're having me on,' said Major Albaz. 'You're really stretching my good will here. Don't you have any respect for your audience? Listen to me, I'm doing you a favour, cutting out all these boring bits. You'd close on opening night without me. And who is this "Avram Blok" on this list you've given me? You boys are skating on thin ice . . .'

Indeed. But the show goes on, Blok, cloven text and all. Branching out of the City into the West Bank, in an old Ford pickup truck and a battered Volkswagen van. Blok, the Jew among a press of Arabs, presented to the bored soldiers at the roadblocks as the show's electrician. Again and again, he sits in the back of the van as the twelve good apostles, six from each car, are lined up against walls for the routine search, men on one side, women on the other (the sensitivities of the natives), one soldier checking them for concealed weapons, another rooting in the van among the backdrops, a third giving him sound advice: 'You may think you know what you're doing, but I can tell you, you don't know these people.' Turning his tattered identity card over and over, with its portrait of an acned teenage innocent, with a full head of hair, alas – 'Are you sure this is you?' Anything's possible. 'What you need is Doctor Jochem's Hormone. I had an uncle who was stark as Yul Brynner. Today he looks like Ringo Starr.' And the parting shot, as the travellers pack back in: 'You know we can't protect you among them.'

Thank you, Sergeant, I shall bear that in mind. On to Beit Jalah, Halhoul, Tulkarm. The rolling brown hills and terraces and fields and sheep and strange people with checkered headshawls, long robes, cracked sandals, stubbled faces of the men, premature age of many women. Blok, passing through the looking glass of the stage to the foreign land which has always been there, just at the corner of the eye, since childhood. Those guttural visitants from another planet beyond the 'Danger, Frontier' signs, sitting before him at every performance, a small multitude of dark-hued wraiths, coughing, hawking and spitting on floors, unwrapping the evening's refreshments, brought from home, not ZIP, but flasks of tea and coffee, pitta with olives or cold chicken legs in greasy paper, shifting about on a couple of hundred squeaky chairs, loudly querying God's wisdom in allocating a Size 15 skull to the Size 10 son of a bitch in front of them, confronting him in the various halls of Rammallah, Kalkiliah, Bethlehem, Tubas, Jenin, through the adventure of the performance in darkness, the barely escaped army raid (irregularities in the use of premises licence, ironed out 'with no hard feelings'), until the night of the fated show at Nablus – but before that – certain impacts, touches, expectations, fragments of dreams:

1) The Hand of Lena Khalili or Blok Fails to Become a Palestinian

Stage night after stage night, throughout Act Number 1, he lies on the old propped-up four poster bed with his pudgy mitt resting softly upon her alien palm. In rehearsal there had been at first no contact of flesh. She sat by the bed, hands in her lap. 'Put your hand on the bed,' said Latif, writer and director. She did so, a full twenty centimetres from the Sleeper's outstretched paw. 'Hold his hand,' Latif said, in the fourth rehearsal, 'Goddamit, he's your brother.' Blok said nothing, feigning disinterested slumber, but raising his upper eyelid just a fraction. He saw her black eyes gazing straight at him, firing mental dum-dum bullets. His palm opened to receive. She placed her own on his, like a cold slab of ham.

But, as the rehearsals and the play progressed, body warmth crept, like an unbidden intravenous drip, down her arm into his own. Her hand trembled, perhaps with normal diffidence and chaste reserve, perhaps with the echoes of charnel houses that lay, as it were, between his blood and hers. But, perhaps by mere routine, the fellowship of the boards, the show must go on, there's no business like, et cetera, the touch became less and less timorous, the electricity flowing more freely, the body heat no longer denied natural gravity, until, at the fifth Jerusalem performance, her hand closed determinedly upon his, in a firm no-nonsense armlock. The grip went right through his body, round his shoulder down into his loins. Thank the Lord he was so liberally swathed in the bedclothes. He opened his eyes cautiously but she had not seemed to notice, her face and attention turned towards the declamation of the Doctor, the dialogue of the two lumpen brothers. When he awoke that night, and spoke in Hebrew, he struggled to hold the sheets above his waist, horrifiedly conscious that the entire cast, and audience, all brothers, as it were, of the Arab maiden, aimed dagger eyes upon him. Slash, slash, slash. But this thought had no deterrent effect upon his subterranean waves, for one has to remember, ladies and gentlemen, that Blok had not fucked for four years . . .

2) The Romance of Lena and Blok (A Fantasy)

They are finally alone, in the abandoned dressing room. Lightning bolts leap from eye to eye. He clasps her hand to his heart. She places his palm on her breast. Thunder claps. The earth moves. [The Eurasian Plate, hurrying towards its billion year overdue rendezvous with the North American tectonic.] Demons of bigotry howl and gibber as their lips meet, sharing salivation. Her soft supple dark fingers fondle his upturned member. The stirring rod of Jacob thrilling to enemy hands. Fate has left them no choice but to elope. They slip across the Egyptian border with false passports supplied by an aged squinting Armenian reeking of third rate aftershave. They linger only for a day in Cairo. The Pyramids, Shepheards, the Nile Bridges, Abdin Palace, Groppi's Café. At her request, a visit to the Tomb of Gamal Abd-el Nasser. Then a slow boat across the azure sea to Athens. Freedom at last! A flea-bitten cheap raucous sleepless hotel by Omonia. Nevertheless, paradise, among the rucksacks of itinerant youth, the meeting of two starved bodies. The two backed beat. The earth moves [the Pacific Plate, moving on its rendezvous with West Asia]. Thumbing lifts, across the European tectonic. West, West, not so young lovers, across the autobahns and far away, far from the East, to freedom . . .

3) But How Do You Think He Is Doing?

'How do you think he is doing?' Avi asked Latif, in the office of 'Bridge Publications'. Under the poster of the Jerusalem porter and the unplugged lips of Kamal Nasser. ('Executioner, strike! We are fearless / Our dark sweat beaded brows are heavy with chains / so the nation may live!' Clap clap clap). The bellows down the corridor of the magazine distributor Kastorak castigating some poor vendor who had dared claim for torn returns of the Rumanian rag *Viata Noastra*.

'He doesn't say much, as you know,' said Latif, 'but most of the comrades feel that he is somehow OK. He is not a liberal, if you know what I mean.'

'Not like me,' said Avi.

'Maybe, maybe. He doesn't have this eagerness to please. He does not condescend. He doesn't ooze solidarity. The man just is. I can't put it otherwise. Of course, there are always dangers. He has an erection, you know, when our Lena holds his hand, although he's very careful to hide it. It's the sort of situation which could be hazardous. But who am I to complain – we are all in deep trouble in that particular department. I have to take cold showers, myself, in the morning, the afternoon and last thing at night.'

'She is very beautiful,' agreed Avi.

'You Jews don't know when you're lucky. I tell you, when men put barbed wire round their women, you don't need any foreign tyranny.'

'To each his own,' said Avi.

'Let's swap for a month, comrade. I'd like to see how you'd last.'

Nevertheless Blok was able to partially escape from this dilemma, between performances, back at Hageffen Street, albeit under the watchful eye of Tolstoy, the Secret Agent With One Testicle, who had passed on routine police snoop reports to the block's House Committee. 'That makes two subversives in our fold,' he told the Committee Chairman, Kadurie, 'as if we didn't have enough with the "Situationist", Basuto,' of Entrance D, Flat 5. 'Well . . .' Kadurie sighed deeply, 'it takes all sorts to make a world.'

Esther phoned him now and again, monitoring his progress, having appointed herself as his big sister, barking curt words of advice in between her own forays into the Social Welfare stew, spending more and more time, it appeared, unravelling the strange case of her oddest client, Ya'akov Ben-Havivo, erring son of the Sephardi mystic and religious leader, the Dayan Ezuz, or 'Mighty Judge', now an ailing seventy-five-year-old. The Dayan Ezuz was famed as a holy man and ascetic, although he was heir to a family fortune which was administered by his seven brothers, including alleged investments in banking, insurance, heavy industry and small arms. The son, rebelling against this burden, lived in a squalid room in the Nahlaot District and stole motorcycles and automobile parts. Esther and Sergeant Tuvia were trying to lure him upon the balanced path of legal thrift and harmony . . .

'I'll see you when I can!' she told Blok, as Adolphe, in the background, clawed furniture.

In between Halhoul and Tulkarm, Blok also received a letter from Yissachar, postmarked, amazingly, Tel Aviv:

HEY, AVRAM!

Yes! I am definitely back in town! Globe trotting over for the moment I can put my feet up and prepare the paperwork for the next blitz on the world! I enclose a cutting from what we call the 'trades', a *Variety* piece on my boss and meal-ticket, our very own Adir Kokashvili! Did I tell you he was once a shoeshine boy in Tiflis? A kopek a brush, resoles extra? And look at him now, the toast of Hollywood! I quote:

'KOK, INDIE, BOFFO DETROIT, HUSKY PHILLY!'

'KOK SCHLOCK HOCK SHOCK!'

'KOK 250G O.K. OHIO,' and so on. We are definitely on the map here! But I'll tell all when we meet. I tried phoning but you've not been in. The old tricks, eh, Avram? All holes look the same in the dark. Call me in between rounds. My private number . . .

He set it aside. Hibernating in the cruelly damp cold of a Jerusalem special winter. Cold rain, gusts of wind, grey skies and an inadequate paraffin heater. Even Mrs Almoshnino was deterred from the usual early morning balcony overture. He sleeps in, parries calls from Papa, ignores the banner headlines of unfolding revolution in Iran: 'THE AYATOLLAH RETURNS!' 'SHAHINSHAH FLEES COUNTRY!' 'FIVE MILLION THRONG STREETS!' Their cries, from television news bulletins: 'Marg Barg Shah! Marg Barg Shah!' Yea, indeed, marg the bastard. But his own show goes on . . .

Finally the big night came in Nablus. The afternoon before the performance, the entire *Zurafa* team rested at Majid Nouri's family house, as this was his home town. His father had a villa on the slope of the hill facing the historic Mount Gerizim, the true site, according to the Samaritan sect, of Abraham's sacrifice of Isaac: the true father lode, not to be confused with that usurping bump two hours' drive to the south, the false Moriah of Jerusalem . . . Nablus, Shechem, Neapolis, about which nineteenth-century pilgrims enthused: 'the whole valley filled with gardens of vegetables, and orchards of all kinds of fruits, watered by fountains, like a scene of fairy enchantment . . . Here the bulbul delights to sit and sing, and thousands of other birds unite to swell the chorus. The inhabitants maintain theirs is the most musical vale in Palestine . . .' But the chords lilting now come from Farid el Atrash and Fairouz, on radio waves from afar, not to speak of the tooting of car horns in the main streets down below. One can almost, but not quite, forget the Occupation, with its frequent patrols in khaki jeeps and armoured cars, in this winter sunlit room with its open arched windows, European armchairs and old pots set on stands, and metal bookshelves crammed with well-handled paperback books printed in that curlicued meandering script of which Blok knows not a single word. An entire universe of his ignorance: Naguib Mahfouz, Fathi Ghanem, Tewfik al-Hakim, Husain Haykal, Taha Husain, al-Manfaluti, Mahmud Taimur, Khalil Jibran, Abd al-Masih Antaki, al-Zahawi, Muhammad Farid Abu Hadid, Farah Antun, Ali al-Jarim, al-Barudi, Matran, Abd el-Rahman al-Sharqawi, Husain Munis, Zuraiq, Karam, al-Arnaut, Abd al-Malik Nuri, Safa Khalusi, Emile Habibi, Ghassan Kanafani, Sahar Khalifa, Darwish, Tuqan, al-Qasim,

116

Rashed Hussein, et cetera, et cetera, et cetera. The passage of many cups of ultra-sweet tea and coffee as the old man and the young players sit and discuss hidden things. Just the sound of the language in Blok's ears as it rolls on, like low-level summer thunder, on into the brief twilight ebbing to call them into the municipal hall, on stage, with the omnipresence of the Military Administration's armoured car around the corner, the knots of soldiers just out of streetlight range and the crowd, filing in. The scent of danger even on an innocent night out, Nablus being after all the centre, the seedbed of nationalist sentiment in the Occupied West Bank. Rumbles have in fact been heard as to the security of the *Zurafa's* Jew. The players surround him, protectively, until he is safely ensconced in the four-poster bed, centre stage, Lena Khalili firmly holding his hand, as the lumpen brothers rage: 'I'm sorry, madam, I said, he probably buried it somewhere else. Oh my God, she said. You must have stolen it! . . . the fucking poodle was jumping up and down . . . I'm lucky I escaped intact . . .'

The beat of the *tambur*. Strains of the *oud*. The Nightingale song of Abu Abbas. The entire cast on stage. Wisecracks of 'Zeppelin' Khalid. The sudden movement of Blok's hand –

'Mother! Brothers!'

'What is it, Adila?'

'His hand! It moved! Abd–el–Salaam's hand moved!'

'Praise be to God! A miracle!' . . .

'Move back! Give him air!' . . .

'Abd el-Salaam! My son! My son!'

He sit up, yawns, asking in Hebrew: 'What's going on, *hevreh*?'

But his movement is too abrupt. The bedclothes fall away. The striped pyjama bottoms are revealed. And through their open fly, the inevitable consequence of unrequited desire, that concealed weapon, the rod of Jacob, a Jewish prick, hard as a policeman's truncheon, turned, in the full glare of spotlights, towards the goggling eyeballs of the *tsamidin*, the stubborn Steadfast of the Land . . .

ASARGELUSHA!

His life does not flash before his eyes –

(Budapest, the immigrant ship *Irma Klein*, circumcision

117

amidships, the promised land, kindergarten sandwiches, Magyar-baiting, three 'R's, puppyloves, Fat Avi, matriculation blues, Armed Forces, Sinai firing lines, bluebottle corpses, victory sweets, demobilization, the fated peephole vision, asylum, true love, therapy, friendship, rivalry and loss, flying pigs, grounding, travel narrows the mind, *la grève sauvage*, burning stocks exchanged, the tall blonde with the curling wisps of smoke, panther blacks, dark and light weltanschauungs, return to sender, an honest living in the vale – Ein Karem, yes, the baby grin of Yissachar, trans-oceanic escapes again, unhappy returns, yes, did this truly happen?! – October War, re-asylum, the fog of internal journeys, the Fall – the black pit of T—t . . .)? No, these are current affairs, written in blood:

BLOK REVEALS ALL TO ARAB NATION!
THE SLEEPER WHO MIGHT HAVE AWOKEN TOO SOON!
WAS IT JUST A ONE NIGHT STAND??

Tumult. Alarums. Confusion. The light goes out. It seems he has one friend in the region. But here is another, grabbing his arm, pulling him away from the crowd. 'There is a back exit!' The voice of 'Zeppelin' Khalid? Rush, rush, stumble, stumble. Out of the womb, baby! And the crowd roars!! Fouled at the hundred yard line, he gets up, desperately trying to tuck the offending object back into those baggy trousers. Crash! A protruding flat. Wallop! The jamb of a door. Thud! Bang! Tinkle! Aaargh! Our hero falling down stairs. 'This way! This way!' An outer door creaks open. The breath of late night fresh air. Mountain aroma. Ah, the freshness! Nevertheless, dark and cold as a witch's cunt. A couple of lit streetlamps, away down the street. The looming prow of an armoured car. The baying sound of the outraged theatre lovers spilling out of the main gate. 'There he is!' The striped pyjamas, blue on white, mark him by the half moon. The stars above. Ah, the clarity! He runs, conjuring more rabid headlines from the trade press:

COCK SHOCK ROCKS FLOCK!
SICK DICK HICK SHTIK!
JUDE NUDE, PRUDES STEWED!

118

Run for your life, *ya habibi!* The armoured car of the Occupier bars his way. He ducks down a side alley. Radio transmitters burst into crackling life. Engines start up. Voices stutter. Somewhere police cars wail. Rising communal verbal thunder:

MOB GOB YOB KNOB!
CLAQUE FLAK SACK MAC!
HIX NIX DIX TRIX!

The running feet of a multitude. Flat against dusty, cold walls he slides in over running gutters. Treading on a slow cat's tale. 'Sorry, Al-Adolphe!' 'Meowwrr! Reowwrr!' The armoured car at the alley's mouth. Running soldiers, clinking metal, heavy breathing, wheeze, cough. Night chill, emphysema. 'Stop or we shoot!' they call in Arabic. *Halto, alie ni mortpafi!* echo Esperanto roaches. He darts under an arch into a courtyard. Stairs leading up to a roof. He leaps, five steps at a time, slithering in a maze of boilers. YID KID HID BID! But the sounds below grow louder. He leaps on, roof to roof, rushing down more steps as lights come on through chinks in shutters, faces poking out, dark fists shaken. Down into a wider, empty street. Angular yellow streetlight on stone. Around the corner. 'Tis the mob again, with looped rope, glinting knives and torches.

SCHMUCK LUCK UNSTUCK!
SHMUTZ CUTS PUTZ NUTS!
RASH FLASH, TRASH SMASH!
HELOT ZEALOTS FLAY, SLAY, LAY PREY!
BACON HATERS MASH HAM!

Backtrack again. Another archway. A door. A family bedroom, occupied: Mother, father, grandpa, grandma, seven children, one chicken. Out the window to backyard. Three more chickens. A goat. Hanging laundry. An *abbayeh* flapping in the breeze. Praise be to Allah! a disguise. He slips the robe on, rushes upstairs. Over another roof, a loose firm plank, placed across the next alley. The stars relentlessly cast their rays, microscopic minispotlights. A minaret, three roofs away, bursts into sound: the rolling cadence of an awakened muezzin:

WOGS, AGOG, FLOG DOG! He flees, over the roofs, in his *abbayeh*, as minarets answer all over town. Now there are shots, fired in the air, the unmistakable clatter of tanks moving in down the mountains. Helicopters over Mount Gerizim and Ebal, the two hills upon which the curse and the blessing of the Law-giver Moses were placed. ('Are they not on the other side of Jordan, by the way where the sun goeth down, in the land of the Canaanites, which dwell in the desert over against Gilgal, beside the Plains of Moreh?') Poor Moses, the worst tour guide in history. But the latter-day zealots of the Block of the Faithful established an illegal settlement there. Jacob purchased the town from the chieftain of the Hivites, Hamor, whose name in Hebrew means Donkey. The modern inhabitants are less inclined to such dumb trust, although all the more stubborn. The Patriarch Joseph is buried here, without his Technicolor dreamcoat.

Blok, his retreat cut off in every direction, sat and leaned against a cupola. The night, in fact, was very clear and sharp, free of mist and tangy. A little too noisy, perhaps, but full of dynamic tension. His erection, he noted, had returned. Poor Lena Khalili. What must she have thought? What consequences might the *Zurafa* suffer from the nocturnal cataclysm? And the redundant Act III of The Sleeper? It had been enacted fully. And still, his boner endured. In the hiatus it could no longer be ignored. The inevitable followed. A searchlight, cutting the darkness like butter, transfixed him in the glare of a jeep which had drawn up in the street below.

'Avram, is that you, fiddling on the roof?'

An oddly familiar voice, amid the white-out. He strained, holding the *abbayeh* down with one hand, shielding his eyes with the other. A recognizable, but long-out-of-mind buzzing sound wafted up from below. The light shifted to allow him some vision as he scampered round the cupola.

'Come down, for God's sake, schmendrick! The whole town is after your ass!'

Thin Avi? No. A somewhat coarser timbre. The wilder call of more impetuous times. His pupils, allowed to widen slightly, could now make out that the jeep below was civilian, though the man standing up in its front seat was dressed in a multi-pocketed camouflage jacket. Strange amulets hung about his neck. A bulky instrument was being held to his eye. Light glinted on glass enclosed in the black Bakelite of a telescopic zoom lens. From his half-forgotten days at Holyland Films Blok dredged the recognition of an Arriflex cinecamera. A battery spotlight was affixed to the top of the machine's magazine. It shifted, as the cameraman lowered his instrument.

'No time left, Avram! Just jump!'

He jumps, the *abbayeh* breaking the speed of his descent . . .

DÉJÀ VU . . . Blok travelling down the rabbit hole of a possibly recurring past . . . if these are the shadows of memories – the smell of *shawarma* . . . spewed billows of fog machines . . . shadows that have slipped their moorings . . . animas and animuses groping for each other in dense mist . . . archetypes who have mislaid their Reserves and Identity cards . . . entire peoples who have not been chosen, threatening to tear the joint apart . . . the descent of Zarathustra . . . the portentous tones of Siggy Freud: 'In the unconscious, Time does not exist' (or was that Armand's silent voice?) . . . further scenes in the camera lens –

Location: Ur of the Chaldees
Call Sheet: God. Abram. Fallen Idols.

GOD: Get thee out of thy country, and from thy kindred, and from thy father's house, unto a land that I will show thee.

ABRAM: Thou must be kidding.

GOD: And I will make thee a great nation, and make thy name great, and I will bless them that bless thee, and curse him that curseth thee.

ABRAM: That's different. [*Exit, jauntily, with kitbag.*]

GOD [*aside, hiding mouth with pseudopoda*]: There's one born every minute.

The smell of *shawarma* again . . .

121

ACT 3 of The Sleeper, As Unperformed at Nablus

The family have assembled for the coup de grâce, the last chance to reclaim their errant son. They have tried cajolery, bombing with love, agitation, revelation, interpretation, education, psychoanalysis, exorcism, rhythmic chanting, son et lumière, rhetoric, maternal threats of suicide, fraternal threats of violence, interrogations in the night, the hard and the soft man, constant light, electro-shock, thumbscrews, mock executions, gnashing of teeth, wailing, all to no avail. Abd-el-Salaam continues to sit in his armchair, reading the Hebrew newspapers, magazines, weekend supplements, puzzle books, glossies, trades, photo-romances. He has never been so well informed about the zeitgeist. But everyone else is tired out. They have discarded period costumes, and are back in their contemporary daily dress of faded jackets, smocks, work fatigues. The Sleeper's bedroom is now filled with cushions, trayfuls of empty glasses, cups, cigarette butts in ashtrays, discarded props such as nargilehs, wooden guns, toy scabbards. Muhammad 'Nightingale' Abbas is idly strumming on his guitar, rendering softly, for private consumption, the luminous poem by Darwish:

> We travel like other people, but we return to nowhere. As if travelling
> Is the way of the clouds. We have buried our loved ones in the darkness of the clouds, between the roots of the trees.
> And we said to our wives: go on giving birth to people like us for hundreds of years so we can complete this journey
> To the hour of a country, to a metre of the impossible . . .
> We have a country of words. Speak, speak so I can put my road on the stone of a stone.
> We have a country of words. Speak speak so we may know the end of this journey.

In the silence that falls there is one sound: the rise and fall of Abd-el-Salaam's snores. The Hebrew newspapers have fallen from his hands. The bastard has gone to sleep again.

All turn to gaze upon him. A spontaneous pulse seems to throb in each heart. They rise as one, seize the tattered armchair with the

122

unconscious figure in the striped pyjamas in its woolen Haganah issue sock cap and, manhandling it in unison, pull and push it across and off the stage, to the sound of a loud crashing and banging and the slamming of a door. Out, Out, Out! Abu Abbas strums vibrantly on the *oud*, and, in a more aggressive, self-confident tone, shouts out the Darwish lines:

> Give birth to me again, that I may know in which land
> I will die, in which land I will come to life again . . .

And the call to the peasant song and dance again:

BUT THE LAND! THE LAND!
OUR OLIVE TREES! OUR PLUMS!
OUR FIGS! OUR VINES!

Linked arms, in rousing *debka*, mass applause, flushed faces, rising chords, *tamburs*. Players and audience, united, and the pain – offstage, cast out, falling, falling –

Down, landing arse first in the back seat of the jeep . . .

'Go, man, go!' shouted Yissachar.

He turned round and dumped the camera, battery pack and spotlight into Blok's robed lap. Moving behind the wheel, yanking handbrake, depressing clutch, accelerator. The jeep shot forward, away from all pursuers, Jewish and Arab, bucketing over potholes, careening round corners, threading the street-maze of the town. Leaving the helicopter, the searchlights, the muezzin, the lynching crowd, army and rebels, oppressors and oppressed, and Lena Khalili, behind.

'The Seventh Cavalry, eh, Avram? So what else are old friends for?'

Blok could not answer. The jeep left the city limits and turned towards the western shoulder of the West Bank, and the alien coast.

'You got my letters,' said Yissachar. 'And no word from the oracle. But I don't jettison an old friend . . . Got hold of our Thin Avi, through your Pa. He told me about this jaunt. I said, that's a scene for me! Got up the old roadrunner and accelerated, just in time for your dramatic exit, Avram! I must say, it was a lulu. But too much energy for no return, brother! You won't catch Yissachar on that kind of beat. Money and power, Avram, and more money! I'm a full-fledged sinner now. Hollywood, comrade! Dreams can come true – don't let them tell you otherwise! You see before you a full partner, no shit, of Kokashvili Leisure Industries! Make 'em laugh, make 'em cry! That's Entertainment! Put on your top hat and tails! Give your shoes a shine! Gotta dance! Positive Thinking, Avram! Forget this one-horse town, the political roachtrap, the small time, for God's fucking sake! You are with Yissachar Pri-On now! The cosmic bellybutton is here!'

BABEL

East to west, Yissachar drove him across the Occupied West Bank to the Green Line – the old borders of the Jewish State – just outside Kfar Saba, joining the arterial Haifa-Tel Aviv highway at the Herzliya junction, the winter glint of a thousand and one headlights on wide thoroughfares passing below the great chunks of apartment and office blocks. Yissachar took Blok directly to a building in the heart of the Big City, a bold new glass and marble tower, with buzzing intercoms and fail safe doors and a gleaming lift up to the fifteenth floor, silenced by reverence for the heavy ambience of cash. They carried the camera equipment into a suite of large rooms, with lean modern furniture and odd pots on stands and film posters upon smooth white walls.

'Nothing is too good for Kokashvili Incorporated,' said Yissachar, adding: 'GMBH.' He moved through the apartment. 'Fitted kitchen. Deep freeze. Sunken bath. Seven-pressure shower mode with finger-tip action. Dimmer lights. Stroboscopic option. Ultra Kwiet air conditioning. Colour TV, 28 inches. Video recorders: VHS, Beetamax, Sony U-matic, both NTSC and PAL-SECAM. New Brain personal word processor. The boudoir – semi-orthopedic double bed with two-speed vibrating option. You have to supply your own partner.'

'Nothing is perfect,' said Blok.

'I usually take what's offered,' said Yissachar.

'You may have struck the right note there,' said Blok.

He showered and changed into T-shirt and jeans, collapsing into a leather sofa along the wall of the parlour. An anglepoise light shone on a pile of bound scripts lying on a low formica stand. He leafed idly through them: 'The Naked Squirrel'. 'The Seven Guns of Moholy-Nagy'. 'Do Caterpillars Dream of the Monaco

Grand Prix?' 'Emmanuelle in Albania.' Yissachar, who had showered second, joined him with wet locks and pink bathtowel to sink into a matching armchair.

'Yes, Avram, it's a strange and daunting world out there, but if you face it like a man and blow smoke rings in its eyes you have won half the battle. Two years I vegetated in Los Angeles, tending Israeli exile bars. Reading the airmail editions of the Hebrew press, joining the queue to teach Hebrew to Jewish kids expected to replace the shortfall in cannon fodder caused by our own defection. After the failure of Irving Klotskashes' Jerusalem venture the old mogul retired up the coast, to Big Sur, not too close to Henry Miller, and though there were rumours, some times, of a comeback, I was left to find a new patron. The City of the Angels, Avram! What a farce! Not one feather of a wing in sight. Icaruses who had all flown up to the sun, and were blood and guts on the pavement. Only Money talked. It said: Fuck off! I floated about, in a battered fifth-hand Chevvy guzzling petrol like crazy, from Westwood to Artesia, from Manhattan Beach to Pomona, from Santa Monica to Santa Ana, from Culver City to Burbank, from Glendora to Yorba Linda, and to the further reaches of Anaheim. Ploughing the freeways, depositing in each furrow a bead of sweat, a gob of spit, a tear. I parked cars in Beverly Hills, took producers' widows' poodles out for walkies, or to the poochie parlour. Once I even washed a schnauzer, in a sunken bath. I dressed up as a Mexican, served tacos and talked like thees, *hombre*. I packed Jewish cadavers into vans, at Mount Sinai Hospital. Despair and madness stared me in the face, but I was not prepared to die. I sat and ate my lunches up against those benches advertising crematoria and mortuaries, watching the signs saying Private, Armed Response, among the Cinderella Palaces, the images of other images, the billboard monuments to ersatz. And then – a Saviour appeared.'

Yissachar rose and went towards a cabinet at the other end of the room, his bathtowel falling in the process. He returned naked, his penis dangling in its thicket, holding a small mahogany box from which he extracted cigarette rolling paper, strips of cardboard, roachclips, and a little mound of pungent weed. 'This should take us back,' he smiled at Blok, 'without the help of the Lord. Colombian, Avram. Just like the old days. But this is passé now, in Dreamland. Everyone sticks white schmutz up their nose. I could never see the point. It's the old-fashioned sins for me. Here's to the survivors. *L'chayim.*' He rolled one joint, lit it carefully so falling ash would not sear his prick, and passed it to Blok, beginning immediately to roll another, while in the pause they could hear the post-midnight jitters of the city, late night traffic along the six-lane thru'way, a stubborn party which knoweth no bounds somewhere in a matching tower block. Someone had been awakened in the flat above, and was perambulating up and down, in what sounded like wooden clogs.

'That is my neighbour, Bentov,' said Yissachar, reclining, a happy man inhaling. 'You may have heard of him, the well-known director of social dramas in the Sixties? His last film was made for Kokashvili. But now he never goes out of his flat – he is working on an open-ended film project completely confined to his own apartment. Though in his time he has been everywhere. You should meet the man. He is a real number. This entire building is full of strange figures: journalists on the make, forgotten authors once short-listed for the Nobel Prize, Iranian refugee carpet merchants, a harpsichord playing chiropodist, a violinist with the Philharmonic who used to dress in rags during the day and open his violin case for coins at a pitch by the Central Bus Station. His wife divorced him but he has now remarried and speculates in real estate. We also have Caspi, the famous ex-torturer, who strangled three Arab prisoners with barbed wire during a reprisal raid into Lebanon, and was pardoned by the Chief of Staff.'

The clog movements ceased for a while. The party wavered. Bentov's apartment toilet flushed. The steps resumed, slow and dragging, this way and that, up and down, receding, approaching, halting for a pause, then resuming. Insomnia, despair, elation? Yissachar shook his head sadly, casting his eyes at Blok's abandoned *abbayeh.*

'The Dispossessed, Avram, what can I do? Don't think I don't sympathize. Nablus, Palestine, Uganda, Iran . . . So many millions of people in shtik, waiting for their messiah. Some saviour who turns into another tyrant, from whom they need to be saved again. Your friend Avi might think the cycle can be broken, but no political nirvanas for me. I've become a convert to the Enemy, Avram, the sucking octopus of Mammon. I now believe in

Capitalism, the true equalizer. The real enemy is State power. Marx was wrong, the State can't be used against itself, you have to shatter it by an alternate force which gives people real power: money. Give your West Bank peasants a real stake in enterprise and they'll break free of all this misery. I'm against the Occupation because it doesn't do this, not because of anything else. Tear down all the borders and let them all fight each other in the marketplace, in company boardrooms, the stock exchange. If Yassir Arafat had real sense he would be demanding a share portfolio for every Palestinian. And it would not be a bad idea for you, either, Avram. We must see what we can do.'

SO, ON THE MORNING AFTER, following a deep sleep, in which the echoes of the mob, the muezzin, the clatter of armoured cars, night sirens, had faded in marijuana resonance, Yissachar woke Blok early, as a cold, bright day dawned, and drove him down to the famous Esplanade by the beach, where he jogged up and down in a purple tracksuit while Blok, wrapped in a borrowed anorak, sprawled on a deckchair watching the tar-smudged waves rolling into the sand and the brave early birds of the Big City, tanned youths and golden girls ignoring the winter, taking the first dip of the day, just happening to pass by the flubbery veterans of daily dawn gymnastics clocking off their seven thousandth session in the shrinking shadows of opening cafés. To their right, the curve of the great tourist hotels. To their left, the long curve towards Jaffa, the old harbour with its low buildings and mosque, the lighthouse poking through the haze. Let's have a coffee up here, Avram.

'This is the life, Avram, flesh and ocean, not your dry mystic Jerusalem.' Yissachar sat under the café awning, rubbing his hands upon an upside down coffee, watching the devout sea fowl. 'I'll admit a soft spot for the Capital City, the rolling hills, the mountain air, but not all of us are asthmatic, some of us would rather have a live show than those golden oldies of the soul. Stay with me here a while, you've seen that huge apartment. I have company now and again, but the place is big enough for three or even four. When did you last have sex, my friend? Don't answer if it incriminates you.'

130

SEX!!

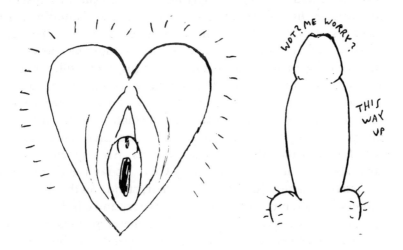

(*seks*, *n* that by which an animal or plant is male or female: the quality of being male or female: either of the divisions according to this, or its members collectively [*arch*., the sex, the female sex, women]: the whole domain connected with this distinction: (by confusion) sect. *Chambers Twentieth Century Dictionary*.) Also, from Roget's *Thesaurus*, entry 951: Impurity, impure thoughts, filthiness, defilement, uncleanness, indelicacy, bad taste, indecency, immodesty, impudicity, shamelessness, exhibitionism, coarseness, grossness, ribaldry, sex, smut, dirt, filth, obscenity, pornography, pornogram, banned book, blue cinema, prurience, voyeurism, et cetera. Esther, Lena Khalili's hand.

'Not very recently,' said Blok.

'You see?' said Yissachar. 'That's Jerusalem all over for you. Have you heard the story of Saladin and the nuns?'

It was this. When the great Salah ed-Din liberated Jerusalem from the Frankish hordes, oppressors of Jews and Arabs alike, tfu, tfu, tfu, importers of their own share portfolios, the Moslem General, having taken command in the Haram es-Sherif, was told of a nunnery, lying south of the City, on the road to Bethlehem, which was said to be brimful with the most beautiful virgins the Holy Land had to offer. Determining to sample this luscious merchandise, he set off towards the Hill of Evil Counsel, laden with gifts of camels and jewellery and fine spices and herbs. But before he could reach the nunnery a runner brought bad news. The nuns, hearing of the evil heathen's designs, had, following the example of their imposing Abbess, removed temptation from the conqueror's path by cutting off their own noses. When Saladin heard this he was deeply mortified, and slunk back quietly to the Haram, handing the camels and gifts to the Charitable Ransom Fund for Christian Women and Orphans. An important lesson learnt about fanaticism in the Holy City. Today the Convent of the Sisters of Saint Claire, said Yissachar, stands on the site of that nunnery. You remember how we used to try and climb the closed walls, take a look-see at the state of the inmates' proboscises? You must have watched it daily from the old Klander asylum, before that burnt to the ground. But no dice. We never saw so much as a single slit nostril, let alone a mons venus. An old tea boy called Ahmed the Gab told me that story, said Yissachar, back in the days of Holyland Films, asargelusha. Now will you stick to civilization?

NEVERTHELESS, Blok returned the next day to 35 Hageffen Street, although he returned, two weeks later, to the coast, to pursue Yissachar's offer of sanctuary, proceeding to commute, City to City, in service taxis, throughout the end of winter, spring, and summer, spending most of his time, though, at Hageffen Street, drawbridge raised, embrasures narrowed: the dawn Vespa delivery, 'FRUITS! FRUITS!', the siren morning call of Mrs Almoshnino, not to speak of his daily fear of the step of Salim, La Peda Nera, the Islamic Vengeance to come, above his head. For the Nablus escapade had not gone without its inevitable consequences: the stopping of the show, the detention of the entire cast by the Military Administration, threats of lethal retribution by the local Islamic Fundamentalists, obloquy, shame, the disappearance of Lena Khalili into the bosom of her family in a remote West Bank village (as far as one could find a remote West

132

Bank village), the 'temporary' but in fact permanent shelving of the play *The Sleeper*, the angry frustration of Thin Avi, accused by some members of infiltrating a fifth columnist, Blok, into the *Zurafa*'s ranks, although Latif told him: 'Don't worry about it. It's a squall which will blow over.' But Blok was visited, on a blustery early March Friday, by a plain clothes Security Branch officer known to all as Pimpled Zito, who took a statement of noncommittal grunts and pauses and served on him an order banning him from future entry into the West Bank and Gaza Strip for a period of one year, occasioning also, unbeknownst to Blok, further discussion in the House Committee, which was sombrely warned, by Tolstoy, of the growing danger of subversion within the building, reminding them of the threat of Basuto of Entrance D, Flat 5, whose Situationist Anarchists were now meeting regularly in his apartment on Saturday nights, plotting, as revealed by Tolstoy's strategic bugs, the complete overthrow of the State and its replacement by a commune of artisans and peasants, with free abortion and rampant sexual perversion of every conceivable kind. The said Basuto, a tall gangling and somewhat decayed youth of thirty-seven, had in fact approached Blok, having heard of his Nablus contretemps, soliciting his attendance at the Saturday night discussions, informing him he was a credit to the Revolution of the Spectacle, a defunct concept modelled after the theories of one Guy Debord of Paris in the 1960s.

But Blok rebuffed him, sinking back into his pre-*Zurafa* daily round, grateful for the non-appearance of Salim/Omar on the roof, exchanging terse words with his fellow inhabitants on the way to the garbage bins, or round the side of the house to turn off the knob of emptied gas balloon Number 1 and turn on the full Number 2, or at Mordechai's grocery store, waiting in queue with the retired merchant seaman Sirkin, who promised to tell him one day the strangest and saddest tale he had ever heard, or the Widow Tishbi, whose loud parties, with her many visiting sons and daughters, complete with breaking plates and stamping feet, were the wonder and frustration of the entire block, as the entire proceedings, being in celebration of traditional family virtues, could hardly be attacked openly, or surviving a visit by Papa, Baruch Blok, whose legs were now so bad that he walked with difficulty with a cane, and talked whimsically about skeleton

133

transplants, and a story he had read of a Californian Institute which cryogenically froze selected patients so they could be cured in the year 2300, a proposition which should, he thought, also attract Blok's mother, since it might free her from the blandishments of Blok's Aunt Pashtida, who wanted both of them to sell their flat in the City and come to live with her on the co-operative farm, among, Papa said, the chicken shit and rednecks. Blok promised to visit more often, and watched sadly as the old man tottered aboard the taxi he had called to take him home, while Tolstoy, peeved as always at the failure of House Chairman Kadurie to take firm action against the Enemy Within, mouthed vague, dire prophecies and disappeared into the maw of his private searches in databanks deep below Mittag's Café for Rabid Sheep, noseless nuns, undead invaders and the most private of his *recherché* endeavours, the fruitless quest, begun in 1960, for his own missing testicle . . .

The Tale of Tolstoy's Lost Ball

The search began in the immediate vicinity of his bladder and round the prostate gland, from whence it proceeded, by rectal inquiry, up the colon, into the large blind pouch (or caecum) and on up the large intestine. Having discarded, by a process of elimination, the kidneys, liver, spleen, pancreas and the peritoneal surface, the quest moved on, by the aegis of Swiss and Californian doctors, into more diffuse spheres. A microscopic probe was launched into Tolstoy's bloodstream, consisting of an entire team of top haematologists and a union approved cinematographic crew, miniaturized by new techniques developed by the US National Security Agency, who were all, however, lost in the lungs due to a sudden coughing fit. Tolstoy began to develop a private theory of his loss, beyond the bounds of medical science, involving secret rays emanating from German scientists experimenting in a secret Egyptian base in the Qattara Depression, not far from El Alamein. These rays were aimed at selected targets within the borders of the Jewish State, with intent to damage or destroy the potency of the renascent Jewish Nation. Later, when he was appointed to the top-secret Department of Apocalyptic Affairs, he became aware of other options, more close to hand, involving occult dabblings and esoteric subversion on a wide scale. He became more and more obsessed, spending long hours of the night shift by the flickering screens, working on complex programmes of his own devising strictly dedicated to the Lost Ball. Hacking, far into the small hours, into medical and bio-warfare databanks throughout the world, east and west, battling through reams of snow and blurred figures, intercepting messages which made his blood curl, reading the bioelectronic drip of mad clairvoyants, and driving his optician into curter and curter warnings of opthalmological doom . . .

IN THE KINGDOM OF THE BLIND
THE ONE EYED MAN IS HALF-BLIND!

★

Blok took the service taxi back up the coastal road, to Tel Aviv and Yissachar. He had already encountered the alienation of thin Avi, and even, it seemed, of Esther, who, while expressing no overt opinion on the Nablus affair, had suddenly became a real busy-bee on the social welfare front, visiting far prisons, making breakfast calls on stunned clients who thought the crack of dawn was 2 pm, comforting distraught mothers and fathers mystified at their offspring's inexplicable errors: 'He was such a good boy! He fell among thieves . . .' So she was rarely at home, and answered the phone, when she was, in a tired voice, saying, 'I really can't deal with anything now, Avram, I'm up to my eyebrows here.' Even Adolphe was absent, when Blok visited the Bak'a apartment, unannounced, to find a dish of catfood, by the doormat, upended, dried glop wasted on the stairs. Avi, too, deep in a demonic phase, working round the clock at the office of 'Bridge Publications', though he told Blok, when they met briefly at the Swallow-Don't-Chew restaurant, with the intimidatory Ezra fuming at every pause between mouthfuls ('THEY THINK THEY'RE DOING THE MOON WALK HERE! EVERYTHING'S IN SLOW MOTION!'): 'I have no beef with you, Avram. The Gods shat on us. We'll get together in a few weeks and talk.' He explained: 'I have this serious problem with an East German deconstructionist – the translator has had a breakdown . . .'

Welcoming him again to Tel Aviv, Yissachar took Blok for a

drive in his new Volvo ('Four-wheel drive! turbo engine, Avram! Note the cassette deck and stereo!') to the suburban town of Ramatayim and Kokashvili Inc. Studios.

'Small beer, Avram,' he confessed, 'compared to Culver City, Paramount, the 400 acres of Universal City Studios! But the Kok has his plans! He's bought a hill, just outside your own city, Avram, the seedbed of the Kokashvili Leisure Centre. He plans to build a totally authentic traditional Biblical village there, populated by animatronic robots modelled on the previous Arab inhabitants of the site, who will all be guaranteed employment as guides, attendants and maintenance personnel. This will demonstrate the joys of modern technology and Arab-Jewish cooperation at the same time. A real scream, don't you think, Avram? But it's all still a gleam in the eye . . . The man is always thinking up new schemes, projects. Sometimes he drives us all round the bend. A very strange fellow, our Kokashvili. He claims descent, would you believe it, from Shabetai Tsvi. You know, the False Messiah? 1666? An odd claim, eh, Avram? The Rabbis have denounced him anyway on nudity and obscene language – a strange alliance with the liberal critics who called him the "cancer of our national cinema", "the scar tissue of our art" . . .'

They rushed up the gleaming asphalt highway, turning down a side track to find the mogul's pre-Leisure Centre rising from sand dunes to the port of the suburbs, a clutch of modest warehouses opening out on to the backlot of his latest picture: a small street in Tiflis, Georgia, with old ersatz stone houses like leaning towers of pizza, washing strewn across the road from fake wrought iron balconies coated with Number 3 rust, but real sewage in the cobbled gutter to ensure the authentic touch. A dreamworld, Yissachar explained, of the mogul's own childhood, and a nostalgic return to the cheapie melodramas which had made the Kok his name as the New King of Schluck before his conquest of the Angel City: *The Lame Soldier*, *The Legless Minstrel*, *The One Armed Cobbler* and his unexpected international megahit, *The Mute Little Beggar Girl From Tabriz*, dubbed from Hebrew into anything from Greek to Tagalog and sold throughout the Third World and the Mediterranean basin, including the Enemy Arab lands . . .

'The Image Factory, Avram! Magic tricks of our time! The present production is *The Blind Seamstress*. A simple tale of true

136

love in the old country. The Actress is Aliza Z—, the rising star of the eastern communities. The wandering knife-grinder-minstrel who is her lover is the famous cassette singer and heroin addict Yosher Osher, the Idol of Youth. There he sprawls with his three companions – the two balalaika players and the spoon and fork man who help the Blind Seamstress in her agonia . . . Note the sturdy crew, our electrician Dubi, Simha the chief grip, Simone, continuity, the cameraman, Feibish . . . the blur you see there pushing chickens across the road is the production manager, Gretz. And now we even have an unimpeded view of the Man Himself – yes, that slobbish shape poured into the Director's chair like plaster breaking out of its mould . . . Observe,' Yissachar enthused, 'the three unshaven chins sunk into his belly button, the worry beads in his left hand, full blast . . . Just the way I first saw him, by a swimming pool under a palm tree in Laurel Canyon, with bodyguards in Calvin Klein casuals and matching shoulder holsters serving him trays of sunflower seeds . . . He took me on as a Production Assistant, and from there I shot to undreamed heights . . . A real miracle, Avram! but the Kok is known for his generosity – giving jobs to all kind of people in need, a real friend of the handicapped – we've had a strabismic focus puller, a sound mixer deaf in one ear, a tea lady who'd spent thirteen years in the booby hatch for poisoning her lover. I'm amazed, in fact, I wasn't asked to chop off my left hand, or drive a nail through my head. Yes, it can get a little hairy sometimes. But Opportunity's knock, Avram! You can't ignore it! When they hand you a ladder – climb, man, climb!'

Meanwhile, Esther,

drawn, in her enhanced professional zeal, into the personal lives of her misfortunate clients, was becoming involved in the somewhat complex family affairs of her star turn, the young motorcycle and spare parts impounder, Ya'akov Ben-Havivo, errant son of the Sage of the eastern communities known as the Dayan Ezuz. The aged mystic was celebrating his seventy-fifth birthday, and wished to reconcile with his prodigal offspring, who was, after all, his sole male issue. The conduit for this peace mission was Sergeant Tuvia, who had arrested the young man seven times, and was now driving the prodigal, and Esther, racing across the

Negev desert, south-east of Beersheba, in a battered Carmel, towards the development town of Arikha, belting out towards the sand dunes the somewhat dubious lyrics of his favourite cassette singer, the Idol of Youth, Yosher Osher:

In the depths of our hearts,
A memory does not fade,
Of the hopes that we had,
Which are now commerce and trade . . .

The hopes of our fathers
Now a counterfeit deal,
Our dreams have been bartered
For metal and steel . . .

In metal and steel,
Our image is cast,
The stranger we fear
Is ourselves to the last.

'What'd'you say?' Tuvia asked Esther. 'Are those words reasonable grounds for arrest or not?'

'I think they are very true,' said Esther.

'Then why does the man stuff his nose with cocaine? Why does he fill his blood with heroin? Eh? Tell me that? Almighty God! The things for which we reward our people!'

'Well, you're singing his song.'

'It's not the words. It's the tune. It gets you in the heart, right here!'

The desert rocks, primeval red under the burning sky. The building blocks of the 'new' town, all identical dust-covered concrete, rearing suddenly out of the sand. It was popularly said there was nothing in Arikha except poverty and religion. The riches of the Dayan Ezuz were only visible in his endowments – the town's school, its single clinic, its barren shopping centre, its five synagogues and its seminary. Each block in town was run by a different clan, but all deferred to the Sage. He himself lived on the seventh floor of a block in an unpaved street, both marked only by numbers. His relatives cocooned him, in declining consanguinity: brothers and sisters on the same floor, daughters and their families beneath, nephews and nieces *et al* on the fifth and fourth floor, the ground floor riddled with his great-grandchildren: little skullcapped boys with sidecurls and girls in long smocks, who surrounded the Carmel as it approached, while a spearhead of their elders emerged from every door and entrance, drawing the two pilgrims and the prodigal into the womb of their welcome, sucking them upstairs, shouting and ululating, embracing the son, the policeman and Esther, pressing into their hands plates piled high with North African delicacies, bombing them with love, showering them with compliments and blessings. 'You are the policeman who arrested our Ya'akov?' 'Seven times.' 'It is a holy number. You have been an instrument of the Lord.' Until, an hour later, there were finally ushered into the presence of the Sage . . .

★

'You know the Arab saying, Avram?' Yissachar yelled to Blok as they drove down the coastal road, away from Kokashvili Studios, 'Life is like a cucumber – one moment it's in your hand, the next it's being rammed up your ass?' Proceeding to enlighten Blok, as they rolled back in the Volvo towards the Big City, as to the complex web of his affairs –

To wit: He was in fact fucking the 'Blind Seamstress', Aliza, who was a married woman with two children. Her husband, a clerk in Bank Barclays-Discount, had refused her a divorce. To complicate matters, the knife-grinder-minstrel and cassette singer, Yosher Osher, was another of her lovers. Yosher Osher was at this point in time at the height of his fame, his recent radical hit – 'In the Depths of Our Hearts' – had puzzled his usual constituency of supporters of Prime Minister Menachem Begin and lead to both Left and Right wooing him assiduously with offers of sponsored gigs, eager to control his considerable 'clout' with the masses of Sephardi youth. At the same time his well-known heroin habit made him the subject of constant police surveillance. Aliza, who was trying to wean him from his vice, often stole his stash, prevailing on Yissachar to hide it in his apartment. The pop singer, out of his mind with withdrawal symptoms and dripping from every orifice, would turn up at Yissachar's building at three in the morning and buzz every tenant's intercom. The police

139

would collect him and beat his brains in before recognizing and releasing the Idol of Youth, who would appear at mass concerts with his limbs in a sling, the living image of police brutality.

To weave the mesh even tighter – Kokashvili, who had a horror of drugs, had his own private enforcers tailing his star, who also reported back on Yissachar's love life, on which the mogul kept a huge file. This, Yissachar said, was a necessary precaution for the Kok, due to the extreme vulnerability of his own business interests: The US Security & Exchange Committee were auditing his accounts, the National Security Agency were suspicious of his searches for audioanimatronic patents, the Mafia were unhappy about a recent due loan, and some Government department whose name no one seemed to know was investigating his contacts with a group of mediums in Bnei Brak, who claimed to be able to raise, en masse, the entire extended family, stretching back four hundred years, of a selected group of clients. Yissachar thought this part of it was harmless crankery, but the Government, oddly enough, seemed to be worried about Kokashvili's claim of direct descendance from the False Messiah, Shabetai Tsvi, whose tenure, short as it was, in the 1660s, had shaken the Jewish faith to its foundations and split the people into opposing factions and who had, at the end of the day, accepted Islam and led his followers into apostasy. Legmen of this shadowy department had been seen shadowing Kokashvili, his employees and their contacts, even their friends and relations. Small wonder Yissachar could not fuck freely, in the tender reaches of moonlight, even in his own apartment, and had, while his beloved curled in his arms, to keep one eye and ear open for the vengeance of husbands, rival lovers, narcotics agents, policemen, secret and not, and countless spirits, steaming in the night, writhing out of Bnei Brak closets . . .

'Do you remember our youth?' Yissachar said to Blok, wistfully. 'Everything seemed so simple then. Ein Karem. Holyland Films. The pornographic paradise. New York. Even madness is not what it used to be . . .'

★

. . . a whitewashed room adorned only with a framed garishly-coloured portrait of the Sage, in a tourquoise robe and white turban. The Dayan Ezuz was now dressed, however, in a dark business suit, black tie, white shirt and cufflinks. He would have looked like a retired undertaker, were it not for his piercing, youthful black eyes, darting about like anti-aircraft guns in search of invading missiles. The returning son, Ya'akov, sat by his side, modestly clad in the T-shirt and jeans of his apostasy and ascension. The old man stretched his hand to the policeman, Sergeant Tuvia, who kissed it and the Dayan Ezuz told him:

'The world is rotten with corruption, temptations of the flesh, of the mind, and the unsatisfied pocket. Youth cannot be kept in a golden cage, oblivious of Sin, held within the sphere of Holiness by Ignorance alone. But you have taught my son the existence of Law and Justice and you have done this fairly, showing the qualities of true Righteousness and Mercy.' Tuvia inclined his head, and a minion handed him a gift-wrapped bottle of Bell's whisky and a signed portrait of the Savant.

Then the Sage turned to Esther and said: 'My daughter, my daughter . . .' The anti-aircraft guns appeared to have locked on their target as she gazed into the eyes of the man about whom so many tales and legends abounded: how he had converted a lifelong member of the Communist Party into a Repentant in half an hour. How he had caused, by the laying on of hands and prayer, barren women to conceive, impotent men to penetrate, imbeciles to display amazing intellect, boneheaded children to excel at their studies. How he could foretell the time of a man's death to the hour and the minute. How, in a burst of anger, he had told an enemy to drop dead, with immediate effect. He was also said to have blessed the nation's nuclear arsenal, which was reputed to lie somewhere in the vicinity of the town, in a secret base beneath the sands. But his voice was gentle as he addressed Esther:

Exegesis One: The Dayan Ezuz, Esther
'I have heard a lot about you, my daughter. And I know more, that is hidden from many, but not from my eyes. My son has told me of your kindness to him and all the spare time you have spent setting him on the right path, and for this we both thank you deeply. But I cannot fail to see you are beset by many troubles. Your heart is a whirlpool of desires. The holy and the profane mingle in your thoughts. In your search for Truth you have

141

opened your heart to foreign voices that should have no purchase in the House of Israel: messiahs of Lies, Socialism, Gods of Ishmael and Christian Edom, Theosophism and the Pit where there is no Faith at all. Persons close to you are at the Gates of the Apostate Kingdom of Shabetai Tsvi and Nathan of Gaza. You have a friend whose brother is a Servant of God but who himself has turned towards the Black Arts. You are living in a State of Sin with a young man who conspires with the Enemies of our People, and you have another acquaintance about whom dark and mysterious forces creep and gibber. I shall speak to you as if I were your father and your mother: immorality is a greater sin for a woman than a man. This is not a matter of discrimination. This is because God has ordained for women the most vital task at the coming End of Days. You will discover the meaning of my words at a time of great upheaval both in your personal life and that of the entire House of Israel. I do not mention all this to condemn or calumniate. Your open heart gathers in these lost souls. But you should learn when to steel and close your heart. The freedom of Choice has been given you. I shall pray on your behalf for seven weeks, Esther. After that, you are on your own.'

He motioned to a minion, who handed him two items which he personally placed on Esther: a jewelled ring inscribed with the word שדי – SHADAI, the divine name, and an amulet upon a necklace of fine silver, with the following inscription of protection against the demon Lilith:

142

'I mean, do you understand what's going on?' said Yissachar, 'do you really grasp it?' They had arrived back in Tel Aviv, parked the car and were at the foot of the Big City towerblock. 'Myself,' Yissachar said, 'I've given up even trying. Hey, Bentov!'

They had almost collided, at the entrance, with a tall, middle-aged man with tousled hair and a deeply grooved face, carrying a heavy bag of groceries. Yissachar introduced him to Blok as his upstairs neighbour, the hermit cineaste and post-midnight clog-pacer. They ascended together in the lift, rising silently towards the upper storeys –

Exegesis Two: Blok, Yissachar, Bentov

(Ascending smoothly in the lift.)

'You are still working with that monster, Kokashvili?' Bentov queried.

'We have just been at his studio,' said Yissachar.

'You know I worked with him once,' Bentov said. Yissachar nodded. 'He is a Neanderthal,' Bentov offered. 'But I liked his own films. Not the garbage he produces, but those he directs. The ones the critics always hated. What was the one with the Yassir Arafat dwarf? *The Blood Beast of Amman . . . ?* I defended it, in *Auteur Magazine*. I wrote he had the touch of an illiterate Buñuel. No one spoke to me for several months.'

'People are strange in this country,' said Yissachar. 'They don't give anyone the credit.'

'It's biological,' Bentov stated. 'Something in the food. All that frying. There is a permanent acidity. I have become convinced it's irreversible.'

The lift had stopped as a balding fifth-floorer tried to wrestle a filing cabinet aboard. They all helped. The man said, 'Thank you. Do you mind holding the door? There's some more.'

'People are always moving around in this building,' said Bentov. 'It's the Jewish genes, I am convinced. They are never happy in one place. It's a fallacy that Jews seek a homeland. They just huddle together for the gossip.'

Blok gazed at the man with his wooden sandals and a face with lines to boggle a cheiromancer had they crisscrossed a palm: the lines of travel, lines of opposition, lines of luck, fate, of intuition.

143

Escape lines, fading into the neck. Rings of Solomon, Great Triangles, Mystic crosses chiselled everywhere.

'How is your own project going?' asked Yissachar. 'I told Avram you're doing film work at home.'

'Excellent,' said Bentov. 'Last week I dollied in, extremely slowly, to the sitting room table. This week I intend to film a chair. You can't imagine the liberation. I was a documentarist, you know,' he said to Blok, as the fifth-floor mover upended a table on top of them. 'The wretched of the earth, lands without bread, *le condition humaine*, et cetera. Hunger, poverty, disease, exploitation, natural disasters, greed. Eventually I couldn't bear the pain any more, especially in war.'

'War?! Tfu, tfu, tfu!' the balding mover spat three times on the lift floor.

'Avram was a war correspondent in his army service,' said Yissachar, 'in 1967, and the Yom Kippur War, '73, isn't that so, Avram?'

'I don't remember any of that,' said Blok.

'My sentiments exactly,' said Bentov. 'Memory is the greatest curse of Man.'

'You're right,' said the mover, loading them each with a chair. 'You must have been married to my first wife.'

'But you remember everything,' objected Yissachar. 'How often we've sat talking about your days in Paris . . .'

'Exactly,' said Bentov. 'It is a great seduction. But therein lies the trap.' The lift was allowed to resume its journey.

'Bentov,' Yissachar told Blok, 'was one of the first critics of the famous *Cahiers du Cinema*. He sat in the gloom of Langlois' cinémathèque in the Rue d'Ulm, in the Fifties, watching endless old American B pictures, with only a few film junkies for company – Godard, Truffaut, Chabrol . . .'

'Astruc, Resnais, Reichenbach . . .' Bentov added. 'Not one person in the audience had changed their underwear in the previous six months.'

'Those are good memories. I would keep them,' said Yissachar.

'I have no choice,' said Bentov.

'I saw a film of Godard once,' said the mover. 'Frankly, I would rather be buggered by a Turk.'

'That too, is an experience,' said Bentov.

144

'Lawrence of Arabia,' suggested Yissachar. 'David Lean. Peter O'Toole. Freddie Young. Now that was cinematography. You should return to production,' he told Bentov. 'We need somebody with your kind of background. I enjoy working with Kokashvili Incorporated, but somewhere, there has to be Art . . .'

'Art!' agreed the mover. 'The Art of Life! My floor here . . .' The lift had halted at twelve. The others disengaged from the wandering Jew's furniture and moved on, towards the ethereal spheres.

'Well,' said Bentov, 'my position is – there's enough art every-where, in my bedroom, my bathroom, my loo. My broom cabinet. I am working up towards the sitting room window. Next year, I might point the camera outside, towards the street, with a telephoto lens. I am no longer prepared to take chances. I have been bitten too many times. Now I want everything I do to be strictly calculated, everything to be under control.'

★

'Controllability!' said Sergeant Tuvia, turning to Esther as they sped, minus the prodigal son, back north across the desert wastes. 'The problem of people one can't arrest! You can arrest almost anybody these days – captains of industry, ministers, politicians of all parties. But a saint? It's a serious problem. What do you think, Esther?'

But she just shook her head, fingering the Dayan Ezuz's amulet, looking out into the sands.

'A real pisser,' the Sergeant said, resuming, in a nasal eastern lilt, Yosher Osher's arrestable song:

> Our eyes, which saw then,
> In our dreams, a jewelled seal,
> Not the death of our sons
> In metal and steel.
>
> Will metal and steel,
> Turn our hearts into rust?
> Will our hopes and our loves,
> Turn to ashes and dust?

145

Further Searches For Tolstoy's Lost Ball

Early in 1967, a team of Belgian urologists repeated the attempt to locate Tolstoy's lost appendage. Dressed in the latest safari gear, they travelled up the urethra, through the fossa navicularis, avoiding the raging chaos of the remaining (right) testicle, to the kidneys and the supra renal capsule. Finding nothing there but a tribe of Latvian Rabbis banished for mail fraud and shchita board malpractice, they proceeded via an interlobular artery to the lower duodenum. Unseen forces, from the gallbladder, cast immense stones which almost capsized their fragile vessel, but they continued bravely, past the oesophagus, floating down the mucus and the peptic glands into the main abdominal regions. Unfortunately, a misjudged bouillabaisse, in a down-market Brussels eatery, precipitated them savagely, while they paused to take readings, into the transverse colon, descending into the sigmoid flexure, buffeted against the rapids of Tolstoy's haemorrhoids, out through the rectum into a downtown toilet, from whence they fled in disarray. Although learned papers were delivered at major international functions as the result of this bold experiment, Tolstoy himself lost faith in Modern European Surgical Procedures entirely, relying, more than ever, on the occult properties, the electronic ectoplasm oozing from his VDUs as he navigated his keyboard through the stored mysteries of the Hechler Box, the Herzl Enigma, the matrix of the Rabid Sheep sightings, the dangerous twists of the Kokashvili–Bnei Brak axis and Salah ed-Din's dreams . . .

★

But Blok returned, again, to Jerusalem on the magic carpet of his own willed exclusion. Promising to consider Yissachar's offer to earn a crust from Kokashvili Leisure Industries by reading scripts sent in, unsolicited, by various doomed hopefuls. 'Money for old rope, Avram. Don't be a schmuck all your life. Come out of that old shell.' Back, by service taxi, to the routine of Hageffen Street, the immune ants invading the orifices of his kitchen due to the whiff of coming summer, the Vespa delivery and 'FRUITS! FRUITS!' and Mrs Almoshnino, the roistering of Mrs Tishbi's offspring and the promises of the ex-seaman Sirkin ('I'll tell you one day the saddest story you've ever heard . . .'), and the cycle of fruitless phone calls to Bak'a, ring, ring, nobody in, Avi nor Esther, all busy ploughing their furrows (doesn't that damned cat ever answer the phone?), and the long walk in the sun across town and the valley, down the Bethlehem Road, pine, eucalyptus, the kiosks, the billboards, the women beating bathmats, the shrill children in the yard, up the stairway to the closed door with the penned messages of other pilgrims who sought in vain: 'Esther, Yoni called. At home tonight.' 'Esther – Rachel, love kisses' ♡ ♡ ♡ ♡ ×× × 'Nahum, 765465.' 'Avi, what's going on? Fuck your mother!'

Spring into summer, in the City, the lazy days following the Camp David Treaty. Further booths, in the town centre, to protest the coming surrender of the Sinai to Egypt. No Withdrawal! spearheaded by the nationalist zealots and the stalwarts of Rabbi Levine. But in Hageffen Street, withdrawal de facto, with the Blokbook, into which he resumed pasting items of the press, sundry random jottings, the rambles of haphazard attention:

JEWISH AGENCY YOUTH INSTRUCTORS IN
DRUG ORGIES WITH OVERSEAS STUDENTS.

ARAB SHEIKHS IN SEX PARTIES WITH
NEW YORK PROSTITUTES.

NOCTURNAL GNASHING OF TEETH, BRUXISM,
CAN DAMAGE TEETH, GUMS, TISSUES.

US ARMY JAILS, DEMOTES, FINES
FEMALE TROOPER FOR
SEXUALLY HARASSING MALE GI.

SAUDI RELIGIOUS POLICE (MUTAWWAS)
RAID RIYADH CHINESE RESTAURANT,
ARREST UNVEILED WOMEN.

KHOMEINI – THE 'OLD MAN WITH LICE IN HIS BEARD'.

YOSSI THE PARROT CALLED AS WITNESS
IN PETAH TIKVA TRIAL.

IRAQ THREATENS WAR WITH IRAN.

147

To which he added, in his own hand:

- The Age of Uncertainty gives Way to the Age of Total Dislocation: Discuss.
- Morality and Ethics are not in the realm of Science: Do not
  bother to discuss.
- the World Conspiracy to Infect us with Guilt: Is Indifference still
  valid?
- (from a Feiffer cartoon) Can you feel oppressed singly, or do
  you have to be part of a group?
- (from the daily press) Youthful rat to father: Tell me, how do we
  know when to desert the sinking ship? Father: What do you
  mean, how? Aren't we the ones gnawing the holes?

And while he was at it, he added the pamphlet the Situationist,
Basuto (Entrance D, Flat 5) the thorn in Tolstoy's flesh, handed
him as he ventured out to empty the garbage, marking the
following passage on page 4:

> In the mythological opera which the society of the spec-
> tacle presents to our no longer astonished gaze governments
> and their numerous subordinate powers have become more
> modest everywhere. The society of the spectacle had begun
> in coercion, deceit and blood, but it initially promised a
> happy path. It believed itself to be loved. Now it no longer
> promises anything. It no longer says: 'What appears is good,
> what is good appears.' It simply says: 'It is so.' Nevertheless,
> those who are aware of the necessity for a radically realist
> solution can only find in this firmer evidence for the inevit-
> able fall of the cities of illusion.

Nevertheless, Blok rebuffed Basuto again, but, some mornings
later, the spindly revolutionary appeared on his doorstep accompanied by a cheerful well-rounded apple cheeked blonde with deep
clear green eyes, who spoke English with a strong Germanic
accent.

'This is Ilse,' he said. 'She has been visiting us, bringing fraternal
greetings from the comrades overseas.'

'Won't you come in,' said Blok. The girl crossed his threshold.

'I like ziss apartment,' she said. 'Look, zere is no propaganda on ze valls. It makes a difference from your room, Basuto.'

'Ha, ha, ha,' said Basuto, in lieu of a laugh. He explained to Blok: 'Ilse has spent two years in Italy, with the Metropolitan Indians.'

'Is that an orchestra or a baseball team?' asked Blok. She laughed and clapped him firmly on the knee. They spent two hours in Blok's flat, sipping his Elite coffee, Basuto rambling on about the ridiculous attempts of the opposition to revive the dead duck of Socialist Zionism, Ilse gazing raptly out of the window at the strange bearded figures now and then ambling by, encased in calf-length black gaberdine in 33 Celsius, with their furry hats and dangling appendages. 'What a marvellous statement!' she enthused, turning to Blok. 'You must take me to see sings in ze city. Viz zese people it is politics, politics, politics all ze day long.'

'Ha, ha, ha,' said Basuto. 'What a good idea! And you can join us for the Saturday Night Group tomorrow, if you want, Avram – no obligation to buy!'

So Blok took Ilse on a Traditional Tour of the City,

to Absalom's Pillar, Abu Tor, the Agricultural Museum, the Allenby Memorial, the American Consulate, the Bezalel School of Art, the Biblical Zoo, the Cave of Zedekiah, the Citadel, David's Tower, the Dome of the Rock, Ecce Homo Arch, the Garden of Gethsemane, the Gates of the Old City (Jaffa, Damascus, the New, the Lion's, Herod's, Zion, the Dung), the Hadassah Medical Centre, the Hebrew University, the Holy Sepulchre, the Islamic Art Museum, the Israel Museum, Jason's Tomb, the Jewish Agency Compound, the Jewish Quarter, the Knesset building, Mahaneh Yehuda market, Mamillah, the Military Cemetery, the Model of Ancient Jerusalem, the Monastery of the Cross, the Mosque of al-Aqsa, Mount Herzl, the Mount of Olives, Mount Scopus, Mount Zion, the Pontifical Biblical Institute, the Rockefeller Museum, the Russian Compound, Sanhedria, Silwan, Solomon's Quarries, Saint Anne's Church, the Taxation Museum, the Temple Mount, Via Dolorosa, the Western Wailing Wall, the Yeshurun Synagogue, the YMCA, Zachariah's Tomb and Zisselmacher's laundry.

Mint tea and eggplant salad at the Artists' House Café, with the

hubbub of the city dwindling towards the Sabbath and the cog-
noscenti beginning to file in for the weekly gossip hour. New
faces, new bodies, the curly hair, beards or fifteen o'clock shadow,
summer-tanned limbs, the flush of feminist youth, sweat drying
on twin peaked T-shirt and tight dungarees, and Ilse, fallen plum
of an alien, once enemy, tree, regaling Blok with tales of student
demos in Turin and Milan, clashes with fascists in Rome, Com-
munists in Bologna, Christian Democrats under every stone.
Burnt-out tear-gas shells on the Via Zamboni. Molotov cocktails
from the best wine bottles. Illegal broadcasts of Radio Alice. How
to be arrested on a charge of carrying lemons (their juice was a
tear-gas antidote). She related to him the slogans of the anarchist
street fighters, opposed to all shades of authority:

'WORKERS' GASTRONOMY! CANNIBILIZATION!
KNIVES AND FORKS – LET'S EAT THE BOSSES!'

'POLICEMEN – THEY'VE CONNED YOU: LICENCE
TO KILL, BUT NO ARMOURED CAR!'

'CARRY THE ATTACK TO THE HEART OF THE
PAPACY! ALL POWER TO THE ARMED CLERICS!'*

'That would not work here,' Blok said sadly. 'The clerics are
already armed.' Ilse's sallies were punctuated by a foghorn laugh
which caused even the most blasé heads to turn, but Blok basked
in such appealing company.

What remained to be said? They returned to his flat and made
love.

LOVE!

> – *luv, n.* fondness: an affection of the mind caused by that
> which delights: strong liking: devoted attachment to one of
> the opposite sex: a sexual attachment: a love-affair: the
> object of affection: the god of love, Cupid, Eros: a kindness,
> a favour done (*Shak.*): the mere pleasure of playing without
> stakes, hence, in some games, no score . . .

Well, definitely a score here, in the Friday night silence of 35
Hageffen, all radios dimmed in deference to the Sabbath, free

---

* *'Gastronomia operaia! Cannibalizzazione! Forchette, coltelli, magnamoce er
padrone!' 'Poliziotto – t'hanno fregato: licenza di sparare, ma ninete carro armato!'
'Portare l'attacco al cuore del papato! tutto il potere al chierichetto armato!'*

reign to the post-supper singing of the orthodox neighbours, Elrom: stamping of feet, clanging of soup ladles on tables: 'When Israel went out of Egypt, the House of Jacob from a people of strange language / Judah was his sanctuary, and Israel his dominion / The sea saw it and fled, Jordan was driven back / The mountains skipped like rams, the hills like lambs . . .' But Ilse and Blok, in the creaking single bed across the stairway, progressed towards their own dominion, the firm communion of ancient enemies, the liquid slap of midsummer tum on tummy, lips, damp limbs entangled, fingers entwined, erogenous zones invaded, a long drought brought to an end by flash flood, the wadi drenched, the desert brought to bloom, water gushing from the struck rock, the Red Sea parted, the springs of hope replenished, the rock turned into standing water, the flint into a fountain, the warm afterglow tones of international brother-sisterhood: '*Caro mio, liebchen, chéri*, oh, honey . . .' wetly licking at his ear . . .

THE FRIDAY NIGHT FUCK, ASARGELUSHA!! copulation throughout the City – couplings of all manner and persuasion, husbands with wives, wives with husbands, lovers of all genders, legal and otherwise, casual encounters in desperation to evade the Sabbath Eve dross, cash and credit card transactions in hotels, major and minor, brief or prolonged moments of ecstasy or disappointment on single beds, double beds, kingsize beds, cots, mattresses, cushions, the hard ground, Kosset carpets, the grass, sand, acts natural and unnatural, animal and mineral, exoskeletal spooning, calls of the wild, the propagation of unwanted species, amphibian and fish fucking, parthenogenesis, artificial insemination with or without registered medical supervision, virgin conceptions, not to speak, to be sure, of the lonely wheezings of solitary consummation . . .

The Friday night fuck!!
  – Esther, lying with Avi, a rare meeting at the old plantation, the Bak'a night stillness, filled with far-off cat yowls, languid thrusting with the mind of each elsewhere, he in the convoluted labyrinth of alien words, she under the uncanny stare of the sensuous old man of Arikha and the gaze of the plaintive thief-son,

151

thinking, too of other caresses amid mountain cricket trills . . .
'This is no fucking damned good . . .'

– Yissachar (in another City) with the 'Blind Seamstress', Aliza,
grappling and grasping each other in mute battle, half an ear
pricked for the buzzer announcing the cassette singer's junkie
hour, the clog, clog, clog of Bentov's insomnia above like a
disapproving minor deity. Life ever on the brink of danger . . .

– Adolphe (behind the distant garbage cans), sinking his teeth
into the scruff of a reluctant female, penetrating with determined
vigour, holding on, tooth and claw, oblivious of any protest,
composing, in his mind, as he went about his business, an
appropriate haiku:

THE POUNCE

The day, the meek can claim,
The night is ours.
Her arse hairs in my face,
Perfumed of flowers.

Cries of lust and outrage piercing the night, framed in the distant
prayers of the old Sage of Arikha, the Dayan Ezuz, twisting and
turning in his desert agonies, his constant kabbalistic meditations
moving his lips silently, curling his beard round his fingers, taut
with the awareness of so much spilled seed, every unfecund drop
of semen a lost soul fallen into the grasp of the *klippah*, the domain
of the satanic powers, which gibbered and snarled at him as he
prayed: Lilith and all her cohorts, Naamah, Rahab and Agrat, or
the demon kings, Samael, Ashmedai, Halama, Maimon, Shem-
urish, Sanoi, Sansanoi, Samnaglof, Kafkafuni, Belial, Beelzebub.
Unclean animals, cats, ferrets, chameleons, monkeys, lobsters,
clawing at his underpants. Shades of heretics cast into the nether
regions rising in his gorge, the false messiahs, Shabetai Tsvi, Jacob
Frank, Yeshua El-Messias, Jesus the Nazarene. The vision of four
men, carrying a sealed box emitting the stench of death, searing
his senses. His ears hearing the glowing heat of flames, his eyes
seeing the roar of furnaces. Drawing into himself all the accumulated pain of impious coitus, Yissachar's adulterous union, the
wasted seed of Blok, all those lost spirits expiring in the *klippah* of
the gentile Ilse's vagina.

152

'The Lord is our God! The Lord is One!'
'I heard you!' rumbled Kokashvili.
Ticker-tape machines coughed in old bourse archives.
Databanks whispered to each other.
The Rabid Sheep claims another victim. Hechler sloshes angrily in his box. Herzl revolves in his tomb.

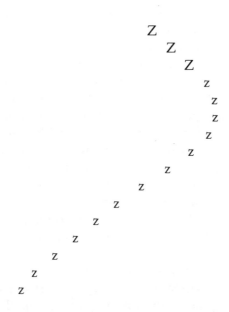

Exegesis Three: The Situationist Cell – Blok, Ilse, Basuto, Paeger, Daniela, Adonis, Za'ater, Ma'alesh, Elvira
(After a long day's lie in and a languid walk with Ilse round Mekor Baruch, Blok had no choice apart from attending the Saturday Night Flat 5 Group Meeting.)

BASUTO: I have to say again – I still believe we haven't come up with the right degree of excess . . .

DANIELA: It seems to me we're going round in circles. You people don't seem to know what you want. We agreed that provocations on the Italian model are useless as everyone takes them seriously. We all remember the farce of the 'Eat the Arabs' petition . . .

MA'ALESH: A hundred and fifty bona fide signatures.

PAEGER: People thought it was just a metaphor for an aggressive policy. You can't be subtle in this country.

DANIELA: We should have put a cooking pot and utensils on the street. Some cuts of meat for example . . .

MA'ALESH: If it would be anything like your lamb curry, you can count me out completely . . .

ELVIRA: It's no use us understanding the irony if no one else gets the message. With people like Rabbi Levine on the streets, we are too close to the reality.

ILSE: Isn't that where you want to be?

BASUTO: Let me reformulate our problem for you. We are living in a fractured society composed of a hundred thousand splinters. Divide and rule ad absurdum. And this by popular demand. The people lovingly massage their divisions, polish them daily, oil their barrels. Our problem is not to call for spurious, bourgeois, 'unity' which just hides behind repression. We want the impossible contradiction: to be the hundred thousandth and first splinter which shatters the whole concept of splinterism. To find the Spectacle which exposes the competing Spectacles in this country – the Religious Spectacle, the Nationalist Spectacle, the 'Socialist'-Zionist Spectacle . . .

ZA'ATER: Does anybody want more tea?

DANIELA: We're all agreed on we're not interested in becoming just another harmless peacenik pressure group. But we've also agreed it's not our task to take part in the Palestinian armed struggle. Our propaganda of the deed has to be seen to be provocative, but definitely life enhancing.

MA'ALESH: I still think we should have a magazine . . .

ELVIRA: Everybody has a magazine. We need a true alternative project . . .

ADONIS: Any new suggestions for squaring the circle?

ZA'ATER: Does nobody want a glass of tea??

Ilse put a hand on Blok's balls. He placed his hand on hers. So many more lost souls in the cauldron, ready to be bounced off her Made In Hamburg diaphragm and expire in her mucous membranes. The night, again in the pursuit of Life Enhancement, bouncing to confound the downstairs neighbours. The new day,

154

wandering the city, sitting in the cafés of the half completed Ben Yehuda precinct, watching the masses struggle for ice cream rather than the overthrow of society. Ilse, nevertheless, informing Blok gravely of his proletarian duties, warning him against the dangers of Stalinist temptation in the form of Gramsci, Althusser, Mandel, pressing on him dog-eared copies of the speeches of Emma Goldmann and the collected works of the Father of the Faith, Bakunin, whom, despite his errors, she still adored, having marked up for him to read her favoured samples of the great toothless Russian boozer's vision:

'Patriotism has its roots not in the humanity of man but in his bestiality.'

'No one should be entrusted with power, inasmuch as anyone invested with authority must, through the force of an immutable social law, become an oppressor and exploiter of society.'

'No State can exist without a permanent conspiracy, directed against the masses of drudge-people, for the enslavement and fleecing of which all States exist.'

'God exists; hence man is a slave.

Man is intelligent, just, free; hence God does not exist.'

'Bakunin believes in God.' Blok concluded.

Ilse threw a cream cake at his head. He did not tell her she was ploughing an old furrow, dimly grooved in his mind: the blocked memory of pre T—t days, post-army-service ventures into the outside world, Paris, 1968, Cohn-Bendit, the burning Bourse, London and another golden shiksa, the Black Panthers, the crackling voice of Bob Dylan, policemen's helmets in Grosvenor Square, Nietzsche: *Ni Dieu, ni maître!* The faded comprehension of old slogans revived in her underlined chapter headings:

DEATH AGONY OF A HISTORICALLY CONDEMNED CLASS. IS THE BOURGEOSIE ALTOGETHER BANKRUPT? DISTINGUISHING MARKS OF A BORGEOIS SOCIALIST. CORRECT TACTICS DURING A REVOLUTION. SOCIETY AS A RESULT OF MAN'S INEVITABLE FALL. ABOLITION OF THE JURIDICAL FAMILY. THE NATURE OF TRUE FREEDOM. ASOCIAL CHARACTER OF METAPHYSICAL MORALITY. CONTEMPLATION OF DIVINE ABSURDITY. HUNGER AND SEX: THE BASIC DRIVES OF THE ANIMAL WORLD. TRUE LOVE CAN EXIST ONLY AMONG EQUALS.

WHAT THE WORKERS LACK. FREEDOM IS VALID ONLY WHEN
SHARED BY EVERYONE. THE ROLE OF A SMALL MINORITY. THE
IMPORTANCE OF CORRECT TACTICS TOWARDS THE PEASANTS. THE
DISAPPEARANCE OF CLASSES. IN TIMES OF REVOLUTION DEEDS
COUNT MORE THAN THEORIES. THE UNIQUENESS OF THE INDI-
VIDUAL. MAN SUBJECT TO UNIVERSAL INEVITABILITY. NATURE AS
RATIONAL NECESSITY. THE LIMITS OF MAN'S UNDERSTANDING OF
THE UNIVERSE. MARXISM AND ITS FALLACIES.

They continued their grand tour of the City, embarking on a long
walk around the Old City Walls, up from Sanhedria through
Sheikh Jarrah to Mount Scopus, Augusta Victoria and the Mount
of Olives. A vantage point with the Old City on one side and the
bare desert falling sharply away from a last pine tree glade on the
other, little dots of goats moving across the bare landscape out
there in search of sparse pasture. On, past groups of ogling
youths, past the high upper wall of the Garden of Gethsemane,
closed, alas, to women wearing trousers, to the Intercontinental
Hotel where the ersatz bedouin poses with his camel for tourists
for a mere one dollar, and down the hill to sit among the ancient
Jewish graves, gazing at the clichéd vista: the battlements, spires,
the cupolas capped with a forest of TV aerials. The golden Dome
of the Rock, the silver of al-Aqsa. And God said to Abraham: 'Lay
not thine hand upon the lad . . .' A middle-aged Arab, with
careful Old City eyes, approached and engaged them in conversation: 'How are you? Where you from? You have many children? I
have had in my life four wives and nine children.' He produced a
thick billfold of snapshots. 'You see – five sons. A man should
have sons, so that his name should not die out, never.' 'We are not
married,' Blok informed him. 'This does not matter,' the man
said. 'You must make children now. There's no time. Revol-
utions, wars, occupations. A man must move fast or be finished.
Very soon, the atomic war, and then it is all over. Nine tenths of
the world will be destroyed. I know a man in the Ministry of
Defence and he tells me it is now imminent.' 'I have already seen
it,' said Blok. 'It is nothing special.' Ilse looked at him a little
strangely.

He took her to an exhibition of sanitation trucks, and to the
Jerusalem Cinemathèque, at her insistence, to see a Festival of

156

Holocaust Films. Millions died before their eyes. Cities burned. Survivors hobbled about in skin and bone. Actors vainly trying to emulate the starving. Then they repaired back into town to Abu Shaul's and ate grilled hearts and eastern schnitzel. Ilse was subdued and wished to talk about Germany. Blok squeezed her hand into silence. They were unable to make love that night, and sweated separately. In the morning they took the soaked sheets to the laundry. Down the Kings of Israel Road to Zisselmacher's in 33 degrees Celsius. Ten degrees hotter within, by the revolving machines, the mixture of steam and stale air, the pasty-faced proprietor in his unkempt white shirt and drenched sidelocks, the all-male customers in black gaberdine, hefting their untidy bundles, all snorting and snuffling with anguish at the sight of the bare-armed blonde gentile temptress. 'Kill 'em with kindness,' said Blok. 'The final solution by other means.' But she still looked extremely perturbed as they walked on down the busy street, past the religious wig shop, Geula Pickles, Grinwald Toys, Moldovan Tailor, Shtisel's Self-Service and Eli Lipsker's Little Soldiers raising the flag on Mount Sinai, scandalizing the devout and making beardless youths hiccup, but stopping short at the junction with Mea Shearim Street, any further progress threatening confrontation with the Vigilantes of the Holiness of the City, who had only the day before thrown acid in the face of an uncovered woman, according to the *Jerusalem Post*.

'I need to get out of this town,' said Ilse. They took a service taxi to Tel Aviv, that seminal Holy Land experience, the travelling debating chamber, hurled by laconic suicidal drivers about the descending mountain bends: 'They say Begin is going to visit Cairo.' 'It's a trick by the Egyptians to kill him.' 'Do me a favour!' 'They'll declare war when we're not expecting it, just like October '73.' 'No, I believe in Anwar Sadat.' 'Some people will believe anything.'

But Yissachar, in his high-rise hi-technology paradise, was too busy to pay them much attention, taking Blok's sudden fortune in the sex stakes for granted, while rooted to long telephone conferences which seemed to span several oceans, tense wrangles about figures, balance sheets, budgets, disrupted schedules, obscure boondoggles. Then he rushed off to Kokashvili's studios for consultations, leaving them alone in the vast apartment, with the deep freeze, the fitted kitchen, the fingertip action shower, video machines, personal computer and semi-orthopedic bed with the two-speed vibrating option. Ilse wished to go down to the sea, and Blok sat, in a tiny oblong of shade cast by a fortuitous café awning, boiling in his pants and shirt as she stripped off and leapt into the Mediterranean, merged in splashing dots, emerging to lie bikinied in the sand. Tanned hairy chested men, like bees attracted to honey, loped in concentric circles. Loud radios. Bats against balls. Tar oozing furtively in to the beach. Ships passed in broad daylight. A large sign proclaimed in English: 'NO MOUNTING ON BREAKERS!' Ah, the horror! the horror! He closed his eyes, vaguely beginning to remember other adventures, or lack of them, in this part of the world. The callow soldier Blok, circa early Sixties, moping along the Esplanade . . . But what is this that casts a shiver? Is it the hand of Lena Khalili? East meets West. Dr Blok, I presume. She returned and dripped water on him.

Taxiing back, the night, to Jerusalem, Ilse parting from him to spend the night at the home of comrade Daniela, with whom she was essentially domiciled. Blok climbing alone up to the Hageffen apartment, to find the ants running amok on the kitchen floor, gorging themselves on pesticides. He soaked the floor with Ritz-Paz, crushing the invaders in their thousands in a succession of wet rags. They protested their fate only fitfully. He dumped the rags in the garbage can, and took it down to the front of house, emptying the corpses into the communal skips, aware of a steady feline gaze.

'Is that you, Adolphe?' he called, cautiously, noting an oddly familiar tang.

But it was just a piss in the dark.

The next day there was no contact. She did not appear, and Basuto was out. He rang the number she had left, but a girl's voice answered, telling him Ilse had just departed with Daniela for a trip down the coast of the Red Sea, the nudist beaches of Dahab and Nueiba, which were all the rage, because they were due to be returned to Egypt in 1982 as the crowning act of the Camp David Treaty. He slept, then ventured down as the sun waned to the second-hand bookshops off the Jaffa Road, stocking up on science fiction. A little Aldiss, a *soupçon* of Sheckley, a dollop of Philip K.

Dick. Two days later, he received a letter from Ilse, postmarked Ophira-Sharm-a-Sheikh:

Exegesis Four: Ilse to Blok

Dear Blok,

This is a wonderful landscape, but probably not for you. I needed time to think things over – your two cities are so confusing! When we get back, Daniela and me, there will only be a few days before I have to return to Europe. I think it's probably best that we don't meet, and classify this as a Goodbye Letter. I have had a good time with you, Avram, but I have also had a problem. You see, I am used to being with people of convictions, who are striving for something they believe in. Not that they don't have contradictions! Most of my friends believe in three different things, all at the same time. But you seem to live in a condition of absolute moral neutrality! You seem to make no judgements at all, everything is on the same plane to you. In the beginning I was refreshed by this absolute, even heroic detachment, as shown by those events in Nablus that Basuto told me of. That you were not part of the arrogant, colonialistic consensus of this strange country, but at the same time you kept your distance from the 'naivety' of the Group. It is true, they are in a difficult position – authoritarianism is in the air of this place, it is difficult to break free. It is also true one cannot walk in the world entirely open to every pang of agony, we all select in what direction our compassion turns. But later it seemed to me that your detachment was just too close to nihilism – a general negation of all values: In Tel Aviv, for instance – that strange apartment with its obsessive luxuries and that charming boy with the air of easy-come corruption . . . That is an atmosphere from which I ran away, Avram. I have two brothers, in Hamburg, who are exactly like that. In the Sixties they demonstrated against Vietnam, and now they have stocks and shares and business interests and portfolios. They discovered Marx was right about Capital: it is a powerful force rewarding the few. I ran away from selfishness and dogmas, and male puritanism disguised as freedom. Blok, there is nothing perfect in any of us – I also don't believe in saints. The Sixties taught us not to expect Utopias, at least to acknowledge our own defects. Everything that we hated in our parents, we discovered in ourselves as we got older (not that I am quite ancient yet, nor you either, Avram!). But I still believe you have to make a stand somewhere! Anarchism is nothing if it doesn't mean looking for the truth at all costs, cutting through all the authoritarian bullshit that calls itself Left and Right. I know, Avram, that you have paid a price for your own search in the past, and you did not wish to talk of that. But I think it is a mistake to stop looking, just to accept things as they are. Despite your best efforts to become transparent, you will be drawn into the process of history. There is definitely something of the artist in you, but you should articulate it somehow. The artist who has nothing to say – perhaps that is the definition of madness! Even in anarchy there must be a structure – voluntarily arrived at. You will forgive me for lecturing you like this, I will have to stop soon, don't worry, my wrist is getting sore . . . But if you float with arbitrary winds, there is always the risk of a shipwreck. Make Order out of the Chaos! Is that a bourgeois commandment? No, because you can make it your own order, freely arrived at, in free association with other whose existence as individuals and whole worlds on their own you recognize. An order created out of the imagination to live another's pain and joy!

I want to tell you one thing more: you can be a good lover. Unlike so many men, you are not impatient. But again, as in life, you expect too little. You are a repressed sensualist. Let that, at least, break free, God damn it! There is an old Italian song:

> *E la vita non e la morte,*
> *E la morte non e la vita –*
> *La canzone e gia finita!*

In other words – *La Lotta Continua!*
Love,
Ilse

160

PS My grandmother had a cure for baldness: a mixture of lemon juice, crushed apples, cardamom and thyme, rubbed into the scalp. It worked for her!
PPS Look after your Hungarian sausage!

★

The summer temperature continued to climb. The columns of ants continued their march. He sealed the cracks at the base of the walls with plaster. An immense cockroach then emerged from the toilet bowl. He sprayed its face with Baygon, then pursued it round the entire apartment with the weekend issue of *Yediot Rishonot*, including the local and the financial supplements. Finally he caught it in the bedroom and finished it off with the end of the broom handle, producing a heart-wrenching crunch. He took it down immediately to the garbage skips, where the scavenging cats grimly converged.

The summer hung on, reluctant to have mercy. The religious denizens of Mekor Baruch and Geula walked about heavily, casseroled in black gaberdine. In safer areas of town, young women disrobed almost entirely. Kiosks ran out of ice cream. Inflation rose to 150 per cent. Yissachar renewed his offer of unsolicited scripts, to be read for money. Blok requested a stay. Avi was absent, somewhere in deepest Galilee, editing a translated anthology of Arab peasant poems of the Land. Esther made soothing noises along the telephone line, but still pleaded pressure of business. Adolphe had returned one day with a large gash in his side and had to be taken to the vet, in a basket, growling and spitting at passers by. 'Armand asked after you,' Esther told Blok. 'Why don't you drop in on him sometime.' He vaguely considered the option.

But one day, which should have been autumn but was still scorching, he took the bus, on impulse, to Ein Karem. Dried bushes and thorns scraping his legs as he toiled up the hill, past the Russian Convent and the turn-off to the Youth Hostel, an empty notepad and pens in a small sidebag ready for any mute response from the Hermit. The stubborn burrs of procreating thistles clung to his trousers, as he tried to recall their brief silent encounter, in the light of Esther's sketchy comments: the Hermit alias the

161

Rabbi's Son, Ein Karem via Brooklyn and San Francisco, Abel to the Cain of Rabbi Levine, scourge of the Unbelievers. If I am not for me, who is for me? And if only I am for me, who am I? But soon the contours of the isolated house appeared in a small thicket of trees, looking as vulnerable in the shimmering afternoon as the gingerbread hut of Hansel and Gretel. The short path, the sign – 'ARMON', the old-fashioned door knocker. But the door was open, and Blok knocked, calling out, 'Anybody in?'

There was no answer. He turned, having sensed a movement somewhere in the thicket outside the house. But there was no one there, and a bird flew out from the top of a tree, down the valley. He entered the house, the short hallway, the arched interior with its mass of bookshelves. There was no one in the room, but cushions and stools appeared to have been flung about, willy-nilly. A buzzing sound attracted his attention to the recessed kitchen. There, stretched upon the slab of the table, was Armand's body, or at least Blok, and subsequently the police, assumed it was Armand, since it was clad in his old tattered T-shirt and shorts, and had his wiry brown-haired arms. For the body's head was missing, and its shoulders ended in a black-red smudge of severed nerves and mastoids, upon which scores of immense flies gorged, leaping about, sucking noisily, flapping their wings, and mockingly paraphrasing, in shrill cacophony, their unwilling host's National Anthem:

> As long as deep within our hearts
> The soul of the Blue yearns,
> And towards far-flung eastern parts,
> An eye to Zion turns,
>
> We have not yet lost our hopes,
> Hopes of two million years,
> To be a Free Nation in Our Land,
> Bzzzzzt! Bzzzzzt! Bzzzzzt!

ACELDAMA

We now ascend to the *Aceldama*, or **Building of the Field of Blood** (Arabic – *El-Ferdus*, Paradise), situated in the midst of the tombs (of the Valley of Hinnom, Gehenna) . . . The Bible does not inform us where the 'field of blood' (Acts, 1, 19) lay, and it has since been shown in different parts of the environs of Jerusalem . . . The present Aceldama has been much revered by Christians, and is frequently visited by pilgrims, many of whom are buried here. The soil is believed to be very favourable to decomposition.

Baedeker's *Jerusalem*, 1876

When Saladin accepted the surrender of Jerusalem, he ordered the prayer niche (in the Aqsa) to be uncovered . . . The Templars had built a wall before it, reducing it to a granary and, it was said, a latrine, in their evil minded hostility. East of the qibla they had built a big house and another church. Saladin had the two structures removed and unveiled the bridal face of the prayer niche . . . The Quran was raised to the throne and the Testaments cast down. Prayer mats were laid out, and the religious ceremonies performed in their purity . . . benedictions were scattered and sorrow was dispersed. The mists dissolved, the true directions came into view, the sacred verses were read, the standards raised, the call to prayer spoken and the clappers (of the Christians) silenced, the muezzin were there and not the priests, corruption and shame ceased, and men's minds and breaths became calm again.

F. Gabrieli, *Arab Historians of the Crusades*

Subject: Cleaning of the Basilica of the Nativity.
(Report of the Sub-Inspector for Holy Places to Sir Ronald Storrs, British Military Governor of Jerusalem, May, 1920)

165

In light of the necessity of the above, the following principles have been agreed:

1. That the Greek Orthodox Community may open the windows of the Basilica throwing southward, for the time of cleaning only.
2. That the Greek Orthodox Community may place a ladder on the floor of the Armenian Chapel for cleaning the upper part of this Chapel above the Cornice.
3. That the Armenians have the right to clean the North face of the pillar on which the Greek orthodox pulpit is placed, up to the Cornice only.
4. That by mutual agreement the following has been arranged:
   a) That the Greeks should attach their curtain tight to the lower nail No. 2 at the foot of the pillar which lies south-east of the left hand set of steps leading to the Manger.
   b) That the Latins should have their curtain fall naturally down the same pillar leaving a space of 16 cm. between it and that of the Greek Orthodox.
   c) That Nail No. 1 be left unused by any of the Communities.

The above arrangements, however, are subject to alterations in case of any official documents in favour of any of the above Communities being produced before next year's cleaning.

Ronald Storrs: Orientations, 1939

'Now don't move, and keep your eye on the ball.'

W. C. Fields

★

ARMAND WAS MURDERED IN THE AUTUMN OF 1979, the year of the signing and ratification of the Camp David Treaty between the State of Israel and the Republic of Egypt, between Menachem Begin and Anwar el-Sadat, under the Cupid smile of Jimmy Carter, the born-again Nazarene. A year, indeed, of marked omens: violent incidents of Jewish-Arab strife occurring frequently on the Occupied West Bank of the Jordan. Many Palestinian political activists arrested by the Military Authorities. The Israeli legislature began debating proposals which inadvertently would legalize bestiality. It was a hot summer. But, in mid-July, Prime Minister Menachem Begin visited Anwar el-Sadat in Alexandria, and was taken for a tour of the famous catacombs of Kom e-Shukafa, an ambience which reminded Anwar of a dream he had had some nights before, and which he now recounted to his new bosom friend:

Anwar el-Sadat's Dream

He dreamt he was the Great Liberator, Yusuf Salah ed-Din, Saladin, drowsing in his tent at the Gates of Jerusalem before the moment of his final glory, and falling, in turn, into a deep sleep in which he had the following dream:

He was entering the Holy City, Jerusalem, Al-Quds, alone, and found its streets deserted. A numinous light illuminated the maze of alleys and arches, but they appeared devoid of any living soul, overhung by an eery pall of silence. Now and again he could glimpse the top of the domes of the Haram peeking between empty washing lines and cupolas, but try as he could to orient himself towards them they ended up further away. Finally, however, he came upon a strange creature which seemed to have slipped its tether: a white ass with a human head, that of a fair-haired, blue-eyed damosel, and the tail of a resplendent peacock, blues and purples shimmering in the glaze. He recognized her immediately as the *buraq*, the holy steed upon which the Prophet Muhammad, Peace Be Upon Him, had ascended to heaven from the Rock of Ibrahim. In her hands, which protruded above her front legs, she held a large ball of twine.

'Mount me, Yusuf,' she said.

Saladin/Sadat mounted, but instead of ascending to the seven heavens, to see Adam, John the Baptist and Jesus, Joseph, Enoch, Aaron and Ibrahim, the tree *sidrata 'l-muntaha* with leaves like elephants' ears and the four rivers, the two unnamed and hidden from human knowledge, and the two manifest – the Nile and the Euphrates, the *buraq* bore him down through the street's paving stones, under the earth, flying through descending caverns. Sitting in the sarcophagus chamber of the Alexandria catacombs,

167

sharing a flask of iced lemon tea with Menachem Begin, Anwar el-Sadat recounted what happened next:

'The first cavern, immense and filled with torches, was clearly that *bir-el-arwah*, the well of souls, where the dead assemble to pray twice weekly. The second, beneath them, was a vast kitchen, where many rabbis, mullahs and priests were overseeing the roasting on a gigantic spit of a number of gargantuan creatures. The third cavern was a colossal stockpile of armaments of all nations and eras: bows and arrows, arquebuses, rotted mangonels, rusted tanks, pikes, lances, Mirage aircraft, Sam and Hawk guided missiles. The fourth cavern was empty. The fifth echoed with the terrible rustling of hordes of vermin, heading for the surface: beetles, cockroaches, termites, rats, serpents and giant lizards. The sixth cavern was empty. In the seventh I was suddenly unseated by the *buraq* in a long torchlit gaming hall. My heart rose, for there, at table, on benches, were fifteen men of the Faith, men with turbans, burnooses, tarbush, fez, takiyehs, their one hand firm on the stem of nargilehs, the other moving backgammon counters. I took the only vacant seat, finding myself opposite the one outsider in the hall, a tall, obviously Jewish, if you will pardon the expression, man in a black coat thrown over striped pyjamas, with burning eyes and an immense black beard. I recognized him immediately as Theodor Herzl, the Founder of your Jewish State.'

'You were still Saladin at this point?' Menachem enquired, politely.

'I was. But Time had lost its thrall.'

'Please go on, brother Anwar,' said Menachem, chewing a home-made macaroon.

'I looked down at the backgammon board. But the black and red counters metamorphosed under my eyes, becoming, each, in itself, a miniature city, pulsing with lights, spewing smoke from cooking pots, chimneys, factories, crematoria: there was Mecca, and there, ancient Tarshish, Baghdad, Pekin, Moscow, Cairo. Jerusalem, London, Paris, Vienna, Babylon, Nineveh, Damascus. A terrible stench arose from Rio de Janeiro. Perfumes and musk from Cordova. Microscopic armies fought in Athens. Black smoke rose from tiny Rome. There were Antioch, Edessa, Pergamum, and also Istanbul and Amsterdam. I pulled my hand back as from glowing embers. Theodor Herzl sat on his bench and smiled.

'"The dice are on your side," he offered. I stretched my hand towards them, but they scurried away, on little spiders' legs. I lunged, but they leapt off the table. Everyone drew up their legs in horror. I jumped under the table, but it upturned. Boards and cities spilled to the ground. I tried to gather them up, but they all rolled into concealed cracks and dark corners. The players beat my back and my exposed buttocks with their nargileh stems, whose jugs burst, filling the cave with hot steam. Wreathed in the steam the Jew just sat there, impassive, in his solar topee.

'"Win some, lose some." he said.'

'I know the feeling,' said Menachem Begin. 'But one should not get discouraged.' They sat in silence in the torchlit catacombs, as their personal doctors injected each with his daily dose of amphetamines, anti-coagulants and cortisone, sighing in unison as they contemplated History.

HISTORY! Spare us your convulsions! your piles of old discarded shoes! GOD, TOD, SHODS CLOD. HAM MAM DAMNS ADAM. CAIN BANE MAINTAINED. The proto-neolithic semi-nomadic half-assed hunting tribes chipping away with flint and bone, harnessing the Ox, the Goat, the Sheep, the treife Pig, growing yams, coconuts and bananas, gossiping village to village by coded drum beats, tattooing each other with secret signs, shamans' hand-me-downs, tall tales of the origins of the world out of the primal vagina or the Creator's primal dung, the bull-god dead and resurrected, reverberating holy names: Tammuz, Ishtar, Nebo, Baal, the Moloch in the Valley of Hinnom. Children thrown into the ovens. When will we ever learn. Later the Jebusites sanctified the hill above the Valley, calling it Jebus, or Jerusalem, and setting up their brazen altar, and a citadel, called Sion, fortified against all comers. But zealous barbarians came from the east, laying the ancient city low. King David, already charging exorbitant rates, the Ark of the Lord on the threshing floor of Ornah the Jebusite, on the hill called Moriah. ABE, ABLE SLAY BABE? KIKE STRIKE TYKE IKE?

'Are you really going to kill me, father?'

'You bet your life,' Abraham said.

And thus our civilization was born. But still the barbarians came, bearing new licence plates, the Egyptian Shishak, the

169

coastal Philistine tribes, Jehoash, the blood brother from a split empire, Sennacherib, Nebuchadnezzar. Slaughter, rape, pillage, captivity. Never a dull moment. NO SOLACE SOL POLIS. But, later, the Temple site regained, taken by Alexander the Macedonian, plundered by Antiochus, freed by Judah the Maccabee, taken again, freed, taken by Pompey, held by the Parthians, regained by Herod, the apostate Second Temple builder: the castle of Antonia, the Citadel of David, town hall, gymnastics area, crucifixion hill. Again, insurrection, massacre, civil war, The Evil Titus, the burned Temple, Aelia Capitolina, Hadrian's Temple of Jupiter, Bar-Kokhba's rebellion, bonfires, the peace of the grave. New vibrations: Constantine the Christian, Byzantium, the Holy Sepulchre. Destroyed by the Persians (AD 614). Many monks disembowelled. New tones from the south: the Khalifa Omar, Abd el-Malik. The Grand Mosques. Et cetera. 1077, the Khwarizmian Turks. 1099, again the barbarians, from the west, bearing Christ. Saladin, Khwarizmians again, the Mongols, Ottoman Turks, and a pause of exhaustion. Pilgrims trekked in to the City, taking in the sites, scrawling their names on gateposts and walls, patiently allowing themselves to be cheated and dispossessed by dragomen of all creeds or punished for a variety of transgressions such as drinking wine in public, spitting, or laughing at Moslems behind their backs. In the summer of AD 1662, the future Jewish False Messiah, Shabetai Tsvi, reached the city from Asia Minor. In the diaspora he had already excited attention due to his esoteric demonstrations: marrying himself to the Scroll of the Torah, placing a large fish in a child's cradle and changing traditional prayers at will. For a year he wandered the narrow alleyways of the Old City's Jewish Quarter, trying to keep a low profile. The Rabbis of the city kept a close eye on him for any hint of eccentric behaviour. Now and again he would leave the City, climb up into the caves in the hills towards Jericho, and listen to the voices of the dead. Buzz, buzz, buzz, buzz. We are the hollow men, we are the stuffed men, our dried voices whisper together. We have absolutely nothing to say, sweetie. You'll have to draw your own conclusions . . .

But Shabetai Tsvi, like so many others, thought he had heard the voice of God –

EAT SHIT, MOTHERFUCKER!!!

The cry rolled over the brown terraced hills, from Anata to Lifta, from Abu Dis to Nebi Samuel, from Abu Tor to Kiryat Zanz and Romema Ilit, across *iftecha de'karta* and the Government Offices, Kiryat Moshe, Givat Shaul, echoing down the pisspoor ages, rolling down the millennium, to affect both fact and legend . . .

Win some, lose some . . .

Further Adventures of the Rabid Sheep

In August 1979, one month after Anwar Sadat's dream, the Department of Apocalyptic Affairs almost succeeded in capturing the elusive critter. A young Australian tourist couple, climbing around the steep hillsides of the Jerusalem Forest, about the area known as the 'Elephant's Rock', claimed, to the Hadassah Hospital Casualty Ward, to have been attacked and bitten by a 'vicious mountain goat'. Blood tests diagnosed hydrophobia. The Department's day shift hit team scrambled from deep below Mittag's Café: Tolstoy's colleagues – Istiqlal, Young Kazha and Gruzini Cholera, with ropes, infra-red lamps and tranquillizing darts, methodically combing the hills, accompanied by Circassian Border Police trackers and a unit of award-winning commandos from the Central Headquarters Patrol . . .

By nightfall they had marked every bush and tree with powerful sheep repellent, but had found nothing except two dead dogs, an old stash of heroin, and some quills of a fretful porpentine. Around midnight, however, Young Kazha, eager for results rather than the mere joy of the chase, reported the sound of growling and gnashing of teeth from the adjacent Military Cemetery. But when the team approached the perimeter all they heard was the normal twang of the dead young soldiers singing: 'A Night of Roses', 'How Pleasant and Good It Is Brothers All Gathered Together'; 'My Love Among the Plantations of Perfume', 'I Once Had a Love So Fair', and other old favourites . . .

With the first rays of dawn it was clear the sheep had eluded its pursuers again. The team retreated down the hill with their infra-red lights, grappling hooks and asbestos suits, leaving the deceased youths to vibrate alone into the early morning hours:

171

Your eyes shine with a green light.
Your eyes are like two precious stones.
My heart thirsts for a moment of silence,
You are going so far, far away . . .

While across the valley, in a cave hewn deep in the mountainside,

the Reverend William Hechler sighed with relief at the passing of the posse: relieved that the odour of his post-death body had not drawn the seekers to his den. For here, in the safety of his central hidy hole, he had allowed himself to spill out of his box, oozing carefully on to the cool rocks, very mindful of the need to keep vital organs from slipping off into rifts and cracks. Two of his four dragomen, making sure, stood by him with little bowls, to catch drips. Being 135 years old and in an advanced state of decomposition did have its unique problems, even when decades of shrewd investments bought the highest grade of protection: to wit, his current quartet of loyal bearers – Shangalay, Charapinsk, Yashmak and Barud – ethnic Assyrians, whose ancestors had scoured the Byzantine East, selling fake relics of Russian saints, pubic hairs of the Virgin, fillings from Judas's teeth . . . Ex-petty couriers in the drug and Dead Sea Scroll trade, they were content to leave the hazards of airport customs behind, for a massive fee, to zealously tend Hechler's person, carry his black box about, and update the maps and plans of his hundred year quest for the Ark, pinned on boards all over the cave walls: the planimetographs, astro-geometrical spirals, triangles of Christ, phi-ratios, megalithic rectangles, parallelogryphs, pyramidologarithms.

And Hechler sighed again, remembering his lost childhood: Benares, his parents' Protestant mission on the Ganges, holiness and bilharzia, his alter ego, dying in peaceful old age in green English pastures. A far cry from the parched Levant with its numinous squeaks and squabbles . . . Promised Lands! God help us! Rubbing his bare eyeballs against the rock, wrapping his ears round the dry gravel . . . In this entombed silence, unbroken by sheep-hunting louts, one can see and hear so many things: immobility, amid continual motion. The timeless dance of positrons, neutrons, quarks. Mind not distinct from matter. Matter not distinct from mind. Whorls of lost souls, lost religions keening.

Faiths that have not stood the test of time. Colossal beasts stirring in chasms. Shopping bags full of skulls. Echoes of international phone calls, secret messages, codes in knitting patterns and tapestries. Endlessly unwinding turbans . . . And, also, along forgotten rifts, that mumble perhaps Anwar el-Sadat hears too, the faded tremor of Pharaohs, counting sheep: one trillion nine hundred and seventy-five billion five hundred and forty-seven million two hundred and thirteen thousand eight hundred and ninety-five . . . one trillion nine hundred and seventy-five billion five hundred and forty-seven million two hundred and thirteen thousand eight hundred and ninety-six . . . seven . . . eight . . . nine . . . OOOOOOOOOOHHHHHH . . .

WHEN WILL IT ALL END??????

A strange reunion, in Armand's house, after Blok's discovery of the body. The incomplete corpse had been removed, after tentative confirmation of its identity by three local residents: Taradash, the grocer, Yadin, from the laundry on the main road, and Father Zak, a Franciscan priest from the Church, who had often discussed theology with the Hermit. There had been a noted birthmark, on the thigh, which satisfied the inspector assigned to the case, for the moment, while hordes of policemen, drafted in from all over the city, pouring sweat, dug up the garden and ground in a radius of two hundred metres, scouring the mountain for freshly moved earth, demolishing molehills and terraces in search of the victim's missing head. Hordes of bugs and vermin ran for cover as they prised up loose rocks and stones, while, in the booklined arched room of the house, Blok, Esther and Avi stood, lost amid the flurry of what appeared to be six petty burglars, but who were in fact plain-clothed detectives ransacking the house, examining every object, dusting every surface for fingerprints and rapidly removing and replacing each book in the packed shelves in search of ephemeral clues.

'I don't know what's happening in the world,' said Esther. 'I tell you, the mind can't grasp it,' as a forensic expert, in white gloves, scraped a gob of dry spit from the kitchen sink unit on to a glass slide.

'The man had no enemies,' said Father Zak.

'A tragedy for our community,' said Yadin the laundryman. The grocer mopped sweat from his brow.

From out of the window, Inspector Kandide, the investigating officer, watched the witnesses gathered within: Thin Avi pacing about, hands behind his back, gazing at the mass of books as if an answer might be uttered at any moment by Jung's *Symbols of Transformation* or *Gestalt Psychology* by Wolfgang Kohler. Esther, shaking her head disconsolately. Blok, expressing no view, impassively rubbing his scalp as if, even without Ilse's grandmother's nostrums, some buds of the lost might be found . . .

Death. Mutilation. Headless corpses. They were the worst, Kandide thought. A killer grossed out on intense finality, determined to underline the act. And, in this case, a cat's cradle of obscure motives and shadowy inclinations, combined, alas, with unlimited opportunity.

Father Zak repeated: 'Such a gentle man. He loved everything living. How could such a man have an enemy?'

Everyone has an enemy here, thought Kandide, simply by being alive. We are born into enmity, facing all those who would rather we had never been born, or wouldn't mind if we were born but would rather we'd stayed somewhere else, or who wouldn't mind we were born and were here but demand we exist in their own image, not whatever we might choose as our own. And by necessity, we so often oblige, and keep a chamber of secret thoughts. Was it this confinement that asphyxiated the Hermit? He motioned to a constable.

'Tell the next of kin he can come up.'

Two figures, hurrying up the path. A small man with a goatee beard, knitted skullcap and a strong air of repressed aggression, like a balled fist rolling up the hill, accompanied by a huge, black-bearded, also skullcapped lout with the familiar paranoid air of a bodyguard.

'Trouble coming,' said Kandide's Sergeant.

'What else is new?' Kandide asked wearily.

Is this the face that launched a thousand leaflets? The defacer of five hundred city billboards? The plug mug adored, loathed, feared, he at whose lifted finger angry zealots pour into the streets, with clubs and broken bottles, ready to avenge Jewish Blood? And this from the same genetic strain, the same heritage, as the gentle anchorite Armand? He shakes Kandide's hand. 'Mordechai Levine, Rabbi,' he says. 'I do recognize you,' says Kandide, 'but we have not had the opportunity before. I am sorry it is in this context.'

'I have not seen my brother since the United States,' says Levine, tautly, 'many many years ago.'

Yes, Rabbi, I have read your files: from Coney Island to the blinding light of Faith . . . The two sprouts of a fiercely Zionist Rabbi, who had once raised funds for Menachem Begin's Irgun. Born within the blare of hurdy gurdies, the lemming hordes of the Amerikan Metropolis rushing to the Atlantic shore . . . One brother digging his heels in the Faith, outzealoting a zealot heritage, spurning the roller coasters, candy floss and candid goyim, the other taking wing, soaring to taste the magic mushrooms of esoteric foreign lore – Buddhism, Hinduism, Theosophy, the Hashbury, the true hellenic heresies . . . The Sixties, man. Know what I mean. But each, on cosmically separate paths, converging, by some genetic irony, on the riven, parched Homeland . . .

'Shall we go in?'

The immense minder scanning the space of the Hermit's room, the Scourge of the UnGodly blinking nervously at the gathering of mourners.

'I understood there would be no one here,' he said, testily, to Kandide.

'I promised to keep the press away for now,' said Kandide. 'With the rest you take your chances.'

'You're Levine,' said Esther, with an air of curiosity, mingled with just a trace of awe, trying to track in those ardent eyes, set in their sallow pasture, looking towards some impossible leap of the dark side of the imagination, the cracked mirror image of the decapitated pacifist . . .

Is Cain able? Should Abel have been cained?

'I was just going,' said Yadin the laundryman, looking warily at the newcomer, nodding to the friends and saying to the Inspector: 'You know where I am if you need me.' Father Zak and the grocer also departed gingerly, leaving Levine and his bodyguard to face the curious gaze of Esther, the dagger stare of Avi, the inscrutable eyes of Avram Blok.

'I'm not staying in one room with this shit,' said Avi, turning to Esther. 'You take the car, I'll take the bus. We'll meet later.' He pushed past the Enemy.

'Don't I know you from somewhere?' said Levine.

176

'From your nightmares,' Avi said, and exeunt, leaving behind a distinct whiff of charred air.

'I always knew you were Armand's brother,' said Esther, trying her social welfare tone, for maximum neutrality, 'but I think he thought you didn't know . . .'

'I know about my own brother,' said Levine. 'He was the one pretending to be someone else.' He prowled about the book-shelves, as if trying to incinerate with his glance all those volumes of foreign necromancy: Gurdjieff and his Remarkable Men, Ouspensky's *New Models of the Universe*, Eliphas Levy's *Key to The Mysteries*, Papus and MacGregor Mathers. And what is the saintly Rabbi Nachman of Bratslav doing among all these blasphemies? He waved his hand at the shelves, addressing those still present as if at a political gathering:

'The rotten fruits! What does one expect? The Jews are always afraid of their own selves! Afraid to admit the Truth is there in your Soul where you start out. It's an old disease we caught, called the "Enlightenment". If we reject ourselves – all will be solved!' He sighed, holding his forefinger and thumb to his brow, then over closed eyes. As if seeing in his mind's eye the end of that betrayal, the severed head lost in limbo.

'I want these people to leave,' he said to the policeman. 'I had a positive commitment if I came there would be no one here. A positive commitment.'

'You can't trust anyone nowadays,' said Blok. The Rabbi turned at this new challenge, amazed, as if a table or chairleg had suddenly spoken up.

'For example,' Blok explained, 'inferior races, religions, saints, idols, your friends, your enemies. They are always doing the unexpected. You must have noticed this.'

For a brief moment their eyes clashed. The sound of ripping sackcloth might be sensed in the ethereal spheres.

'I will eventually deal with people like you,' said Levine, and turned away towards the door.

'You will hear from me,' he told Inspector Kandide. 'I have legitimate rights. I am a candidate of my party.' He stormed off with the orthodox hulk in tow, brusquely banging the front door.

'What a strange man,' sighed Inspector Kandide. 'His followers give me such a lot of trouble . . .'

177

Outside the uniformed policemen toiled on, digging in vain for Esau's head, while Jacob and his guardian angel swept down the path, brushing the autumn hills with their wrath, pausing only to flypost the Virgin's Fountain with the leaflets of their Party Manifesto:

Vote for the Party of National Purity!

FOR THOU HAST CHOSEN US FROM ALL THE NATIONS!
THESE ARE OUR UNSHAKEABLE PRINCIPLES:

THAT the Nation of Israel is a HOLY and ETERNAL Nation, chosen by the G-d of Creation, of Present and Future Times, who determines the history of the entire world in accordance with His Will.

THAT the ETERNITY of Israel will not lie! The State of Israel is the COMMENCEMENT of Our Salvation as the Commandment of the Hour of the Lord Blessed Be He, with His Outstretched Arm, with signs and wonders. The Lord has determined to END the agonies of his people Israel and no power on earth can prevent the State of Israel from carrying out this Holy task. Even the Jews themselves cannot, by their hesitations, prevent this task from completion!

THEREFORE! –

We must utterly REJECT all defeatist policies, all hesitations and doubts based on 'what the gentiles might say', any WEAKNESS in facing the eternal enemies and utterly breaking their will. For Our Salvation is in Our Own Hands, and does not depend on the gentiles, and THEREFORE we must steel ourselves for the coming challenges, to face the Whole World, which is full of hate for Israel and its Messiah, for we know we are 'a nation which dwells alone', and we should give no quarter to false and foreign ideas, such as 'territorial compromise', or a 'Palestinian people', who exist only in the imagination! for THESE ARE OUR TASKS:

1) To return to every centimetre of our Holy Land, and to our Holy Torah, the Source of our strength.
2) To EDUCATE our children to our Traditions of the Commandments of Our Creator, to open our eyes, and

178

reject the blindness which makes us say: 'We are a "normal" people like all the others.' (!)

3) To make clear to the Strangers in our midst that they are here on our sufferance alone, and those who cannot accept this should Return to the Lands of their own Ishmaelite brothers, by means of organized and humane Repatriation.

4) To make sure we are not polluted by foreign concepts, and to adopt, by means of our own Parliament, the Laws of our Halacha and Traditions.

5) For only thus will we be worthy to begin the task of Rebuilding Our Holy Temple in Our Time, in Our Holy City of Jerusalem!

OUR ENEMIES – WE SHALL BREAK! For the Destiny of Israel is Glorious Victory!

OUR HOLY LAND – WE SHALL NOT FORSAKE! For we shall settle every inch of its soil!

OF THE SALVATION OF THE LORD – WE SHALL PARTAKE! For how Pleasant is our Fate and how Beautiful Our Inheritance!

VOTE The Party of National Purity – Rabbi Levine to the Knesset!

But the electorate showed no signs of elevating Rabbi Levine to Parliament, and Inspector Kandide made no headway at all in the investigation of Armand/Levine's murder. The missing skull remained missing, despite the strip mining of almost the entire hill of Ein Karem, while Kandide constructed elaborate theories to be sifted one by one:

a) The Cain and Abel scenario, scotched by the zealot Rabbi's iron-clad alibi, which also tied all his Party's known strong-arm boys to a 'Conference On Arab Violence Against Jews' held at the time of death way across town.

b) The possible tie in with the unsolved petty assaults of the so-called 'Hairy Beast of Ein Karem'. The anonymous miscreant and nuisance earned this name for his habit of laying his reportedly hirsute nude body beside those of

179

sleeping women, whose company he gained by climbing through open windows, fleeing silently the moment his victims woke, noticed his presence and screamed. But he had never been known to offer the slightest hint of violence, and had been dormant for almost a year.

c) The possibility of a random act of racial violence against Armand as a Christian by someone who did not know he was a Jew. Grenades had been found primed, twice, at churches in the area, with anonymous leaflets promising 'Death to the Missionaries', repudiated stoutly by Levine's Party. The proliferation of small groups of freelance bigots was a constant thorn in Kandide's flesh: the Sons of Judah, the Brothers of Israel, the Mothers of Dissension, Rabbi Nachman's Right Arm, God's finger, the Prepared Table's Left Leg, and so on.

d) The possible connection with Armand's occult library: his known dabblings with the esoteric and the hidden, leading to hints in his police file of a security dossier in a shadowy Department of State Kandide knew of only by rumour and innuendo. He had filed a request for further material with the relevant Internal Security Office, as yet to no avail. Again he submitted his application. But there was yet a fifth area of entanglement –

e) Murder for a sexual motive. For, in the bathroom cabinet of the 'Hermitage', Kandide's searchers had found several tubes of personal lubricant of the Californian Fruit Flavoured variety: Strawberry, Peach Melba, Mango, Guava and Passion Fruit, hinting strongly at a homosexual life style. Deep penetration agents in the local 'gay' community had uncovered rumours which lead to certain cafés in the depths of the Old City. Perhaps, after all, the solution was quite simple, one the zealot Rabbi might well applaud: *cherchez le wog*. But Kandide still kept an open mind on all options . . .

While winter came, and did its deeds, and went, and spring, and summertime, amid growing tension in the Land of too much certainty and dispute – more incidents of violence between Jewish settlers and Arabs in the occupied West Bank: Arab youths throwing stones at Jews passing in cars, armed settlers firing back, dead and wounded, random assassinations of settlers by Arabs, the army firing at groups of demonstrators. A new joke was extant: Palestinians could fly. Bullets officially fired in the air kept striking them in the legs or torso. In May Arab guerrillas ambushed settlers on their way to a religious class in Hebron. Six dead. In June booby trap bombs planted in cars simultaneously maimed two Arab mayors known to be leaders of the nationalist resistance in the West Bank.

In late March, Salim's hitherto dormant cell of the Popular Front for the Liberation of Palestine had received three functioning grenades. In April Lena Khalili left the West Bank for Jordan in a bus crossing the Allenby Bridge. In July the *Zurafa* submitted a new play to the Censor, devoid of any Jewish role. Also in July the UN General Assembly, in special session, passed a resolution calling for Israeli withdrawal from the occupied territories of the West Bank and Gaza Strip. Back in the Homeland, the Israeli Ministry of the Interior finally proposed the legalizing of bestiality. The Justice Ministry had wished to legalize homosexuality, in line with Enlightened Opinion in the European West concerning sexual matters. The religious parties objected, however, offering, as a substitute, the legitimizing of unnatural acts between man and woman, and those between man and beast.

But, earlier than this, on the Eve of the Passover, Esther appeared on Blok's doorstep, at 35 Hageffen Street, bearing, in a ventilated box, an extremely disgruntled Adolphe, having previously telephoned to beg of Blok the favour that he might keep the beast for the holiday.

'I remember you two got on, when you stayed with us,' she had said. 'Both Avi and I will be away.'

They had not met since the aftermath of the Armand murder, when Esther had recounted to Blok the missing tale of the Hermit's Coney Island origin, the two brothers, Zev the Doubting Jew, his escape On The Road, to the Hashbury, his sudden sighting through the dense local mist of a headline, one foggy day in '67: ARAB–ISRAEL WAR INTENSIFIES: JERUSALEM UNDER FIRE. And how, two months later, he landed at Lod Airport, fired by old genetic prophecies . . .

181

It gets us all one time or another . . .

'But that's a feral beast you have,' Blok protested. 'Doesn't it look after itself?'

'He wanders off, but two weeks is a bit much. The flat hasn't been empty so long before.'

He opened the door to the sight of a bilious yellow eye glaring at him through a hole in reinforced cardboard.

'Let him out of the box and see if he kills,' he said. Adolphe made a beeline for the kitchen.

'Don't feed him tuna or sardines,' she said, laying out of a rucksack a round dozen tins of catfood. 'They give him terrible wind. He can be an awful farter, but it's all for show. He has the constitution of a buffalo, really. How are you getting on, Avram?'

He made an Elite coffee, and she explained the general layout. Avi was off on a mini-conference of Arab poets and other artistic members of the Rakah Communist Party in Nazareth, followed by a sojourn at an ex-colleague's marijuana farm near Rosh Pina. She had been invited to join the Passover beano at her ex-client, the Prodigal Ya'akov Ben-Havivo's family apartment block in Arikha.

'A real North African event, Avram. All the trimmings. They say the Old Man always prophesies after the Seder songs are over. He's very frail, they don't give him long to live. Then young Ya'akov will be the Dayan Ezuz, the Spiritual Leader of his people. The seven daughters don't qualify, of course . . .'

'What will you do there for two weeks?' Blok asked.

'You'll think it's funny, but we're going to meditate in the desert.'

'I must say I think that's funny,' said Blok.

'Armand's murder did something to me,' said Esther. 'It made me think about things I thought I had solved for myself . . . or maybe that's not entirely true. It's not easy, Avram. There are so many deceptions . . .'

'You were having an affair with Armand,' said Blok.

'Aren't you the sly one, God help us,' she said. 'You pretend to be asleep and then see through the walls. Avi warned me about you, I remember. I suppose there can be no real secrets in this town. Except from the police, who never asked me . . . You have to realize, Armand was quite a character. He'd done those things

182

we often fantasize about doing – changing identities, trying new roles . . . really looking for his true self – I know that sounds like the oldest cliché . . .'

'What about Avi?'

'He has his own flings. We're trying to live out another cliché: the liberated modern couple. Maybe we should have just got married instead. But it's difficult, you know, to do what's expected of you out of your own free will.'

She sipped Blok's coffee, as growling sounds from the kitchen indicated Adolphe might have met a cockroach and was considering his options.

'He had quite a life . . .' she mused, 'Armand, the Hermit . . . he had a whole bunch of groupies once, in California. Hippies who followed him up and down the State, sitting together on the edges of cliffs, watching the kestrels buzz the coastline.'

'Who do you think killed him?'

'God knows. The police don't, I can tell you. It's probably a random case of some madman who didn't like the idea of a free man living out there . . . But the thought of his head, still missing . . . Forget it, Avram, let's talk about you. What have you been up to? Time passes so quickly . . . I sort of start, and it's next year suddenly.'

'I have begun reading scripts for Yissachar,' he said, 'my friend from Tel Aviv, in the film business.' He motioned towards a pile of manuscripts on the cracked salon table.

'What are they like?' she asked.

'Nothing on earth,' he replied. 'The usual.'

She picked up one, pointing out the title: 'SCORCHED EARTH'.

'A soldier, shattered by combat,' he said, 'hides in the Judaean Hills. He lives on roots and wild gerbils and suffers from chronic flashbacks of his friend who died by his side in battle. One day he hears shooting, and an army patrol warns him that Arab guerrillas are in the area. Setting out with his hunting rifle he tracks them down to a hidden cave and takes them prisoner. As he has no radio, he decides to force march them across the desert to the army. Then they overpower him, but have to keep him alive, because of his survival skills. A strange rapport emerges between the two sides, but it all ends in blood and tears.'

'And you get paid to read this?'

'I have worked it out,' he said. 'At five new agorot the page. At going exchange rates that's about 0.0016 US cents per word.'

'Better than nothing,' Esther observed. She peeked at him over the edge of a chipped coffee mug engraved 'BEING A JEWISH MOTHER MEANS NEVER HAVING TO SAY YOU'RE SORRY'.

'What happened to that German girl,' she asked, 'Ilse?'

'She writes me postcards,' he said, 'from Bavaria. Further recipes against alopecia.'

'I was glad you found somebody, at least,' she said, gingerly. 'It would never work between us, you know.'

'I tried the squeezed lemon idea,' he offered. 'Several hairs sprouted, for a short while.'

'Baldness isn't the problem,' she said. 'I told you long ago. Look at Telly Savalas, Yul Brynner. But there has to be a spark, somewhere, *comprende*? I'm sorry, it's just the way I'm made.'

'And Armand had the spark?'

She sighed. 'Oh, Avram, what are we going to do with you?' Unwittingly echoing past imprecations . . .

'Pickle me in brine,' he suggested.

A vast crash interrupted them from the kitchen. A coal-black form dashed out, faking alarm. Blok rushed in, to find a box of chocolate biscuits, hidden in a wall cabinet, open on the floor, its contents scattered and broken.

'I shall roast the beast, and make soup of its bones,' he vowed.

'He's such a pain in the neck,' Esther sighed again. 'Maybe he'll really be too much for you.'

'Leave him with me,' said Blok. 'I will deal with him.'

'Just without violence, for God's sake, Avram,' she said. 'Violence makes him really nasty.'

'Say Goodbye to him. You might never meet him again.'

'Goodbye Adolphe,' she said. 'I must run.'

But Blok had to postpone any moment of reckoning with Adolphe due to the advent of the Passover: the Festival of Freedom, presaged by the smell of freshly baked matzohs, the massed hard boiling of eggs, the scraping of the bitter herbs, hoarding of bread by the irreligious and its purging by the devout, not to speak of the preparations of the zealot settlers of the Greater Land of Israel Movement for their annual Passover march across the heartland of the Occupied West Bank, with advertisements placed in all the papers:

THE ERETZ YISRAEL MARCH – BLOCK OF THE FAITHFUL: Bring all the necessary equipment, including a Happy Mood!

עלֹה, עלה ונעלה !

Necessary equipment: Two full bottles of water; head covering; strong, comfortable walking shoes; sleeping bag; torch, food for two days; toilet paper; warm coat; garbage disposal bags. Owners of musical instruments and firearms are asked to bring them along.

Blok had prepared none of these items, but was still manoeuvred into festive collaboration, dragging his bones reluctantly to join his ageing parents for the Passover *seder* beanfeast, held this year at the apartment of the daughter of Mama Blok's vaguely third cousin, Brigadier Nachman (retired). For the last two years, since his release from T—t, Papa and Mama, Baruch and Rosa, had dined quietly alone *en maison*, resisting the blandishments of

185

Blok's Aunt Pashtida to venture north for her annual mass blow-out down on the co-operative farm, but this year the formidable surviving kinswoman had come south, latching on to the retired Brigadier, who had emerged from his own hibernation on the coastal plain to invite the Bloks to his family *seder*. Elchanan A., Papa's last surviving blood tie, had died during the previous year, leaving the only begotten son, Avram, as the last head of cattle to the snared by the umbilical lasso and complete the tribal round-up. All over the country, normal life ceased for this ancient ceremony: Avi, pulling in the cool smoke of home grown at a herbalist do in far Rosh Pina. Esther, reclining with the women downtable from the Prodigal Son and heir of the Dayan Ezuz, replete by the right hand of his illustrious father at the head of an immense table, festooned with ornate candlesticks and goblets, silver utensils and salvers, the elder guests topped by whorls of turbans and reading from old goldleaf volumes of the Haggadah handed down from Father to Son. Back on the coastal plain, at Adir Kokashvili's villa, Blok's friend and new employer, Yissachar, sat in the midst of an even more dazzling show of multicoloured embroidered caps and gowns, ornate Georgian tapestries and wall hangings, the mogul plastered on three dozen cushions, groaning and grunting his own private version of the text, dreaming of Shabetai Tsvi, emitting strange beeps, trills and rasps, smoke signals from his hairy nostrils wafting through open windows and across the fields and orchards and freeways to Bnei Brak, where his hired mediums conducted their own readings in piles of plucked chicken feathers to keep away male and female demons, while they ploughed through the Haggadah, backwards, from 'Had Gadya' to the Wine Blessing, disgorging from their gullets entire chickens, boiled eggs, matzoh-shmura and matzoh balls on to prepared plates, the youngest person present, the halfwit Dudu Diskin, reciting, in the 'B' language, the traditional Four Questions:

HOW IS THIS NIGHT DIFFERENT FROM ALL OTHER NIGHTS?
    – That on all other nights we eat leavened and unleavened bread; this night, only unleavened bread.
    – That on all other nights, we eat all manner of vegetables; on this night, bitter herbs . . .

Too true. Blok's father, Baruch, took him into the bathroom on a pretext of requiring physical aid, while the other celebrants rushed about from the kitchen to the dining table and back. In the last few months Baruch's leg problems had worsened and he was now travelling about in a wheelchair. Rosa, suddenly rising from her bed of nails, the Book of Psalms, Lamentations and Recriminations, bustled about, fetching and doing where previously she had been virtually prostrate and dependant on Baruch throughout the decade. A miraculous and ironic inversion, but not one that Papa Blok enjoyed. Locking the R. family bathroom door behind him, he wrestled from under the wheelchair seat a flat half flask of Johnny Walker whisky and, taking a swig, passed it to his son.

'Fortification, Avremel. Drastic measures are called for, or neither of us will survive the night. Here, let me pretend to shit, in case the forces of darkness see through walls.' He manoeuvred himself, waving away filial aid, trousers down on the toilet bowl, sighing and puffing and running his hand over his own thinly covered scalp.

'We should book as a double act,' he said, viewing the desolation upon his son's shining cranium. 'The Two Hard-Boiled Eggs. I tell you, Avremel, life is really shittier than you think. A shot of the old firewater? Or are you still taking those pills?'

'No, Papa, that was just when I came out of the hospital. Two years already.'

'As long as that? My brain has gone soft as putty. Since my legs turned to plasticine I've been in prison, like Rudolph Hess alone in Spandau. Your mother does all the supporting roles, the US, British, French and Russian warders. A bit like the time we both, your mother and I, spent hiding in rooms during the war, in Budapest. When we came out, you were made. But this time there will not be such an afterglow. And then we were only hiding from the Nazis. This time it's God himself who's after me.'

'I'm sure he has other fish to fry,' said Blok, not knowing how to console his father.

'No,' said Baruch. 'It's a personal vendetta. You feel these things, deep in your bones. For God's sake, drink and pass me back that bottle.'

Determined knuckles rapped on the bathroom door. 'Are you two OK in there?' rasped Aunt Pashtida.

'He's helping me pull it out!' Baruch shouted.

The loud silence of a cold retreat. 'Tell me, is this what it was all for?' asked Baruch. 'To die in the Holy Land, surrounded by one's kith and kin, the very people you should have spent your life avoiding?'

'You're not going to die, Papa,' said Blok. 'You're going to shit on all their graves.'

'To do that I would have to be tracking twenty-four hours from cemetery to cemetery. How does one accumulate so many hates? Do you think it is the climate?'

'I met a man who said it's biological,' Blok said, remembering the Tel Aviv hermit, Bentov.

'We shall return eventually to Gobineau,' said Baruch. 'I think he classified us with the Phoenicians. He was nice to us, he said we have a touch of the Aryan. But Adolf Hitler didn't think so. Do you think he was right?'

'Who?'

'Hitler.'

'No.'

'I also think he got it wrong. But there is definitely something askew with us. Or is it just the universal norm?'

He drank to drown the cock-ups of humanity, the fear of death, of cold hard-boiled eggs and bitter herbs and disappointment, the dinner gab of Nachman R., who had come to resemble something out of an old Alec Guinness movie, the senile General moving pepperpots on the table. Recycling old tales of his triumphs in 'black' propaganda, how he had convinced the Arabs our forces had the atomic bomb back in 1948, and how he had persuaded Kwame Nkrumah, first Prime Minister of Ghana, that the Akan people, from whence he came, were descendants of the Lost Ten Tribes. 'We milked those Lost Ten Tribes dry,' he said wistfully, 'from Ireland to Indonesia. But then the oil money came, and no one wanted romance. They just put out their tongues to suck crude.'

'You can suck mine, any day,' Baruch said, under his breath, but Blok put a hand on his shoulder. They had finished off the flask before coming forth, relieved, from the ablution chamber, their sins manifest on their breath and in their glazed demeanour, but everyone pretended not to notice while at the same time

188

emanating the crossbow darts of disapproval. 'We will soon be pin-cushions,' Baruch hissed to Avram, as Aunt Pashtida's ratchet eyes wheeled. And Mama clucking over both of them, literally laying eggs, cold and hard boiled, on their plates, long before the apportioned reading allowed this, in fear they might both starve to death. 'Not yet, Rosa! Not yet!' called Aunt Pashtida. But no one could stop Mama's largesse. 'HOW MANY GOOD THINGS WE HAVE TO THANK GOD FOR –

'– If He had taken us out of Egypt, but left them unharmed – It would have been enough . . .

'– If He had harmed them, but left their Gods still armed – It would have been enough . . .

'– If He had harmed their Gods, but not killed their first born – It would have been enough . . .

'– If he had killed their first born, but not given us all their wealth – It would have been enough . . .'

'Have we already had the Ten Plagues?' Baruch asked Rosa.

'Yes, Baruch, long ago,' said Rosa.

'How could I have missed my favourite passage . . .' Baruch slumped grumpily in his wheelchair. But Blok had noticed them fitfully, spraying the air, spittle struck from the craggy rock of Nachman: BLOOD. FROGS. LICE. BEASTS. BLIGHT. BOILS. HAIL. LOCUSTS. DARKNESS. THE SLAYING OF THE FIRST BORN.

And his forefinger, dipped in the wine, spotting the white tablecloth. Always the uncomfortable part of the text, the righteous joy in revenge. The grisly Lord, perhaps, of Rabbi Levine, rising from the noodle soup tureen. Old Shadow Boy, with his talons and horns, stretching those webbed fingers forth over Baruch with his failed legs, Nachman R. with mortality written all over his once-muscular frame, now like the girders of an old building waiting for the wrecker's ball, Aunt Pashtida, preserved in bile, Rosa, newly risen to an old love, even the young, fresh innocence of Nachman's descendants, he, a washing machine salesman with the Amkor Company, she a part-time kindergarten teacher, and their two young ones, one male and one female, as Noah had took into the ark, and yet, for them too, it would come to pass: And God blessed Noah and his sons, and said unto them, be fruitful, and multiply, and replenish the earth. And

189

the fear of you, and the dread of you, shall be upon every beast of the earth, and upon every fowl of the air, and upon all the fishes of the sea, into your hand are they delivered. But whoso sheddeth man's blood, by man shall his blood be shed: for in the image of God made he Man. As Nachman's granddaughter rose to open the door in the traditional welcome for Elijah, the invisible prophet who wanders through the world, for whom a chair is set aside at every circumcision in which the 'Godfather' who holds the baby ready for the chop sits, a brimming cup of red Carmel wine waiting for him on the Passover table. But no one approached except a stray black cat, which Aunt Pashtida shooed away, while Nachman, alone relishing the consonants and vowels, intoned the terrible excoriation:

POUR OUT THY WRATH UPON THE PEOPLES WHO HAVE NOT KNOWN THEE, AND UPON THE KINGDOMS THAT HAVE NOT CALLED THY NAME. FOR THEY HAVE DEVOURED JACOB AND LAID WASTE HIS DWELLING PLACE. POUR OUT THY INDIGNATION UPON THEM AND PURSUE THEM WITH THY WRATHFUL BREATH. PURSUE THEM WITH THY BREATH AND DESTROY THEM FROM UNDER THE HEAVENS OF THE LORD.

Of course, we don't really mean this.

But is there really something in the air?

The Reluctant Terrorist

When, just before the Passover, Salim's cell of the Popular Front for the Liberation of Palestine received their consignment of three grenades, they also received instructions to disrupt as far as possible the Jewish Festival of Freedom. In a matchstick lottery held with his brothers in arms, Lutfi and Abd el-Mahmud, Salim drew the first short stick. Hiding the grenade in a blue canvas satchel, under a pile of similarly tissue-wrapped oranges and Hebrew newspapers and magazines, he took the Number 19 bus from the Jaffa Gate to the back of King George. Pushing and jostling with his enemies in the mid-spring sweat-box, voices raised, complaints rumbling, small talk leaping seat to seat. Familiar landmarks oozed past: the General Post Office, the office block of Beit Yoel, the great empty site of Zion Square where some vast tower block was in eternal construction. People scurrying about with shopping bags to catch the last pre-Passover shopping squeeze. He alighted at the Hamashbir Department Store and mingled with the crowd at the entrance. Traditionally, this was one of the busiest days of the year, so Lutfi had remarked, with enthusiasm. Salim skirted the fringes of the crowd and moved in on the back trade entrance. Two years earlier he had painted the roof of this building, so he knew its ten storeys well. The bag check man at the front diligently peeked into housewives' stashes, men's briefcases, tourists' rucksacks, a thousand and one holdalls. The obscure contents of women's handbags swum in his nights before his eyes. But at the back, an abandoned security booth was Salim's only obstacle. Had it been manned he would have tried his luck at the front. But Murphy's Law prevailed. However, as he approached the service elevator, a rush of voices drove him on a detour, down first floor corridors to the main concourse, and up through the trading floors. Riding the escalators with the masses, overladen women, yapping children, grim men faced with the onerous task of spending, ridding themselves of useless shekels. Currency devaluing by the hour, like Germany in 1923, thought Salim. And it will also end the same. A woman trod on his toe and begged his pardon, eyeing his face with some suspicion. A nation of sniffer dogs, trained to tell the inferior races from the chosen. He passed the second and third floors, lingerie department, bed-linen, children's wear, kitchen tools. The fourth floor, electrical goods, garden implements, Do-It-Yourself, radios and televisions. Fifth floor, furniture department, edging out on to the service staircase. A clear run to the top of the building, and a vantage point fixed in the memory: an open window, right by the service elevator on the seventh floor. He looked out upon the store car park below, raucous with horns and passing dots. Shoppers traversing the back exit/entrance laden with their gotten gains. A steady stream of human ants in and out, the functioning discourse of trade and tradition fuelling the pariah state. He opened the blue canvas bag and took out the tissue-wrapped grenade, putting away the tissue carefully among the small cache of usurped citrus.

191

As he had hoped, there was no one about in this part of the building at this hour. Tea break for office staff on floor 5. He held the grenade aloft, hooking his finger through the pin. Then he looked down again. The people moved on, oblivious. So this is what it is like, striking a blow for one's Nation. He wondered which of them would take the random force of the dropped egg of death. Would it be the fat, waddling woman in the blue flowery dress? The bald man with hairy arms humping three shopping bags as if sentenced to ten years' hard labour? The religious family with their gambolling brood, little dancing figures in black skull-caps? The uniformed soldier and long-haired girl friend, arm around each other's shoulder? Throw the fucking grenade! voices called to him from his mother's bounteous tapestry: the prophet and his *buraq*, the Khalifa Omar, Abd el-Malik, the liberator Baibars, although Yusuf Salah ed-Din the Merciful seemed to purse his lips in silence. And another Yusuf, his father, the housepainter of the Jewish City, thrown by Menachem Begin's milkchurn bomb out of the window of the King David Hotel. 'I had just one little patch left to do, in the corner . . . !' Bang! into a casuarina. The mass death of Arabs, foreigners and Jews. And look what it got them – the Jewish State. Violence pays. His arm was getting tired, poised at the window, sweat pouring down his face. He could not believe he could not be seen by everyone, leaning out, holding Death. Surely someone should be heard coming along the corridor, allowing necessity to randomize the toss. But he appeared to be entirely alone, with all of Time to decide. This hesitation was ridiculous. The Nation would not forgive a cissy. So many sacrifices already in the struggle, so many brethren cut down. Generations of humiliation, dispossession, slaughter, thousands crushed like so many roaches. No quarter, no mercy given by them to the woman, the child, the aged, the sick. He pulled the pin from the grenade and leaned out of the window. Scanning, spying suddenly an empty patch in the throng. Two cars had locked bonnets, trying to exit the car park, closing off a corner of the compound. He lobbed the bomb with all his strength in that direction, then ran past the service elevator, down two flights of stairs, into the crowd, the shattering thud echoing in his ears. Slowing down and mingling again, down the escalators, as the massed shoppers stirred. What was that? A car backfire? The usual sonic boom? No, that was too close for comfort. Let's get out of here, God help us! The crowd surging out front and back. Running policemen trying to hold them back, shutting the doors in mid rush. But Salim was already out in the car park. An acrid smell and black smoke from the ground. Shattered glass everywhere, pieces of car chassis. A male voice screaming in hysteria: 'My car! They got my fucking car! The murderers!' Then he slipped away in the muddle. His cell comrades, Lutfi and Abd el-Mahmud, were not pleased. 'In that crowd, how the hell could you have missed?' they screamed at him. 'It was the luck of the throw,' he said lamely. The second grenade was entrusted to Abd el-Mahmud, who threw it, several days after the Passover, at an ice cream stall in King George. Five passers-by were killed, and seven more maimed for life. The Front's commanders broadcast their congratulations, from Damascus, in the Martial Music Hour. But Salim hid the third grenade in his cupboard . . .

★

'When the noise of the shelling stopped in Pest,' said Blok's father, 'your mother was the first to climb up the stairs and look out of the window, though I called on her not to be stupid. The Russians were still shelling Buda, the west side of the river, and we were sure there were still Nazi snipers. I remember the date exactly: January 18, year of Jesus Christ 1945. The exact date, we later found, that the German army evacuated their beloved Auschwitz. I climbed up after your mother and saw what seemed like the end of the world in front of us: great apartment block buildings collapsed into rubble, mounds of brick, stone, ash, twisted girders, charred joists hanging in mid air. Familiar newsreel images today, but we had never imagined such a thing. I was struck dumb by the awful beauty of the scene: an apocalypse of liberation. As you know, we had been locked away indoors for months, first separately and then together, hiding from the final transports and Ferencz Szálásy, the Hungarian saviour. A Russian tank rolled into the ruins of what had once been Ipoly Street, dithering and bucking over the débris like a child's toy. Tears stood in our eyes from gratitude.'

Mama had gone to sleep, after Blok had accompanied his parents home, freed of Nachman R. and Aunt Pashtida. Baruch had squeezed out of his wheelchair on to the ragged old sofa with its musky smell of the 1950s, lavatory cleansing, Ama soap on the floor tiles, soggy galoshes, hot milk toddies. Baruch had directed Blok to the old drinks cabinet, in which a half bottle of Slivovitz had survived.

'The Russian soldier stood up in the tank. He had those high Mongol cheekbones. A few people like shattered rag dolls stood on the girders and half waved at him. He made a gesture of smoking, begging for a cigarette. But nobody could find one for him, until a twelve-year-old boy, with a rifle and ammunition belt, rushed up and threw him a packet. He sat there inhaling in ecstasy, like your generation, Avremel, I've seen do with your marijuana. One little happy wisp of smoke curling up from that great heap of embers. Then the women and the men starting to emerge from the rubble like moles out of their little burrows, picking their way through the bricks, the fallen power lines, the burnt-out armoured cars, and carcasses of men and horses. Those dead horses, in particular, kept us alive. We didn't eat the dead Germans. But we did burn their bodies, in little bonfires. It was a very frozen hell. People warmed themselves as best they could, then began searching the ruins for food, clearing away the rubble in their buildings, setting up pathetic shards of home. And pretty soon, the politicians arrived, with their red armbands and their hammers and sickles, and we knew, your mother and I, that we had to move on, elsewhere, south, like the migrating homeless birds. You were already there, with us, though we didn't know that till a few weeks later, that we already carried with us an entire new world . . .'

Adolphe's Tale

PSHAW! A NEW WORLD?!! A likely story! Look at the man! I ask you: is this the stuff that dreams are made of? Just take a gander at this *lemech*, shuffling about the house like a snail in its own crapulent shell. The human race! Do me a favour! Give me crack corn any day! The whole apartment block is full of deadbeats. Even their garbage lacks the merest trace of finesse, all chicken bones and orange peels. Ah, but their hopes! Their aspirations! Their night thoughts and crepitations!

PHAUGH! But let them dream! Let them masturbate in the hours of opportunity! For my time will come. I know what I know and I have heard what I have heard . . . The rest is mere whimpering and whining –

TSAUGH! But even I have to take care, for they have physical strength on their side. I, agility, lightness of mind and of wits, beauty and spiritual awareness. But nevertheless, I curl myself round his leg, nuzzling his shoes (EGH! PTAH!) as he returns from his tribal *Walpurgisnacht*, having done my bit to keep his flat free of vermin. The idiot puts poison down to trap the ants, not knowing they thrive on adversity. My presence, on the other hand, turns them away, to torment other geeks in the building. Biology, not chemistry, is the answer. But they will never learn. The roaches, on the other hand, are a problem. They fear not man, beast or God. Succulent morsels though they may be. I deposited one, half eaten, on his bed one morning. The milk of feline kindness. Did he thank me? I don't have to tell you, comrades. There is no point in lowering one's guard. I composed another haiku:

> Nature, red in tooth and claw.
> The widow's flower bed is eaten.
> Honesty, the fools adore,
> Lions with a teat on.

The two weeks of my abandonment by Esther passed slowly. The timelessness of the bald madman's daily round. First light, the spasm of the early Vespa. One hour later, the Arab vegetable woman, even in the High Holy Days, followed by the neighbours' bovine morning moos, which drag Baldie into the bathroom. Even myself sitting lightly on his face fails to vary this routine. The finjan of water to boil on the stove. The curse at the empty refrigerator. The gloomy stare at kitchen walls. He has some of his newspaper items stuck up, with Blu-tack, round the cabinets, some new, some yellow and crumbling with age, carried through from long-forgotten wanderings:

195

SOLDIER SHOOTS HIS MOTHER BY MISTAKE

SECRET ATOMIC WASTE DUMPED IN DUSTBINS

DRILL YOUR OWN WATER WELL

BLIND FISH BROUGHT TO LIGHT

AL GREEN BURNED BY SUICIDAL GIRL FRIEND

REVOLUTIONARIES RESCUE TROTSKY'S DEATH MASK

POLICE WOO THE YOUNG

STONING TEACHES PEOPLE A LESSON, SAYS
AYATOLLAH KHALKHALI
*(Iran's Most Feared Cleric Chats About Death
Over a Tub of Vanilla Ice cream)*

There's a man after my own heart. Not like this one, nailed to his cross of inactivity and disinterest. Mind you, he does spend an hour or two every day reading through the varied scribblings of idiots his friend Yissachar sent him from Tel Aviv. Take, for example, the following piece of garbage, a 'treatment' *noch*, gormlessly entitled 'The Bitter Tears of Mrs Almaliah' (a brief synopsis will suffice):

A widowed mother living in a small hut in a slum on the outskirts of Tel Aviv wins a vast sum in the Payis Lottery with a ticket she found in the street. She divides the money among her three sons and two daughters, who each spend it in their own way: The youngest boy buys a motorcycle to help him in his drug pushing. The middle son invests the lot in the Bourse and loses it in a collapse of the market. The elder takes his cut and leaves for West Germany, where he becomes a wealthy brothel keeper. The older daughter falls for an Arab, who uses the cash to buy arms for a group of terrorists. The youngest daughter, shocked by all these horrors, becomes a Repentant and gives all her money to an ultra-religious trust. The mother dies of a heart attack and in the last shot of the film 'small boys with skullcaps and sidecurls run joyfully from the school playground to immerse themselves in the Torah.'

To this melange Yissachar appended a note saying: 'Beware! The Saints are really marching!'

FAUGH! PSCHITT! The Human Race! You better believe it, brother! Eventually Esther came and took me away. Not that she is much of an improvement on Baldie, with her non-feline instincts of help and succour to the down-and-out and the depraved. Or that arse Avi, Changer of Universes! PEWK, RATTLE, SHAKE, CRAW! The same ilk as 35 Hageffen Street's pustule, Basuto of Entrance D, Flat 5! Continually bending old Baldie's ear: A new plan, Avram, Comrade Paeger thought of it, we'll declare ourselves an Independent State! Fly a flag out of the apartment window, stop paying taxes, water, telephone bills. They'll repossess your television set, said Baldie. That made the pillock go pale. Already his group are threatening to split into three factions, pro, con and a combination of both, one group having decided to eschew factionalism in favour of Unity, another intent on holding a public debate on whether the 'Movement' should go underground, and the third consisting of just Basuto and his girl friend Daniela, whose parents are pressing them towards marriage, and have offered them a luxury flat in Gilo, which is in what was once an Arab suburb that had been conquered by the Israel Defence Forces in the good old Six Day War. Boring! Boring! Boring! To cap it all, a postcard came for the madman from West Germany, which I read, standing on his head, and kibitzing over his left shoulder:

> Dear Avram! You won't believe this, but I am becoming respectable! I have joined the new Green Party. It seems I am going to stand for local elections, in the Rheinland-Pfalz District! Next year, who knows – Parliament! Your Always Loving Sister,
>
> Ilse!
>
> PS Have you tried my grandmother's recipe? It puts hair on billiard balls!

I dug my claws into his scalp. He threw me off, and pursued me about the apartment with a broomhandle. This at least I can appreciate: some old red-blooded hostility! But it never lasts, with the nebesch. Lapsed back into that glazed look of implacable contemplation. Then out on his aimless wanders, ploughing the town, or alternately stretched out on the bed with the movie scripts which are now his bread and butter. God! am I glad that my stint is over, even though I used the time to some profit firming up the local territory. Proving to the local moggies who's boss! These things take time, but is this not Jerusalem? Empires are not built in a day . . .

Indeed not. As Blok entered, Adolpheless, the post-Passover period, the days of the Counting of the Omer, leading up to the Feast of Pentecost, *Shavuot*, God's presentation of the Torah to Moses upon Mount Sinai. In between, the hodge-podge of Holocaust Day, Remembrance Day, the Day of Independence, leading on to the 33rd Day of the Omer, Bonfire Night, upon which small Bloks, in their day, burned effigies of President Gamal Abd-el Nasser and sang robust songs commemorating Bar-Kokhba, the rebel who lead the zealots to glorious defeat in the 130s, AD. He was the one the Rabbis of his day called Bar-Kuziva, the Son of Deceit, holding him responsible for a useless massacre. But the new leaders of the Jewish State, and especially Menachem Begin, idolized him madly. The skeletons of some of his fighters had been dug up in caves in the desert only the other day, and it was said an official State Funeral of dem ancient dry bones was being planned . . . Rumours, *über alles* . . . But the orthodox celebrated the night as a purely religious event, devoid of nationalism, gathering round their bonfires in the Mahaneh Yehuda court-yards, as Blok chanced upon them, in his wanderings, men and boys in full regalia, beards, sidelocks, fringes, linked in a great slow circle, their women and girls watching separately from above, on the wrought iron balconies. No light but the red of the fire glimmering on rapt, enraptured faces, the oldest men, white whiskered, propelling the circle round with slow deliberate steps, chanting one line over and over again, in a rhythmic, rolling chorus:
'THIS IS THE GATEWAY TO THE LORD – THE RIGHTEOUS WILL PASS THROUGH IT.'
Quite so. Reading the scripts of the hopeful (free of Adolphe's sneers) by night, wandering the City by day, an old Blokkian

custom: down the Kings of Israel Road, past the military barracks of Schneller, into Geula, past the nut and pickle stores and Zisselmacher's laundry, up into the old stone red-roofed houses of the Bokharan Quarter, avoiding the new concrete eyesores of Ramot Eshkol and the Ammunition Hill, down Yoel Street into the true hard core of the medievalists and acid throwers, his 'sock' hat enabling him to pass safely among the Guardians of Chastity, past the tiny pischifke shops of holy utensils, candlesticks and *kiddush* cups, *siddurs*, prayer shawls, memorial candles, old-fashioned hole-in-the-wall cobblers, groceries, ironmongers, wigs for devout women who shaved their own hair on marriage, set unsettlingly on faceless leather dummies, tiny leaning alleyways leading to ghettolike squares of residences, synagogues, seminaries of a dozen score competing Rabbinical schools, Vishnitz versus Gur, Vilna versus Satmar, Riga versus Lodz, round fifteen thousand and still no knock-out in sight . . . And everywhere on the walls the tightly printed posters, shrieking fraternal pain and venom:

ABOMINATIONS! CRY, ALL YE FAITHFUL! SLAVES RULE US, WE HAVE NO DELIVERER! OUR HOLY CITY IS BECOME THE SINK OF INIQUITY! OUR SANCTUARIES THE DEPOSITORY OF THE FILTH AND POLLUTION OF EVERY ADULTERER AND EVERY FORNICATOR! CRY, HOLY CITY, DON SACKCLOTH AND ASHES, ROLL IN THE DUST TO MOURN THY DEFILED SANCTITY! LOOK DOWN, O LORD, UPON OUR PITIFUL, INTOLERABLE SHAME!

Wherefrom, this terrible cry of lamentation, this sweet agony that cannot be forsworn? Time, stand still! Sun, freeze at Gibeon! Twentieth century – surrender! But still it oozes into them, through every reluctant pore, making them twitch and itch with the fear of thought-crime, inadvertently sinning in their minds, ogling unchaste women, brushing up against them in buses and supermarket queues, devouring pornographic magazines in toilets, sneaking tokes of hash in corridors . . .

LEAD US, KNOT, INTO TEMPTATION . . .

The days, the weeks, the months pass.

TIME, gentlemen! So what's Time, in the annals of this sodding City? From the tall tales of creation, the old shamans' reach-me-downs: MADAM HAD'EM, SAYS ADAM. MOSE GOES, CLOSE FLOWS. Old news, wrapping magic fish. CHRIST SHYSTER? HEIST KEISTER. Incoming barbarians, all zones: David, Saul, Solomon, Sennacherib, Alex the Greek, Antiochus, Herod, Nail 'em Up Pontius, Omar the Saviour. Franks'n'Saladin. Hulagu and his Kitbag and the wily Turks. The incoming Voice of God, calling:

EAT SHIT – MOTHERFUCKER!

Words, crackling in the brittle air. Roaches scurrying, mumbling darkly. Wiry trackers of Apocalypse crawling stealthily on a cold trail of sheep poop. Fearful decisions taking shape in the Prime Minister's Kitchen Cabinet, behind the kedgeree and the Osem Oven Farfel . . . A media personage, who used to shine shoes in Tiflis, emits bubble dreams of Fujicolour ancient glory, as the centuries roll on back . . .

A SILVER POT
AT THE END OF EVERY RAINBOW!

The Voice Rolls Over the Brown Terraced Hills,
gathering dust, down the streets of the walled City, striking the ear of Shabetai Tsvi, the False Messiah, as he stands, in the throes of his pre-Shabbes shopping, with a plastic bag, at the corner of El-Wad and Bab el-Habs Streets, at Ibn-Habub's grocery, arguing with the phlegmatic vendor over a random cabbage: 'Look, a beetle has dunged in here, my good man.'
  'It is God's will, Reb Shabetai.'
  The dry autumn of 1662 . . . A full three years to go before the Prophet Nathan Ashkenazi of Gaza (whom he had not yet even met), would proclaim Shabetai's mission to the faithful, precipitating the Great Messianic Upheaval of 1665–6, when half the Jews, East to West, believing in the imminent Redemption, would pack their suitcases, sell their houses and property and make ready for their magical transportation to Zion and the End of Days.

Some would even climb on roofs whenever a cloud came by, in the hope this was the promised vessel.

But Shabetai, still seeking, at this early point, a sign of that as yet unformed drama he knew lay somewhere in his destiny, continued to pursue his bi-weekly sojourns in the caves around the City, closing his eyes, opening his soul to the battle he had already come to recognize between the *shekhinah* and the *klippah*. The spark of the Divine and the husks of Evil. Till suddenly a voice he had not heard before spoke: 'COME OUT, OUR KING, LORD SHABETAI TSVI, OUR LORD AMIRAH, WHEREVER YOU ARE!'

He stepped out of his cave, and found himself facing a construction site of the most amazing nature: on a flattened plain carved as if by God's knife out of the summit of the gravel hill stood a web of girders, wooden and metallic, supporting the fronts of a row of shops and houses giving out on to a main street paved with a hard grey surface. Immense glass lamps hung from giant turrets, adding, for no logical reason, an orange glow in the desert afternoon. Great silvery planes reflected the light blindingly into his eyes. He dropped on his knees, daring to raise his eyes after a while, to view the prosaic shapes of three men and two women, the men bearded and sidecurled, the women properly coiffed, with their hands raised in the attitude of supplication, and another, massively fat but squat shape, seated like a wrinkled watermelon on a small wicker chair, his right hand flicking a ring of worry beads, his left hand holding out a sheaf of papers.

'Mr Shabetai Tsvi?' he said. 'You don't know me, but I am your far descendant. You will eventually have a son, Abraham, who will survive you, but that's not important right now. My name is Adir Kokashvili, and I am a producer of motion pictures. I want to propose to you a little business venture. To begin with, please sign here, here and here.'

But the False Messiah turned and fled, away from the glare of the great 10 K's, down the chalk flank of the hill, scratching his legs on the desert brambles, scrambling across a gully to a wide, hard, neat road, again with that grey metallic surface, upon which varying sizes of horseless vehicles roared up and down at an astonishing speed. Grinning faces looked out at his plump figure, garbed in his old fasting robe and green cap. Suddenly one of the

201

vehicles stopped, a great, shuddering hulk of metal, puffing and steaming, carrying upon its back a large, precarious load of wooden crates packed with citrus fruit. The driver, dark, unshaven, with a weather-beaten peasant's face, held open the door by his side; and called out in Arabic: 'Stop abusing those feet, friend! Hop aboard! Jerusalem, yes? Al Quds?'

'Al Quds,' the False Messiah agreed. He sank back on the dusty leather seat. The vehicle bucked and roared forward, up the wide grey road. 'Which village are you from?' the man continued in Arabic, a language Shabetai knew a little. He shook his head and spread his palms. The driver shrugged, plying his steering wheel. 'A man's life is his own. You are a Jew, aren't you?'

'Yes, I am a Jew,' said Shabetai.

'God made us all the same but different,' said the driver, 'but it is hard to know what He had in mind. In his own time, maybe He will sort things out.'

'You have spoken the truth there,' said Shabetai.

'You shouldn't wander the desert alone,' said the driver. 'These are disgusting times.'

In a few minutes of bone jarring, headlong travel, the City of Jerusalem stretched before him. The familiar walls, spires, cupolas, and mosques, although the Dome of the Rock gleamed with a spectacular sheen of gold it had not seemed to have in 1662. He motioned the driver to set him down, refusing an offer to drop him at the precise point of his destination. 'A man must keep his own mysteries,' said the driver, and rattled off. Shabetai began walking on the hard path down the valley towards the walls, taking note as he walked of the further changes the landscape seemed to have miraculously undergone: the air was not as clear as it should be. There were strange massive buildings on surrounding hills. An entire new city appeared to have arisen beyond the City walls. 'Lord, guide my soul,' he prayed. Though I walk Through the Valley of the Shadow of Death, I am the Meanest Son of a Bitch in the Valley. He continued walking, noticing the strange iron posts with unlit glass lamps lining the side of the road, and the startling new Christian edifices in the crook of the valley: onion-shaped domes over a great basilica with a brightly-coloured mosaic of the Agony of an earlier aspirant Messiah. He began to climb the slope towards the walls, but the familiar battlements and the Gate of the Lions trembled in the summer heatwave. A red haze was descending before his eyes. A boy, standing by a box-like wheeled cart, shouted some obscure message at him. Letters on the cart, inscribed in Latin and Hebrew, formed slogans he could not recognize: PEPSI COLA. SEVEN UP. KINLI. TEMPO. CASSATTA LUX. He fell, face down, tasting the red hot dust. Slipping away from his moorings: he dreamed, a dream full of unknown echoes and strange names and concepts, in the City of his deepest fears and desires:

Shabetai Tsvi's Dream: The Centripetal City
All roads lead to the City, and the City is never full. All day and all night, along the mighty bridges linking it with the trans-oceanic hinterland, one can view the giant trucks and caravans of railway carriages pound down the tracks and highways, bringing steel from the Ruhr Valley and Ohio, timber from Scandinavia and Vermont, iron ore from Silesia and Pennsylvania, beef from Buenos Aires and Texas, exotic fruits, paw paws, mangos and kiwis from Florida and Marks and Spencer. A mere twelve-hour journey, along the maritime bridges, from the high towers of Manhattan and Coney Island, the vast savannahs and plantations of West Africa and Patagonia, the mills of Manchester and Massachussetts, to the perimeter of the City. Or one might glimpse, in the fast lane, the speeding limousines of high servants of State, flags aflutter, bullet-proof windows opaque, bearing civilian or military master-planners swiftly across the Mediterranean isthmus, flitting past the Athinai-Roma Junction and straight on to the twelve-lane coastal highway running into the Jaffa Road. Disgorging a gaggle of perturbed witnesses to the darker side of the City's blessed centripetality: to the south-west – the expanding suburbs of the twin cities of Cairo-Algiers, teeming shanty towns of dispossessed fellaheen spilling over Emanuel Olswanger Road, hordes of fetid itinerants hawking their wares at the doors of the Kiryat Yovel Supersol – cheap vegetables from the Nile Delta, dried camel meat, pharaonic artifacts, pornographic videos. To the south, within sight of the Ramat Rachel swimming pool – the barbed wire of the thin Johannesburg Corridor, conscript troops guarding the bullion trains coming through, double trenches, booby traps and sandbags keeping the Ethiopian Wars at bay . . .

203

South-east, too close for comfort, the border posts of the closed Cities, Mecca–Medina, with their constant complaints about nude bathing within sight of the Holy Kaaba . . . But above all, the north, ever the north which is the City's true bed of nails – just beyond Sanhedriya and Ramot Eshkol, on a good day with the naked eye one can easily spot the looming menace of the Russian Wall: the barbed watchtowers, the constant searchlights, the jangling alarms set off as the Brethren trapped beyond the ramparts break through or come over, climbing over the weak points, tunnelling under like moles, floating over the blind spots in balloons despite the ack-ack, even shooting themselves out of cannons. And then the slow trek across the minefields, toe by toe, elbow after elbow, the dull popping sound of a departed comrade or relative fraying the survivors' nerves, or the terrible rumble of the massive Antonov helicopters rising over the wires, dusting the killing grounds with jasmine or powdering them with lysol, choking the nostrils and throats of all the City's inhabitants, forcing them to go around for days masked in muslin dipped in vaseline. But still, the miracle remnant come, climbing, parched and bleeding out of free fire range, merging with the hordes of other refugees, merchants, trippers, tourists, nouveau-poor, gast arbeiters and Arab villagers touting for work in the lee of the Damascus Gate, or in the long queues forming at the Municipality, an endless burden for the Guardians and Councillors of the City, written in so much blood, sweat and tears . . . ingathering, proliferating, spitting, smoking, jabbering, jousting, jitterbugging, compelled like moths towards the flame of Affluence, Salvation, Freedom . . .

★

Saladin dreamed that Anwar dreamed that Menachem dreamed that Hechler dreamed that Herzl dreamed that Shabetai dreamed that . . . that . . . that . . . that . . .

★

READ THOSE SCRIPTS, ASARGELUSHA!
DON'T LIFT YOUR HEAD ABOVE THE PARAPET!

MEKOR BARUCH

(THE BLESSED SOURCE?)

Parables.
Psynopses.
Antiverbs.

The world is my oyster, I shall not rant.
It faketh the sighs of umpteen pastors,
It leadeth me in the path of sightlessness for its own sake,
It forecloseth its toll.
Yea, though I stake out the cadeaux of the tally of pests,
I see and hear no evil,
For thine art is with me,
Thine clods to laugh, and dump on me,
Thou prepareth a fable for me in the essence of my enemies,
Thou appointeth my bed with trolls . . .

★

THE DESERT MONOLOGUE: (Pscript 1)

Samir and Samira live in the wilderness in the Desert of Tsin
(retreat is the decade's big theme). There is nothing in the desert
except scrub and tumbleweed and old red rock and scorpions, and
the hut built by Samir and Samira in the lee of the mesa of Hor
Hahar. By day, they stay in their shady enclosure, squeezing a bare
sustenance from cactii, arguing about Nietzsche, Schopenhauer,
Spinoza, Sartre, Lacan and Wittgenstein. At night they venture
forth under the gloam of moonlight and lie in wait for lost
travellers. These, when found, they kill by strangulation, and
leave as monuments to the pitilessness of nature. One day, they
find the photograph of a child in the wallet of one of their random
victims. Something in the angel-likeness of the features moves
them to doubt their way of life. They set out towards the city,
hitch-hiking with a variety of frontier types. But, in the city, they

discover the photograph is over twenty years old, and the child has grown up into a ruthless gangster, controlling gambling dens, houses of prostitution, protection rackets and contract murders. For the first time in their lives, they resolve to commit a rational, motivated crime . . .

★

THE HAPPY IMMIGRANT

It is the early 1950s, the teething years of the State. Yosef is a new immigrant from Rumania, a young medical student who has fled the interminable speeches of Gheorge Gheorghiu-Dej to freedom in his new adopted country. He is put to work planting trees and breaking new ground, hassled by bureaucrats and illiterate foremen, but loves every moment of it. In the displaced persons' camp he meets a Yemeni girl, Aliza, whose entire clan has transferred from the Yemen in the 'Magic Carpet' project. They converse in broken Hebrew, the renascent language, and fall hopelessly in love. They marry, give birth to a beautiful coffee-coloured child and go to live in a spanking new apartment in Kiryat Malachi, where Yosef becomes the town doctor. In the last scene they wander off into the sunset, she big with child, he dangling stethoscope, below the skeletons of rows of apartment blocks vigorously under construction.

The author wrote: 'I wish to counter the flood of pessimistic garbage which seeks to drag our State down into the dust. I believe a strong, positive presentation would be both popular and highly valid from an artistic point of view.'

Blok merely scrawled an X, consigning the positive to the dustbin.

★

ITEM (from the Blokbook, which remains a refuge from the Afterbirth of a Nation):

IRAN IMPORTS 80,000 FALSE LEGS
FROM GERMANY (Reuters)

The War with Iraq has taken an immediate toll of the Islamic Republic's medical resources. The savage fighting taking place around the Shatt el-Arab waterway has caused untold casualties to both the Iranian and the Iraqui forces, including a vast number of cripples. Evidence of this is the order, revealed by *Der Zeit*, of 80,000 new prosthetic limbs from the Baumann Gruppe GMBH in Dusseldorf, which specializes in such aids. It is also revealed that France, the Soviet Union and Israel are supplying armaments to the combatants . . .

★

A man came to Blok's door, fleshy, red faced and sweating in his ultra-orthodox coat and waistcoat.

'To marry my son,' he said, throatily.

'Excuse me?' said Blok.

'To marry my son,' the man repeated, wiping his forehead with a handkerchief.

'I don't understand,' Blok said.

'Money,' the man explained.

'No,' said Blok, closing the door. The man retreated, huffing and puffing down the stairs, mumbling heavily under his breath.

★

SALON DELILAH

Samson Mishnikoff is an ultra-orthodox Yeshiva student who lives in Mea Shearim. He falls in love with Delilah, a hairdresser in the Gaza Road in Rehavia, a fashionable secular part of the town. He abandons his studies, changes his traditional dress for modern clothes, and allows her to shave his sidelocks and beard. Delilah, who is the daughter of the local Chief of Police, initiates Samson into the high life of society, sex and drug orgies and skinny dipping. But when he falls for a blonde Tel Aviv floozie named Mokie, Delilah turns against him and vows revenge. The next time she cuts his hair she douses him with a chemical which twenty-four hours later renders him blind. In terror he finds his way to Mokie's Tel Aviv villa but she, spurning him, locks him out of the house. He hides in her garage, crazed with horror and shame, and that night, when her guests arrive for the usual party, he approaches the house with a can of petrol, douses the house and burns it to a crisp, perishing himself in the flames. In the last scene of the film Delilah, in her salon, is welcoming another quiet young man to her barber chair, this time a chartered accountant . . .

Blok wrote in his report to Yissachar: 'Faye Dunaway and Charles Bronson?'

★

ITEM: WELCOME BACK TO AUSCHWITZ 1981 (*from the imported foreign press*)

> Next June, a giant reunion of Jewish survivors from the Nazi Holocaust will be held in Jerusalem. They will be housed in a 'survivors' village', near the centre of the city, where each tent will be named after a death camp – Auschwitz, Treblinka, Belsen, etc. Under each name will be listed the participants who have survived from that particular camp, so that they can get together and reminisce about the old days. A torchlight procession of survivors, from the Knesset to the Wailing Wall, will come as a climax of the event. All those taking part have been asked to bring along mementoes from the extermination camps, such as the striped pyjamas which were once their uniforms . . .

> (*Sunday Times* [UK] 17.8.1980)

★

LOVE ON THE BEACH (alternate title: THE SODA JERKS, Hebrew: THE GAZOZ KIDS)

Yosske, Nakhtsche, Elik and Boaz roam about the Tel Aviv beach in the mid-1950s, desperately chatting up the girls, Dina, Rina, Ditsa and Hedva, who pass the time ditto, being chatted. In between chats they devour ice popsicles and fizzy drinks, and play practical jokes on the elderly keep-fit fanatics who exercise their flab on the beach. They watch ships pass on the horizon and

210

fantasize about foreign lands. At night they try and smuggle Goldstar Beer into their mixed dancing parties, writhing to the new, raucous music of Elvis Pelvis Presley. They attend a cinema screening of *Rebel Without A Cause* and the girls fall in love with James Dean. In order to impress the girls, the boys decide to steal a van and army jeep and stage a 'chicken run' up north by Ramat Aviv. But both vehicles get stuck in the sand, and the kids beat a shamefaced retreat. Meanwhile, the Suez Crisis has struck, and their fathers are being called up to the front. The kids decide to contribute to this Real Life game and set off towards the Sinai Desert . . .

(Blok wrote: 'A money spinner, *milacek!* But haven't I seen this somewhere before?')

★

ITEM: Censors, hard at work, Bismillah! in the offices of the Ministry of Information in Cairo, painstakingly scissoring the State of Israel out of Atlases and Maps in books and magazines . . .

★

Misheard over the BBC Overseas Radio: 'Mr X, who had his name amputated . . .'

★

ITEM (Reuters): . . . The Afghan rebels doused themselves in petrol and hurled themselves on the invading Russian tanks . . .

★

ITEM: CHIEF OF STAFF 'RAFUL', TO UNIVERSITY STUDENTS: 'WE WILL NEVER BE ABLE TO REACH A SITUATION WHERE THE ARABS WILL NOT WANT TO DESTROY US.'

★

ITEM: PEACE IS A DECEPTION (Book Review, *Yediot Aharonot*):

Sadat's Conspiracy by Paul Eidelberg, translated by Moshe Atar. . . . the entire Sadat initiative is not intended to bring

211

about peace, but the destruction of Israel by sophisticated means, by weakening her at home and damaging her position abroad, and the Israeli Government's acceptance of this is a major error that amounts to a complete loss of the senses. Many quotations and proofs are brought to bear on this theory, in order to arouse public opinion . . .

★

TÊTE À TÊTE (Hebrew title: IN FOUR EYES. Alternate title: THE TWO-HEADED SEMITE):

A head transplant film: The head of a Palestinian Arab terrorist is grafted on to the body and head of a Gush Emunim Jewish settler. The film begins with a helicopter chase in the desert: Abu Jihad, the most wanted Arab terrorist, is captured in a fire fight but is close to death from multiple torsal wounds. However, he holds in his mind the secret location of a nuclear bomb the terrorists have purchased from an enemy superpower. A volunteer is sought to sacrifice his life by donating his body for a head transplant to be carried out by the country's top surgeon, Doctor Paradis. A fiercely patriotic Gush Emunim settler, who has terminal brain cancer but whose body, from the neck down, is healthy, volunteers. But in the interim period of the operation, when both heads are sitting on the one, volunteer body, the settler, Elyakim, discovers life, in any form, is better than martyrdom, and the two heads agree to escape before the next stage of the operation, when Elyakim's head would be severed. Together they roam the countryside, hunted by the massed armed forces of land, sea and air, at first bickering and arguing about their intransigent loyalties, but eventually coming to realize that their predicament binds them to a common fate . . .

Blok wrote: 'A hundred and fifty carats!' But Yissachar replied: 'Alas, the times and Kokashvili are not yet ripe.'

★

From an essay by Buñuel: There is no need to hypothesize God if one accepts as real the world of the imagination.

★

212

MEANWHILE, IN THE DEPARTMENT OF APOCALYPTIC AFFAIRS,

Agents Tolstoy, Lermontov, Rashi and Istiqlal were wrestling with the steady Chinese drip of unsolved, clueless, pending metaphenomena, gathering pace as 1980 crept by and 1981 loomed outside in cumulus clouds and cold rain, though twelve levels below Mittag's Café there were no seasons, no day or night, merely the nerve-tingling hum of neon and the tick of digital tocks. Artificially induced lunch hours spent scanning the *World of Puzzles*, purchased from Kastorak's dwarf vendor just up across the Jaffa Road. Istiqlal in particular proud of his savantry in unravelling the Esoteric Crossword:

ACROSS

1. Baggy pants Hezekiah (8)
2. Tetrahydrocannabinoline? (3)
3. *Coniunge ergo filium tuum* (5,4)
4. Cuban missile crisis? Hotzli Potzli! (5)
5. Second Treatise of the Great Seth (9)
6. Fuck my wife? The Holy Serpent! (5)
7. Ethical Dualism (2)
8. The moth plays about the lamp till dawn (7)
9. Zöe (fanning herself): 'I'm melting!' (7)
10. The lightly burdened shall be saved; the heavily laden shall perish (5)
11. Valdemar! The box! the box! (7)
12. The Fourth Maggot (9, 5)
13. Congolese sauerkraut (5)
14. Noah's quark? *A bi gesunt! Mittelpunkt* (3,4)
15. *Isat pragbhara?* Gross matter! (8)
16. *Hazal al layali, ya Juha!* (6)

'Come on,' says Istiqlal, 'it's not that difficult. Number 6 is Sarah, the harlot wife of the False Messiah Shabetai Tsvi. Number 12 is from the *Shang Tzu*, the Chinese Machiavelli – 'sincerity, truth' is the answer. Fifteen – "*isat pragbhara*" is Sanskrit for the Slightly Tilted. Number 10 is from the Sufi Hasan. Nine is from James Joyce, *Ulysses*. Number 8 is a Sufi text as well.'

'Number 3 is OTRAG,' offers Lermontov, 'the German rocket range in Zaire.'

And so on and so forth. Tolstoy always complaining. 'I really don't see the point of all this waste of energy. Why don't we just run it through the machines?'

'The machines, *toujours* the machines!' scoffs Istiqlal. 'Why don't we just chop off our own heads? Where's the old Jewish brain, Goddamit! Standing, pickled, in a vase! Where's your oomph?! Where's your fucking birthright?!'

But no one could provide him an answer.

Hechler, in his box, directing his minions as they plant coloured pins in his complex maps of the cosmic flux and flow, rasping through a speaking tube, his voice weakening by the month as his decomposition increases, the stench flowing out from the Givat Shaul cave, drawing the attention of scavenger dogs and small boys, forcing him to burrow deeper along the City ley lines, penetrating defunct civil defence tunnels and abandoned workings of the old Judas Shuttle programme, cancelled through lack of government funds, sending its chief planner, the old firebrand General Zetz, off to Central Africa in despair, to new veldts of business opportunities . . . the four Assyrians, Shangalay, Charapinsk, Yashmak and Barud, dragging along their pillaged army K-rations . . .

The databanks chattering, jittering, nattering, throwing out their ectoplasmatic analyses, occult signs, tetragrammatons, the seventy-two main names of God (and the nine billion spare subsidiaries), dot matrix printers rendering three-dimensional graphs of the *sephirot*, paraseismic needles leaping to register the jerk as Kokashvili once again urges his hired mediums to locate the lost False Messiah, who had only just slipped his grasp: the mogul, in person, descending to the Bnei Brak basement garage of the Exorcist, Eitan Feibush, a dealer in second-hand station waggons to the orthodox by day, and black kabbalist by night, with the aid of his wife, Totta, their half-wit son, Dudu, the bespoke tailor Manoach Diskin and Matilda 'The Witch' Sharabi, forming a group of five, half a religious *minyan*, representing the five configurations of the Godhead, the divine faces or *partsufim* of the

Lurianic Kabbalah: the entire process being, of course, in total contravention of High Rabbinical authority – the materialization of the dead, in particular, usurping God's prerogative, meriting certain excommunication – but Kokashvili had plans, asargelusha! three days and three nights, locked in the basement, until gross visions of kebabs on giant skewers and colossal mounds of sheeps brains and grilled hearts tormented him constantly, when suddenly, at 03.17 hours, Matilda Sharabi and the half-wit son Dudu keeled over simultaneously into the centre of the hexagram formed on the garage floors by chassis of old Toyotas, re-tread tyres, rusted hubcaps and synchromesh gearboxes, foaming at the mouth, vomiting green slime and ululating in tongues, as, between them, a smoky wisp slowly formed into the flesh, bone and blood of a familiar, dumpy, middle-aged man with a clean-cut brown beard and sad eyes, dressed in an old *jalabiyeh* and red slippers, with a green turban on his head.

'Well,' said Shabetai Tsvi, 'here I am again.'

★

ITEM (*from the Blokbook, undated local press cutting*): I AM OFFERING MY BODY FOR SALE; DOES ANYONE NEED A KIDNEY OR EYE?

> asks a resident of Rehovoth, aged 29, who has incurred heavy debts. 'I am ready to sell any part of my body, separately. Perhaps someone needs a kidney, or an eye. They can be very useful. I am ready to sell myself into slavery, if only I could be freed of my creditors,' says the heavy-set, bedraggled and haunted debtor. 'They are pursuing me and threatening my life,' he explains, 'I have even considered suicide. But maybe I can be saved, if I can sell the only thing I still own – my body. I live from day to day, in fear and desperation. If no one wants to buy my body, suicide will be my only way out.'

★

ITEM: DEBASEMENT OF THE NATIONAL FLAG (*Yediot Rishonot*, 6.4.81):

> The trial of a youth instructor of the 'Young Guardians' movement, a member of Kibbutz H—, who is accused of

215

besmirching the honour of the national flag, will open today in Haifa. I. G., aged 20, is accused, in the course of an educational session, with teenage cadets of the 'Young Guardians', of spreading the State flag on the floor and instructing his cadets to wipe their feet on it. At the time, it was said in defence of the instructor, he had intended to carry out a debate after this act on 'the Sanctity of Symbols and Values'. The instructor is also said to have tied a towel on the window and instructed the cadets to sit and sing the national anthem under it. Several cadets protested and stopped the session when the instructor took hold of a Bible and began burning its pages with a candle.

★

ALI AND ALIA (Pscript 6: A Tale of the Pioneering Days)

Alia is the daughter of a Jewish pioneer from Poland in the new settlement of Zichron Ya'akov in turn-of-the-century Palestine. Ali is the youngest son of an Arab farmer from the nearby village of Ma'ara. Both are five years old and, without the knowledge of their parents, they roam the pristine countryside together, among the cowpats and the dells, the new-mown hay and swamplands. Through their eyes, we observe the changing relationship between the Jewish pioneers and the Arab villagers. At first there is mutual respect and profit, as the Arabs help to work the Jewish land. But as new, radical, Marxist-Zionist migrants appear, a sharp conflict of interest develops. The new 'Workers of Zion' demand that Jews should stop employing Arabs and give work only to their own brethren. The Arabs begin to fear the encroachment of the new settlers on their ancestral lands. Ali's father organizes a sabotage raid on a warehouse belonging to Alia's father. The children are forbidden to meet each other, but, so deep is their friendship, they run away into the fields. To feed themselves they steal from both Arabs and Jews, and each group, unaware that the marauders are children, sends out a posse with guns and dogs to suppress them. Both vigilante groups converge, at night, on their prey, but only the golden dawn reveals the pathetic bloodied corpses of the two mites, clasped in each other's arms . . .

The author wrote: 'My script shows the future belongs to the children.'

Blok wrote in his comment for Yissachar: 'Not so. His own script shows the future belongs to vicious old men with heart disease and palsied trigger fingers.'

★

ITEM, MISHEARD OVER BBC WORLD SERVICE:
'. . . many suffering from post-fatal depression . . .'

★

But Blok, having read his quota of scripts, and finding himself unable to raise Yissachar by telephone, decided on a quick sortie to Tel Aviv, as he still had his friend's apartment keys. In the lobby of the building, however, in a repeat of the past, he met the upstairs neighbour Bentov, carrying his daily bag of groceries.

'Your friend is not in,' Bentov said. 'He has many enemies.'

'Don't we all?' Blok replied.

'Why don't you come up for a coffee,' Bentov said. 'I was just thinking I could do with an assistant today. Nothing technical. Just a third hand.'

Then entered his apartment, which was a peculiar clutter of misarranged furniture: chairs standing on sofas, cabinets on their sides, oddments spilling out of drawers. Framed reproductions of Impressionist and other paintings leaning against the walls. Cardboard boxes of old black and white postcards. Prints of Olde Palestine. Wooden phalluses. Miniature brass Eiffel Towers. And everywhere, books, not neatly arranged, as in Armand's hermitage, but in vast piles around the walls, on the sofas, chairs, cupboards, tables: tomes on film, photography and art, tattered French and American paperbacks, Hebrew novels, dictionaries, encyclopedias. In the centre of it all a 16mm Canon cine camera, on a wooden tripod. And, on tripods and rails below the ceiling, an array of professional lights, with barn-doors, filters, scrims, snoots, et cetera.

'I was preparing a flashback,' Bentov explained. 'But with your help we'll diversify. I would like to film you, hands and wrists

217

only, unloading these groceries in the kitchen. I was going to wait for my wife to do this, but *hélas* . . . As you can see, we do not live together. She elected to remain in the public domain, directing successful feminist pictures. You have seen perhaps *The Testament of Tamar*? No? It won the Harp of David Award.'

Later, over a cognac which Blok did not refuse, Bentov told him his story:

Bentov's Tale

'I first arrived in this country at fifteen years of age. I weighed only forty-five kilos. People assumed the Holocaust was responsible but in fact it was sheer nervousness. My father had brought me directly from Paris, where he had gone just before the war, which we spent in Spain, a neutral country. We pretended to be Christian émigrés from our birthplace, Rumania. But when I arrived in this country the kids here called me "soapy", their slang for concentration camp survivors. People were hard in those days. A bit like the Wild West. Nevertheless, there was a Vision . . . the true heroic act of shovelling shit for a Cause, or canning grapefruit segments . . . Today's jobs for Arabs, or immigrant women, or gentile volunteers. I was only briefly tempted, too hungry to try my luck at Art. Painters, sculptors, all sorts of eccentrics, I found them all in the City. But my father hated being here, once the initial burst of romance had worn off. The Provinces, he scoffed! What's wrong with Bucharest? And he took ship back to Paris, where he died three years later. I went to bury him, met some cinéastes, became a movie buff, sat in Monsieur Langlois' emporium, and then I met the great documentarist Joris Ivens, who had just shot a film in China, called: *Six Hundred Million People Are With You*. I thought: what a noble sentiment! Suddenly I found myself accompanying him to Cuba! Ah! the real thing! 1960, Fidel . . . revolution . . . genuine mass power . . . I joined up with some Cuban cinéastes, and toured the Latin subcontinent: Colombia, Peru, Brazil, Uruguay, Argentina, Chile. What can one say? The staggering tale of poverty, illiteracy, repression – under democracies as well as others . . . And the others! – when you arrived by plane in the Dominican Republic, at the capital, Ciudad Trujillo, you saw a huge sign, big as a house: "GOD IN HEAVEN. TRUJILLO ON EARTH." In 1961, thank God, they shot the bastard . . . We lived in South America with Indians in the mountains, in peasants' huts, in shanty town hovels. In Lima, Peru, I nearly died of dysentry because we had no cash to pay the city hospital. The Israeli Embassy baled me out. And thus, full circle, I renewed my contact with my first adopted home . . . Back to the land of the Six Day War, the Greater Israel, marriage, divorce, Adir Kokashvili . . . Did Yissachar tell you I made a film for him once: *Do Not Cry For Me, Buenos Aires*? A film in Spanish, about a homesick immigrant. He dubbed it into Moghrabi, Ladino and Farsi, renaming it every time. You see, when sentiment is established for sale, anything goes, real feelings perish. The old problem, I suppose, of the Siamese twins, Art and Money. Myself, I have run a sword between the two. And here I am – content to live with the scar.'

The reason for Yissachar's Tel Aviv absence, as discovered by Blok later, was this: He had taken his girl friend, the 'Blind Seamstress' Aliza, off to the beaches of the Red Sea, in order to escape harassment by her other lover, Yosher Osher, the cassette singer and idol of youth, who continued, nevertheless, to pound daily on the doors of the Tel Aviv building, buzzing buzzers in vain, yelling into all the intercoms at the other hapless tenants, being rebuffed coolly by Bentov, who simply told him: 'Yissachar is not at home. He has emigrated to Australia.' Leaving Yosher Osher, his veins shot full of the white stuff that fries the brains and the gonads, to stagger off, weeping and wailing, into the hot, humid, sex-permeated, cosmopolitan night. Although later he wrote a hit song about this experience:

Yosher Osher's Song: Broken Bones

The pedestal
beneath the skies
was the altar
of my sacrifice.

The ladder's steps
greased with tears,
were they your curses
or your cheers?

I slipped and fell
breaking my skull,
a treacherous storm
crushed my hull.

They set my bones
in the museum,
Mondays and Thursdays
you can see 'em.

And you, my love,
drinking from my skull,
my empty skin the pelt
of your annual cull.

★

But autumn begets winter, winter begets spring, and the nation
adapts itself to Blok's mood and constitution, as the General
Election campaign of 1981 creeps up upon the unsuspecting. Four
more years of Menachem Begin's government up for the Nations'
yea or nay. Once again, the neo-kabbalistic symbols of the hopeful
score of parties pasted over every billboard and wall: the long
discredited אמת – EMET – 'Truth' of the fallen Labour Party,
the more obscure מחל of the chemically euphoric leader,
Menachem Begin's Likud coalition, the magic charms of the
Religious Parties, the fringe hopefuls, Right and Left, the Com-
munists, the ethnic minority lists, and of course Rabbi Levine and
his MATAH – the Party of the Purity of the Nation. The Brave
New, Fully Exclusive World. New echoes of apostate brothers,
missing heads, lost souls, for whom rallies, meetings, party
caucuses abound, the carmagnole of the Irgun Leader's supporters, snaking through summer nights, faces alight with the fire of
their idol's rhetoric, braced upon the podium, not so much the
respected Prime Minister of the land but still its premier rebel, the
man who confounded all his detractors, who smote the leviathan
of Socialism, and threw its beef-steak cuts to his adorers. Bread,
circuses and inflation. Stacks of cash, man, in your hand! You've
never had it so good! Piss on the moaning minnies, economists,
bleeding heart intellectuals, people who wear glasses. The crowd

roars. This is the man they love to acclaim, the man who tells the world to fuck off, who made Sadat of Egypt his lackey: 'BEGIN! BEGIN! KING OF ISRAEL!' the chant arises, ripples, soars. Young men tear their shirts open in trance-like frenzy, tears roll down men and women's cheeks. Arms flail the air, hands grab at heaven, which is just within one's reach. Hair is torn out by the roots. 'BEGIN! BEGIN! BEGIN!' Over in adjoining streets, cars and vans with stickers of the opposition Labour Party have their windows smashed, tyres ripped, one party van overturned and set on fire, its driver barely escaping the unleashed fury of the mob, who pursue him with sticks, down the side streets, smashing shopfronts on the way. Who Is Not With Us Is Against Us. **BEGIN! BEGIN! BEGIN!**

Avi and Blok, meeting again in the Swallow-Don't-Chew restaurant. 'GET ON WITH IT, LADIES AND GENTLEMEN,' Ezra cries, 'I'M GETTING POORER BY THE MINUTE!' Avi meticulously drawing out his slow mouthfuls of humus and ful. 'Yes, Avram, things are coming to a head. You can feel it in the air. Everyone tells you Begin is scaring off the voters but I tell you the schmuck is in control. Go to the development towns and you'd think the Messiah, or Rod Stewart, has arrived. Daddy is coming, they tell you as they stand there platzing in the desert sun. And this time it'll be no namby-pamby liberal coalition. This time it's the hard core. Trouble, Avram, with a capital B.'

'ANYONE WHO'S VOTING AGAINST BEGIN CAN LEAVE RIGHT NOW AND MAKE WAY FOR THE NEXT CUSTOMER.' Ezra, desperate for any excuse. But Blok was considering the latest of his paranoias, finding mothballs in one's pubic hair . . . Not to speak of the ants, who might abandon the kitchen out of sheer boredom, to seek darker dominions. Waking up blind was another fear which had survived the winter, as well as the obsessional silent conversations, in the dead of night, with Adolphe, long departed back to Bak'a and Esther, but returning often in the form of a jet black sarcophagus with lazy eyes and a slow drool:

'A funny thing happened to me tonight on the way to the catbox.'

'You don't say.'

'I couldn't believe my ears.'

'I never do.'

'There are fifty billion cockroaches under the earth, waiting to take over.'

'Tell me something new.'

'War is inevitable.'

'The earth is round.'

'Those you think are with you are against you.'

'I carry no passengers.'

'Millions of microscopic creatures still call you home.'

'I repudiate them all.'

'Love is blind.'

And attempts to conjure other visions by means of the meagre offerings of native pornography, seventh-generation black and white copies of foreign magazine colour photographs overlaid with Hebrew commentary: 'She thrust her vulva against his erect member, emitting moans of extreme pleasure.' Indeed. Where are the old days of Liam O'Habash, of the triple frisson of the forbidden, the illegal, the smuggled in old overcoats? Now dangling for all to consume at every bus station kiosk. More Baygon sprayed in every crack. But the ooze of the world continues. The failure to find Armand's murderer. The stubborn leaked sightings of the Rabid Sheep, the smell of the Hechler box, post-fatal depression, the decline of the currency along with the boom in the Bourse shares magically rendered in the weekend financial supplements Blok uses to block the dripping toilet pipe:

Shilton A	75TB	288.0	+4.5	+6.4
Leumi Industries	1142	8.7	−1	−0.1
Merkaz Kablanim	239TB	166.0	+12	+5.3
Klal Leasing	333TB	20.0	+30	+9.9

Insurance Companies:

Arieh 1.0	463TB	98.6	+28		+6.4
Ararat 0.1	641	76.2	−22		−3.3
Hadar 1.0	300			+	
Hasneh	778	482.0	+25		+3.3
Haphoenix 0.1	1055TB		+55		+5.5
Menorah 1.0	3030	97.7	+40		+1.3

Trade & Services:

Intergama 1.0	290	85.0	+13	+4.7
Meir Ezra 1.0	525	80.0	+25	+5.0
Kristal 1.0	190TB	50.0	+12	+6.7
Supersol A 2.0	1580	11.9	+58	+3.8

Real Estate & Construction:

Abraham Gindi	358TB	900.0	+18	+5.3
Oren Construction	197	208.1	(−)	
Africa 0.1	1815			
Arazim 1.0	139	6.6	(+)	
Drucker 1.0	280	38.2	(−)	

And so on and so forth.

Nevertheless, in the night, incomplete figures continue to batter Blok's rapid eye movements: the unavenged pacifist, Armand, minus his head, with the ring of bluebottle flies circling noisily over his severed trachea, humming pioneer melodies (We Have Come to the Larynx, To Build and To Be Built There; Arytenoids, Arytenoids; This Is Our Cartilage, Land of Our Fathers, et cetera) and shitting blood on the bedclothes . . . the disembodied hand of Lena Khalili . . . while Esther, pounding down the Arikha-Beersheba desert highway in Ya'akov Ben-Havivo's chauffeur-driven Citroën limousine, bends her ear to the prodigal son of the Dayan Ezuz, Sage of his People, legitimate heir to the moral asceticism and investment portfolios of his clan:

'I need your help, Esther. I am lost in a fog. I have eyes, but I cannot see . . .'

The shifting sands creeping over the asphalt roads, the relentless entropy of a stern Lord, Blessed Be He, not many miles from the underground stockpiles of the Atomic-Bacteriological-Chemical Corps. She has tried to initiate him into the global wonders of the world of Jung, the speculations of Velikovsky, the folk homilies of George Ivanovitch Gurdjieff:

I AM THOU,
THOU ART I,
HE IS OURS,
WE BOTH ARE HIS,
SO MAY ALL BE FOR OUR NEIGHBOUR.

'People expect me to be like my father,' said the son, 'to prophesy, to provide answers to their pain and their confusion. But I feel nothing in myself of – what was it you called it, the luminous?'

'The numinous, Ya'akov.'

'There is nothing of that in me. Only my own pain, my own confusion. I cannot speak to my father of all this. He is sunk in his own strange wanderings. He is now exclusively prophesying the End of Days – the sparks rising from the feet of Adam Kadmon – the Messiah Son of Joseph . . . I understand none of it, really. Will you help me, Esther? You've read all these books. That Chinese book, with the sticks. Teach me what all those wise men say.'

'I can't teach you, Ya'akov, I can't teach anyone. You have to find your own way.'

★

ITEM (*Yediot Rishonot*, from the Children's Page):

> Shalom, Boys and Girls!
> What can we do when the situation at home is not good: there are many needs but not enough money, the parents are sick and on top of all this the walls of the house are cracking? Should one pretend everything is all right and nothing has happened, and continue to waste money and keep making more and more demands on the poor parents? And what about the cracks in the walls? Should one just plaster them over from outside or perhaps repair the foundations so that no cracks should appear in the future?
>
> The answer is plain: first one should gather all the people of the house, children and adults, and tell them the truth in good faith. One should find out the causes of the difficult situation and ask everyone to help. One should also make less demands on the parents, and cut back on the expenses, and work hard, so that the house should stand and the income should be more than the outlays. And the parents should sack the servants and charwomen and stop travelling abroad.
>
> One does not have to labour the point, children: what is the parable here? The house is the State, the parents – the

government, and the people of the house – ourselves. And there is nothing more to add.

★

(Snip! Snip! In Cairo, castrated atlases pile inexorably up to the ceiling . . .)

★

'BEGIN! BEGIN! BEGIN!'
    Is it biological?

★

And Blok continued to walk the City, on days the early summer weather permitted, allowing the whiff of a breeze from the Mount of Olives, propelled out of Hageffen Street and off the new batch of scripts sent by Yissachar by the morning foghorn of Mrs Almoshnino, the nasal greeting of the plate-breaking Mrs Tishbi, the huffing ex-merchant seaman Sirkin passing him on his morning jog: 'I hear you're working with some film people, Mister Avram, you must come in for a glass of tea some time – I can tell you a story that is so strange you will think I have made it all up for you. But it is the holy truth.' Indeed. Down, past the raucous packed market stalls, the sweaty press of shopping baskets, past the lurking Agrippas Street Gang, guarding the great rubbish skips with fang and claw, little beady eyes peeping out of dustbins, past the bag repair shop, the Biscuits & Bakery, Household Goods, Salon Eden, the Eden Cinema (showing a local comedy – *To Petah Tikva and Back* – an Adir Kokashvili production), the Paladin Hotel, Etti's Flowers and Dani's Jewellery, past the Falafel & Shawarma King into the hubbub of King George and Ben Yehuda Streets, where, one day, an odd event occurred:

He was sitting minding his own business in one of the cafés sprinkling the new pedestrian precinct, sipping an upside down coffee alone at a table under a brightly coloured awning, ignoring the loudspeakers of the various party workers trying to snare floating voters, not to speak of the touts of Rabbi Levine's Party trying to raise signatures on their petition to rid the country of all 'strangers' and unbelievers, and quietly perusing the small classified ads of the free weekend *All the City* magazine –

225

Companion sought for trip to India this summer.
Religiously observant preferred. Alon, Tel. 432543.

New student dance group seeks boys whose knees don't
tremble. Knowledge of folk-dances not essential. Come to
Sprinzsak any Thursday at 8.00 pm and ask for Irit the
Instructress.

I have two tickets for the special Rod Stewart concert and
am looking for a female partner to join me. Tel. 925674.

Pantomime Studio: Yo'av Aristotle, Tel. 645321. Summer
Course, Beginners and Advanced: Mime Technique,
Creation of Illusion, Control and Balance of the Body,
Relaxation Techniques, Expression, Improvization,
Performance with Masks.

– when a petite cheerful brown skinned black haired girl
approached and said to him: 'Do you mind if I sit at this table?'
 'Please,' he said.

★

The Balm in Gilead

She sat and called out in a loud voice for a very cold fresh orange
juice. Then she turned to Blok and said: 'My name's Shuli. I don't
think I've seen you around.'
 'My name is Avram Blok,' he said. 'I have been trying to keep a
low profile.'
 'I know the feeling,' she said. 'I often have it too. I mean, why
get up in the morning?'
 'I don't know,' said Blok. The orange juice arrived. 'I've never
found a good answer for that one.'
 'I mean look at all this nonsense,' she said. 'Labour, Likud, the
Religious Parties, Humpty Dumpty. Is it for that we were born
into this world?'
 'I have no answer,' he said.
 'Why are you wearing that funny cap?' she asked. 'It reminds
me of my old boy friend's father. Are you bald?'

'Yes,' he said.

'I don't care,' she said. 'I'm not prejudiced.'

'It'll return, I'm told,' he said, 'when the Messiah comes.'

'I don't care about all that nonsense.'

'Do you come here often?' he inquired.

'On my off-shift. I have four days off every three weeks.'

'You work in a factory?' he asked, with muddled images of Charles Chaplin's *Modern Times*.

'I am a policewoman,' she said, dumbfounding him. 'Do you live here, in Jerusalem?'

'I think so,' he said, his mind revolving like the steel drum of an empty washing machine. 'If you can call this living.'

'I know the feeling. I mean sometimes you think, what the hell.'

She consumed her drink, through a straw, in one draw. 'Do you work,' she asked, 'or are you a student?'

'I read film scripts,' he volunteered, in lieu of sharp lights and thumbscrews. 'People write them and send them in. I reject them.'

'My ex boy friend is an editor at the television,' she said. 'Do you know him, his name is Avishai?'

'No,' he said. 'Television scares me.'

'I know the feeling,' she said. 'Isn't it terrible?' She looked at her watch. 'Listen, there's a new Paul Newman on at the Orion. Do you want to come with me to the matinee show?'

He sat beside her in the half dark cinema basking in her sheen as the ageing star struck a hockey puck around the screen amid a stream of robust obscenities. A rag bag of scattered idlers around the theatre cheered, rolling bottles of Coca-Cola and Kinli down the pitted aisle. 'Pathetic,' she said to him. 'These people are from broken homes, that most of them broke themselves.'

Suddenly he was holding her hand, for a brief instant, before she disengaged. When they emerged from the cinema the heat of the day had snapped into a dry mild evening. 'I generally cook myself a meal at home on my days off,' she said. 'What do you say to stuffed aubergines?'

He could raise no serious objections. She lived in the German Colony area, in a cool pied à terre in Emil Zola Street, which she had inherited from a girl friend who was now in the modelling business in Greece. 'Isn't that a dream? She offered to get me into

227

that line, but I like my work,' she said, removing silver paper wrapped items from the fridge on to the kitchen table.

'I thought you had trouble getting up in the morning,' said Blok.

'I do,' she said, 'every day.'

★

ITEM: MIRACLES DO HAPPEN: A 'BEWITCHED ROAD' IN JERUSALEM – CARS LEFT ALONE ROLL UPHILL!

Magical roads exist in Jerusalem, despite the skepticism of scientists who claim it's all an optical illusion! A couple, Yitzhak and Sarah G., left their car for a moment to look at the view on their way up Shmuel Ben Adaya Road, leading up to the Mount of Olives, when to their complete amazement, they saw the vehicle roll on its own power away from them up the hill! 'At first,' Yitzhak said, 'my wife thought I was hoaxing her, but after we tried leaving the car with the brake off ten times she became as convinced and stunned as I was . . .'

★

ITEM, by an Israeli columnist: 'I am not one of those people who are tearing their hair because the Likud is going to be re-elected. I am simply one of those people who are tearing their hair.'

★

– I'm not your idea of what a policewoman is, am I? Shuli told Blok. You are a victim of stereotyping. Have I bashed in your skull with a truncheon yet? He admitted not. Well, don't push your luck. She had been in the force two years, she explained. Mainly on traffic duty. But she was due for a course on special investigations: her ambition was the homicide section. They discussed the famous case of Armand's murder. You found the body? she said. How disgusting! A body without a head. It really

228

makes me shiver. It's a dangerous world out there. That one's really driving them spare, she said, the investigation got nowhere. Sometimes you just can't crack a mystery. You just have to accept life is life. It turned out Shuli also knew Esther, slightly, by her social work, and Esther's friend Sergeant Tuvia. There are a lot of good guys like him on the force. And also, like everywhere else, some animals. Blok found himself telling her the chapter headings of what he could glean of his long-forgotten life story: sparks rising from the feet of his old Adam, from closets long sealed. The old peeping incident of 1967, his descent into the mental asylum. 'I knew you were crazy as soon as I set eyes on you,' she said. 'But I don't care. Life is Life.' He found himself telling her of his useless longing for Esther. A half baked rerun of buried and forgotten precedents (Nurse Nili, Malka Halperin . . . did they ever truly exist?) . . .

'You're not really in love with Esther,' Shuli said. 'You just think you ought to try, but you feel guilty, because she's your best friend's girl.'

'Yes, officer, it's a fair cop. You got me clean to rights.'

'Why punish yourself,' she said, 'when there's such a fine set of law enforcement agencies paid to do that professionally? I think everyone should spend six months in jail. And that includes the policemen.'

'By all means, the policemen,' he agreed, as she shovelled stuffed aubergine on his plate. But he had held back his more dubious political exploits, the *Zurafa*, Nablus, the Hand of Lena Khalili, the footsteps of Salim/Omar on the roof, the constant threat of hot air balloons, instead dredging from his addled memory vague images of the fleshpot West: Paris, May, 1968, the timorous echoes of the London of Wilson and Heath . . . 'Why did you come back?' she asked him. 'The money ran out,' he said. 'But also, I suppose my genes were rumbling.'

'I know the feeling,' she said. 'I got as far as Cyprus and had to turn back. It's human nature. An instinct. You belong where you belong.'

They sat, idly watching the television, a religious programme about the Burial Society, demonstrating, with the aid of a professional model, the correct way to wrap a shroud. His hands turning the pages of the *Police News* magazine which he found on her

coffee table: 'COCAINE? ARE WE APATHETIC?' 'MURDER
FOR THE FAMILY HONOUR: A REASSESSMENT.' She put
the sound up for the nine o'clock News:

GOOD EVENING. OPINION POLLS AGAIN PUT THE LABOUR ALIGN-
MENT AHEAD IN THE ELECTION RACE, BUT THE GAP WITH THE
LIKUD IS NARROWING. MORE VIOLENCE AT A LIKUD PARTY
RALLY. CLASHES BETWEEN LEFTISTS AND MEMBERS OF THE
'MATAH' PARTY OF RABBI MÓRDECHAI LEVINE. RELIGIOUS DE-
MANDS FOR THE NEXT COALITION WILL INCLUDE A TOTAL BAN
ON ABORTION. SYRIAN PRESIDENT ASSAD IS SAID TO BE SERIOUSLY
ILL, IS A CHANGE IN DAMASCUS IMMINENT? MORE INCIDENTS IN
SOUTHERN LEBANON. WE HAVE A SPECIAL REPORT.

'What's on Jordan Television?' said Shuli. She switched over to the
Shirley Bassey Show. He kissed her. She responded carefully. He
removed his cap. Hair began to grow. It sprouted, gently, out of
long lost pores, a dark brown, flecked with strands of grey. A
tentative but fertile welcome mat, flowering over neglected
wastes. Tears flowed from his closed eyes, trickling down his
cheeks and arms into the sofa, on to the tiled floor. In the cracks
between the tiles, small buds thrust through, opening into the
fragrant petals of orchids, cyclamen and anemones, rose bushes
curling up around the armchairs, vines climbing up the walls –

– O my dove, that art in the clefts of the rock, in the secret places of
the stairs, let me hear thy voice – My beloved is mine, and I am his,
he feedeth among the lilies . . .

(– Shabetai Tsvi, acclaiming the home-made humus Kokashvili
has laid before him . . . domiciled in the annexe of the film
mogul's large, isolated Savyon villa, while his mentor ponders on
his next move . . .)

(– 'WHERE IS MY BELOVED GONE?' cries Hechler, retreating further and further from Mount Herzl . . .)

(– I went down into the garden of nuts, to see the fruits of the
valley . . . Adolphe, scoffing: A policewoman?! PTSHAW! the

man has hit rock bottom! there's no further he can go . . .
[continuing his scrabble for power in the City's garbage cans] . . .

(But Saladin, waiting on the Mount of Olives to ravish his
betrothed, still dreams . . . Who is this that cometh from the
wilderness? Set me as a seal upon thy heart . . .)

(The databanks chattering under Mittag's Café, new threats and
promises by the hour . . . graphs plotting the computed probable
movements of the Rabid Sheep, Tolstoy and partners rejoicing in
its imminent capture, its long overdue comeuppance . . . ['Any
sightings of your lost object, Tolstoy? I've heard strange reports
from the Amazon basin . . .') Many waters cannot quench love,
neither can the floods drown it . . . If a man would give all the
substance of his house for love, it would utterly be contemned –]

(The coup de grâce in the election campaign, as Menachem Begin
sends a fleet of bombers off to raze a nuclear plant in Baghdad: a
conflagration worth one Parliamentary seat per minute . . . and
the payoff: certain Victory – a new, zealous, narrow coalition,
committed to No Surrender and National Pride . . . celebrations
in the Kitchen Cabinet, frolicking in the *Kiddush* wine . . .)

– The tears flow, thundering down the ravines of the Syrian–
African rift, down the Jordan, through the Dead Sea, under the
Arava and the Gulf of Suez, the waters closing about Anwar
el-Sadat, the last Pharaoh, as his cherished Peace crumbles:
October 6, 1981 – assassins, running towards him at a parade
called to mark his past glorious victories, riddle him with bullets
in the chest, knee, arms, neck and face. It was said that he rose
towards them in the podium, thinking the men were rushing
forward to salute him in person. Dozens of world leaders attended
his funeral, but the Egyptian people stayed at home. Perhaps he
was acting out, in his death, the wry simile of one of his past Prime
Ministers, Mahmud Fawzi:

'In the Middle East, we are like an audience in a theatre where there
is no play. There is scenery, there are sound effects, lights, a
curtain – but there is no script.'

231

SALEM

Bright ides of March, amongst unsolved murders. Thin Avi riding down the Gaza Strip road in a bright blue and yellow Egged bus with forty-five other civilians-turned-soldiers, heading for his annual army Reserve service with unusual eagerness, as he exchanges nips of genuine bourbon with his seat companion and fellow officer Captain Pandis, alias Yasu, whom he had met up with at the Ashkelon rendezvous.

'*L'chayim!*'

'Skol, pardner! My, look at all these long faces! You'd think they'd been asked to castrate themselves!'

'They don't want to fight fellow Jews.'

'One can't bash Arab heads in all the time. Variety is the spice of life.' He threw a shrewd glance at Avi. 'Of course, you never served in the West Bank and the Strip, you lucky schmuck, the bastards let you keep your halo.'

They had been called up for a special tour of duty down at the Rafah Gap, to assist the evacuation of the last part of the Sinai due to be returned to Egypt, in six weeks' time, in line with the Camp David Treaty. (Despite Anwar el-Sadat's death by Islamic vengeance, one murder void of any mystery.) But hundreds of zealots of the Greater Land of Israel movement, the Block of the Faithful, the Renewal Party and Rabbi Levine's followers were crossing the lines into the Jewish settlements and the town of Yamit, beyond Rafah, which were due to be dismantled. Everyone knew the government was turning a blind eye to these incursions, in order to demonstrate to the world how tough it was for Jews to give up their land, although the settlers who lived there had already accepted financial compensation to leave.

'To absent comrades!' Yasu, throwing his head back, imbibed.

235

The bus rushed down the straight die of the asphalt artery, tangy orange groves on either side, here and there an Arab with traditional robe and headdress, a little boy selling fruit, sand intruding on the road, turrets and TV aerials peeking through, motes of the eyeless city, Gaza, sprawled in dust to their right.

'You know my friend I told you about,' said Avi, 'the one who came out bald from the lunatic asylum. He fell in love with a policewoman, and now his hair's grown back again.'

'We shall drink to the return of your friend's hair,' said Yasu, 'and all the fruits of the field. And how is your redhead? Still kicking?'

'She's become obsessed with one of her clients. A pauper who's about to become a prince. Anointed by God with family shares.'

'They are the best libation, *habibi*. May the bush be never consumed. Do you think they'll issue us clubs, or will it just be bare fists against the Chosen of the Lord? Speaking of which, I haven't seen our Captain Karish anywhere. Do you think he missed the transport?'

'He's probably joined the demonstrators,' said Avi.

'That would be nice,' enthused Yasu. 'We could bust him for mutiny in action, and put him up against the wall.'

'He will die proudly,' said Avi.

'To Karish's martyrdom!' Yasu swigged. The dunes rushed past, the coastal scrub, palm trees, the city-free whiff of blue salt sea. The lazy sprawl of Dir el-Balah, the gloom of the squalid refugee camps by Khan Yunis, the crisscross of the old defunct railway, winding back and forth across the road, perhaps due to inebriated planners, closing in on the old, soon to be re-established, international frontier . . .

– But Esther had again headed south, again to meditate in the Negev desert, within reach but out of sight of the nuclear store-house, overlooking the riven rocks of the Small Crater with their multicoloured seams, the vast emptiness of the dark blue late afternoon sky like a gigantic wedding canopy. 'One cannot deny God's work in this place,' said Ya'akov. Esther did not try. The young man had acquired a glimmer of self-confidence, as he sorted out the anchovy sandwiches, uncorking the thermos flask, his two beefy minders keeping a discreet distance in a dark brown

Land Rover. His father, it was said, was sinking rapidly, oozing out his last months of life on the seventh floor of his Arikha apartment block, while family lawyers prepared the transition of corporate and spiritual power to his heir.

'Will you take a look at that star!'

Once again she had had to abandon Adolphe, who had taken to vanishing anyway on long absences, from which he would return sporadically, scratching at the door and lying low for a day or two, licking an endless series of wounds: a frayed ear, a lump out of the buttock, a bitten leg, clumps of missing fur, sustained in God knows what battles in skips all over town. This time he had not been seen for three weeks, and had in fact turned up on Blok's doorstep, snarling, blood stamped on his nose, making a beeline for the kitchen. Blok had phoned Esther.

'It's a blessing, Avram! I'm so glad he's safe! I'll call you when I get back . . .' Though Blok was ill equipped to chaperone the animal, as he now divided his time between 35 Hageffen Street and Shuli's dream pad in Emile Zola, accompanying her whenever police schedules allowed, doing the rounds of her own private version of the centripetal city – her cafés, her restaurants, her favourite falafel stands, newspaper kiosks, grocers, stores, patiently listening to drones of gossip with girl friends and inter-locutory flurries: 'You don't say . . . I know what you mean . . . they all think they're who knows what, really . . . why don't you tell him to get lost . . .'

And her banter with the streetfolk of the city, the picture postcard salesmen, the Arab vegetable women, the blind beggar by the railings outside Steimatsky's: 'Byelaw Number 27, Mordechai!' 'Very good, Miss Shuli!' 'How's the Bourse portfolio going?' 'Ha, ha, such good jokes, lady!' Or, by Beit Yoel, stopping to chat with a moustached cop checking two Arab workers' ID cards: 'Constable Amikam – Avram Blok.' 'Any friend of Shuli's, I'm sure . . . have you heard the latest increment offer? The bastards want to starve us out . . .' 'It's difficult to make a living,' agreed the Arab worker. 'Did I speak to you?' Amikam asked. Further chit-chat with the garbage men at the corner, loading the previous week's litter of the Purim holiday: the costumed 'street carnival' of the city's students, with joke stalls of 'kosher fried shrimp', 'Biblical' *shawarma* and 'glatt kosher

Japanese tempura', 'Mexican Jewish chili' and 'Texas frank-furters', a float of Adam and Eve cruising through the cheering crowds with a giant papier-mâché penis pulled up and down on a pulley. Despite protests, no arrests were made as the throng was pelted by confetti, bunting and bubble gum. But pretty soon the City got back to normal, buses scooping up irate passengers, taxi drivers cruising, shoppers laden with shopping bags, Bourse gamblers crowding round plate glass windows behind which shares flickered on VDUs. Moving on, as fortune fades from the frame, in the old Jerusalem soft shoe shuffle, sandals flip-flopping, keyrings disconsolately wound and unwound round lazy index fingers.

Normal service in Blok's neighbourhood streets too, as Mekor Baruch and Geula fill with the most devout of all the ultra-orthodox Hassids greeting their visiting sage, the great Rabbi of Satmar, who has deigned for the first time in living memory to leave his stronghold in Brooklyn, New York, and set foot in the Holy Land – a commandment he had heretofore avoided due to the heretical rule of secular Zionism: pouring in their thousands out of the Street of a Hundred Gates, halting and snarling the traffic, his personal guards, in traditional striped robes and headgear, making sure no woman appears in the sage's eyeline to tempt his soul away from perfection. Marching away by the arms an obese Sephardi lady overcome by curiosity. 'But I'm sixty-two years old!' she cries. 'I'm ugly! I've had thirteen children!' No matter. Principles are at stake. The bearded heads bob, dance, sing. The rock of ages flutters his eyelashes . . .

Yea! other eyelashes fluttering against Blok's bare chest, preceding even the Vespa delivery and 'FRUITS! FRUITS!', waking him to the realization that Shuli, curled upon him in fetal warmth, has to depart early to enforce the law. The crackle of dawn, her short-wave radio emitting the spit and fuzzle of static and taxi drivers' patter breaking in on the band: 'I have one at Borochov and one at En Gedi.' 'I have one at Rivka and one at Costa Rica.' 'Who made these allocations?' 'Levi.' 'Tell him to boil his head on a plate . . .'

She stands before him in her short-sleeved uniform, with her twin V of Corporal's stripes and gleaming 'Police of Israel' Badge, having blow-dried her hair. 'I arrest you,' he said, 'for exceeding the beauty limit.' 'Where's your authority?' she replied. He showed it to her. She kissed him on the forehead and disengaged. 'I'll see you tomorrow evening.' Turning and exiting, closing the main door quietly but failing to escape the peeking eye of Mrs Bejerano opposite, clip-clopping down the path, raising a finger to Adolphe on the garbage enclosure fence. 'You just watch it, don't shame us all now.' He bared his teeth in defiance. Blok lying in bed, allowing his tumescence to ebb. Yoghourts, a fresh roll, a tin of pickled cucumbers, and another pile of Yissachar's resumed manuscripts: A city man goes to live down on the farm, where he falls in love with a teenage cowmaid . . . Two prisoners escape from the Gulag Archipelago, and hijack a plane to Freedom . . . Sharks attack the holiday resort of Eilat . . . A woman falls in love with the anonymous donor of her artificially inseminated pregnancy . . . Two soldiers on patrol in the West Bank kill two Arabs and hide their bodies down a well, and then they go on to become successful businessmen vending computer equipment to new settlements, till one day . . . A Jewish patient falls in love with his Arab lady dentist . . . A tale of cocaine among Tel Aviv footballers . . . A corrupt Knesset member is killed by his wife . . . A modern Western with Arabs as the cowboys and Israeli Jews as the Indians. 'It's an old wives' tale,' Blok wrote. 'I thought it had promise,' wrote back Yissachar. They had taken to communicating by the tender mercies of the post, as Yissachar struggled in Tel Aviv with the Kokashvili Leisure Company's everyday business while its proprietor was alleged to be locked away with some mysterious guest on a private project which he would disclose to no one. 'I don't know how long I can keep this up,' Yissachar wrote, 'perhaps I should bale out of this madhouse . . .' He also sent Blok, for his famous scrapbook, treasured cuttings from the US, which he knew Blok was fond of, from the *National Enquirer* magazine:

SADAT WAS VICTIM OF MUMMY'S CURSE:
HE DISTURBED REMAINS FOR KING TUT EXHIBIT

PERFECTLY NORMAL MAN WANTS TO BE RETARDED

GOD HELPS NINE YEAR OLD LIFT INCREDIBLE WEIGHTS

Which Blok added to his ongoing portfolio: EGYPT BANS FURTHER *DALLAS* SCREENINGS; ISRAEL HAD THIRTEEN NUCLEAR BOMBS READY DURING YOM KIPPUR WAR – 'Golda was told: The war has started. She said in Yiddish: *Nar das felt mir* – that's all I need . . .' DANGER! CULTS ARE HUNTING YOUR CHILDREN – Our Correspondent Among the Hare Krishna – An Insidious Force In Our Midst; NEW LUXURY JAIL TO BE OPENED NEAR NABLUS; EX-GOVERNMENT SECRETARY: BEGIN IS KEPT ALIVE ONLY BY DRUGS. And the unfolding drama at the edge of the Sinai – PSYCHOLOGISTS PREDICT 'WITHDRAWAL SYMPTOMS' . . .

And even these left his cup strangely empty as he plied his routine wanderings round the city, intoxicated by a new-old wine. LOVE! Could this be true, after so many false alarms? The streets imbued with a new catharsis, a new patina on the stones . . . He loved Big Brother. No, don't mislead us: he loved the city, its walls, its gardens, its unkempt streets, its strange corners, its centripetal buzz, beggars, with Bourse portfolios, ascetic gluttons, aggressive pacifists, placid hysterics, revolutionaries of the spectacle, armchair fanatics, sensual repressives, the doubly glazed dream factories belching ghosts, all its onion layers of illusion. All the roads that lead out of the city that need never be taken. The bottomless womb. He could embrace the quarried stones. MAN HELD FOR INTERCOURSE WITH WALL. (How full would the jails be then.) Levitating, at night, in Shuli's apartment, Emile Zola Street, off the Valley of Ghosts Road: he clasps her warm body, they break through the ceiling, melting tar freed by lack of recent Arab coolie whitewash, up, glowing in the night sky, a clear double blip on radar – the waters of the Isthmus lapping below them, Shuli's gendarme colleagues, riding on luminous broomsticks with official number plates, waving them through empyreal intersections, her parents, stout Iraqi immigrants, lolling on clouds as they pass, and his – sweat pouring off Mama's forehead, Papa leaping from cirrus fibre to fibre, trampolining with his wheelchair, old friends gesturing from stratii, married Nili, dead Nietzsche and Flusser . . . a porcine snort, the grab of teeth on his ankle, just before the pearly gates, over which a blue police sign winks on and off:

'STOPPING HERE', or, as on some smartass buses: 'I HEARD YOU THE FIRST TIME.'

Never a dull moment, *hombres*.

Troops waved Thin Avi, in his Egged bus, through the perfunctory roadblock at the old-new international border between Palestine and Egypt, brushing them on into the Rafah Gap, the swathe of coastal sand dunes peppered with wire fences, salted with the watchtowers of the Jewish settlements set up after the 1967 War. Strips of green cultivation, low houses and fruit trees, opening out into the large town of Yamit, built by the now dead one-eyed General, Moshe Dayan, as the harbinger of a brave new world. Tree-lined avenues and lawns around low whitewashed houses and apartment blocks set up on land partly inhabited before by Bedouin tribes who had become farmers. In 1972 they had been served with expropriation orders, their hutments and crops bulldozed, their water wells capped, sent wandering about the desert in long human convoys, carrying their belongings in pathetic bundles. Then Avi was among the protesting left-wingers gathered to denounce this brutal act. Some of the Bedouin Arabs were eventually allowed back to new quarters, while others found work on the Jewish farms and now, ten years later, watched from their employers' gardens and plots as the Jews, in turn, packed their belongings and prepared to leave. And knots of stalwarts, almost all skullcapped and bearded, clustered round the descending soldiers to hand out Bibles, prayer books and anti-withdrawal leaflets, slapping them effusively on the back. 'Welcome! Welcome in True Peace to Yamit, the Town of the Future!' Many soldiers looked sheepish, but Yasu merely slapped the zealots back heartily, saying: 'You look in good shape, comrades. You'll look even better in traction, won't they, Avi?'

'So they will, so they will.'

The landscape was overshadowed by a tall jagged tower, a great circumcised concrete phallus, surrounded by immense steel rods, a monument to the fallen of the Six Day War, topped by the national flag and draped with a huge banner saying: 'THE VOICE OF THY BROTHER'S BLOOD CRIETH OUT FROM THE GROUND,' while bobbing heads of those who had climbed up to the top shouted defiance to the sea and the sands. Other banners and flags were raised over schools, clinics, post offices and banks.

'If this is not the Land of Israel, what is?' a bearded man buttonholed Avi enthusiastically.

'Don't give me that crap, fascist pig,' said Avi. 'If it were up to your lot we'd be having wars every three years for the next five centuries.'

The mournful baby face of his commanding officer, Colonel Adashim, the Sorrows of Young Werther, loomed in the dust.

'Don't annoy the natives, Ben–Gur. You know they get excited easily.' Yasu handed him the last of the bourbon. 'We're having a briefing in the schoolhouse.'

By the side of the road Arab labourers loaded a van with fridges, washing machines, sofas and a grandfather clock, watched anxiously by an extended family of Jewish settlers, the new breed of chequebook refugees . . .

Later, Avi, ever living in hope, wrote the following letter to Esther:

Calling Home Base! Is anybody there? Anyone returned from the Saint's desert lair?

I've just spent the entire day chasing fanatics from one end of this crazy town to the other. Out of the clinic and into the school. Out of the school and into the post office. Out of the post office on to the beach. And all this under strict orders of 'No Excessive Force, These Are Our Brothers.' There are also special units of women soldiers who have to shoo the ladies about. One of our girls is already in an ambulance with a cracked skull, brained with a 'brotherly' flower pot. One lunatic tied grenades round his body and threatened to blow himself to blazes.

(Avi had told him: 'Well, it's a quick death, comrade.' 'Is that how a Jew talks to a Jew?' the man raved.)

An army chaplain untied him in the end. Reinforcements landing on the beach, in dinghies, like the troops at Iwo Jima, sticking the national flag in the sand. I tell you, when we

242

talked about this country being a madhouse we didn't know how far we'd go . . . Meanwhile, the actual inhabitants of the town have been quietly packing and trekking out. Only the hard core remain. God, the folly of it all! The full circle – fifteen fucking years building the town and the buzz is they're going to bulldoze the whole shmeer into the ground, so as not to leave it to the Egyptians! If no Jews are to live here, let it revert to the wilderness! Don't you love what they're doing to this country?? I remember sitting around on this beach – up by El Arish, in '67, watching the little crabs come out of the sea at sunset and smooch around in the abandoned rubbish of war – army boots, tunics, messtins, upended steel helmets just as in *The Longest Day* . . . Remember all that garbage about having a 'bargaining card' for Peace? A lot of soldiers here are confused by shedding blood for a place then having your head cracked in by your own countrymen for letting it go back to 'the Enemy'. Their conclusion: If you've got it, keep it! 'Peace' is an abstract word they can't grasp at all. The addling of an entire nation's brains. There should be a new concept: Crimes Against Rationality. Maximum penalty: Life under the Yamit Memorial. There they go again: 'Blue and White, Blue and White . . .' It's enough to make you join the Fatah. And how's your own madhouse up there, steeped in holiness? Any news from the Saint of the Negev?

> Despite it all, Love! Roger and out,
> Your greying haired
> Son of Werther.

Esther, having just returned from the Negev, wrote back:

Dear Wolfgang,
Your sorrows do sound deep and ominous but didn't you go off fresh and eager? Anyway while you swan about there on the beach the whole town has filled up with soldiers who must have been pulled out of the Sinai bases. You'd think we were under occupation ourselves, as the poor souls wander about the streets, looking for an uncrowded café or a short queue at a falafel stall. But as you know, I just sail on doing my deeds. While you're out there worrying about the soul of

243

the nation there are still a lot of ordinary people tormented by simple things like illnesses and doctors' bills and breaking legs, and losing a job and having to deal with a parole board or a court appearance. Even in the midst of the apocalypse men still steal cars and smash windows and beat their wives and knife each other in gambling dens. Girls still get pregnant without wanting to and marry the wrong man and can't get a divorce and run away from home. Such is my dreary round but I still enjoy every minute. Your problem is you give yourself a heart attack every time somebody doesn't think the way you do. End of personal criticism (for the time being). Keep hauling! I saw our romancing couple in the street yesterday – the newly blossomed and the police-woman. Mooning about (she was off duty) as if they were sixteen years old. I tell you it's TRUE LOVE. I know about it from books and movies. They didn't see me, they didn't see anything. They were in their own world. Don't you think it's wonderful? In the midst of crisis they find their answer! The Saint of the Negev is OK, as you ask, if a little confused. You may not believe this but the boy is actually sincere, he has real obligations waiting for him in the strange world he'll soon inherit . . . People have good will, not only in your particular path. But you're a grown boy. You can open your eyes!

Love,
'Lotte'

Pupils widening in the dark. Shuli, out on her night shift. Checking suspicious shapes in dustbins, odd packages left against walls, chasing up late angst in Musrarah, disentangling whores from their clients, gossiping with the old codgers of the Civilian Guard patrolling with old Mauser rifles and berets last worn in Montgomery's Eighth Army. Blok, alone at Hageffen Street, wrestling with the night noises trickling through the wire meshed windows, the snores of the ex-merchant seaman Sirkin, pots and pans moved post-midnight somewhere in Entrance B, the furious scrabble for power of Adolphe and Co at the dustbins, nagging late night radio from God knows where, strange shrieks, from the Old City? Or hyenas at the Biblical Zoo? Tolstoy, perhaps, masturbating loudly right across from Entrance D, lost testicle or no, his life impoverished by the dead quiet registered by his bugs in Flat 5, above, due to the total dissolution of the Situationists, Daniela having left Basuto to pursue a medical degree at the University, leaving him furiously but silently scribbling a final tract denouncing the ideological disease of Mandelist-Revisionism. Tolstoy, left haranguing the House Committee about the depredations of Avram Blok and his new amanuensis, Adolphe: 'One understands a pet. But this monster? It's intimidating all the children!' Committee Chairman Kadurie, ever the Reconciler, soothing: 'It hasn't bitten anyone yet, has it? Let's give the poor beast a fair hearing.' Nevertheless, Tolstoy began keeping precise records of Blok's late and early comings and goings:

> Tuesday, April —, 1982, 8 am: Avram Blok, Entrance A, Flat 8, returns bedraggled from a night obviously spent elsewhere in dissolution and depravity. The Black Beast wraps its filthy paws round his leg as he rounds the entrance. The Pact between these two raises serious questions. Must check dept. databanks for correlations. Idolatry. Feline succubii. The Old Ache again. Is there a Connection? Must attach . . . B apartment . . .

And so on and so forth.

But as Blok entered the door of his apartment, with Adolphe, livid at his abandonment for mere female company, clinging to his trouser leg, the phone rang, emitting the voice of Yissachar:
'Hey there, Avram! Where the hell have you been? I've been trying to reach you for a week!'
'Things keep coming up.'
'You bet they do. What's this I've heard you're going out with a lady copper?'
'I cannot deny this.'
'Is it true they use the special technique of unarmed combat to good advantage?'
'Professional secrets, *habibi*.'
'The hell. Sock it to 'em, baby. Listen, things are moving this end too. Forget about all this script reading crapola, all those sticky-palmed Ernest Hemingways and Dalton Trumbos with their

245

wet dreams and half cock brainstorms. We can find some film school graduate to do all that. I have some new ideas brewing.'

'You don't say? What is Kokashvili up to now? I've heard he has been reviving Shabetai Tsvi.'

'You heard that too? You can't beat the grapevine. The man has really gone into hiding. People at the Company are getting worried. Projects tumbling, accountants tearing their hair, impending tax raids, lawsuits like confetti, over-optimistic turnover forecasts, amortization, breach of contract . . . Between you and me, we need an alternative for the day the house falls down. I've been sounding out some odd jobs, like in the old days. Remember our days together, Avram? Holyland Films and the three old dwarfes? Me editing, you as soundman? I've been doing a bit of camera lately. I think we can branch out, find some freelance work. Keep up the vibrating bed, the Sony-Umatic, the good life, now that junkie Osher is off my back, Avram, thank God, following Aliza's trail now she's gone off to Greece, shooting some soft core in the Peleponesos, *evharisto poli*, Olympic Airways. So how about it, old buddy?'

'Whenever you're ready, Yissachar.'

'What's that, Avram? The fucking line's bad. You sounded upbeat. Is it the policewoman?'

'It could be.'

'Fuck 'em and feed 'em beans.'

But on April 12 an incident took place which shook the entire City. In the mid-morning of the Christian Easter Sunday, a gunman, who turned out to be an American immigrant serving his three-month basic training in the Israel Defence Forces, burst into the Haram esh-Sheriff and shot his way into the Dome of the Rock, the site of Muhammad's ascent into heaven. His bullets killed a Moslem guard and wounded a policeman, whose life was saved by a pocket calculator kept in his breast pocket. The gunman, dressed in his army uniform, took up position inside the mosque, below the fabulous stained glass mosaics and the wooden balustrade of the Holy Rock itself. When Israeli police arrived, he surrendered and was hustled out through outraged Moslem crowds. These clashed with policemen and armed Jewish vigilantes, and another Arab was shot dead. Meanwhile, in the

246

gunman's delapidated hotel bedroom, police found a multitude of empty food cans, broken furniture, leaflets from Rabbi Levine's party, and garbled scribblings in English and Hebrew on scraps of paper: 'NATIONAL LIBERATION', 'SELF DETERMINA-TION' and 'LET MY PEOPLE GO'.

Other events of the day, as reported in the press: the Pope warned of war between Christians and Christians in the far off Falkland Islands. The banned Polish leader of the 'Solidarity' movement appeared in public, with a beard. The visit to the Holy Land of Harry Oppenheimer, Chairman of the Anglo-American Gold Company and said to be the richest man in the world. One hundred and sixty drowned in a ferry accident in Rangoon. Two terrorists captured in the Jordan valley. The singer Lulu arrived on holiday. Demonstrating milkmen set fire to the 'Teneh-Noga' Dairy. Israeli Druse declare: We are still loyal to the State. Masked men stole 25,000 shekels. An Egyptian child named Begin after Camp David is due to meet his famous namesake. The Defence Minister, General Sharon, says *Newsweek*, told the US Embassy Israel will invade Lebanon and reach as far as Beirut. Official sources deny the story. One hundred zealots committed to stopping the withdrawal from Sinai arrested for crossing army road-blocks. The government reiterates all measures will be taken to ensure the final withdrawal takes place on time, and in an orderly fashion. Nevertheless, clashes between the zealots and the army were said to be escalating . . .

– Sun, stand still over Gibeon, the moon in the Ayalon Valley . . . On the summit of the Armoured Division Memorial, loud-speakers belt forth Homeland and religious songs. Figures dance below the stars . . .

'What I wouldn't give for a sniper unit!' Yasu moans, in sleepless fury. 'This is all your fault!' he makes a feint at Karish, their zealot colleague, who has finally turned up, reluctantly, bearing anti-withdrawal leaflets. Karish dodges the blow. 'You want to obey a shitty order, suffer for it!' he says, moodily chewing a chocolate wafer. They all glance towards their commanding officer, the baby faced Adashim, Colonel the Sorrows of Young Werther. But he is stretched out on a bed in the evacuated clinic, with a white sheet pulled over his head . . .

247

Shuli and Blok, in bed at Emile Zola. Becalmed amid storm warnings. He enters her. She enters him. They lie together. Levitation at any time. The cool breeze through the open window brushes the drops of their sweat. Sleep does not come. They take a late night walk in the neighbourhood. The strange cluster of foreign name streetlets: Lloyd George, Wedgwood, Wyndham Deedes. Echoes of a colonial past. Past the apartment blocks of Jan Smuts Street to the single track railway. The Ottoman gauge lifeline to the coastal artery. Grass and gravel between the wooden sleepers. Pine and lemon trees from adjoining backyards. Snoozing cats, Adolphe-free. Mutual unshaken memories of youth: games of chicken and bravado, running across the lines in front of the oncoming slow diesel engine, belching black smoke and honking at fully three kilometres per hour. One had to be in cahoots with the timetable or one might die of starvation, waiting for the rare chuffing passage . . . In the lee of Lloyd George, the Semadar Cinema, Two Tarzans at 10.00 am, 350 prutot, now 0.00000001 of a shekel. The past shrinking through the materialist lens. Johnny Weissmuller and Lex Barker.

'What was that?'

A low shape flitted across the road.

'Come here, doggie doggie!'

'That was no dog.'

'Pretty big for a cat, wasn't it?'

'That was not a cat, either.'

'A pig?' he suggested hopefully.

'Looked like a sheep,' said Shuli.

'A bit zippy for a sheep, don't you think?'

They peeked behind the rustling bushes at the side of the road, but could see nothing but a trail of turds.

Another Jerusalem mystery. They continued their walk, crossing the Valley of Ghosts Road, round the back of the Natural History Museum, the old stone walls of the leper hospital, the new bulk of the Jerusalem Theatre. Culture for the reborn. They sat on a rock, in the glade behind Dubnow Street, their feet scrabbling gravel by the half-hearted playground of see-saw, slide and metal rocking horse held to the ground by steel girders. Overlooking the dark silence, dappled by streetlights, the opaque windows of the city sleeping, their faces caressed by the brisk mountain breeze oozing through the evergreen pines.

'What should we do,' said Shuli, 'about us?'

'We live happily ever after,' said Blok, looking up, as if counting the stars.

'No, but seriously . . .' Shuli said. 'I don't care if we just go on as we are, but if we start to think . . .'

'Always a dangerous procedure.'

'You know what I mean, if we have something special . . .'

'All right, let's get married,' he said. 'Kids, a house in the country, a yacht, a garage. We can have ten children, our own private army. We will train them to shoot to kill.'

'Don't kid me, you hate children, you think they're poaching on your grounds. I can see you're not into the future, Avram. That's what drew me in the first place to you. I hate the future too. But sometimes, you just have to think . . .'

'I'll do whatever you want,' he said. 'I'll meet your parents. I'll have a barbecue with your brothers. I'll introduce Adolphe to the family dog. We'll take bets on which one survives.'

'My family can stay in their own world,' she said. 'But we have to work out our own.'

They left the conversation hanging on the breeze, bobbing away like a scattered puffball, proceeding, hand in hand, to tap their way home. Behind them, the Sheep came out of hiding, resuming its stealthy pad, hugging the stone fences, down Gedaliah Allon, 29th of November Street, into Bustanai, hoping to lose itself in the labyrinth of the bourgeois German Colony, baring its teeth at the large Alsatian at Number 17, which retired yelping in a tremble, followed, with ultimate caution, by the black-clad balaclavad trackers of the Apocalyptic Department, dragging their nets and curare-tipped harpoons, determined this time not to fail . . .

Sun, stand still at Gibeon . . .

Nevertheless, dawn over the Yamit memorial:

Dear Esther,

Yes, the day of the big show has come, four days to the End of our Mission and then home in time for Independence Day!

Yes, ironies still piling up. The town will definitely be destroyed. From where I sit I see bulldozers silhouetted in the first light, poised on the dunes to smash the buildings and tear up the roads. We've been issued with some special kit to deal with the last barricades – most people have already left. But we have the real hard core, up on the monument, or sealed inside abandoned houses. The main hoo-hah, though, is over familiar ground, our old friend Levine's warrior boys. They've locked themselves in a bunker and are threatening suicide, Massada fashion, unless the government cancels the Withdrawal! Shock, horror, alarums. Brass gathering. You must be seeing all this on TV, or have you given up? I waved to the cameras, but was I visible among all the other khaki robots?? . . .

– Standing guard in front of a nine-foot-high concrete block, the top part of an air raid shelter, its off-whitewash walls daubed all over with an aerosol mishmash of Biblical and secular scrawls:

IDF SOLDIERS BEWARE – THERE ARE GAS
BALLOONS BEHIND THIS DOOR!

OUR BLOOD IS UPON YOUR HEAD, BEGIN!

HE WHO ABOLISHES THE KING'S EVIL DECREE
ON THE SABBATH IS JUSTIFIED
(Rambam, 'Hilchot Melachim' 80:9).

FORM YOUR PLOT, IT SHALL FAIL!
LAY YOUR PLAN, IT SHALL NOT PREVAIL,
FOR THE LORD IS WITH US!

ONLY THUS CAN WE STOP THE WITHDRAWAL!

Onlookers, evacuees, fellow zealots, officers, soldiers, police, politicians and press, who have been officially banned from the area but have infiltrated through, mainly in the guise of skullcap-ped demonstrators, crowd the bunker, pushing and shoving for a better view, taking pictures amateur and professional, shouting calls of support or questions that cannot be heard, debating the pros and cons.

'It's a tragedy, they mustn't be allowed to do it!' An orthodox, coiffed woman pleading.

'What's the point?' a tougher lady, with folded arms. 'If they want to commit suicide they should do it in Jerusalem where it counts and the whole world is watching.' 'Bazooka the lot of them!' mutters Captain Yasu. But the orders are to stand down, awaiting the arrival of the party leader himself, Rabbi Levine in person, called in to calm his disciples. He appears, in a phalanx of newsmen and generals, having been helicoptered in from the north, grinning widely as he basks in his sudden centripetality, climbing on a rickety table supplied to put his ear to the fist-sized air vent set high in the bunker wall. From the Armoured Memorial, the continuous strains of patriotic vocals. The thokka-thokka-thok of helicopters, the revving up of bulldozers. Levine climbs down. 'They are adamant. I cannot move them. This is what happens when a government betrays its people.'

'You promised to talk them out of it!' an appalled General says.

'I said I'd try. We are a democratic party.'

'Give this man some coffee,' the General commands. The only pot around is Yasu and Avi's. Reluctantly they serve the zealot. 'Some spare ribs, Rabbi?' Yasu taunts him. 'I lost my taste for them long ago,' the Rabbi answers. Avi trying to skewer him with glances. 'It's strange, where people meet, isn't it, Mister Levine?'

'I don't remember. Was it last summer, in Judaea?'

'An estranged brother,' said Avi, 'dead in Ein Karem. A man who somehow lost his head.'

'There are many estranged brothers here,' said Levine. 'And you all seem to have lost your heads. Why are you helping to throw Jews out of their own country?'

'I enjoy it,' said Avi. 'It makes a change from knitting.'

'You talk like that,' said Levine, 'but inside, where it counts, you are eaten up by contradictions.'

'String 'em up,' Yasu mumbles in the background. 'It's the only language they understand.'

'The Chief Rabbis are coming!' someone cries. Avi shakes his head. But this is no jest. Sweeping down the sandy, sunbeaten path, the two chief clerics of their respective Ashkenazi and Sephardi flocks, Abbott and Costello of the faith, bear down on the Levine bunker. The beards, the velvet cap, the robe of office, opaque sunshades against the glare. Bodyguards and Generals lift the Ashkenazi primate on the table. He speaks to the hole in the wall:

'Do you hear me? You young people who are in there. . . Your threats have anguished the highest in the land . . . I have with me here the First of Zion, a great force, a known giant in the Torah. The greatest interpreter of the *Halacha* in the world. I am mere dust at his feet. He will talk to you and explain that the *Halacha* completely forbids suicide . . .'

Oh dear, oh dear, oh dear. (The helicopters whirl. The static of walkie-talkies. The click-click-buzz and whirr of cameras.) Later, in the relative calm of the abandoned clinic where Avi's unit had its base, after the kamikaze ground crew had relented and exited, singing devout songs of praise, Colonel Adashim, the Sorrows of Young Werther, swathed in his sheet, exegeted:

'What is man? A boiled beetroot, an apricot stone, stuck in the throat . . . And all his travails level with the grass, and all his hopes Blue Band Margarine . . . He crawls upon the earth, sniffing at an anemone here, a discarded fag butt there . . . His head is a pricked balloon . . . His eyes sacks of crushed bones . . . pus runs out of his ears . . . His balls are tied around his neck, he carries his guts in his pouches . . . He pits his arsehole against the world, and polishes his eyeballs with Brasso. Fit him with wheels and he'd be your grandmother. Jack him up he might break ground. His brains have already been removed. Take him up in a B-102 and scatter his entrails to the winds. Who cares about the *kashrut* certificate? Every person should at least once taste the flesh of one of his or her own limbs . . . Every man or woman should bathe naked in the gas chamber of life. All men are created equal. A villa and Volvo for every citizen. A nuclear bunker for each child. A triple womb with all-risk coverage and de luxe lining for every woman. A bone for every dog. A cat for every flea. Free cheese for mice who have been converted according to the laws of the *Halacha*. A free pack of ants for armadillos. They are almost blind, you know: when attacked, they curl into an invulnerable ball. Batten the hatches! Close the vents! Stock up with ten months' worth of shaving powder! Disembowel the quarter-master! We who are about to God knows what salute you: *Veni, VD, vici.*'

Midnight and the final briefing. The tower songsters reduced to nostalgia: 'Those Were The Days – We Laboured and We Struggled . . .' One had fallen asleep under a loudspeaker, his snores relayed across the battlefield. In the old schoolhouse, maps unfurled of the town, arrows, circles, dotted lines, each company and platoon assigned their quota of houses and streets to be cleared, picked crews dispatched to man the Special Equipment, cages, foam squirting fire hoses, giant lifting cranes. Plastic shields, but no clubs or weapons. These Are Our Brothers, Handle With Care. Yasu slapping Avi on the back. 'It'll be misty, maybe no one'll notice if you give someone a good whack with an axe haft.' 'Kill 'em with kindness,' said Avi.

The sand rolls in off the dunes. The holy men gone from the streets, empty lawns, trampled gardens. Don't tread on the flowers, comrades! The bulldozers begin work on the fringe. Dawn chases the fog back to the sea, revealing little knots of people on each rooftop, with their banners and flags. Children hiding in irrigation trenches, women sitting down in trash-strewn entrances, ready to be dragged away. The press, ready and eager to serve posterity. The soft purr of ENGs –

ACTION!

The troops dash into frame, the brave defenders raising the flag! T-shirts emblazoned 'NO TO THE WITHDRAWAL!' thrust in the faces of authority: khaki, pouches, waterbottles, steel helmets to guard against objects cast down. No boiling oil, but steel hooks and staves, bricks, Coca-Cola bottles, crates, bedposts, chairlegs, plastic bags full of sand, earth, ash, dung, abandoned household appliances, lamp posts, plugs, hair dryers, plates, mugs, broken toys, garbage sacks, old boots and shoes, thrown down on the invaders hoist aloft inside the steel cages by the giant cranes, with their fire hoses, operators below opening the cocks on the hoses to shoot foam on to the defenders. Now the Philistines are on the roof, rushing out of their cages, wresting steel bedposts from limp hands, foam from below enveloping both sides, drenching clothes, blinding, turning the battlefield into a giant bubble bath. The zealot hordes are hauled, pushed, shoved into the cages, then winched up, over the roof parapets, brought down to waiting police vans. The sound FX: Cries, shrieks, whistles, singing: 'IF I FORGET THEE YAMIT, MAY MY RIGHT HAND FORGET

253

ITS CUNNING! BELOVED YAMIT, WE SHALL RETURN TO THEE!' Foam-covered men packed and locked in the vans. Army radios crackle: 'Street B cleared.' The bulldozers move in: blades outthrust, crashing into ground-floor walls. A brief glimpse of a residence: a light bulb, a wall with the empty spaces of framed photographs – then the upper floors cave in. The bulldozer grinds back, forward, eager for another bite. Concrete cracks. Girders buckle, plaster crumbles. A job worth doing is worth doing well. *Dunam* after *dunam*, boys! Ruthlessly the machines worry at the fallen flakes, the shards of balconies, compartment walls, a few remaining household goods, a broken ironing board, discarded cooker, an old army tunic, cracked boots . . . Dust to dust. Ashes to ashes. The houses are punched into the sand. Wilderness to wilderness. Primal scream. All the onlookers have fallen silent. The forces of the Law and Resistance, together, standing on dunes just outside the city limits, watching the bulldozers graze, the whine of treads, the crash of steel on concrete, and, to administer the coup de grâce, the sudden appearance of giant air hammers, lofted by cranes, like Martian war machines from the War of the Worlds, moving in on the Armoured Memorial, circumcizing it in two. Charges laid by sappers blast the base from under it. It crashes, shatters on the ground. Even Yasu is silenced, shaking his head, his hand rests on the shoulder of a bearded protestor he has just dragged bodily out of a last ditch, determined to remain behind . . . Colonel the Sorrows of Young Werther looks at his watch. 'I wonder what's keeping the helicopters?' he mutters, adding, as his officers look at him quizzically, 'the ones that are to strew the salt . . .'

The Defence Minister declared: 'No Arab army has been able, or will be able, to destroy an Israeli city. Only we, with our own hands, had to destroy Yamit, had to wipe her off the face of the earth, in order to comply in time with our Peace Treaty with Egypt and to avoid the spilling of Jewish blood. Let us therefore bind up our wounds and sink our differences so that we can stand up to the coming campaigns . . .'

But Anwar el-Sadat, who had intended to take the town over intact and transform it into a tourist paradise, with ice cream parlours and scuba diving and watersports and the entire jiveola, appeared, a bloody wraith in the ruins, staggering about the dust in his deathtrap uniform, oozing red from two dozen wounds, as he shoos away the Bedouin scavengers gathering with old Jaffa crates and boxes, looking for a wristwatch left behind maybe or the coil of a cooker, or some old re-usable screws, the ex-President pop-popping on his eternal pipe, shaking his halo sadly, tut-tut-tutting, wheezing in tears, the afterglow of disbelief in his assassinated eyes –

WHY? WHY? WHY?

★

'So you see,' Kokashvili said to Shabetai Tsvi, as they tucked into a fine shashlik and salad at A—'s Restaurant at the Yemeni Vineyard, in Tel Aviv, 'so much may appear to have changed but nothing is changed. People are still as afraid as ever. Yearning to be free. To have and hold a little piece of paradise before they die. And after that . . .' He watched the False Messiah spear a chip, nervously, worrying at the unusual fritter. 'I thought I would give people pleasant dreams, redemption in this world, not the next. But no one likes a dreamer, in the real world – the lawyers soon had me on the ropes . . .'

'You failed to amortize,' said the False Messiah. 'It's in black and white in your portfolio.'

'Well,' Kokashvili said determinedly, 'I won't make the same mistakes this time . . .'

★

Saladin, looking down on the City walls from his tent on the Mount of Olives (still between Abu Sneima's kiosk and the Intercontinental Hotel), notes the frenzied scurrying and acceleration below, the panic buying of groceries, the realignment of guards at battlements and embrasures, the hurried removal of laundry from washing lines, lowered TV aerials, the hogtying of redundant lawyers, accountants and scribes to the front ramparts, as a human shield running from the Golden Gate to Saint Stephen's. The mass smashing of tourists' cameras and bonfires of foreign journalists' notes.

255

'When will they ever learn?'

The noseless nun sucking his penis. The virgins of the convent supine behind him under the thrashing bodies of his lieutenants. Violated hymens snap delicately like so many pinned butterflies. Saladin closed his eyes briefly again. But a Sufi message, imprinted on his retina, flamed like a row of Roman candles:

THE DEVIL CANNOT ENTER A MAN'S HEART,
UNLESS HE DESIRES TO COMMIT A SIN.

He looked again at the City. The City looked back at him, with a pitiless and hoary gaze.

★

The PM tossing and turning, in the Kitchen Cabinet, behind the pepperpots and Telma Steak Seasoning, convulsed in the perpetual heartburn of his public and private angst, trying to soothe himself with seminal memories of the old days of Struggle and Achievement (We Fight, Therefore We Are. Have We The Right? Land Of Our Fathers) . . . The ghost of Anwar el-Sadat appears to him, peeking from behind the Champignon Sauce: the gaping red wounds in his dress uniform, the annoying pop-pop of his briar pipe, mispronouncing, as usual, his 'P's:

'Beace in our time. This we have both bromised. And I expect bromises to be kebt.' Pop, pop, pop, pop. 'You and I, we have sworn an oath of friendshib. But evil men wish to destroy all hobe of beace between our beobles. Let me give you some advice, from my own exberience: always wear a bullet broof vest.'

Ghosts, proliferating in the City. Armand's headless corpse, garnished with flies, reported leaning towards patrons of Chinese restaurants, as they stepped out in the spring breeze; Tolstoy's lost ball, sighted on the 'Ammunition Hill', bouncing outside the Police Training School; Jimmy Carter's presidential re-election prospects, seen slouching towards Bethlehem to die; Yamit settlers, clutching their six-figure compensation cheques, searching shadows of the Bourse; Kokashvili Inc. scripts, expiring in turnaround; past masters, retracing steps –

256

'We shall go to Jerusalem, Reb Shabetai . . . I have a location all prepared . . . we were going to build an audioanimatronic centre . . . but the powers that be let me down . . . we are always fenced in by insane "regulations" . . . haven't you found that to be so? The lack of imagination and oomph of those who "lead" the masses – never ready for the bold moves, don't you think? But don't worry, we'll show them times have changed, we are made of sterner stuff now – we won't piss in the same wind twice . . .'

★

If You Will It, It Is No Fairy Tale . . . In his sealed box, hidden deep in the toilets of the City's nuclear bunker, the only part of town the scavengers are not attracted to his increasing putrescence and decay, the Reverend Hechler never forgets Theodor Herzl's adage. Wisdom of The Founder, safely entombed in his black marble sarcophagus on the hill which bears his name. Brooding in his final hideaway, well aware of time running out as his rotting extremities fall off, scooped up and reattached by his faithful bearers, Shangalay, Charapinsk, Yashmak and Barud, the Assyrian Quartet, financially loyal to the end. He has never felt so close to his goal, but there remains one confrontation to be undertaken, one piece to complete the jigsaw puzzle, data only a dead man can provide . . .

He sets out, oblivious to the first echoes of Independence Day looming in the streets above – the little festive plastic hammers, as yet tentative, so as not to encroach on the preceding sombreness of Remembrance Day, the day of mourning for the fallen of Holocausts and wars . . . Carried in his box through winding corridors, up redundant liftshafts, stepping aside while robot trucks purr by under the neon lighting, bearing their own sealed cargoes, germ warheads, binary chemical shells, neutron payloads, vanunutons . . . Proceeding by leaps and slithers along the labyrinth, the Quartet, lifting him, hand to hand, up flues, emerging finally in the staff toilets of the Beit Hakerem Supersol, deserted for the holiday. Scurrying past darkened shelves of tinned meats and vegetables, catfood, kitchenware, detergents, coffee and tea, tinned humus and orange squash, imported cornflakes, home-made cheeses, Emek, Regev, Adama . . . Breaking the lock of the emergency exit and out into the spring air, at the closest point to his objective, up the hill ahead of him – Mount Herzl, the national shrine – just as –

BANZAI!

Across town, by the German Colony district, at the cul-de-sac of Yordei Hasira Street, back of Number 32, Bustanai, the dogged trackers of the Department of Apocalyptic Affairs (Tolstoy, Istiqlal, Young Kazha and Gruzini Cholera) in their asbestos suits and breathing masks, wielding their reinforced nets and tranquillizer darts, their little brushes and pans, finally corner their prey, up against the apartment block garbage cans, trapped in the detritus of municipal tree surgeons – achieving their own grand apotheosis: the live capture of the Rabid Sheep . . .

Drugged, trussed and borne down Mishmar Ha'am – The Guard of the People Street – in triumph, and then driven off, horns blaring, down Palmah, President's Street, and Ze'ev Jabotinsky, opposite the panorama of Mount Zion, in the Department's old battered Volkswagen van marked 'Moch, the Good Laundry' . . .

All aboard, for Independence Day!

Stock perversions at the Swallow-Don't-Chew.

'GOOD GOD! IT'S THOSE TWO AGAIN! ONLY NOW THEY'RE THREE! CAN'T YOU GO RUIN SOMEONE ELSE?'

'Avram, you remember Amnon, my old partner from Bridge Publications . . .'

'Haven't seen you for a long time, Avram . . . Have you been abroad somewhere?'

'The man has been hob-nobbing with the forces of Law and Order. Literally in bed, would you believe it. Three humus with ful, Ezra.'

'TWO DOLLARS COVER CHARGE FOR YOU LOT. NO SHEKELS OR YUGOSLAVIAN DINARS!'

'Your trousers are at half mast, Ezra; is it for Remembrance Day?'

'WHO ALLOWED THIS MAN TO SPIT ON THE FLAG?'

'It's kosher Jewish spit, Ezra.'

'!!??★★!???!!'

'This place is getting really desperate. A man returns from serving his country in the boondocks and what does he get? Lousy service in restaurants, his girl friend absent again, no candle in the window, and his oldest friend jumping ship. What's with you, Avram? I thought you were keeping an eye on our Esther. Yesterday you were head over heels in love with her. Then you dump her for Mrs Kojak. The day before it was that German chick, Ilse. What the fuck happened to her?'

'She's probably in the Schleswig-Holstein Parliament by now, for what's-its-name, the Green Party.'

'You can't found a Jewish planet with alien shiksas! But what happened to old-fashioned loyalty? Goddamit! The whole country's out to lunch. Mark my words, something terrible is about to happen. Sometimes I feel, Avram, that you never left the madhouse, and we're all living inside your head. Or maybe the Fatah has dumped LSD in the water supply. God alone knows.'

'THREE HUMUS WITH FUL, *HEVREH!* YOU'VE GOT EXACTLY FIVE MINUTES! I HAVE A HUNGRY QUEUE OUTSIDE.'

'Have you heard,' said Amnon, 'they're going to go ahead with the state burial of those skeletons they dug up in the caves. The Bar-Kokhba warriors. It's official. They're also planning a TV miniseries.'

'*Allahu akbar!* Where is this magic policewoman of yours, Avram, who grows hair on barren heads? Just look at this thatch, Amnon, can you believe it? The boy defects to the bourgeoisie and immediately he's thick as Samson. Is this justice?'

'Justice is blindfold,' said Amnon.

'I always thought it was an eye infection. So give, Avram, *nu*, where is our reverse Delilah?'

'She's on duty tonight. Crowd control.'

'Yes, the celebration of Freedom! The night of the hammers, *Sieg heil!* I vote we give the whole shebang a miss. How's your old Fiat, Amnon? The great escape. How about a drive to the Dead Sea?'

'SWALLOW, DON'T CHEW, GENTLEMEN! THE SECOND SHIFT IS WAITING!'

The streets outside filling with revellers, a knot here, a knot there, clustered round the cardboard boxes of the vendors of the plastic Independence Day hammers. The soft flanges at either end, squeaking shrilly as heads are struck in festive joy. The magic inscription on the handle – Martello Musicale; a tradition dating back to the depths of Time, at least to Purim 1969. And several thousand of these expected on the streets tonight, click-clicking in mass cadenza. Homeland tunes blaring through loudspeakers. Accordions. Entertainment platforms. Joy at the founding of the Jewish State, thirty-four years ago . . .

'Why don't we go into the Old City?' said Amnon. 'Lend our ears to the *Zurafa*'s new play . . . remember them, Avram? They have a new text, another original . . . the performances were held back because of the Arab commercial strike, but I hear they're opening tonight at the old High School, just to snub the Zionist holiday . . .'

'Oh no,' said Blok. 'Count me out of this one.' Seeing the looming hand of Lena Khalili.

'I wouldn't worry about your Nablus contretemps, Avram,' Avi hastened to reassure him. 'They don't hold that against you. Except that quiet, suspicious fellow, Salim, and he's left them. 'Zeppelin' Khalid's always asking about you. He says Nablus was the high point of his life. But seriously, it's all under the bridge.'

'We've been thinking of a revival of translated Arab plays,' said Amnon. 'Get our show on the road again. Open a new office . . .'

'I'm not going into the Old City tonight,' Blok said.

Proceeding inevitably, with his two friends, up the road, pushing through the gathering hammer bearers, nik-nik-nik, the plastic locusts, get away from my head, happy holiday! happy holiday! the loudspeakers, yodelee-yodelo! I Once Had A Love So Fair! red wine in little paper cups, open-air kebabs, grilled hearts at Abu Shaul's, coloured lights and paper bunting. Leaving the Jaffa Road and the crowds behind to venture up Helen the Queen Street, past Levy's Steakhouse, Bank Tefahot, the turreted Sergei Building and the Ministry of Agriculture, skirting the remand prison /police station in the old Russian Compound, its small heavily meshed windows set in the moss-grown quarried stone, the lit white façade of the Russian cathedral opposite with its ten green capped domes, '. . . bought by the Russians in 1860, and built up after the Crimean War as a centre for all the pilgrims that flocked to Jerusalem before the revolution . . .' the guidebook says. 'In front of the cathedral a cracked stone column some 12 metres in length has been uncovered. Herod used this area as a quarry and it seems quite possible that the pillar was in the process of preparation for the Temple when the stone split . . .' But Blok's childhood, trickling back into his brain, reminded him it was the finger of Goliath, snapped off and turned to stone . . . as they walked on, down the street of his kindergarten years, with its old stone fence and roomy houses, the very window railings in the ground floor of number – where he had stuck his head, having to have it prised loose by the entire staff of the Voice of Israel Radio, down in the next block . . . spitting into the long vanished matzoh bakery, and Papa Blok, in his Haganah tin hat, reading *Ujkelet*, surrounded by refugees escaping the sporadic fire across the then border with the Hashemite Kingdom of Jordan, only a half kilometre down the road, which they now traversed, into the Street of the Prophets, past the gravelly plot of empty ex-No-Man's-Land, now a car park for trucks and the site of watermelon stalls doubling up as video-watching cafés, Arab youths drowning the revelry of the Jewish City with reruns of American TV movies, War, Horror and Romance, the street opening out on to the Damascus Gate and the splendours of the Old Walls, the great arched portal with its reliefs of patterns and flowers, the ornate battlements decorated with Israeli soldiers on patrol . . . Within the walls, the locust hammers diminishing into the nag of far-off crickets, the blank stone façades and shuttered shops of the Moslem Quarters purveying their usual message: Fuck off Jew, Tripper, Barbarous Occidental Scum. Becoming lost in the narrow alleyways, up against cul-de-sac yards, old iron gates, creaking shutters, barking pariah dogs, the ubiquitous, lurking donkey turds, all the weaponry of the poor . . .

'I did this on LSD once,' said Amnon. 'I'm telling you, you wouldn't believe the half of it . . .'

'Don't try us, Amnonke.'

'Well, perhaps another time.'

They pressed on, meandering in spirals, in search of the performing arts . . .

★

. . . While the Reverend Hechler, sloshing in his sealed box, is carried on by his four Assyrian bearers, out of the Beit Hakerem Supersol, into Denmark Square with its strange monument of a jagged iron boat, braving the small knot of local revellers striking their plastic Independence Day hammers on their stoic, broad foreheads – 'Hey, Moishe, watcha got in that box? rotten eggs?' – crossing the traffic lights of Herzl Avenue, past the Flower Shop, the eight storey buildings of Yefe Nof, the Sonol petrol station with its graffiti hailing the Jerusalem Hapoel football team, up the hill with its weed-grown verges sloping down towards the Jerusalem Forest, the night smell of spring pine, the bearers' feet

crunching torn cartons and broken Cola bottles, approaching the
turnoff to the Military Cemetery (its denizens all kibitzing
tonight) –

'Slow down! Slow down, Goddamit! We don't want to catch
the ceremony!'

Indeed not: the lighting of twelve immense torches on the parade
ground at the top of Mount Herzl: the gravel summit leading to
the granite Tomb of the Founder, ringed by flower bushes and a
low iron chain. On a makeshift podium the President and the
Chief Rabbi of the Armed Forces wrapping up their official
speeches sealing the Day of Remembrance and opening the
Independence spree:

'Thirty-four years of the Full Sovereignty of the Jewish People
in its Own Land . . .' .

> (INDEPENDENCE: the state of being independent – not
> dependent or relying on others: not subordinate: completely
> self-governing: thinking or acting for oneself: too self-
> respecting to accept help: [*math.*]: not depending on another
> for its value, said of a quantity or function: [*Chambers
> Dictionary*])

Twelve youths, representatives of the ingathered communities of
Israel, light the torches with petrol-soaked brands. The assembled
dignitaries and invited guests rise to render the National Anthem.
A minion whispers in the PM's ear, at this apotheotic moment, the
good news of the Rabid Sheep's capture. The Leader is wreathed
in smiles. He breaks out in song. 'TO BE A FREE NATION!'
Fireworks erupt from the lee of the Founder's Tomb, dazzling
colour in the sky. Hechler's bearers, having put down their burden
by the Military Cemetery, a couple of hundred yards off, watch
the show.

'Asargelusha! Trojan fizzigigs!'
Hechler slithers in his box.

Meanwhile, back in 35 Hageffen Street, across the way from
Blok's abandoned apartment, the ants making hay, Adolphe,
locked out, venting his fury at the dustbins, up on the third floor of

Entrance D, Flat 5, the Situationist Basuto, long reduced to the ignominy of his one-man fraction, performed the final act of revolutionary purity by hanging himself in his apartment. He had purchased a rope the previous day from Malachi's hardware store round the corner, and had tied it to a bracket he had screwed into the ceiling with an electric drill borrowed from Shemesh of Flat 1, below, saying: 'Just a couple of holes, Shemesh. I have to put in a new cabinet.'

'Don't we all,' dryly observed Shemesh, who, though a Likud voter in '77 and '81, had grown disillusioned with the Begin government. The Russian immigrant, Arkadi, in Flat 7 above him, stamped on the floor indignantly as Basuto plied the drill. He climbed on an armchair and placed the rope round his neck, following the meticulous illustrations in a juvenile encyclopedia in the entry on Scouts' knots. On his black and white television the Mount Herzl ceremony was approaching perihelion. The torches of Remembrance had been lit by the representatives of the Dispersion – Europe, North Africa, Yemen, America, Russia. The President expressed his thanks to History and the Nation. The rest of the night's viewing was to consist of:

> 20.00: Chamber concert with Pnina Zaltsman and Uzi Wiesel.
> 20.30: Message of the Prime Minister for the Day of Independence.
> 21.00: 'Entertainment Stage.' With Yehoram Gaon, the Peace '82 Ensemble, the Givatron Group and two hundred dancers of 'Tsavta' from across the country. A special show for Independence Day featuring Israeli folk songs and dances.
> 22.45: Feature Film: *Cast a Giant Shadow*, with Kirk Douglas as the Jewish American soldier who fights for the Hebrew cause in the War of Independence of 1948. Also starring John Wayne, Yul Brynner, Frank Sinatra, Senta Berger and Topol.
> 01.00: Biblical verse of the day and News summary.

'I therefore announce the Day of Mourning over, and the Day of Joy commenced.' The President raised his hands. The sirens blasted. Basuto leapt off his armchair. Upon the still live television set he had left a pile of unpaid telephone, water and electricity bills, his Final Tract on Revisionist Mandelism and the following itemized note:

1. IN THE BEGINNING WAS THE IDEA. IN THE END WAS THE IDEOLOGUE.
2. I AM NOT A HUMAN BEING! I AM A REAL NUMBER! (The Prisoner, episode post hoc.)
3. WHO ARE WE? STALE CLAY. WHAT ARE WE? THE VANISHING INDIVIDUAL.
4. THE CARAVAN BARKS, BUT THE DOG MOVES ON.
5. To my parents: apologies for the sorrow. I know you cannot keep the Rabbis' hands off my body. This doesn't matter, as we become void. I would like the anthem of the Spanish anarchists to be sung at some stage over my grave. A tape or cassette recording will do. I know I have been a disappointment to you, but I had to go my own way. I consider that I have snatched a victory from the jaws of defeat: that I have never been co-opted.
6. To Daniela: I love you, but the IDEA is stronger. I am leaving as THEY proclaim their 'Independence'. I know you will understand but not accept this. I bow to your comradely critique. I bequeath all my books to an auction in aid of orphans of IDF reprisal raids.
7. DEATH TO IMPERIALISM, STATISM AND THE HIERARCHICAL DOMINATION OF MAN OVER MAN (AND WOMAN).

He also left on the pile a top copy of a film script, which he had submitted, under an assumed name, to Kokashvili's company, a 'satirical' Western with the Arabs as cowboys and the Jews as Indians, and which had been returned with a reader's note stating:
    'A strange mélange of Andrew V. MacLaglen and early Mexican Buñuel, with a touch of Jodorovsky at his worst. Signed, A.B.' to which a scribble had been appended:
    'Who the hell is Jodorovsky?? Y.'

★

265

'What can I tell you, Avram? You should have been there when the town was punched into the ground. It was like one of those third-rate Hollywood Bible epics, but where the hell was Victor Mature? With the jawbone of an ass they slew ten thousand homes . . . Why do we do this to ourselves? People hear the word "Peace" and go wild with panic. They have a need for instability. It's a psychiatric problem, dammit. An inbred need to be abnormal.'

Sitting on the battlements for a joint produced by Amnon from an innocent pack of Marlboro. Ahead of them the pale ghost of the Mount of Olives and Augusta Victoria, under the night sky's moon.

'Was it like this in our youth? Or did we just not notice? The short-trousered hikes, the pirates in the cesspool, the endless nagging at the groin. Don't tell me you remember none of that, Avram. You know what? I believe with you it's all a pose. But as you know, you can't blank out the Terror. It will still trickle through the pores. The hell with the Good Old Days. The fucking present's all we have. You know things are really over between me and Esther. She's balling the boy saint now. Before it was the hermit of Ein Karem, and he was having it off with half the Arab boys of the City. Talk of fraternity and solidarity. We're all recycling the same germs. But we carry on, somehow, in that apartment. At least you took that cat off our hands. You have to laugh sometimes when you see what God handed out. Not that I'm acknowledging the bastard.'

'Who do you think killed the hermit?' asked Amnon.

'I would like it to have been that bastard Levine. But it was not his style. He's clean there. No, it was some random maniac, who hated strangers. That's our speciality. Kill the nigger, even if he's yourself.'

'We'll miss the show.' Amnon managed a glance at his watch. They climbed down the walls and back in the labyrinth. But when they eventually reached the site of the Khalidiyah High School they found it shut, with two policemen standing guard and a small knot of people in the road. One of them, a small tubby familiar figure, darted over and gave Blok a hug.

'Ibrahim! It's really good to see you! Where have been all this time?'

266

'Here, there. Where the wind blows.'

'The wind, this place, is always ill,' said 'Zeppelin' Khalid. 'As you can see, we've been cancelled again. Theatre closed because of "fire regulations". They didn't like us performing on their "national" day. There was a bit of a row. The police came. They arrested Salah, Yassir and Mouna Elias. She kicked a police-woman on the shin. I think they're in the Moscobia.'

'That's the Russian Compound,' Amnon explained the local argot to Blok. 'A fucking scandal.'

'Normal procedure,' said Khalid. 'Latif and Ali have gone looking for the lawyer. He's probably celebrating his "Inde-pendence". But they should be out by tomorrow. Remember, Ibrahim,' he clapped Blok on the shoulder, 'when we were all stopped in Beit Jalah? We smuggled you out through a wine cellar, didn't we? Or was that at Tulkarm?'

They found themselves sitting on cushions in his apartment, around the corner, whitewashed stone, old posters, knickknacks, cuttings. The ubiquitous porter carrying Jerusalem, frozen silent on the wall. A bottle of Johnny Walker to match Amnon's hidden joints. Rapping on old times. Oh, that night in Nablus, Ibrahim . . . ! A legend . . . the Hand of Lena Khalili . . . ! Hearts broken like matchsticks, Ibrahim . . . you know she rejoined her family, then crossed to Amman, something she had planned a long time. Not your fault, Ibrahim, she hated all this here, provincialism, self-pity . . . some say she's joined the Armed Struggle . . . the blowing wind, eh? Liberation! Which one of us will live to see that? When a person can be judged as a person, not a thing or a giraffe? When will we be free, eh, comrades? You, Jews, give me the answer, I dare you! Do *you* have this INDEPENDENCE, this plastic hammer in your hand? Are you free? tell me true!

Freer than you, Khalid.

And you, Ibrahim?

Another drink, I'll tell you.

Independence? Fuck my arse!

Liberation? Fuck my arse!

Equality? Fraternity? Fuck all their arses!

Peace? do me a fucking favour . . .

Amnon: You have to believe in something . . .

267

– This bottle! This piss-coloured liquid! This is my God, today!

– That's what they want you to think, that Peace is a pipe dream . . . but if the political context forces their hand . . . they gave the Sinai back to Egypt, didn't they, despite all the kicking and screaming . . .

– Yes, and they'll give the Himalayas back to Nepal, and the Andes back to Peru, and the Kalahari back to the little bushmen, but Palestine, my foster brother? Palestine, eh, tell me, will you return that?

PALESTINE!

PALESTINE!

Bouncing echoes fill the room, ricocheting off the bowed porter, the old Arab saddlebag, the mop stuck in a bucket in the corner, the creaky shelf of half a dozen books and little piles of magazines, the cracked tiles, the old stone walls, escaping out of the small arched window, through the mosquito netting, out over the cupolas, washing lines and spires and maze of TV aerials, leaping like the *buraq* over the Temple Mount, the Haram, the great golden and silver domes. Palestine!! Palestine!! A mother calls for a lost child . . . Go to missing persons, *ya umma!* the baby's gone with the bathwater . . . gurgling down there under the earth: BALESTINE!! BALESTINE!! The wraith of Anwar el-Sadat shaking his gory head: I tried to do my best, brothers, but they shot me full of holes . . . 'Zeppelin' Khalid chases him out of the room, with a broomstick . . . he vanishes, wisping and whirling over the cupolas, wailing:

Always wear a bullet broof vest!

Palestine!!

Palestine!!

Bouncing back from the Mount of Olives, across the Valley, Gei Ben Hinnom, Gehenna, to Abu Tor, Bak'a, the Valley of Ghosts Road, leaping over the YMCA and the King David Hotel (just that little piece left undone in the corner!) the banks, shops, supermarkets, art galleries, souvenir emporiums, sneaking round the perimeter of Mea Shearim, touching Mekor Baruch and Hageffen Street, where Tolstoy was beginning to be suspicious about the full blast of the Prime Minister's speech to the Nation on Basuto's television, a clear sign of something gone awry, causing him, against his professional judgement, to climb the stairs to the door of Flat Number 5 and rap nervously on the door. 'Mister Basuto, are you all right?'

Palestine!

Palestine!!!!!!!!!!!!

. . . The last sparks of the fireworks waning, the cleaners moving in on the parade ground, the guests and VIPs scattered, official limousines and Egged buses rolling down Herzl Avenue. The Reverend Hechler's bearers carry him round the back of the hill, skirting the Military Cemetery, up past the Tombs of the Presidents of Zionist Organizations and those of the Founder's family, over the iron chain and the flowerbeds right to the black granite sarcophagus, its plain rectangle marked only with the great visionary's name in Hebrew, thus:

הרצל

Moving swiftly and stealthily Shangalay, Charapinsk, Yashmak and Barud attach the Hechler box to the Tomb, hard granite to cold metal. Hechler has paid this visit only thrice since the remains of Theodor Herzl were transferred from Vienna to the Jewish State in 1949. From the first he has been aware the Founder stirred continually in his solid lead coffin. Humming old Yiddish tunes, vaguely reciting the text of his unpublished plays, or dictating unwritten essays and missives to long deceased, overthrown, or forgotten world leaders: 'Dear Willie, it is true we failed to reach agreement in our last meeting. However, as Herr Goethe says . . .' 'Dear President Loubet, your immortal name . . .' 'Dear Prime Minister Giolitti, I know you are having troubles in Milan, but . . .' 'Abdul Hamid, *mon cher*, about these so called "Young Turks", I think I have found the solution for you . . .' Between times he simply revolved in his grave, spinning like a top, this way or that. Tonight, however, having been shaken up by the annual fuss, he is sitting up in his sarcophagus, trying to improve, in memory, his backgammon game by recalling his Hoyle: '. . . a leading principle is to "make points" whenever you fairly can, especially in or close to your home table . . . avoid the leaving of "blots", particularly where they are likely to be "hit" by your adversary . . .'

'Pssst!' Hechler whispers, urgently. 'Theodor, it is I, William . . .'

'Get lost,' Herzl says. 'I'm busy.'

'I have very little time,' Hechler whispers. 'I am as close as we are now to the final goal, the true location of the Holy Ark, actual gnosis. But I need clarification on one vital point . . .'

'"There are only three throws,"' Herzl rumbles, '"that will enable the adversary to hit the blot, and your next throw will in all probability enable you to place it beyond the reach of danger . . ."'

'For the love of God, man,' pleads Hechler, 'for the Love of Zion, of Our Cause . . . My time is almost up, the pre-death hypnosis will wear out in the shortest time . . . I shall return to dust and ashes . . . the entire venture lost . . .'

'". . . to avoid this, some, for a hit, play one man from the same point to the deuce . . . but the bolder play is to be preferred . . ."'

'For the love of Truth, Theodor!!!'

★

The neighbours cut down Basuto's body, placing it on the old run-down sofa which had played host to so many verbal contributions to the debate on correct theory – Shemesh of Flat 1, Cohen-Deshen, the fan of the Jordan TV Hebrew News, Kushnir, the retired writer of Flat 4 and Arkadi, the New Russian immigrant who had stamped on the ceiling while Basuto prepared his exit. And Tolstoy, looking grave and self-possessed as he slid about the apartment professionally noting its contents, taking charge of the script, essay file and note which had been left on the TV, leaving the unpaid bills untouched. Neighbours from other entrances also ingathered: the House Committee members, Kishonski of Entrance C, Flat 5, Kimchi of Flat 2, the Chairman, Kadurie, the widow Tishbi, clucking like a crucified hen, the grand bulk of Mrs Almoshnino with her husband peering round her smock.

'If only I hadn't loaned him the drill . . .' Shemesh twisted in his self-reproach. 'How was I to know what he would do with it?'

'He was always a strange boy,' Kimchi said.

'Will somebody switch off that damn TV . . . ?'

270

'BRING OUT YOUR DEAD!'

Old tin cans and empty whisky bottles rapped against the cool stone wall of the Russian Compound perimeter.

'Amnesty! Amnesty!'

'Free the prisoners!'

'Shush! people will know we're drunk,' said Amnon.

'Have you ever seen a drunk Jew?' Avi croaked. 'Everyone knows we're famous for not being able to cut it – one glass of carrot juice and we're wobbling.'

'More carrot juice!' cried 'Zeppelin' Khalid.

Blok struck the remand prison walls with his Independence Day hammer. 'Open Sesame! First time round Jericho! Toot! Toot! Toot!'

'Most of the remand cells are in the inside . . .' said Amnon, pointing to the heavily meshed windows set in the old stone walls. 'These are just offices . . . but I'm not going in there . . .'

'Follow me!' said Avi, staggering towards the gateway. Rounding the entrance into the Compound, they assaulted every available wall, fence post and parked car, rapping on the door of the Russian cathedral. 'Come out, Rasputin! All is forgiven!' Khalid, trying to sing 'God Save the Queen' by the closed entrance to the Hall of Heroism with its unused British gallows, preserved to educate the young, switched to the Palestinian *Biladi! Biladi!* as they passed the Supreme Court building, back down into Jaffa Road, round the WIZO souvenir shop and the Union Bank, second time round the walls, bang, bang, click, click, in the gate, right up to the deserted entrance of the police station.

'What the hell? What sort of a country . . . ? Man can't even get arrested . . .'

Ribald voices from within, beyond the desk sergeant rapping with three other colleagues at his post and a pickpocket who was nursing a paper cup of red wine. A cop waves at Blok:

'Hey! Remember me? Amikam. You'll find Shuli through there . . .' waving them on into an anteroom decked with bunting and flags, portraits of President Navon, peeling traffic code posters, Fight Crime! an ad for Yosher Osher's Police Benefit, Prime Minister Begin, Elvis Presley, coloured balloons, cigarette smoke, sweet smell of *Kiddush* wine, sweaty bodies in pressed uniform, crisps crunched underfoot, the buzz of post-midnight coptalk:

. . . I tell you the man just slipped . . . he would have gone under . . . the whole crossing was jam packed . . . so often in Latin America . . . life is getting just as cheap here . . . back in Bulgaria . . . over the hill . . . retirement pension . . . double mortgage, triple loan . . . a good handlock on his foot . . . how's our Sherlock Holmes then, Kandide? . . . right there on the fucking clothesline . . . a very similar case in Austria . . . a row of torsos, fished out of a lake . . . two videocassette recorders . . . a whole fistful of his hair, man . . . unsolved murders . . . Chaim Arlosoroff . . . let's face it, everything's running down . . . so I told her, not with me, honey, that's not my truncheon, girl . . . is that somebody singing in the cells? . . . quadruple interest savings fund . . . Hey, Shuli, your boyfriend's here! . . . spot margins on the yen . . . so I tried a Boston Crab on him . . . commodity spot margins . . . what on earth are you doing here, Avram? Oh my God, you're stoned as shit . . . will somebody shut up that remand cell crooning . . . *Biladi! Biladi!* . . . wait a minute, Avram, don't go down there . . . hey *hevreh*, this is an off duty party, don't spoil it, for God's sake . . . Salah! Yassir! . . . this way, comrades! . . . Palestine! . . . hey, you there, where you going . . . ? Avram, please . . . Is that you in there, Yassir! Khalid! did they get you too? . . . Stand by for your Entebbe rescue, comrades! . . . who the fuck has the keys . . . Avram, this is getting stupid . . . sorry, *hevreh*, you can't go in here . . . listen, I'm speaking to you nicely . . . let's not spoil a festive day . . . *Biladi! Biladi!* . . . I'm asking you again, sir, back off . . . shit! fuck . . . aargh! . . . get the bastard! piss . . . ! Oh my God, Avram! Tuvia, you know him, do something . . . calm down now, All Israel Are Brothers! Ow! shit! sister's cunt . . . ! Reinforcements! Mad Jew! Mad Jew! Mad Jew! –

The flotsam of the day's night, along the Jaffa Road, eight pm, none but the Arab street sweepers among the torn paper-chains, squashed cigarette packets, matchboxes, smashed light-bulbs, discarded plastic hammers, ten thousand paper cups, gunged remains of kebab and chicken legs, gnawed to the bone, hard pitta shreds and rotting green salad. Cats wandering stunned amid the inexplicable mounds of manna. An Arab sweeper extracts a whistle from the pile and blows it melancholily. Strung in twos along the pavement – Blok and Shuli, Avi with Esther, called in by Shuli in the small hours, *punkt* on her return from another southern sojourn, Amnon trailing in the rear.

'What do you want, Avram? I don't understand. I thought you were completely uninvolved. But God help us, what did you think you were all doing, going in there stoned flat . . . I know you smoked it all, but they could have found the grains on you, probably all over your clothes . . . God, you were lucky Tuvia and me were there, you could have all been in jail for weeks, and your friend, punching Amikam in the stomach, if it was someone else you wouldn't have got off . . . high spirits, drunk on the day, but what did you think you were doing? Were you really going to free the prisoners? What are you, Paul Newman in *Exodus*? It's not that I care what people think of me because of you, I just don't understand at all! Are those your friends? You should have seen them at that school, kicking and hitting the police . . . that girl who got me right in the shin . . . what are we supposed to do? We do our job, that's all. We enforce the Law. Arabs and Jews alike. I have to live in the real world, Avram, I don't make the politics. Their lawyer will get them out anyway, in twenty-four hours.

273

And what sort of name was that you gave the sergeant? Ticho Brahe? What sort of shit is that?'

'I just said what came into my head.'

'Your head ought to be boiled in oil.'

'Butter me and put me in the oven,' he said.

But he was at least spared that. Staggering alone up the road to 35 Hageffen Street to find a small knot of neighbours standing like onlookers of a spent fire at the portals of Entrance D. 'The student has committed suicide,' Kimchi informed him. 'The *hevra kadisha* have already been.' Indeed, the religious Burial Society had taken away Basuto's corpse, just after midnight, in their deep blue van inscribed: GATES OF HEAVEN: JUSTICE WILL WALK BE-FORE HIM. 'That poor boy . . . so young . . . a terrible tragedy . . .' Mrs Tishbi shook her head at Blok. But the ex-merchant seaman Sirkin took his arm: 'Don't listen to them. They're a bunch of hypocrites. They would have hung him themselves if they could. Who can blame an idealistic youth for despairing in these days?' Who indeed. 'But are you all right, Mister Blok? You look as if you've had a hard night. Can I get you a good Turkish coffee? One skill at least I've preserved from floating around the world . . . I fed your cat, by the way. It was raising hell at your door. Elrom almost took a spade to him. Well, any time, any time. I'll tell you my story – it's the saddest thing you'll ever hear . . .'

The arrival of a tearful Mrs Basuto, abandoned mother, her face covered with a handkerchief, at the house, ushered upstairs by the phalanx of busybodies as Blok watched from his window. Sinking back into post-scandal routine: nagging Adolphe, the invading ants who discovered a new highway to the kitchen – round the back of the old lumber on the balcony in through a crack in the high windowframe, down to the kitchen cabinets with their condensed milk and honey. Ah! the promised lands! Even Adolphe can't get at them this way, the black beast of Amalek . . . Blok devastates them with Baygon powder, watching them scat-ter, down, up the walls, back into the old cartons, fruit crates, rusted tin cans, shaking their mandibles stubbornly: plenty more where we came from! Adolphe, sneezing from the swirl of poison dust. Retching and running to the door. Human swine! I'll get you yet! Ducking the stones of the Almoshnino offspring in the yard:

'There goes that ugly pussycat again!' 'You missed him! You missed him!' 'No, I didn't!' No compassion here for the fallen of life's battles. No sanctity for holy days . . .

As the anniversary passes, April fades into May, again the days of Counting of the Omer, bringing in the sheaves, the bonfire night of the 33rd day thereof, the dancing devout, linking hands, THIS IS THE GATEWAY TO THE LORD, THE RIGHT-EOUS SHALL PASS THROUGH IT, the State burial of the Bar-Kokhba skeletons finally taking place in the Judaean desert, army buglers and the last trump, through to the Festival of Pentecost, *Shavuot,* marking God's gift of the Torah to Moses, Blok, waking to the dawn chant, dwarfing FRUITS FRUITS and the Vespa and Mrs Almoshnino's foghorn, of a phalanx of wor-shippers, seventy strong, proceeding up the Street of the Vine wrapped in prayer shawls, returning from all-night prayers, bouncing their war cry off the apartment block walls, scattering early morning slugs and caterpillars and dumbfounding the cats in the garbage skips, causing the trees and the shrubs to sway to the repetitious chant of God's Name:

'YAH-YAH-YAH YAH-YAH-YAH, YAH-YAH-YAH-YAH YAH-YAH-YAH!
YAH YAH YAH-YAH-YAH, YAH-YAH-YAH-YAH YAH-YAH-YAH!
YAH-YAH-YAH YAH-YAH-YAH, YAH-YAH-YAH-YAH YAH-YAH-YAH!
YAH YAH YAH-YAH-YAH, YAH-YAH-YAH-YAH
YAH-YAH-YAH . . . !'

After they passed, a soft calm descended, broken slowly by trucks and armoured cars revving in the Schneller barracks across the Kings of Israel Road. A sound which raised no particular qualms in the post-panic days following the return of the Rafah Gap to Egypt. An air of crisis abated, return to the semi-normality of small time *Sturm und Drang*:

SOLDIER FIRES SHOTS FROM JERUSALEM HOME

Said to be distraught at the absence of his dog, a soldier on leave yesterday fired several shots from his M-16 assault rifle from the second storey balcony of his home in Jerusalem's

275

Nahlaot neighbourhood before surrendering to police 20 minutes later. No one was hurt. The suspect in the shooting was charged three years ago with stealing a firearm from a car. He then escaped from jail and climbed a supermarket roof and threatened to kill himself. He was persuaded not to do so by police Staff-Sergeant Reuven Mizrahi, who also persuaded him yesterday to surrender.

NAKED SWORDSMAN STARTLES OLD CITY (May 12, 1982)

A naked man brandishing a long sword ran through Jerusalem's Old City market yesterday, scattering passers-by and shouting, 'God lied to me.' Police say the man, a 34 year old US tourist, began his escapade in a shop where he was purchasing the sword. When the shopkeeper asked $800 for the blade, the tourist stripped off his clothes, grabbed the sword and ran off down the street . . . A Border Police patrol caught up with him and managed to restrain him after a short struggle, in which no one was reported injured. He was taken into custody wrapped in a keffiyeh donated by an onlooker.

'So what do you expect Avram?' Yissachar bawls down the phone at him. 'You played with the matches of the dispossessed again and got burned. I thought you'd learned your lesson. What profiteth a man if he gaineth the whole world but loseth his immortal ass? Harken, rather, to the voice of tinkling cash: I have set up this truly crazy freelance deal. Don't ring off when I tell you: it's a wedding. But don't misunderstand, comrade – this is the Big Time, no Kodak Brownie bukisriki. Do you know what people pay for video nuptials now? There's this big do, in Herzliya: the daughter of our biggest armaments dealer is marrying the son of our greatest Rabbinical scholar. Everyone but everyone will be there. All the leaders, public and hidden, of the Nation. From the head of Mossad down to the PM. An entertainment platform. All the chicken legs you can eat. So wha'd'yousay, Avram? Will you come and do sound for me? Just like the old days? Holyland Films? You still don't remember . . . Whad'youmean, No? I thought you were game for action! Snap out of it, schmendrick! this is real

276

money! don't slip back into your bad old "moral" ways! If we don't do it, someone else will!'

And Avi, equally perturbed down the blower: 'What's that, Avram? the girl denies everything. She says her play with the boy saint is platonic! She's helping him overcome his fear of inheriting the responsibilities of his daddy when the old magus finally goes. People will expect poor Ya'akov to heal the sick, tell fortunes, make the blind see, the lame win the Olympics. The laying on of hands, cholera! Just let him try that shit with me! How about that laying on at the police station? God, I enjoyed that hands-on experience! Even if they did all jump on me afterwards. You have to fight back sometimes, dammit! They can still charge me if they fucking please . . . But how are you and the policewoman? You know she and Esther have become quite pally. They meet in coffee shops and welfare centres. Discussing the horrors of the male of the species, you and me. Not the miracle worker, no! He's all right, a sensitive soul, a real caring person! Can you believe it?! Everyone's gone mad in this country. Did you read this morning in *Ha'aretz*? Some geek in the Jewish Agency has published his plans for the future of the Area: we shouldn't be striving for peace, because that's an illusion, we should go to war to overthrow the whole applecart: re-conquer the Sinai, dismember Egypt and set up a Christian Coptic State there; split up Syria between the Alawis, Sunni and Druse; tip over the Lebanese domino, conquer Iraq and split her into city-states around Baghdad, Basra, and Mosul. The whole Arab world is just a tower of cards which a mere flick of the toe will bring down. And this garbage is put out in an official journal of the World Zionist Organization. Listen to me, Avram – don't be lulled into a false confidence: the shit is really going to hit the fan!'

RESERVE OFFICERS TELL OF ARMY 'BRUTALITY' IN AREAS:

Six reserve army officers who recently completed service in the [occupied] territories yesterday charged that the government's policies were resulting in IDF brutality, trigger-happy reactions and indiscriminate collective punishments. The six stressed that while public attention was roused by specific sensational events, 'the daily reality in the territories is one of violence and brutality.' . . . The Defence Ministry spokesman said last night that Peace Now was trying to make political capital out of the IDF soldiers, but said their allegations would be investigated. Earlier in the day unnamed Defence Ministry sources had dismissed the officers' charges as 'groundless' . . .

MASS EXPORTS OF THE NEW 'UZZI' PISTOL WILL COMMENCE SHORTLY,

reports the Army magazine 'B—h'; the weight of the new 'Uzzi' is two kilos, thus giving it good stability; it can fire 9mm bullets, in magazines of 20, 25 or 32 shells; the Military Industries' spokesman said it is hoped to repeat the great success in world sales of the other members of the 'Uzzi family' . . .

Ah! the mundane, rolling on! Today's temperatures: hot and dry. No change expected: Jerusalem: 18–29, Tel Aviv: 20–30; Haifa: 16–28; Beersheba: 23–32; Gaza Strip: 20–31; Eilat: 22–34; Golan Heights: 17–29; (the Sinai is no longer with us) . . .

Warnings of drought. A headless corpse, seen walking in Ein Karem in broad daylight, no clouds obscuring the sun. Rumours of quiet agreement, in the PM's Kitchen Cabinet, among the jars of jam and olive oil. Shuli sees Blok but does not bed him for the moment. Esther is busy with social welfare appeals. Tolstoy is busy, debriefing the Rabid Sheep, which has begun speaking in tongues, deep beneath Mittag's Café, purveying the juiciest of information to the massed Intelligence Chiefs of the Land. To cap it all, on a hot Saturday, the merchant seaman Sirkin finally corners Blok, on the pretext of borrowing an Eshed yoghourt, and relates to him his long promised saga, the saddest story he has ever heard:

THE MERCHANT
SEAMAN'S
TALE

(The Saddest Story Blok Had Ever Heard)

It was in the mid Fifties', you wouldn't remember, you would still have been in short trousers . . . the first years of the State, ah, all that nostalgia . . . but some of us have other memories . . . We had just got over the trauma of the great seamen's strike of 1951, the first painful battle between us Hebrew workers and the Jewish State. Of course, the State won. We lost. But then I travelled all over the world, on an old leaky cargo vessel, the *Berl Katznelson*, sailing under a Panamanian flag. On this particular winter we were cruising down the West African coast, south of the Island of Fernando Po, along the Cameroons and Gabon. Then part of our crew was transferred to a river boat, at the mouth of the Zaire, at Matadi, to pick up a cargo of groundnuts upriver, at the capital, Leopoldville, which is now called Kinshasa . . .

Onwards we ploughed into the depths of the Dark Continent, lulled by the dank, stifling heat of the tropics, inching past the languid forest stretching into the unknown. Strange and disconcerting cries came, day and night, from monkeys, birds and insects in the trees. We were wary of the upriver populace, due to the cryptic advice given us at Matadi: be sure they don't sell you tadpoles! We were at a loss to understand this advice, until, at one of the ramshackle ports we hove in at, several of our crew bought pet monkeys off local pedlars, which died a couple of days later, having been torn from their mothers' arms unweaned, 'tadpoles' in the local parlance. We had to throw the pathetic little corpses overboard into the muddy waters. But I had bought nothing, until we docked at a tiny river settlement whose name I just can't remember, where we disembarked and sat at a tiny café of rotting wood and warm beer. I grew bored and left my companions to wander up the crumbling jetty, to the very edge of the rainforest, where a small, wizened old man beckoned to me from the shadows:

'Come, you want to see good thing!' he said in broken French.

Anything to break the tedium! I followed the old man into the forest, down an almost invisible trail. After one hundred yards I had lost sight of the river or any trace of man. The trees almost obscured the sun. 'Come, good thing, you buy!' said the old man. I held back, but he took my hand. I followed him, sweating and cursing my stupidity, mad images of missionaries in cooking pots floating through my mind. But, suddenly, we emerged into a clearing, facing a small hut of reeds and branches. 'Come! See!' said the old man, 'you not see better thing anywhere!'

My eyes adjusted slowly to the darkness inside the hut, and I saw a shape moving strangely on a creaking wicker rocking chair. A red ember glowed in the shadows. The old man removed a reed shutter, and there in the low filtered daylight was a chimpanzee, the size of a large child, rocking lazily and smoking an immense cigar.

'Is good, no?' said the old man. 'Only fifty francs, Monsieur! You do not buy him, people eat him. They say he *maphula-mbembe*, bad spirit, they cook and eat, burn brain. I beg you, he is like my son.'

The beast ambled over and took my hand, pulling me itself out of the hut. As if by pre-arrangement with the old man it led me back along the path to the river. There it tugged my arm to squat beside it and passed me the still lit cigar. It had a strange air of serenity, and, also, a great melancholy, that despite my rationality pierced my heart. We smoked, in turns, for a while, and when I started up to look around me the old man was nowhere to be seen. I left fifty francs with the café owner and departed on the river boat, with the ape. My fellow crew members adopted him as their mascot, naming him Winston, for the cigar, and keeping him supplied with cigarettes when the cigar was done, as he sat, aboard the *Berl Katznelson*, upon the deck or bridge, smoking peacefully as he gazed out towards the Atlantic waves . . .

What could I do? We had become inseparable. In Dakar, Lisbon, Naples, Athens, we walked about hand in hand. He sat with me in cafés in Aristotelous Street sipping coffee, ouzo. He had a certain knack of communication, waiters served him as just another customer, young ladies gave him their seat on the bus, and building workers called to him: Hey, Papagos! from their high girders. But at Haifa port, the customs officers rudely shattered my dream. You can't bring this animal into the country, monkeys belong in the zoo. They took him away and stuck him in a wooden cage, where he sat for several days cadging cigarettes and pitta sandwiches off the stevedores. A week later they came with a truck and hauled him off to the Haifa City Zoo, where he stayed for three months, delighting the children and gazing sadly at the adults. I was allowed to visit him when I wished, and on Sabbaths, when the Zoo was closed, they even allowed him out with me for a walk within the closed walls. But the zoo keepers did not allow him to smoke, they said it was an abuse of his nature. Nevertheless, on our walks, we would hide under a tree, puffing on the Ritmeesters I brought him like two furtive schoolboys. I decided to take a rest from the sea, and I took a job a friend had offered me in a garage by the Tel Aviv beach. But I could not leave Winston behind, so, one night, I broke into his cage and stole him.

For one full year I was able to live happily with Winston in Tel Aviv. The zoo keeper at Haifa had guessed what had happened but did me a good turn: he told the police the ape had broken out by itself, and they hunted it for some weeks round the Carmel with nets and tranquillizing darts. Then the story died. Winston helped me in the garage, holding wrenches and spanners, keeping his distance from any petrol when he lighted up. Everyone helped me to keep the secret, such as it was. The local policeman was a friend, those were more easy-going days, no one hassled you if you kept your head down. Winston was a perfect gentleman of the old wharfs, sitting on the stone jetties, looking out to sea, with a cigar whenever we could afford one. I would cook at home, he washed up. He never broke a plate or cup. We slept in separate beds, but spoke to each other, in our thoughts, in the small hours. We lived life for the moment. It was my happiest time.

But happiness does not last, my friend. Suddenly politics, armies, war. The Sinai crisis, Abdul Nasser, Egypt, Britain, France. You were in short trousers then. Now we're immune to the whole schmeer. The siren goes, we rush to the shelters. The soldiers go out, they come back, or don't. I did my stint in '48, but the hell with that. In '56 they called me up for Civil Defence. I went round with a tin helmet and torch, shouting at people to put their lights out. Coming back home in the small hours to find that small, tell-tale red ember glowing in my ground floor window. One thing I could not make Winston understand was the blackout. He lit cigarette after cigarette, put on house lights, climbed about on streetlamps trying to screw in new bulbs. It's a war, Winston, I told him, sadly, boom, boom, falling down dead. Legs chopped off. Men blinded. Women crying. Babies orphaned. But he just grunted and presented me with a flea he'd just found in his rump. Poor Winston. Or rather poor us. He was just outside it all.

One night I returned home from my beat around Allenby to hear three shots fired in quick succession. I ran, my heart in my mouth, to find three soldiers crouching by my block, rifles at the ready. What's going on? I asked. Someone attacked us, they said, an infiltrator, smoking a cigarette. The nerve of the bastard! I ran into my flat. Winston wasn't there. That's not an infiltrator, I told the soldiers, it's my chimpanzee. He's harmless. You're crazy, their officer said, the bastard tried to strangle me. They brushed me aside and ran off, as trucks roared up, pouring troops on to the beach and Esplanade.

That was how my nightmare began. Can you imagine it? You're a young man, there must be someone in the world you care for. Can you imagine them being hunted down, by soldiers, on trucks, tanks, armoured cars, searchlights, all the modern weapons of death and mutilation – dum-dum bullets, flame-throwers, phosphorous bombs? They would not believe the shadow they were hunting was an ape, a dumb animal with a tobacco habit, who would not hurt a fly . . . The alarm escalated – reports spread of armed guerrillas in the streets, equipped with climbing gear, which they were using to scale walls and set up sniping posts in the city. Helicopters were called in. By dawn the entire coastal plain was in a turmoil. I was at my wit's end. I called in at the central police station, told them about Haifa, begged them to check the old zoo story, but they elbowed me aside: Who cares about your fucking escaped monkey? We have terrorists in the heart of the city! I went home with a heavy stomach and listened to the bulletins on the radio. Sightings reported from every quarter – from Kiryat Shalom, from Bat Yam, from Ramat Gan, Giva-tayim. Wild rumours, that they intended to move on the Capital and attack the Heads of the Government. I went out and walked all over the town, from Ussishkin right into Jaffa. I had a hunch he might have headed to the old fishing port with its old stone houses, its crumbling mosques, its lazy wharfs and jetties. I approached the Arab fishermen who had seen me with him on happier days. But they had not seen Winston and were sunk in their own melancholy. I remember, the sea was so blue and calm that day, oblivious to our pain. The sea, the sea that never cares, that's been here all the time and will roll over our ashes. Robinson Crusoe I was on that day, searching for a missing Friday. And the town was emptying out, of all those who were called up to the war looming in the headlines: ANTHONY EDEN WARNS NASSER: GREAT BRITAIN WILL NOT STAND IDLY BY. EGYPT MASSES TROOPS. And, lower down: INFILTRA-TORS ON THE COASTAL PLAIN: BNEI BRAK NOW UNDER SIEGE. I walked the streets around Allenby – Sheinkin, Bialik, Pinsker, Hess, peeking in the little parks where we used to sit on the old wooden benches, puffing on our cigars, watching the children on the swings. What could I do? I felt the sun go down over the pit of the Mediterranean. Dusk, and an eerie silence. And then the air raid siren. I stayed in the house as people rushed to the underground shelters. Listening to the radio. General call-up codes for the various Reserve units were read out over the airwaves: Red Melon, Empty Bucket, Salted Fish, Clean Hands, One Law, Dried Ashes, Lemon Popsicle, Stewed Prunes. I sat with my head bowed by the crackling wireless set. Life had passed me by. I had made a friend, but lost him to the blind cruelty of fate. Now and again I thought I heard a grunt, and sprang up, but there was no one there. The call-up codes rolled on: Pickled Herring. Damned Spot. Lord of the World. Peeled Banana. Acid Drop. Boiled Porridge. Sweet From the Strong. White as Snow. And then the first tales of battles, the Mitleh pass, Abu Agheila . . . Blood and fire in the desert . . . And then the item I had dreaded. A large ape, which inexplicably appeared in the centre of the city, had been shot dead by a Civil Defence patrol while apparently breaking into a tobacconist's store. Finding no heed taken of three calls to halt, the Civil Defence man, a pensioner named Lorach, had fired low, to hit the robber's legs. Imagine his surprise when he approached cautiously to find a three-feet-high ape, dying on the pavement from a stomach wound, clutching an imported cigar. I did not mean to kill the poor beast, said Lorach, adding: I shall never forget those eyes . . .

'What conclusion do you draw from it all?' Blok asked, politely, when the merchant seaman had finished.

'It is very difficult,' said Sirkin, 'to be an outsider in this country.'

But there was worse to come.

GEI BEN-HINNOM

I have a candle, a candle thin and cute,
Why haven't they packed the reserve parachute?
Because the main chute hasn't opened, as I feared,
And upon the floor I am sure to be smeared.

Parachutist's Hanukkah song,
reported by Daniel Marmari, age 6

'**R**edemption!'

– Kokashvili said to Shabetai Tsvi. 'That, at the end of the day, is the issue. The name of the game, the only game in town. There is only Salvation or Destruction. Either or. One or Zero. Was that not the view the Sages took?'

'But the People?' the False Messiah asked. 'Are they prepared and purified? Is the generation worthy?'

As they sat, chewing *pulkes* from paper plates, overlooking the rising site of the half-built Leisure Centre, poised opposite the walls of the City. All about them papier-mâché flats being hammered into a replica of the Holy Temple, insofar as research could prescribe it. Electricians, painters, carpenters, gofers, rushing about in honest labour.

'There is a risk in every project,' said Kokashvili. 'You have to accept this, Reb Shabetai. If I had waited for the people to be worthy I would still be shining shoes in Tiflis. You have to roll up your sleeves and get to work if you want to shift this stiff-necked nation. If you'll pardon the familiarity, you can't just sit on your arse and wait for the cosmic rearrangements. You did your part in your time, but the people blew it. The result, you died in exile, alone. In Yugoslavia, Goddamit! I wouldn't wish that on a dog. In your day you were too dependent on Shank's Pony. The bush telegraph, the wooden cart with clapped-out nags, sandalled feet, corns and blisters. But we are at the portals of the twenty-first century, *habibi*, the digital age. The flick of a switch that can enlighten people or darken the whole screen . . . Mind you – I retain world rights, whatever the outcome, including subtitled and dubbed versions . . .'

★

289

'Theodor! Theodor! Wake up!'

★

Ring, ring! Ring, ring!
  'Where the fuck are you, Avram? Don't you know the shit has hit the fan?'

★

'DON'T BOTHER ME NOW,' said the Prime Minister. 'I am preparing my apotheosis.'
  A vintage reek arose from the little pot on the primus stove in which this was being stirred . . . (Jasmine, and honeysuckle, and myrrh, and pine, citrus, barley, fresh bagels and turkey schnitzels, blintzes and sour cream, Siberian lice in kasha, gulag farts, stale gaberdine, blood libels and scorched earth and old apfelstrudel, falafel, gun-powder plots and printers' ink, congealing wounds, putrefying corpses, freedom's whiff, blood, toil, tears and sweat, lashings of hot air . . .) The DM, rolling into the Kitchen Cabinet on tank tracks, tasted it with qualified approval. 'A little more paprika,' he suggested. 'Now about this piece of talking mutton . . .'
  (The Rabid Sheep, with its powers of prophecy, having been wrested from the Department of Apocalyptic Affairs, was transferred from the Ministry of Religion to Defence, as the National Interest required. The miracle of its inexplicable survival despite several years of terminal illness compounded by the stream of useful information pouring from its putrescent slobber, expressed mostly in defunct semitic languages – Aramaic, Assyrian, Egyptian, Habiru – although Greek, Latin, High Dutch, Afrikaans and Esperanto were also in partial evidence, ending up with the convenience of modern Hebrew, garnished with the juiciest street slang. A cornucopia, in exegesis, of military and strategic information: troop movements, political alliance options, consequential forecasts, secret clauses of warplans, enemy missile dispositions, systems breakdown, sigint codes.)
  'Ineffable! Marvellous!' cried the DM, 'The Guardian of Israel never sleeps or slumbers!' Procuring the PM's signature on his considered plans, he rolled back out of the Kitchen Cabinet, firing on all cylinders . . .

★

290

'Regrettable interference with the Beace Brocess . . .' Puff, puff, puff . . .

★

From the Situationist Basuto's Last Will and Testament:

> 'NO ONE SHOULD BE ENTRUSTED WITH POWER.'
> 'TRUE LOVE CAN EXIST ONLY AMONG EQUALS.'
> 'FREEDOM IS VALID ONLY WHEN SHARED BY EVERYONE.'
> 'PATRIOTISM HAS ITS ROOTS NOT IN THE HUMANITY
> OF MAN BUT IN HIS BESTIALITY.'
> 'AN EYE FOR AN EYE MAKES US ALL BLIND.'
> 'IDEOLOGY AND SCHIZOPHRENIA – TWO SIDES
> OF THE SAME COIN.'

And, as an epigraph, he had written:

> '"When ideology, having become absolute through the possession of absolute power, changes from partial knowledge into ideological falsehood, the thought of history is so perfectly annihilated that history itself, even at the level of the most empirical knowledge, can no longer exist." (Debord)'

★

THE WAR BEGAN IN LONDON

(Bulletin – 2 am: Israel Ambassador in London Shot
The Israel Ambassador in London was shot last night in front of the Dorchester Hotel here by an assassin who was later identified as an Arab. He was hit three times in his head and upper body and was reported to be in critical condition. His Special Branch bodyguard opened fire and hit the attacker behind his left eye. The Ambassador was first taken to the Westminster Hospital and was later transferred to the National Hospital in Bloomsbury which has sophisticated neurological equipment. Aged 52, the Ambassador has served in London since 1979. He is married and has three children. Latest reports indicate he may not survive the attack.)

– and then seethed in the kitchen of Esther's apartment as Thin Avi blundered about, shaking the table, dislodging salt cellars and paint pots, knocking ceramic garbage off the loose shelves, tearing a poster of the twelve months of the zodiac off the wall and brandishing his Call Up Form Eight. A Sergeant-Major from his unit had brought it to the door, at one thirty pm, Friday, just as they were making ready for a pretence of domestic harmony, a walk to the Jerusalem Cinematheque to see a film by Federico Fellini, the obese Italian cinemaestro, *Giulietta of the Spirits* ('Fantasy mixed with reality: a middle-aged woman discovers the fraud in her marriage and seeks to attain self-consciousness'), Blok, on a rare occasion of general reconciliation, having joined Esther and Avi for this treat.

'What's this?' Avi asked the Regimental Sergeant-Major, whose military nickname was Dipshit Banki.

'They're calling up the unit,' the RSM said. 'That's all that I can say.'

'It's Lebanon, isn't it?' Avi said. 'The Big Banana. The fuckers finally found an excuse.'

'Don't give me politics, please, Avi,' the RSM spread his hands. 'You have a beef with the army, that's your problem.'

'Tell the bastards I'm not coming,' said Avi. 'Let them stick this one you know where.'

'I've done my duty,' said Dipshit Banki, and turned and went down the stairs.

'The hell with them,' shouted Avi. 'I've had that shit up to the eyebrows long enough. Let them find some other dumb bastard to carry their garbage cans. Some other dumb bastard whose picture they can stick on the cover of *Life* Magazine – The Brave Soldier Schweik, saluting the flag. In his death he gave us life! In his wheelchair he gave us another parliamentary term of office! With his one foot he made us stand on both ours. He gave his colon for his country. Let the Goddamn bastards do their own dirty work! If they want to kill Palestinians let them start degutting their gardeners! Let them act out their own fucking perversions! I've hung up my butcher's cleaver! Send the fucking politicians themselves to the frontline with RPGs and full gear!'

'I made the same suggestion ten years ago,' Blok remembered, 'but no one took any notice.'

'If you want to refuse, refuse,' said Esther. 'No one expects you to go this time.' Haven't you given them enough blood? There it is, upon the floor. Oozing through the cracks in the floor tiles, drip, drip, drip into the Friday night couscous of Mrs Danoch downstairs. In five hours, the air raid sirens will usher in the Sabbath, as is their wont, which a little boy on a bicycle used to usher in with a ramshorn, pedalling furiously across the town. TOOT-TOOT! TOOT-TOOT! TOOT-TOOT! The City, no longer alerted by amateurs, but with the full blast of the State.

Esther told him: 'Do what you feel you have to do.'

'You go and have fun, children,' he said. 'I am not in the mood.'

He stayed behind, drained and prostrate on the rolled mattress in her bedroom, smoking a Craven A, while Blok and Esther, leaving him to wrestle with his soul, walked slowly in the sun down the Bethlehem Road towards the Cinematheque in the Valley of Hinnom, Gei Ben-Hinnom, Gehenna, Moloch town, where even King Solomon practised abominations, and after him, King Ahaz made his children pass through the fire, and sacrificed and burnt incense in the high places, and under every green tree, therefore the Lord his God delivered him into the hand of the king of Syria, who smote him, with great slaughter, and later Theodor Herzl, arriving on the Sabbath Eve from Jaffa, had to traverse the Vale by foot, from the Ottoman railway station, cursing and grumbling as he tottered towards the City on his cane, but now, in the defile, the Cinematheque nestles in a rebuilt Arab building, looking out towards the Walls and Mount Zion from the tasteful terrace of its café-restaurant, where the beautiful people, male and female, bask in the aura of clean sun-bronzed limbs, having ordered a Waldorf Salad, or a Warner Brothers Fruit Flambée, or Bogart-Chicken-in-the-Basket.

'What do you want, Avram? They're out of natural juice.' King Josiah finally tamed the Valley. He made it unfit for any religious use by filling it with bones, offal and other rubbish, whereby it became the city's cesspool, latrine and central privy, polluting the River Kidron, chasing it away so that it has not been seen for two whole millennia, rendering the city dry as a dead dingbat, parched and hanging out its tongue.

'A Kinli will do for me,' cries Avram. 'I can't stand that natural stuff anyway.'

293

A bell rings to summon them to the surreal Italian. The bijou sets, the Nino Rota jangle, the multicoloured winged angels of the optical illusion. (Programme Notes: 'For me, Fellini says, everything is realistic. I see no line between the imaginary and the real. I am indefinitely capable of wonder, and I do not see why I should set a pseudo-rational screen in front of this wonder.') A woman in white sits on a white deckchair on a beach of white sand. In Bak'a, Avi lies on Esther's bed, raging against the dying of the light. A raft floats by with three horses. A trapeze artist swings above a bed.

'Shuli would have loved this,' says Esther.

'Yes, I'm sure she would,' says Blok.

'You shouldn't let her go,' Esther says in his ear. 'She's a real person. You need someone like that to anchor you down.'

Like the Pequod, tied with harpoons to a rampaging Moby Dick. Avast, the white whale! The dark policewoman, bearing summonses. Since the Russian Compound, he had been seeing less of her. A love down-scaled. More déjà vu . . . 'I don't care what you do, Avram, but you have to find a balance, somewhere . . .' The blind scales of justice, falsely weighted. On the screen, a little girl playing a martyred saint is tied to a burning grill by angels.

Later, they walked back in the easing harshness of late afternoon, the hint of a breeze, the deepening blue of the sky, the dappled dark and light greens of trees, the sharper contours of fence stone, back across the old Ottoman railway lines, Vaknin's grocery, the Orgil laundry, falafel hut and glazier, all shuttered and closed, the anonymous siren blaster all set with his Rabbinate-issued calendar, his finger on the button, the electronic wail set to slither over the lazy rooftops, curling along the telephone wires. They hurried their pace a little in concern over the reluctant warrior, but when they reached Esther's apartment they found him risen, no stone rolled from his tomb, but a note, left on the kitchen table, held down by an ashtray full of butts:

FUCK THEM ALL! I CAN'T LEAVE MY BOYS OUT THERE TO THE MERCIES OF THAT BASTARD, KARISH. HE'LL LEAD THEM INTO AMBUSHES, WAVING THE BIBLE, SHOUTING OUT VERSES FROM

THE TALMUD, WAVING MAGIC CHARMS AND TALISMANS. IF I
HAVE TO FACE WIDOWS AND ORPHANS OF MY SOLDIERS I'LL DO IT
ON MY ACCOUNT, NOT OTHERS.

GOD ROT THE GOVERNMENT, THE STATE AND THE WHOLE FUCK-
ING NATION WHICH HAS COOKED THIS PUTRID STEW! SORRY
ESTHER. I'LL TRY TO WRITE AS OFTEN AS I CAN. TELL AVRAM HE
WAS RIGHT ALL ALONG.'

'What on earth did I say?' Blok asked.

They sat in the house, as the day faded, allowing the quiet of the
post-siren Friday evening to seep into their bones, mingled as it
was with the muffled gabble of the Sabbath profaners two floors
down. 'I'll paint your portrait,' Esther told Blok. She had gone
back to her oldest and neglected joy, daubing canvases with
coloured goo. The faecal experiments of innocence.

'Do you recognize this one?'

'The Jaffa Road intersection at rush hour,' he said.

'No, you clown. This is Armand.' The amber splodges resolved
themselves into eyeholes, in the midst of robust whorls. 'I did it in
a burst of desperation last year. You can call it the Missing Head.'
She turned the painting to the wall and rummaged for a fresh
canvas. 'God, it all seems so long ago. Nothing seems to be
resolved. I started about eight different projects, but that's the
only one that got done. This was supposed to be Ya'akov, the next
Dayan Ezuz . . . I'll do you in the same sort of style . . .'

'Whatever turns you on,' he said.

'God, that's an ancient phrase!' she marvelled. 'It makes me feel
like Methuselah's grandmother. What are we doing here, in these
1980s? Why couldn't we have stopped, like Peter Pan?'

'It's biological,' Blok stated, remembering Bentov.

'Just sit there, I'll get my shit together.'

The silence and the strong smell of clean dirt remembered from
vermillion tinted schooldays. Daub, daub, daub. Idle thoughts,
fears, procrastinations swirling in the dabs and whorls of gouache.
Absent friends. Shuli, in the routine of weekend shift, pushing
paper at the Russian Compound, scouring the empty streets for
malpractice. Yissachar, burrowing after new freelance deals after
his Grand Wedding triumph. The nuptials of armaments and the

spirit. The Duality harmonized. 'Everyone was there, Avram! You should have seen it! The two Chief Rabbis, the entire Kitchen Cabinet, the Chiefs of Staff, top bankers, film stars. And Yosher Osher – can you believe it – warbling his latest hit song! Fresh from his bust in Greece, rescued by contacts – you gotta know the right people, for God's sake!' Indeed? Whorls and whirls of brush on canvas . . .

'Remember those evenings,' Esther said, 'when we used to sit here with Avi, and Adolphe, and us doing the I-Ching?'

'Ah,' he nodded.

'I haven't opened the book or thrown the sticks since Armand. You know, the enormity of not knowing . . . A friend, a lover dies, horribly, you never find out why, and life just goes on. A sharp pain and then it all rolls back again. What does his absence amount to anyway? Where are the unhealed wounds, Avram? Where are the lessons we're supposed to learn? OK, so we accept "Life is Meaningless" as the motto of the age. What does that acceptance bring us? Enlightenment? Resignation? Where does that all get us?'

He shrugged.

'You all laughed at poor Ya'akov Ben-Havivo,' she said, 'the "boy-saint", as Avi always called him. But now he lives in a world which has real roots and traditions, which tells its members clearly who they are. We may think they're primitive, with their prayers and white magic, but who are we, Avram, all we unhappy, un-"civilised" skeptics?'

'Ah? Who? Ah! Hmm,' he opined.

Meanwhile, back in Mekor Baruch,

Adolphe sensed the advent of the national crisis in the growing tension of man and vegetable, the brittle hardness of tree bark, the weeds standing like dried raised hairs on the ground's scalp, the taut breath of the inhabitants hurrying home to catch the early evening newscasts, willing time to stand still. He prowled down Hageffen Street, turning up Takhkemoni, bounding across the Kings of Israel Road to sidle under the main gate of the Schneller army barracks. He scurried across the parade ground, noting the unusual bustle for a Sabbath Eve, the revving trucks, the soldiers with kitbags, Women Army Corps clerks rushing about with files under the ornate weathercock tower with its chiselled acorn, lamb and corn eaves and the gothic legend '*SYRICHES WAISENHAUS*'. A Protestant missionary, Ludwig Schneller, built his orphanage here in 1860 to turn destitute Levantine children into productive Lutheran craftsmen. But what the hell do I care, Adolphe thought. Now that he co-habited with Blok and lived almost totally out of bins, he had abandoned the last vestiges of domestic geniality which had been necessary with Esther in Bak'a. He followed a lunch trolley being trundled across the building's inner yard by a scraggy kitchen staff worker, who flashed his pass at the two guards sitting by a door marked: '305. NO ENTRY.' They allowed him into a neon-lit corridor leading to the dead end of a liftshaft, unaware that a small black furry bundle now nestled behind the soup tureen. With much clanging and banging the scraggy hand manoeuvred the trolley into the lift and departed whence he came, leaving the trolley and Adolphe to be conveyed automatically down five underground levels. A burly Colonel pulled the trolley out of the lift, shouting out 'Vittles, *ya manayeg!*' to the assembled top brass. Colonels, Generals, Department Heads in mufti, Hypnotists, Idiot Savants, Strategy Consultants. Adolphe scampered unseen past stampeding trouserlegs and perched, crouched very low, on top of a tall filing cabinet, taking a clear look at the maps, monitor screens and scrawled blackboards festooning the room, but riveted, his gaze attracted unerringly to the incongruous, astonishing apparition at the chamber's epicentre, as the news of the first air strikes crackled over the intercom . . .

– Can you hear anything, Reb Shabetai?
    – Perhaps a touch of tinnitus in the ears . . . I am a martyr to Menière's disease, an affectation of the organ of balance . . .
    – There is definitely something going on out there . . . perhaps the window of our opportunity . . . I'll send out a boy to buy the newspaper. Has anyone got a ghetto blaster? –

Saladin's Third Dream
– It seemed to Yusuf Salah ed-Din that, attacked by a sudden revulsion, he turned his back on the City and began to stride down the eastern slope of the Mount of Olives, towards the bare ochre

gullies leading towards the Jordan Valley. But as he walked he felt the earth shake beneath his feet, and heard heavy rhythmic panting noises closing in on his rear. He turned back, to find the City dragging in his wake, in the shape of an enormous aged crone, whose massive robes were made of a hundred thousand broken, pulverized bricks, whose toothless mouth was the black arch of the Damascus Gate, and who wore the chipped battlements of the City like the bedraggled ornaments of a faded, crumbling crown. Her breasts were the twin domes of the grand mosques of the Rock and Al-Aqsa, with the dome of the Christian Holy Sepulchre as a cancerous scab upon her navel. The countless other domes, spires and cupolas were like so many pimples of unnamed disease on her dry, wrinkled skin, upon which a thousand thousand maggots crawled.

'Yusuf! Yusuf!' she cried, with the croak of a giant vulture drawn from the very Valley of Perdition. 'Come, couple with me! It is destined! A marriage made in heaven!'

'I know you well,' he said, standing his ground, with the Dead Sea shimmering in haze a little off his left ankle. 'You are the very Mother-of-Calamities the seers and kadis warned us of . . . I refuse you!'

'Couple with me!' cried the great crone. 'Show us your rampant zabb, o conqueror of a thousand and one latrines,' laughing as she waddled forward, the battlemented walls of the City billowing about her with the clatter of a hundred thousand pots and pans. Her black mouth yawned, and the fetid odour of rancid grease, over-roasted coffee, ten-day-old falafel and open sewers hit him in the face, throwing him down upon the ground.

'Fuck me, you son of a bitch!' Her drawers, composed of the tatters of tarpaulin and old carpets, dropped, to reveal, to his astonishment, a male organ, in the shape of the Citadel of David, thrust erect towards his mouth. He clenched his teeth, turning his face into the dry, burning gravel. The revealed hermaphrodite laughed again, pounding the earth in its derision.

'You fear a frontal assault? Then take me from the rear!' The monster turned and thrust its anus, which was indeed the Dung Gate, right on to Saladin's member, which had become erect from sheer terror, causing him to ejaculate his seed clear through into

298

the Jewish Quarter, across the Mughrabeen and spilling over the Jewish Western Wall into the Haram esh-Sheriff.

'Eat shit! Eat shit!' the vile apparition cawed with triumph, rising and leaping over the hills and valleys to vanish in the haze of the west . . .

– Can you smell anything, Reb Shabetai? ? ? ? –

. . . Adolphe found it difficult to countenance, but nevertheless there it was: below the scrolling maps, the flickering monitors, by the podium on which a blindfold idiot savant pointed out advised lines of advance, the Defence Minister, whom Adolphe had often seen on television, sprawled on a red velvet diwan in the full glory of his several T-bone steak per breakfast bulk, cradling in his massive arms the shit-encrusted, mangy-coated shape, malignantly dribbling over its host's khaki fatigue shirtfront, defecating in his lap as it spewed out, in a low, morose croak, a string of topographical co-ordinates, mixed with expletives, the unmistakable shape of –

No! This cannot be!

★

Bulletin

. . . THE FIRST TWO TARGETS, HIT AT 3.15 PM ON FRIDAY, WERE NORTH OF BEIRUT'S INTERNATIONAL AIRPORT. ONE WAS FATAH'S COMBAT TRAINING SCHOOL WEST OF THE BOURJ-EL-BARAJNEH REFUGEE CAMP. THE COMPOUND CONTAINED EIGHT BUILDINGS, TENTS, HUTS, AN OBSTACLE COURSE, MACHINE GUN POSITIONS AND AT LEAST 10 ANTI-AIRCRAFT EMPLACEMENTS. HUNDREDS OF TERRORISTS HAD BEEN TRAINED THERE, A MILITARY SOURCE SAID. THE SECOND TARGET WAS AN ARMS DEPOT SITUATED UNDER PART OF THE GRANDSTANDS OF THE SOCCER FIELD NEAR THE SABRA REFUGEE CAMP. 'THEIR AMMUNITION KEPT BLOWING UP ALL NIGHT LONG,' A SENIOR SOURCE DESCRIBED . . .

. . . REPORTS INDICATE WIDESPREAD PANIC IN SOUTHERN LEBANON, WITH THOUSANDS OF CIVILIANS JAMMING THE ROADS

LEADING NORTHWARDS FROM SIDON AND OTHER TOWNS AND
VILLAGES, APPARENTLY FEARING THE LONG AWAITED LAND
OFFENSIVE BY ISRAEL AGAINST THE PLO . . .

THE FIRST ENEMY SHELLS WERE HEARD IN ISRAEL AT 5.11 PM,
WITH KATYUSHA ROCKETS FALLING ON THE GALILEE PAN-
HANDLE, CLAIMING ONE ISRAELI LIFE AND INDIRECTLY CAUSING
THE DEATHS BY HEART ATTACKS OF TWO MORE ISRAELIS IN BOMB
SHELTERS . . .

From the *Jerusalem Post*:

FOR THE PEACE OF GALILEE!

The die is cast: it is war in Lebanon now. To the accompani-
ment of an intense bombardment from the air, the sea and the
ground, armoured units of the Israel Defence Forces, aided
by paratroops, pushed north across the border to destroy the
PLO's infrastructure in Southern Lebanon, and to roll the
terrorists themselves back . . .

Saturday night the cabinet, by a large vote, gave its
approval to the one strategy that seemed practicable under
the circumstances – a powerful thrust into Southern Lebanon, designed to clear an area 40 kilometres deep from
terrorist presence. The Security Council's bid for a cease-fire,
issued early yesterday morning, and later President Reagan's
appeal for restraint, coming from Versailles, thus fell on deaf
ears. Israel was out to solve the terrorist problem, ONCE
AND FOR ALL . . .

for all . . .

★

Go, child, walk around the City, the quiet streets of unviolated
Sabbath, the sunwashed stone bricks standing guard over abandoned asphalt, with the sparse traffic of unbelievers, even the
rubbish collectors are off duty, putting their feet up in the cafés of
the Ishmaelite sector, the steam of a bubbling finjan, the small
white china cups, even the hubble-bubble sometimes of an old-
fashioned nargileh by the tourist-strewn steps beyond the

Damascus Gate, in search of history, Stars of David, the Crescent and the Cross, the cartfuls of Arab bagels, the Licensed Money Changer, the vendors of sesame seeds, painted plates, talismans, souvenirs, but in the New City, a hush, and the clip-clop of sedate pedestrians, ambling along the hidden web of family obligations –

Shabbat Shalom! Shabbat Shalom!

Sabbath Peace, et cetera. Even the cats drowse. From inside synagogues, the keening of ritual trickles through grilles and barred windows. Worshippers float in and out at the appointed hours. How Good Are Thy Tents, Jacob, Thy Abode, O Israel. Men lounge about in pyjamas, listening to the morning radio newsreel. Staccato talk of war wafting its lost way into the ether between the instrument and the human ear. Déjà vu, as yet unscrambled. A dairy brunch on the kitchen table. Yesterday's bread, coffee, yoghourts, perhaps a cucumber, a tomato. How would you like your eggs? Guests splash in hotel swimming pools. Brown bodies stretch and tease. Children mercilessly splash their elders. Semi-cold drinks in cans. Refrigerators hum in households. Sabbath clocks tick in some. Toilets flush. Videocassette recorders and small fans revolve. Weekend news-paper supplements unfold and scatter over tables, divans, chairs, chests of drawers, pouffe cushions, bathmats, floors. Languorous coupling proceeds in sluggish shuttered rooms. Midday sunbeams punch through slats dappling arms, legs, buttocks, breasts. Lips on lips and tongues in earholes. Sweat soaks crumpled sheets. In secret kitchens heretics discreetly unveil hidden cuts of ham. The lure of the forbidden at top pitch. Blood rushes to the brain. Siesta time, but still one might hear, in the calm, far-off tweaks, twinges, twists of weariness and despondency, muffled discontent and mumbles of complaint and pain.

Tick, tick, tick. Pensioners doze, handkerchiefs drooped over their eyes. See, hear, speak no evil. It's too damned hot. The temperature is at an early high for June of 31 degrees. Sweat gets in your eyes. Pity Blok, as he walks home to Mekor Baruch through the sweltering heat of high Jerusalem noon, after a night being painted and a lazy morning spent on Esther's spare mattress, proximity but no touching, staggering back again across the trafficless railway line, the Sonol petrol station, down against the panorama of Mount Zion, the Dormition and the Jericho hills, the Valley of Hinnom, across the ancient *sabil*, the bridge of the fountain, past the 'Sultan's Pool', up, below the Citadel, through Yemin Moshe, the first district built outside the Walls (1860), the picturesque renovation of the old almshouses, transformed into a guest house for foreign artists, and art galleries, and recording studios, and well-kept flower beds, and mulberry and eucalyptus trees and fine cactii, and the best kosher French restaurant in Israel, and passion flowers and morning glory, up, past the shady landscaped park where the Peace People were wont to gather and protest once upon a time, past the stationary buses opposite the Jaffa Gate, the thin stream of mad dog tourists braving the midday sun with their blue and white *tembel* hats and name tags and cameras and the few weary Arab vendors and shitkickers, and on across Mamilla Square, renamed the Israel Defence Forces Circus, round the back of the Municipality, up the Tribes of Israel Road, evading Mea Shearim, up the Street of the Prophets, across Freedom Square, past the closed market, down Takhkemoni to the Street of the Vine, Hageffen, staggering up the path to Entrance A. Climbing the stairs and sprawl . . . Sweat runs down the bed, to the neglected floortiles, upon which small beasts scurry free, bathing briefly in the salty fluid, before they pass on to the sacked pantry.

'Adolphe!'

No answer.

Tick.

Tick.

Tick.

Tick.

Tick.

June 5 creeping by. The day, fifteen years ago, that Blok, fresh and piebald, catapulted into the Sinai desert, Nagra and notebook slung round his shoulder, on the army magazine *Babasis*'s jeep, with Said T—, the gold-toothed driver flashing the star of innocence at him: 'We're in the hands of Yehoshua!' Rotted bodies like dead locusts on the desert sand. Miles of smashed and burnt trucks, tanks, armoured cars. The bullets with his name and incorrect address on them, the close shave heightening life. Life!

The joyful returning heroes! Men, women, children, lining the streets, throwing sweets on to their laps as they cruise by with six days' growth of dust and beard – Victory, and Jerusalem the Golden! How time fails to fly. Tick. Tick. Tick. Tick.

Ring, Ring, Ring, Ring, Ring!
   – Goddamit! Avram, what the fuck are they doing to us? Just when we thought we had God by the balls! I was all set for a whole sheaf of assignments of Joys and Festivities, Weddings, Bar Mitzvahs, Anniversaries, Divorce Parties of the Rich and Famous, film or video, staggering fees, you wouldn't believe your own eyes! Even Kokashvili has surfaced, building sets in Jerusalem for some massive comeback project, we've all been asked to pitch in when – Zammo! A call up, would you believe it, to put on the khaki and shoot film up in the battlefield, as a Reserve cameraman! I cried off, Goddamit! Pressure of affairs! They told me to go boil my head. What they're looking for is enthusiasm, you got that? They want people to love their new war, *icho de putana!* No way, Jose, I told them! So I'm holed up at home – barricaded on the fifteenth floor, *hombre!* Come and join me, we'll drink and smoke our way through this madness in luxury – the whole shtik – the vibrating bed, the sunken bubble bath, the freezer stacked with three weeks' worth of everything, old classic videos, hard core, video games – Space Invaders, Killer Gorilla, Pacman, Frogger, The Castle of Death – Bentov is hibernating as well, above me, all the shutters down over his windows – you hear? Come up and fiddle with us while the world burns! Eh, Avram? It's definitely biological! Come on, old pal! What do you say?

Ring, Ring, Ring, Ring!
   – Avram? Shuli. Where've you been? I've been trying all day. Isn't it awful? They've put us all on extra duty, God knows what they're expecting, a revolution? It's really depressing, and who needs it? You know what I mean. Violence only begets more violence. Any policeman with half a brain knows that. Although some people – but are you all right, Avram? I know I've been a bit distant lately, but you know how things are – I mean my personal life has to have some balance when everything else is such a mess. Remember we talked about the politicians? Now look what a

fucking stew! I've seen Esther at the station, she's a really sweet person. She told me your friend Avi has gone up there . . . God protect him . . . you know what I mean. I thought he was crazy – that day at the Compound, but who can judge at this time? I mean, try and be normal in this country. I have to go now, look after yourself . . . I'll be in touch . . . Don't get too depressed – huh?

Ring, ring, ring, ring.
   – Avram? Amnon here. I phoned Esther, she told me about Avi going. We shouldn't talk on the phone, but there are some contacts – we're already trying to get something moving – a protest demo at the University – Even at this early stage we have to do something – Have you heard, they're pushing on towards Beirut, bombing the shit out of Sidon and Tyre – complete lies about the casualties, theirs and ours – It's a whole fucking blood-bath – civilian centres plastered – crap about a limited operation – Peace for Galilee! What a farce. The government, the opposition, the Americans, General Haig, all in cahoots, the Russians sitting back enjoying the horror show, the Arab world spitting words from its arse – the people out there dying. We have to fucking well do something – even a flea biting an elephant. Tomorrow at three – the University campus – they'll probably murder us, but what the hell – are you there, Avram? Are you there?!

Ring, ring, ring, ring.
   – Are you all right, Avremel? They haven't called you up or anything? I know they wrote you off, after the Hospital, but you never know . . . In times like this they drag in everyone, the halt, the lame, the blind, the deaf . . . Getting stuck in that nuthouse might have been the best thing you ever did, I should wash my mouth out with soap . . . Difficult to speak as a father to son in this . . . You try to be patriotic, but when you see . . . I always said Begin was an arsehole . . . So are they all, all arsehonourable men . . . But you're not going to volunteer or something dumb? OK, OK, I only asked. Even your mother doesn't want you to serve in this. She's as well as can be expected, a little bit more bowel trouble . . . The doctor says it's the heat. Thirty-two degrees, asargelusha! Who can take it? Thirty-six years in this country and what have we got to show for it? Cholera, blight,

boils, syphilis, plague of the first born. Don't tell me about their potash plants, flowers and cattle shit blooming in the desert. Aunt Pashtida has been at us again, we should go live with her down on the farm, renew our health in open air. Give us your poor, your huddled masses . . . I should have told her to stick a rooster up her arse! What have we done to deserve this? Lucky we don't believe in God, Avremel. But don't try to convince your mother. When are we seeing you? No, don't feel pressured . . . Whenever you feel . . . Look after yourself, you hear me – don't let the bastards get you down!

Knock, knock, knock.

– Good morning, Mister Blok. What is that smell? Is there something wrong with the drains? I'll get Almaliah to look into it. I'm just collecting for the House Committee. Whatever people can give for our boys up north. Not perishable goods. Things like shaving cream, razors, brushes, bootpolish, food in tins, wafers, biscuits. Books and magazines, if not too bulky. Music cassettes, lots of boys have those little recorders everybody carries nowadays. Mrs Shemesh gave us a supply of heavy socks, and Mrs Tishbi is knitting strong sweaters and caps for the winter, if, God forbid, our boys are still stuck up there then. You know how it helps your morale when you're at the front to know the people at the rear are behind you. Anything you can give will be appreciated. I understand, you've been away a lot. But there must be something in the house? Shaver batteries? Bootlaces? Soap? We're especially low on salving cream, for chapped lips, it's going to be a hot summer. I remember in the Sinai, in '56 . . . but I've got the other entrances to call on . . . You're sure this tin is all you can spare? Well, you know where to find me if . . . Hair shampoo, combs, pen and paper, mosquito oil, anything will be welcome. Let's pray this only lasts a few days. No one wants these wars. I don't have to tell you. But that's our fate. The Jewish story . . .

Dear Blok,
You will probably be surprised to get a letter from me after so long a time. But I am sending this Express as I don't know how long it will take to reach you in these difficult days. You may not know that I am now a Member of the Lower Saxony

Parliament for the so-called 'Green' Party. I have just come back from organizing a protest meeting about the war you have now in Lebanon. This is a terrible thing, which I am sure you feel as well, as any person who still has human feelings has to see at this stage. The suffering, the killing, the dispossession, is too horrific to think of, except that we must, wherever we are, make our voices heard. I want to express my solidarity with those people in your country who are against this militaristic, ultra-nationalistic war. We all appreciate how difficult it is to be in opposition to a government at a time like this. Be assured your protest – and I know you too are with us – will be echoed in the world. We, especially in Germany, know where these wars of aggression lead. Can you pass these words to Basuto and whoever is there of his group? I have written in the last few months to both him and Daniela but have got no reply. I feel very much for the 'peace' people in this time of trial.

Love and Solidarity,
Ilse

Beep! Beep! Beep!

– Here is the News, and first, the headlines . . . Pincer movement with other forces which had moved up from the south. The Phalange Forces radio said Israeli forces had entered the city . . . the army spokesman could not confirm this report, but said heavy fighting was continuing in and around the city of Tyre . . . confirmed that the Beaufort Fortress, Nabatiyeh and Hasbayah have fallen to the Israel Defence Forces. No figures of IDF casualties have yet been given, but will be issued later today, the army spokesman said . . .

And now for the news in detail . . .

Beep! Beep! Beep!

Ring! Ring! Ring!

– Avram? For God's sake, turn down that radio! What do you say? It's not yours, it's the neighbours'?! I know, it's the same everywhere. It's as if they're transmitting in your head! And you can't switch it off, can you? What's that? I also tried to close the windows, but you're right, it makes the flat like an oven. As you say, who needs the gas pellets? At least you can joke at this time! I'm going completely mad. I've become like an army wife, it's just like my worst nightmares. Phoning up people to ask about casualties, to ask where Avi's unit went to . . . The whole city is full of rumours, nobody knows the truth about anything. They say there's about two hundred casualties . . . I don't want to think about it. You know what they were showing at the Cinematheque yesterday? You won't believe it – *La Dolce Vita!* of course, I couldn't face it. Remember *Giulietta*? That seems about ten years ago now. I feel like a wrung-out old hag. No, don't come over, I have to handle this myself. I've been talking to some other women, who've been talking about some demonstration . . . I can't believe I'm getting into this . . . It all seems like such an awful time machine . . . a macabre déjà vu . . . What'd you say, Avram? What's that? I just can't hear you in that noise . . .

Ring, ring, ring!
  Ring, ring, ring!
  Ring, ring, ring!
– Avram, you're still there? . . . You heard? You saw? The TV poison in our veins . . . no, don't come over . . . I get here three a.m, whacked . . . I'll call . . . yes? . . . No? . . . Choking on our own shit . . . why don't they stop those Homeland songs? Is this how it ends? Drowning in saccharine nostalgia? Mogadons? Arsenic's the only cure . . . Yes, Avram, everything's A-OK here, I've got Clint Eastwood, Greta Garbo, Buster Keaton, Groucho Marx . . . the Good, the Bad and the Ugly . . . Avram! This is your Aunt Pashtida! Of course the line's bad, we're at war . . . ! Your mother and father . . . we only have your good at heart . . . Still no word from Avi? He might phone you . . . sometimes he doesn't want to speak to me . . . Hallo, hallo, is this 615423? Goddamn the fucking meddling bastards . . . Guess what? I saw Esther, yesterday, at the women's demonstration . . . embarrassing is not the word for it . . . people spat at them, called them whores . . . men are animals . . . but the police force is trying to stay fair . . . you saw our advertisement, in *Ha'aretz*? . . . Peace – Yes, War – No, what else is there to say? . . . We've called a demonstration on the Saturday, in Tel Aviv, God knows who'll turn up . . . Hallo, hallo, is that Zelda? What'd you mean No? The

same to you, fuckface . . . No, Avram, not tonight . . . Love? Are you out of your mind, Avram? How can you even say that word? . . .

Beauty?
Faith?
Truth?
Compassion?
I think we have a crossed line . . .

Beep! Beep! Beep!

CLASHES WITH SYRIA ESCALATING – IDF TIGHTENING NOOSE ON BEIRUT – ISRAEL READY FOR CEASE-FIRE – SAM MISSILES KNOCKED OUT – OUR CHANGING WAR AIMS – DAMASCUS NOT BOMBED – MANY PLO FIGHTERS SURRENDERING – SYRIAN THREAT DEPRESSES STOCK MARKET – WHY WE SHOULD WIN ANOTHER SIX DAYS WAR – POLICE BREAK UP UNIVERSITY DEMO – ISRAEL SEEKS DIALOGUE – LEAFLET BOMBS WARN BEIRUTIS – A NEW ORDER IN LEBANON? – 134 FALLEN SO FAR – OPTIMISM ON EARLY CEASE-FIRE – REAGAN RAPS BREZHNEV – CAIRO WON'T SEVER TIES OVER INVASION – BE SURE TO GIVE SOLDIERS LIFTS! – COMPLETION OF IDF MISSION NEAR – POLICE FIRE TEAR-GAS AT JERU-SALEM ARABS – CRIMINAL ATTACKS ON INDIVIDUALS DECREASE – LEBANESE LEADERS MEET 'TO SAVE THE NATION' – FURTHER CLASHES WITH SYRIAN FORCES – OUR REPORTER AT THE FRONT REPORTS:

'Underfoot, browning Lebanese wheat crushed by tank treads. Overhead, circling storks and pregnant helicopters, supply packets slung beneath their bellies, heading northwards . . .'

Northwards . . .
Northwards . . .

The siren call of loudspeaker wails. Crossing, criss-crossing Hageffen Street's windows, a jeepful of bearded patriots patrolling up and down the Kings of Israel Road, crying: 'A Voice Calls in the Desert! Be Comforted, My People! Come, everyone, to the Grand Synagogue of Mea Shearim for a Prayer for the Wellbeing and Victory of the Warriors of Israel . . . Tonight at Seven O'Clock at the Grand Synagogue . . . a Prayer for Wellbeing and Victory . . .'

Hesitating to respond to another knock on the door, but succumbing, Blok found Shuli on his doorstep, in uniform.

'My God, Avram! How can you live here? The place is a fucking pigsty!'

She threw open all the windows and retired into the bathroom for a shower, calling out: 'Clean it up, Avram, for God's sake!'

'Let God clear his own rubbish . . .' he mumbled, but surveyed the battlefield. Columns of ants marched across the salon floor, skirting the puddles of sweat around the bed, up the wall to the east facing window in a long dual carriageway, one bearing, one advancing to bear more of the sack of his kitchen cabinets: peppercorns, sugar grains, rice, farfel, shredded biscuits, dried fruit segments, a whole packet of Osem chicken soup mix with egg noodles despoiled and methodically hoisted like the booty of some Lilliputian treasure galleon.

'Where the fuck is that cat?'

Adolphe-free, the small red roaches scurry agilely over the floors, up walls, table and chairlegs, some foraging on the ant horde's stragglers who are nevertheless replaced instantly, with automatic precision. Ruthlessly, Blok sets to work with Baygon, squirting the poisonous powder up and down the escape routes like a grim Luftwaffe air ace strafing endless refugee columns.

'Eat Spartan death, Athenian dogs, Scythian scum, spawn of Ashmedai!'

Shuli emerges, *sans* uniform, wrapped in his bathtowel, drawing up her legs on the bed as he sloshes down the corpses with detergent in water and a soppy reserve schmutter.

'You ought to change these sheets.'

'OK. OK.' He rises on the bed to mount her.

'Take a shower, Avram, you smell like an old goat.'

He accedes, and returns to find her sprawled on her back, head on her arms, dressed in one of his T-shirts.

'Were you going to hide here till the war's over?' she asked. 'You can forget it. It's set for long distance. Remember I told you about my ex-boy friend, the film editor? He came over the other day, all shaken. He's been cutting the war footage at the television station, with the Censor looking over his shoulder. This yes, this no. He said they cut out ninety per cent. Terrifying things, shocking scenes, shots that made his hands tremble. The talk is it'll go on for weeks, even months. Maybe for ever. I don't know, Avram . . . I never really bothered about these things, they were

309

part of life, like nightmares. You tried to live without thinking about it. You know what I mean? Abuse of power, authority . . . I knew about corrupt policemen. You had inquiries, you found and fired them. As far as I knew the system worked. Let the government get on with governing . . . But this . . . oh shit, what am I saying, Avram? Next thing I'll be demonstrating . . .'

'How about a demonstration of carnal lust?' he said.

'All right,' she said. They both proceeded. Taking the conventional, missionary position, he kissed her lips, her neck, her breasts and nipples. She responded and pressed his back with her fingertips. He entered her and began thrusting. She locked her ankles behind his thighs. Her hands seized his new-born hair.

'You should have shaved as well,' she whispered.

'Unh! Unh! Unh! Unh!' he replied.

Later, she said: 'You might become quite good at this, sometime.'

'Practice makes perfect,' he suggested.

'It's a funny world,' she said. 'You know, that night at the Compound, I was so furious at you you can't imagine. But now it seems like a thousand years ago . . . I saw Esther at that demonstration . . . Women Against the War . . . There were about a hundred women, sitting there, on the lawn opposite the department store . . . just across the road from the travel agencies and American Express, the traffic passing by . . . A few small kids and babies, and some men standing with them . . . But the men passing by were really bitter, I was amazed to see the hate in their faces . . . Why should it be such a threat? Some people with placards, what's the problem? I see them around all the time . . . Stop The War . . . Well, isn't that what we're all supposed to be about, everybody in this country? Against war?'

'Most people seem to enjoy it,' said Blok.

'If I believed that I'd have to shoot myself.'

He raised an eyebrow.

'I know,' she said, 'I never cared about all this, I came out in a rash at the TV news time, even if the set was switched off. But I've changed. Haven't you ever changed, Avram? Have you always been able to hold this distance? Even when it's blaring at you inside your brain? Even when it ties up your guts?'

'I shtick my neck out for nobody,' he said in English, trying out his Humphrey Bogart.

'Well,' she said. 'I'm not converted to the bleeding hearts but I want to know what's going on. My weekend's free. I can shed this khaki. Will you come with me to this Tel Aviv demo people have been talking about?'

He threw a slipper at a roach which had braved and survived the deadly ring of Baygon. Nevertheless it escaped, scurrying . . .

Northwards . . .   Northwards . . .   North-west, climbing through the Jerusalem hills on a late Saturday afternoon with a busload of determined oppositionaries of mostly youthful mien. Some veterans of a long chain of cause and circumstance, glazed starers in the eye of history. Others were new embarkees on the Odyssean cycle of dissent, listening intently to the BBC Overseas Radio News. The bus spilled them on to the plateau of Tel Aviv's Square of Kings, to join an angry crowd around a makeshift podium, a generous mix of young, middle and old, with many weary-faced couples, clearly parents of those drafted to the siren call of army Form 8. Pained speeches from the podium denounced the war: Can We Remain Silent? Can We Remain Oppressors of Another People? Where Will This Bloodbath End? A pop singer sang of a conscientious objector. A war veteran indicted the government. A scholar called for a minute of silence for the fallen of both sides. People pressed Shuli and Blok with leaflets, but they were looking about, searching for Esther, with whom they had been unable to make contact. 'Amnon should be around here, too,' Blok said, but they could not see him in the crowd, which swirled and eddied, circling the podium, forming little knots around counter-demonstrators who had come to point out the errors of their ways, a skullcapped dapper young man in a neat suit puzzled at the lack of patriotism, a hook-handed Christian fundamentalist waving the Old Testament, a determined youth floating through the crowd, handing out little stencilled mock telegrams saying:

To the 'Peace Lovers':
The ring of steel is tightening around us in Beirut stop Please continue to do your best to break the spirit of the

People of Israel and its Army stop You are our last hope
stop Signed Yassir Arafat Beirut.

But a larger group gathered, as if drawn by a tangible empathy,
round the figure of a man and a woman enclasped, his arm around
her neck, her hand supporting his holding up a large placard
naming the guilty heads of government and armed forces and
declaring in thick black letters:

BEGIN – SHARON – RAFUL –
MURDERERS OF MY SON!
NEVER MORE!

Ten thousand people around him in the Kings of Israel Square but
he appears to see none of them, except the woman, clasping his
clenched fist on the wooden placard pole. Gazing through the
crowd, through the solid bulk of the Tel Aviv buildings about the
Square, out across the night blackness of the sea, through the stars
to a galaxy undiscovered by either science or inspiration. Or
perhaps it was just a glance that was blind, halted by an invisible
veil drawn across his eyeballs, deflected within, to the volcanoes of
his mind. He had written a letter, to the Prime Minister, which he
had also sent to the editorial offices of all the national newspapers.
It said:

> Dear Sir,
> I am the descendant of a family of scholars, the only son of
> M— F—, who fell as a heroic fighter against the Nazis
> among the partisans of Riga. I survived the Holocaust and
> came to Israel, where I served in the army and raised a family,
> and was blessed with a son, G—, who grew into a handsome,
> strong and honest young man with a pure heart.
>   I nourished my son with unlimited love and was proud of
> him as only a father can be. Deep in my heart I saw him as a
> symbolic link in the chain of our history, and, with others
> like him, the realization of our people's renewal.
>   When the time came for my son to be drafted into the
> army, he volunteered for an elite unit and served faithfully,
> becoming due for demobilization a few weeks ago. He had

many plans for the future. Like my son and his friends, I knew the real character of Israel's present leaders, and we lived in constant fear. Each night I went to bed praying that war might be avoided. But every child could see that you were looking for an excuse to invade Lebanon, to start the first war in our history that was not defensive. A shot fired in London gave you that excuse to send lethal war machines to spread death into cities and villages. My beloved son G— was sent with his unit in great haste to a bloody battle near N—, in which he fought bravely, but found his death.

Thus was severed the chain of unending Jewish generations, ancient and full of heroism and suffering, and the life that had just begun to flower was cut off. But before the blood dried on the battlefield you hurried, in your helicopters, with photographers and movie cameras, to declare and sound forth with vanity, not even pausing to remove your shoes and ask forgiveness for your dark chauvinism and blind adventure. And the voice of our son's blood cries out from the ground!

— D— F—, Kibbutz —

Saladin's Fourth Dream

He dreamed he had returned to the Valley of the Bones, and the fair lady with the ball of twine enticed him further and further, until he came to a realm of utter desolation, without a trace of even the driest vegetation, only sand, gravel and low rocks, scalding his feet under the merciless sun. Commending his soul to his Maker, he trudged on, until he could walk no longer, and then lay down in the lee of a shadeless boulder, drawing his tattered, crumbling robe over his unprotected head. A vulture, alighting from the steel grey sky, scraped through the sand towards him and began to eat his left foot.

'It is not meat that a bird of carrion should consume the Chosen of Allah.' he thought. But he found he could not move a sinew. The vulture completed his feast of the left leg and began to work upon the right, swallowing the flesh of both legs up to the haunch and noisily sucking the marrow from the bones. Then it proceeded to the groin, swallowing both testicles, tearing off the

313

male organ and commencing to pull out the Great Sultan's intestines.

'By Allah, this is going too far,' thought the General. But he remained helpless, as the beast climbed upon his chest, tearing out his heart and devouring it, ripping open his throat, devouring his larynx, tearing off his lips and nose, finally thrusting its beak through his eyes and sucking out his brain. His spirit departed, soaring above his ravaged body, gazing piteously down and lo! where the blood of his veins spilled out on to the sand, blades of grass and green bushes and scrub began to grow, cyclamen and anemones curled up from the barren ground, date palms, olive and pomegranate trees thrust up from the rocks, and before his ethereal gaze a garden flourished, flush with fruit trees, cypresses and pines, ringing with the sparkling calls of hoopoes, sparrows, bulbul, crows, wagtails and pelicans. The calls of laughing children were heard, and the mechanical crash and tinkle of fairground shows and merry-go-rounds. Candyfloss and hot-dog vendors cried out their wares, pickpockets plied their trade in the throng, gangs of ne'er-do-wells vied for a go on the dodgems, punters were whirled about on the wall of death, and the happy clatter of a thousand and one cash registers could be heard again in the land . . .

– LETTER? WHAT LETTER???

The PM burrowed more deeply in the kitchen cabinet, knocking over the sugar and saccharine tablets, spilling the crude table salt, floundering in the potato flour. Desperately hoping his private secretary would not follow the powdery line of footprints leading to his hiding place behind the bag of matzoh meal.

– Sir, Sir, Your Excellency –

– GET BEHIND ME, SATAN!

– But Sir, the cri-de-coeur of a bereaved father . . .

– I AM BEREAVED TOO – THEY'RE ALL MY CHILDREN!

– Please, Sir . . .

His back to the rear of the cabinet, the PM thankfully made out in the wall the contours of a defunct mousehole. Squeezing his frail frame through, he scurried nervously into the space between the brickwork. Flaking plaster, crumbling bricks, rusting girders and

314

stanchions, the detritus of several decades of the kitchen cabinet spillage.

– Sir! the daily casualty report . . .

A gathering sneeze – Eheu! Eheu! –

Fading echoes down the plughole . . .

Adolphe pricked up his ears, arched his back and set every black hair erect as quills upon the fretful porpentine as he slowly circled the Rabid Sheep's cage, keeping his eyes fixed on the beady peepholes of his malevolent rival. The Map & Planning Room empty for the night, a red emergency glare dimly illuminating the abandoned chairs and cabinets, the curtains drawn over the blank screens on the walls and the cage in the centre of the room, within which, warily guarded by the soothsaying beast, lay the messtins with its latest supper: chicken bones and gristle, cows' udders, intestines and tripe. Adolphe, his last stolen meal of scraps from the Planner's mess already a fading memory, inched his stealthy way forwards. The Sheep growled, dribbling copiously and pawing its filthy bed of hay. Adolphe hissed, flinging a gob of his most rancid spit into the creature's eye. It retreated a little into the centre of the cage, pulling its messtins with it. Adolphe crouched down for a long wait, ears pricked, pitch-black nostrils trembling, bathed by the red emergency glow.

'Wake up, Theodor!'

'You think anyone can sleep through this noise? Helicopters flying overhead. The sonic booms of fighter planes. The wailing and gnashing of women's teeth. Television and radio sets at full volume. Long queues at the pearly gates. What is all that racket?'

'It's the Jewish State, Theodor.'

'Well, at least they're not dull . . .'

'Are you ready, Reb Shabetai?'

'As the Lord wills,' the Messiah replied, quietly.

★

'Vitamins and cornflakes!' cried Bentov. 'Sugar-coated pills of wisdom! Wasn't there a cartoon series once with that slogan, in the

315

silent days, what was it called? *Aesop's Fables* . . . My heart bleeds
as well as the next man's, but protests like this will shift nothing.
You can't fight barbarism with half measures! Don't talk to me
about the Peace Movement! I've seen them parade past my
window – my camera out, telephoto lens on, a hundred and
twenty millimetres . . . With Swiss expertise I pick out their fresh
faces and their placards and banners. Ah! Such well brought up
liberal youths! Don't tread on the hyacinths, Yossi! It's not nice to
kill other people! Vitamins and cornflakes! Yes, I see the agony of
the bereaved father and mother. Yes, the anguish of dead friends.
Yes, the moral revulsion at the atrocity of it all. But all this for a
personal cleansing – a ritual bath of one's own self-righteousness?!
Do me a favour, comrades!'

'But what do you expect them to do?' asked Shuli. 'Sometimes
you have to stand up to be counted.'

'You can be counted quite effectively lying down,' said Bentov,
'or sitting in flowerpots. But what are you standing up for? If it's
just to hear the sound of one's own voice I can hear that adequately
in my kitchen.'

'What about the voices of others?' said Shuli, who was sitting
uncomfortably in the eye of Bentov's personal domestic cyclone,
the opened chests of drawers, the piles of books, the upended
settee, the spotlights. Bentov on his knees composing a pan across
their feet, tilting up to encompass Yissachar's slippered trotters,
drawn up on an armchair.

'Ah, yes,' Bentov agreed, 'the problem of youth. The terrible
fear of solipsism. The need to feel not alone.'

'But what's your solution, I don't understand?' she insisted,
throwing out: 'Revolution?'

'That might be one option,' Bentov squinted into his view-
finder. 'But I do not necessarily advocate that one. It plays hell
with the free flow of film stock.'

'You'll not get an opinion out of Bentov!' laughed Yissachar.
'He's an adept at avoiding the world.'

'I eat, I shit, I fornicate on occasion,' said Bentov. 'I shoot film,
therefore I exist. Can you move your foot a little this way?'

'That man is crazy,' Shuli said, a little later, one floor down, in
Yissachar's luxury hermitage. Wonderingly wandering about the

316

massive deep freeze, the sunken bath, the vibrating bed and triple videocassette recorders. 'He ought to be locked up.'

'He is,' said Yissachar, 'by his own hand. The war's put all of us on the defensive. Bentov has been ranting about putting up a machine gun in his window instead of the camera. "A mass murderer at a great height can do tremendous damage," he told me.'

'I knew he should be locked up,' said Shuli.

'So should we all,' Yissachar began making real coffee in the kitchen. 'The floor has fallen out of the fantasy market. Reality has become far too grisly. The Apocalypse's arrived as expected, on TV, in ninety-minute news bulletins. Did you see our Great Leader's Hannibal speech? The flanking armies closing in on Beirut? Maybe Kokashvili has the right idea, rebuilding the Temple with hardboard and plankwood. Most of his crews have answered the Call to the battlefield but he's forging ahead with Belgian cameramen. Remember our Judas Pig extravaganza, Avram, in the previous volume of your saga? The one and only Irving Klotskashes of Hollywood, now retired? Kokashvili is trying a similar trick: he wants to merge the movies with real life. He who controls the image controls the substance. Poor Basuto, who died because we turned down his dreams . . . How he would have loved this inferno.'

'Poor bastard,' Shuli murmured, but it was unclear whether she meant Basuto, or Yissachar, or Bentov above, or Blok himself. Retaining her sombreness as they left the Big City, squeezing like manufactured sausages through the railings of the Tel Aviv Central Bus Station, Platform 3, Jerusalem (Express 401). The impatient hordes, pressing forward. An unusual dearth of soldiers. The radio news reported the night's peace demonstration. Spontaneous arguments en route erupted:

'Traitors! They should hang the lot of 'em!'

'They are the conscience of this country!'

'Your brothers' blood cries out!'

'This neo-fascist government!'

'Jews!' sighed Shuli. 'It's always high drama. Maybe you're right, Avram, we should remain offstage.'

They walked from the Jerusalem bus station to Hageffen Street savouring the silence of the capital, ambling past the old houses of

Romema and the new dual carriageway, past the concrete box of the Israel Television, where Shuli's ex-boy friend and other slaves were burning the midnight generators. The air sparkling clear under a canopy of story-book stars. Look, the Big Dipper. Look, Cassiopeia. Look, Orion. The smell of lemon trees in gardens. Gently swaying casuarina. The moss between the worn stones of the Schneller barracks' wall.

'I love this city,' said Shuli, 'ten times more at this shitty time than ever. Ten times more just because the times are so shitty. Do you understand that, Avram? I want to live and die here.'

'In that order, I hope,' he said, disengaging from her briefly to allow two orthodox men in full regalia to sidle between them, unsuccessfully pretending not to ogle her bare arms and the velvet of her thighs. 'Let's go up to the flat,' he proposed. 'By now it should be crystal clear of roaches.'

'No,' she said. 'I want to go home now, to Emile Zola, alone. I'll take the Number 15 part of the way.' She indicated the bus stop opposite. 'You understand, Avram. I'll call you when I can.'

The night, streetlamp lights etching out the quarried stone, the old wrought ironwork of balconies, the slatted iron shutters, light behind the bars of the Yeshiva of the 'Beginning of Wisdom', silhouettes of hatted, sidecurled heads bobbing to and fro in rhythm. The Lord said this. Rabbi so and so said that. There is nothing new under the moon. The familiar billboard and poster:

SON OF THE TORAH! TAKE HEED!

HEAR THE WORDS OF THE TORAH FROM THE LIPS OF OUR TEACHERS AND RABBIS – UNTIL WHEN WILL OUR CRIES GO UNHEARD? UNTIL WHEN WILL THE SWORD OF HERESY AND IMPURITY BE FLOURISHED OVER OUR HEADS? ARISE AND CRY OUT, AGAINST ABOMINATION, AGAINST THE ASSAULT ON ALL OUR VALUES, AGAINST THE OBSCENE, SECULAR EVIL . . .

But the rest had been torn away. He turned into Hageffen and climbed up to the apartment to find the telephone ringing. Unlocking the door rapidly he ran in and picked up the receiver to find his premonition confirmed. It was Esther.

'Avram! Can you come over? I've got a letter from Avi.'

318

Dear Esther,

Where to begin? Where to end? A cog in the machine turns non stop. You'll have to unscramble whatever you find here. It won't make sense. Not that it should. Why don't I describe my surroundings? Let's see: a lot of sleeping bags on a hill. Stone terraces, olive trees, an allotment of fruit trees. Not unlike Ein Karem. Is there still an Ein Karem? Down the slope – some destroyed houses. An Arab with a horse and a plough moving in the line of sight. No. This is idiotic. Try again, from the top –

At the expeditionary camp: The usual havoc of transition. Off with the civilian rags of freedom, on with the khaki badge of slavery. The ill-fitting, coarse cloth, already smelling of the sweat and piss a thousand laundries can't wash off. The armoury and the sweet-sour smell of gunoil. Familiar faces in the dark: Yasu, Karish, God help us. The mournful glide of Colonel Adashim, the Sorrows of Young Werther: 'Briefing in half an hour.' A school reunion in a nightmare: the maps, routes of advance, et cetera.

What is it that makes us such cowards? I'm absolutely aware I shouldn't be here, I should have reported straight to jail, with kitbag. Yasu sings in my ear: 'Greetings upon thy return, O fair bird / from the far southern climes to my window . . .' Karish ecstatic, leaning forward, asking questions, the perfect junior officer. Adashim, as usual, looks asleep, as if all this does not concern him, but someone else, whom he has left at home. Daybreak, we climb aboard the 'zeldas'. The fucking armoured cars. Living targets, hemmed in by steel. The soldiers sit huddled like canned beef. We get off, we get on. Going nowhere. 'We're fooling the enemy,' says Yasu, 'ourselves. Tonight we get to blow our own heads off. Captain Jekyll versus Captain Hyde.' No, its Captain Hyde and Captain Hyde.

The columns move. We cross the border on a highway over-looking the sea. Mountain scenery, brown hillsides, pines, rocks. Morose soldiers of the United Nations, in their toy blue helmets. Crisp and clean air. Surreal feeling of a joyride. This did not last long.

War, Esther. What does it conjure up? Sunflower seeds in the Semadar Cinema? John Wayne and Iwo Jima? Cemeteries, hospitals and crutches? You look at the view and watch for hostiles. Then you just become a machine. At the beginning we are cosily hidden behind the tank column's arse. Fire from ahead, we pass a burnt-out jeep, a smashed Mercedes, bodies on the hill. Everyone at the ready. No Peaceniks in a 'zelda'. The more you kill of them, the sooner it's over and you can go home . . . Your metabolism tries to fool you. Moral scruples are just wisps on the wind.

The hell with the Censor, I'll give you details: (I'll try and get this to you by hand somehow, some lucky bastard might sprain an ankle . . .) Proceeded north from Rosh Hanikra up the main coastal road, joyriding with minor skirmishes past Iskandarouna and Mansoura to the fringes of the refugee camps of El-Bas, Nebi Mashuk, Bourj Shimali and Rashidiyeh. Skirted these and went past Tyre, watching other units break off and go down towards the camps and town. (The irony of it all is the explicit orders with which we started out: avoid large civilian casualties. My God, what innocent spring flowers we were − just seven hours before . . .)

Artillery and aircraft fire. Plumes of smoke. We ate our K-rations. Camped for the night in a football field, the tanks forming a circle with their cannons pointed out, like a corralled waggon train. Every now and again they fired into the dark at random, to discourage night attacks. Not a brilliant lullaby, as if anyone could sleep. More briefings, more maps, moments of choice, mad thoughts of fomenting rebellion. Far too fucking late. I am signed, sealed and delivered. Wartime camaraderie, here we're all together again, the happy family of robust warriors, far from the responsibilities of home, wives, job, mortgage . . . Politics be damned! This is another story, a very deep atavism . . . Karish, Yasu, Colonel Adashim and all the rest . . . we might tear each other to

320

shreds in normal times, but in abnormal – the band of brothers!
Goddamit, Esther!

That damned night! Brainwashing myself into believing I could
do my stuff and not be soiled. And the tanks – firing into the
darkness . . . Karish, wandering inside the ring, trying to figure
out the proper direction for his morning prayer, each of us ragging
him in turn: the east's that way, Krishna! no, that's the south!
Listening to the news on Yasu's Walkman, but those are dis-
patches from Mars, nothing to do with us at all. Our reports tell of
heavy fighting in the camps, stronger resistance from the 'terrorists' than expected. The fucking generals who promised an easy
time! Cleaning out the 'nests of the murderers' . . . Pleased to
meet you – signed, The Broom.

Dawn and back into the 'zeldas'. End of any sane illusion.
Spectacular mocking sunrise of gold, red and blue. A breakfast
munch of the rations and down the road behind the tanks' arses
again. When did all this destruction happen? Buildings smashed,
pits and craters, burnt cars, fallen pylons. And the shock that
literally froze my penis, I remember feeling it disappear, shrivelled
inside me with the remains of my stomach: the sudden streams and
streams of people – the lost inhabitants – almost all women, old
men and children, running in the road like chickens escaped from
the slaughterhouse. Where did they all come from? Black-clad
women, holding babies, running at the side of the tanks. The great
steel monsters with their giant schmucks, raping the land, ya'ani.
Against all logic I turn, gesticulating to Yasu in the half track just
behind me, pointing at the mass. He flings his arms up in the same
incomprehension. For a moment we seem united by a sort of silent
scream, but it's not us doing the screaming. Mouths open and shut
below us, drowned by the treads of tanks and armoured cars – and
the radio, scrabbling on in our ears, its talons in our eardrums.

Sidon in front of us, more plumes of smoke. Cannon and
aircraft bombing a city. So what's the big deal? Haven't we seen it
often enough in the movies? But we move off the road, to the
right, into the refugee 'camp', Ein el-Hilwe, whose name, I'm
told, means 'sweet spring . . .' Massive concentrations of PLO
fighters in evidence right away. One tank already hit. A 'zelda'
RPG-ed. Does this make any sense to you, Esther? These stupid
words, what do they mean? In short, the shit itself, in person. A

321

dozen soldiers depending on decisions I have to make in a mouse-trap. They train you well, those fucking bastards! It all becomes purely technical. You run, you try and find a way through, the fire's too heavy, you retreat, re-group back up the road while the higher ups argy-bargy: call in the air force, wipe the bastards out. No, there are thirty thousand civilians in there. Thirty thousand potential terrorists! Wipe 'em out while there's still time! Fuck that, this is not the Wehrmacht, *habibi*! Fuck you, stop living in the past . . .

Oh, we are so fucking righteous! Lucky for me my brain switches off. For me, not the victims . . . Oh! Karish was so incensed! There are Scum in there, the Eternal Enemy, the Two-Legged Animals, Human Dust! How dare they put up such resistance?! It's our moral weakness that they sense. Shut up, Krishna, says Colonel Adashim, You're making my arsehairs curl. Someone turns up with giant loudspeakers. Our clever planners have thought of everything. All the little printed leaflets, which they showered all over Sidon: To All the Inhabitants: Get Out, Gather by the Sea. Allow Us to Fight the Terrorists in Your Houses Without the Stigma of the Slaughter of Innocents. Un-armed inhabitants are called on to come out, armed ones to surrender forthwith. The camp is completely surrounded, gentle-men! There Is No Hope! Give up now!

'Would you give up,' asked Yasu, 'if your wife, your children, all your family and friends were in there?' 'No,' I said. 'So why are they wasting their breath?' 'Because we're so fucking humane,' I told him.

In short, the shit continuing to go down. Hair-raising scenes in the 'battlefield'. If this letter gets to you, show it to Avram, remind him of the 'good old days' – anyone remembers the Six Day War – the 'clean' combat of soldier versus soldier? Out there in the desert, where men are men (until they're joints of roast-beef) . . . Or even '73, when my hair turned white – when we were on the receiving end . . . Can you believe this nostalgia??!! And they called Avram Blok mad . . .

A maze of unpaved streets and alleyways, stone fences and low stone and concrete houses. Most of the outer part already reduced to rubble by the tanks. Behind each pile of rubble, a fighter with a rifle or rocket-propelled-grenade. Mortars somewhere inside, so you can be schnitzelled from above. Every stone, every mound of garbage is a defender's paradise. One of the *hevreh* is hit in the leg, another torn by shrapnel. I am up to my tit in medics. Retreat. The medic gets shot. A ten-year-old-boy, or thereabouts, peeps over the rim of a fence, pointing an RPG. I shoot the boy. I drag the medic. A tank rolls up to cover our back.

You read, Esther? I shot a ten-year-old boy. This is Mama's Avi speaking. It was him or me, pardner. And he was soon lost in the mass. Later we heard about those who hesitated, and were shredded by these '*ashbal*'. I could have remained both pure and dead. Do you hear, Esther? The voice of Karish from my bowels! I'm only a minor murderer. If I had been a fighter pilot, or an artillery gunner, I could have bagged fifty at a time. Do you think I can plead this, come the day? Karish says we are all going to be judged. I think, though, he means a competition for bodycount. Do not forget the Amalekites! Still avenging ourselves for the Pentateuch. The three-thousand-year memory. Myself, I can barely remember breakfast. Well, stop wailing, Avi, and be a man, eh? Stand up and be a proud Jew!

This letter seems to have self-destructed. The best thing would be to throw it away. Confession is not a very Jewish trait. Save it for Yom Kippur, asshole. Anyway, I've reached the end of the notepaper, there's nothing left but the back of these mad Sidon leaflets –

(The rest of the letter is written on the back of these yellow flyers, each with a map of Sidon and designated gathering areas, with arrows showing the permissible safe routes out of town towards the sea, and the peroration, signed by O.C. Northern Command – 'the Armed Forces of Israel will not flinch from carrying out their duty with speed and precision, whatever the cost.')

– but I can't pretend that too much soul-searching took place at the time, at all – in fact this is the first break I've had to sit down and think for seven days! Going back on that jumble of action and torpor, with Yasu and Karish and all the others and me lolling about in an abandoned Fatah school, with the Sorrows of Young Werther stretched on three schooldesks under a portrait of Yassir Arafat and kids' drawings of tanks, explosions, guerrillas and

323

guns. You know he is a lawyer in real life. Real estate deals, would you believe it. Yasu teaches gym and dabbles in the Bourse. Karish, would you believe it, sells security equipment, burglar-proof locks, bolts and systems! I don't think I ever told you that before . . . it all seems an absurd dream . . .

Making plans all night for death, carrying them out in the morning – aircraft sorties, heavy artillery, the works. The wonderful jargon: 'softening up', 'light precipitation of fire' . . . then the first day's gauntlet all over again. The bombing has just made the rubble higher, better barricades for the defenders. One by one we have to sort out the underground bunkers, the hidy-holes, the booby-trapped cellars . . . Repetition, the true evil, God help us, being condemned to do again and again what you know you shouldn't have been doing from the start . . . the sheer fucking evil of it all. Stupidity and incompetence, yes. Arrogance and self-delusion. But the sheer evil of it all. Remember all those theoretical discussions in earnest adolescence: How Does One Become a Nazi? Fucking easy! I have met the Enemy and he is me. Down the line, from Central Europe, through Vietnam, Biafra, Afghanistan – to yours truly! Our Avram might revel in this grisly joke, wouldn't he? Our fate as grotesque, murderous clowns – caked with dust, heavy with lead and pouches – us and our surreal enemies – the 'terrorists' – our own fond creation . . .

So we continue, manufacturing them by the minute: I see them, bouncing on their mothers' backs – holding their grandfathers by the hand, gazing at us with blind, all-seeing eyes. A mass of people like some apocalyptic movie of the damned. Clustering about us, clamouring for food and water. Some of the men give them their K-rations. Others sneer and wave them away, shouting 'Go to Arafat!' I see men who at winter manoeuvres gave their last blanket to a friend who was caught short, acting like insane hyenas. I see the unit gathering prisoners marking their arms with black spots . . . I see high-ranking officers, in charge of water carriers, standing over their closed taps smiling above the thirst-crazed throng. I hear expressions of contempt that raise goose pimples: 'They're less than animals.' 'They should be poisoned, like vermin.' 'They should be put in gas chambers.' I can't believe my ears. I step down and ask the soldier who said this whether he wants to die now or later. I put the barrel of my gun against his throat. Yasu pulls me off, in panic. Colonel Adashim pretends to see nothing. We have each retreated into a private world. Only the overwhelming force of the machine holds the cogs in place now, stopping them from flying off into space, to orbit Uranus or Pluto . . . I see the face of fear and smell its reek of piss, shit, sweat and tank petrol. Have I already made this statement? I see my own face, smashed in mud and tank treads. My fucking mangled conscience. Wasn't it all so fucking predictable? Didn't we foresee the whole thing? That's what makes it so fucking stupid – I just seduced myself. Nobody forced me. Nobody dragged me screaming out of bed. What a farce. What a fucking stupid farce.

So here I am, Esther, one sleeping bag among a cluster on a steep hillside. Stone terraces, an orchard of olives, a couple of allotments of peach and plum trees. An Arab with a horse and plough has just moved out of line of sight. One less target! My mind is just a blank. I am reduced to a cipher. No, I have reduced myself. No hiding behind State or Duty. Or is it 'I was only following orders'!??? I've spoken to other colleagues here from the move-ment . . . The laugh of the century! The Peace Party that wages war . . . ! Perhaps we were all born askew, crippled by a genetic confusion, puppets of our inheritance, just as Karish and all the other pious bastards think. I repeat the past, therefore I am. God, how I loathe that idea. What price the whole Zionist enterprise, the Brave New World of total change? Despite everything I suppose I believed it had some meaning, some grandeur still sticking to it. People who moved their arse. The spade, the pickaxe and Tolstoy. Land of Our Fathers. Sanctity of Toil. Human Brotherhood, hooray! While others moved off to the Marxist-Leninist bunker I still thought there was something to be salvaged from the wreckage above ground. Fucking pathetic, no? Another Arab has moved into sight, with another horse. Or is it the same one? Perhaps he ran round behind the hill to reappear, or circumnavigated the globe. I suppose we're just doomed to the treadmill, chained to our cowardice and fears. Enough. These leaflets are driving me round the bend. Just keep going, fuck it all, despite it all. Regards to Avram, Amnon and whoever else is left. Tell the world. Love, etc,

Avi

★

325

Adolphe pounced. The Sheep, wearied of its eternal vigilance, had dropped its head on the hay in the centre of the cage. Worming his way through the bars, Adolphe rushed at the messtins and began dragging them off. But the clatter of the tins woke the Sheep instantly, and it sank its teeth in Adolphe's leg. Adolphe turned, burying his fangs in the Sheep's arse. With one fart, the Sheep flung him off, stunning him against the bars. It moved in for the kill, but Adolphe recovered, biting the beast on the fetlock. The Sheep leapt back. Adolphe lunged, raking its face with his claws. The crapid hay smouldered and steamed where its blood drops fell. Its mouth foamed. Adolphe rushed in, claws unsheathed. They met in a terrible hacking mêlée of torn black fur and ripped wool. The cage shook and collapsed, the battle proceeding upon the Forward Planning floor, the muffling force of five basement levels concealing the struggle from the night shift guards outside the liftshaft's upper maw, waiting lazily for the summer dawn.

A letter to the Editor of the *Jerusalem Post* (June 27, 1982):

Sir,
As we struggle to retain our sanity during these tragic times, we turn to TV as a source of distraction. The programmes are beyond description. Why we must see war and murder on our screens during these tragic days, I cannot fathom. Surely we have enough of it all around us without having it brought into our living room too.

We pay high TV taxes. Is it too much to ask for not too old, decent, pleasant films for those of us who must be distracted from the nightmares we are forced to live through? Surely you can see to it that the programmes are more suitable.

F—L—, Tel Aviv.

From *Ma'ariv* (undated):

Dear Sir,
Your columnist N.D. described the hardships of people whose neighbours tend to hold noisy all-night parties. May I bring to your attention an equally upsetting problem which afflicts a close friend of mine: My friend lives on M— Avenue in Tel Aviv, close to the central Police Headquarters. He

complains that every night he can hear dreadful screams of people who have been arrested, giving my friend and many of his neighbours terrible recurring nightmares. I have myself, on two occasions when I visited my friend, heard blood-curdling cries which appear to be of a person in agony and also cries of pain in Arabic, which went on until 3.00 in the morning, when I had to take my leave. The second time I heard this I phoned the Police H.Q. number and was put through to a duty officer who said he could hear nothing. 'This is impossible,' I said. 'I am only a few houses away from you, and I can hear the screaming very clearly. You just cannot hold people in a residential area. Children and elderly people cannot sleep, and the value of the apartments depreciates.' Is there anyone who can answer the frustrated calls for help of the long suffering residents of M— Avenue?

Yours sincerely,
Meir K—

PLO VOWS TO FIGHT ON – BEGIN: 90 PER CENT OF TERRORISTS 'LIQUIDATED' – LIBYA's GADDAFI TO PALESTINIANS: SUICIDE BETTER THAN SHAMEFUL SURRENDER – A HUNDRED THOUSAND DEMONSTRATE AGAINST WAR – A DEATH BLOW TO ARAB RADICALISM – ANTI-WAR PROTESTORS A FIFTH COLUMN: KNESSET MEMBER – A VICTORY FOR HUMANITY –

LEBANESE WAR HERALDS NEW ERA FOR TOURISM

Tourism Minister Avraham Sharir: 'Soon we shall see the wonderful results of the war – a new era of prosperity for the tourism business. We'll be able to add one more state to the package tours to Israel and Egypt. This is already a reality, the possibility of a real peace, without the threat of war in Israel.'

Dear Avram,
We were so glad to hear about and see on television your big demonstrations against the Lebanon War. It is heartening to

know that there are so many people who are willing to be counted and to stand up against neo-fascism and the militaristic state machine. You will be glad to know that demonstrations in solidarity with the oppressed Palestinians and the Peace forces in Israel are being held all over the world, here in Germany and also in France, Great Britain, Italy, the Netherlands and Scandinavia, and of course in the Third World and even in the United States! Two days ago I marched in a big rally in Munich . . .

Adolphe staggered half dead out of Schneller, evading capture before the inevitable panic which would follow the discovery of the Rabid Sheep's carcase. Most of his hair was gone, he had lost one eye, his whiskers, his tail, and one forepaw. But he triumphantly cawed this song, as he trailed blood across the Kings of Israel Road, down Takhkemoni towards Hageffen Street:

> Ours not to question why,
> Ours not to weep and sigh,
> Ours but to bite their arse
> And tear their fucking balls off.
>
> Ours not to contemplate,
> Ours but to lacerate,
> Mangle, savage, maul and scratch,
> Catch them with their smalls off.
>
> Give no mercy, show no ruth,
> Hold no punches, be not couth,
> Vengeance only blood will sooth,
> So tear their fucking balls off.

At the entrance to the apartment block the native garbage skip dwellers, whom he had terrorized for the past several months, closed in on his wounded, shattered frame, eager for the coup de grâce. But Blok, who had returned late from his commiseration with Esther over the reluctant warrior's screed of pain, and then stayed up, unable to sleep, pasting the backlog of newspaper items into the Blokbook, heard the unusually fierce mêlée and came running down the path to chase the mob away and gather the bloody, spitting black bag of bones to his chest. Bearing it upstairs, he knocked on Sirkin's door to request the use of the old seaman's Red Star of David first aid box, boiling up kettles of hot water while the retired wanderer laboured firmly with bandages and iodine, trying to avoid the flailing claws of the ungrateful beast.

'Keep still! Keep still!'

'Aarg! barg! marg!'

'Will you eat anything before you get going?' Kokashvili asked Shabetai Tsvi, settled crosslegged on a pile of cushions in the ersatz Holy of Holies the mogul had constructed with movable walls, to facilitate every conceivable camera angle. 'You can't expect to wrestle the demons of the *klippah* on an empty stomach, can you?'

But the Messiah waved him away, sinking swiftly into a deep trance, his eyelids closing slowly as dimmerlights reduced the kilowattage mercilessly trained upon him. Gaffer's assistants moved coloured filters in and out of the barndoors of spotlights. The Messiah's lips moved, as if manipulated involuntarily, mumbling over and over slurred phrases which seemed to come from a foreign source and accent:

'The Beace Brocess . . . the Beace Brocess . . .

. . . always wear a bullet broof best . . .'

★

'They're coming! You're next!'

With a loud cry the Dayan Ezuz jackknifed up from his sickbed, thrusting a skeletal, withered right hand at the circle of his relatives, gathered in dewy-eyed force around him, with no route of escape, the prodigal son and heir, Ya'akov Ben-Havivo, kneeling tearfully by the spattered sheets:

'THE RABBLE HAVE REACHED THE GATES OF THE CITY!' And, sweeping his finger around, he misnamed his relatives one by one for the dark rulers of the Other Side: 'Halama, Samael, Kafkafuni Zutar, Ashtoreth, Lilith, Samnaglof, Sansanoi, Zumzumit, Zauba'a, Ba'al Zevuv, Agrath, Na'ama, Shemhurish, Maimon, Ashmedai.' Then he fell back, having given up the

329

ghost, on his pillows, with a look of mingled triumph, pity, satisfaction and disappointment.

★

'No point in trying to find eternal rest,' said Theodor Herzl, bowing to the inevitable and climbing out of his grave. Leaning his arms on Hechler's box and dusting dirt from his clothes while the Assyrians passed him a hot corn on the cob. The helicopters droning on above between Schneller and the Prime Minister's bunker. An ashy silence fallen over the young men's tombstones in the Military Cemetery. The brown hills, the road twisting towards the Jerusalem Forest of casuarina, cypresses and pines.

'It's very peaceful here,' said Herzl. Hechler gurgled assent in his casket. 'Perhaps I got it right after all,' Herzl mused. 'Do you remember my novel *Altneuland*? The saga of the future Jewish State? People called it a mere utopia. But what do the critics know? For myself it was pure presentiment – a dream and yet far more. Do you remember my Afterword? – "The Dream and the Deed are not as separate as some appear to think. For all the deeds of men derive from a dream, and unto the dream they shall return."'

'A fine turn of phrase,' said Hechler.

'What one seeks is always within one's grasp,' said Herzl. 'But unshaken Faith is the key.'

He looked out, brushing stray corn hairs from his beard, as the summer sun rose over the City.

ALTNEULAND

And when they came into the balm of the Old City, the first sense of the exalted atmosphere descended upon the crowds of pedestrians. For now they no longer found within the ancient walls of Jerusalem the filth and noise and ordure of twenty years ago . . . The streets and alleys had been paved with new stones, and were as neat, smooth and clean as the floors of a good house. No private homes remained in the Old City. All the buildings served the purposes of charity or ritual . . . The Old City in its entirety was an international territory, and the people of all nations were wont to see it as their homeland. For this place was the habitation of that most human of experiences – Sorrow . . .

And now we stood upon the threshold of the Temple of Jerusalem. It had been rebuilt, for the time had come, and, as in the days of yore, was constructed of hewn stone, chalk stone brought from the surrounding quarries and hardened in its contact with the air. And here again were the bronze hewn pillars before the Temple of Israel. The left pillar was named Boaz, and the right, Yachin. In the courtyard stood a great copper altar, and the great water reservoir that is called the sea of copper, just as in the olden days when Solomon reigned over Israel . . .

Theodor Herzl
Old-New Land (Altneuland), 1902

The Illusion of a Future

Shabetai Tsvi floated over the centripetal city, noting the changes since his first dream. The elongated bridges, stretching the distance between the city and its hinterland to breaking point, disrupting schedules, breaching contracts, causing riots at bus and railway stations where passengers waited for days and weeks for transport that did not arrive. The desert, encroaching on the town from north, south, west and east. The exiled brethren, diminishing behind receding barbed wire. Migrating fellaheen unable to reach the metropolis, their bazaar cries fading, their skeletons whitening in the growing No-Man's-Land. Even the service taxis from the coast failed to get through the wasteland and lay, huddled piles of rusting metal in sand dunes, vultures picking the commuters' bones by the dried-out husks of looted petrol stations. He soared, avoiding the surveillance drones, the satellite probes, the SAM missiles. The Old City appeared dour and empty, but in the New City, despite it all, life continued, petty commerce flourished, art galleries preened, hot-dog vendors vended, café klatschists kvetched over dry cheese omelettes, stranded tourists gambolled in international hotels, the Number 18 bus still climbed down from Mount Herzl, traversing the city's centre, gorging and disgorging overladen shoppers. Bank clerks at every corner still struggled with mounds of rapidly depreciating banknotes, the souvenir shops continued to sell strange memories, small children in prams protested in a vague premonition of they knew not what, so far. The pageant of everyday tit for tattle, little people, scurrying up and down the old thoroughfares under the hammer of the sky –

Wallow, Don't Stew!
As Blok walked down the Jaffa Road, from the ice cream kiosk, past the shops under the pillars, Freiman & Bein, Amkor electrical goods, Singer Sewing Machines, Nili's Eatery, Carmel Carpets, carrying Adolphe, growling but inert in a cardboard box, on his way to the veterinary surgeon. Just outside the Snow White toy store he met Esther coming in the other direction.

'Is that Adolphe?' she asked.

'Yes,' he said. 'I am taking him to the vet.'

'Allah have mercy on him,' said Esther.

'I'm afraid he's dying,' Blok averred.

'I suppose I should have looked after him,' said Esther. 'But he was so wild.'

'Any more news from Avi?'

'A letter. A phone call. Still the same. Despair.'

'And you? Have you been avoiding me?'

'Things are mixed up. I can't take anything on board.'

'I love you, Esther, in my own strange way.'

'I love you too, Avram, but what can I say? And Shuli?'

'Shuli doesn't love me any more. She has become an active pacifist.'

'You're wrong, Avram. I've seen her and she's still all for you. But she also has to sort out her mind.'

'We all love each other but it makes no difference. It's this fucking loveless City. Did Shuli tell you she was in love with the City? But the City loves nobody.'

'Don't let despair consume you too, Avram.'

'I'm not in despair. Look – positive action: I am taking the cat to the doctor.'

'I'm grateful, Avram. You know I can't deal with it.'

Blok bowed and continued on his way.

The Echo and The Id

All the alarms tripped at the Department of Apocalyptic Affairs deep below Mittag's Café. The ascent of Shabetai Tsvi and the raising of Herzl, in tandem, sent tremors through the whole system. Databanks coughed and bleeped, figures and graphs roiled on the display units, and two fully equipped field teams scrambled. Tolstoy, Lermontov and Rashi rushed off to Schneller, to liaise with the armed forces, while Istiqlal, with Young Kazha and Gruzini-Cholera, set out towards Mount Herzl, unaware that the Founder, trailing after the Hechler box, had already turned off into David Wolfson Avenue and was bypassing the Hebrew University, breathing heavily and mopping sweat from his brow.

'A beer, a cold beer . . .' he gasped desperately, 'a pint of Bass, for the love of God, or even a flagon of Schmeck's Pilsen . . .'

But the Assyrians continued to bear the decomposing Hechler towards the centre of the City as the temperature continued to rise, to 33 degrees Celsius, 90.4 Fahrenheit in the shade . . .

The Psychopaternity of Everyday Life
(or The Philatelist's Stones)

'Difficult times, Avram, I can tell you, even for professional
ostriches like your poor besieged father. I don't know how much
longer I can resist your accursed Aunt – I smell chicken shit in my
twilight years – they'll bury me in the Moshav's manure pile. Ah,
the soil! Asargelusha! This God person doesn't give up, does he?
Now he has my left leg as well as the right. A wheelchair
permanent on the fourth floor? Even I can't hold out now. And
gallstones – it's His new idea. Kick old Baruch Blok when he's
down. Your mother, thank God, seems to be getting stronger.
She has a deal with Upstairs. All those decades of Psalm reading.
Preferential treatment. Listen, when I go, I want you to put a large
club, with nails, in my shroud. But don't say a word to your
mother. When I get through the gates, up there for Judgement, I'll
take it out and Whop! let Him have it . . . Let's see Him pee blood
for a change. Fuck them all. It's good to hear your voice, Avremel,
but you know, it's perfectly legal to visit. Are you OK? Have you
got rid of that diseased cat?'

Moses and Mononucleosis

She loves me, she loves me not, as he flicked ants off the cracked
kitchen marble, watching them scurry on the floor, cut off ab-
ruptly from their tribe. The eternal booming of the neighbours'
radios, in one ear and out the other, yesterday's, last week's,
next week's newspapers spread out all over the floor: ADVANCE
OF ARMOUR IN BEIRUT: IDF LIMITS WATER, ELEC-
TRICITY SUPPLY: HORSE-DRAWN CARTS IN BESIEGED
CITY: DUM-DUM BULLETS AND ELEPHANT-
HUNTING ROUNDS FOUND IN TERRORIST WARE-
HOUSES. Mush! Mush! Solar topees crawling through the
Lebanese underbrush. The giant kefiyaed beast unfurls its trunk,
bellowing to the sky. And still no sign of Shuli, gone to ground
after her last plaintive phone call: 'Do you think I should stay in the
police force, Avram? Do you have a point of view?'

Jung and Innocent

Continuing down the Jaffa Road, on the corner of the Jordan

Bookshop and the Alba Pharmacy, Blok ran into 'Zeppelin' Khalid.

'Ibrahim!' cried the fat actor. 'It's good to see you! What have you got in that box?'

'Just a cat I am taking for his medical appointment. He was badly mauled in a fight. Twelve against one.'

'I know the feeling. Especially these days. Life is really shit, isn't it . . . We haven't met since the Russian Compound . . .'

'You survived that all right?'

'Normal procedure. Charges dropped, till next time. But you never saw our new play . . .'

'I never even knew its name . . .'

'These are shitty days . . . it all seems so pointless . . . so much slaughter going on up there . . . what can we do? Anything we try simply emphasizes our futility . . . but come round, Ibrahim, we're in Zaroubi's Café . . . even in these days – you are always welcome . . .'

He passed by, going towards the Zion Square crossing, waving: 'Good luck with the sick pussy . . .'

Sylphization and Its Discontents

Meanwhile, Esther, contemplating her meeting with Blok, proceeded up the Jaffa Road to the second-hand bookshop where she was wont to cool her pains in a cup of coffee on the terrace with the proprietress, Dina L—, whom she had met at the Women Against the War demo and whose boy friend was also serving reluctantly out there for the glory of those he despised. Then, as the afternoon heat ebbed, she crossed over to the shoe shops under the pillars, idling at Freiman & Bein and the schmutter shops, then crossing back to catch the Number 18 bus in the direction of the Cinematheque, tonight due to show *Der Blaue Engel – The Blue Angel* (Joseph von Sternberg, 1930), to be followed by *A Respectable Life* (1979), with Kenta and Eva Gustavson and Stufa Swenson ('a difficult film, at times brutal, criticizing Swedish social welfare society, and raising the problem of heroin addiction, which both the authorities and the public in Sweden prefer to ignore') but at the last moment, deciding she could face neither Marlene Dietrich nor the failure of Swedish socialism, she walked back down the

Bethlehem Road, across the railway tracks, past the petrol station, the billboards, kiosks and groceries, to her apartment, which she reached at the tail end of twilight, fixing up an omelette and green salad, then, picking out the long untouched book of I-Ching and the set of stalks, made a throw. The hexagram which appeared was that of Hsu – Waiting, or Nourishment:

> If you are sincere
> You have light and success.
> Perseverance brings good fortune.
> It furthers one to cross the great water.

The individual lines, however, were less promising:

> Six in the fourth place: Waiting in blood.
> Get out of the pit.

Lotuswise, Esther sat and waited. The phone rang. It was the young prodigal son, Ya'akov Ben-Havivo.

'My father, blessed be his memory, has passed away,' he said. 'The family have elected me in his place.'

'I'm so sorry. What a terrible responsibility . . .'

'I'm inviting you to my coronation.'

Alte Neuland, Alte Schich

Refreshing himself under the fountain at France Square, Herzl resumed his walk with the four Assyrians, inconspicuous in their dress as Arab labourers conveying Hechler's box on a trolley. The ripe smell now palpable from within the casket was assumed by passers-by to emanate from the unwashed pores of the inferior race.

'I am impressed,' said Herzl. 'Neat parks, tall buildings, hotels, flower gardens, clean streets, frequent public transport. Just as I had predicted. My dream has truly come true.'

Floating along the streets of Rehavia, the wide swathe of Ramban Street, the narrow interlinks of Abarbanel and Ibn Ezra, quiet middle-class residences fronted by foliage and gardens, lemon trees and casuarina, pot plants and domestic cactii. Cosy

Pensions and Youth Centres. Nose against the plate glass of the Viennese Pastry and Cake shop in Keren Kayemet, closed, alas, for siesta. Herzl leaves his saliva on the window, brushing away the Assyrians' offer of a dry crust of *kümmel*. Curious students of the Gymnasium High School's summer course crack feeble jokes as they pass. 'Theodor Herzl, eh?' 'Get his autograph.' 'Is that the man to blame for it all?'

Into Ussishkin Street, with its low, long, red-roofed houses. The old quarried stone. Obituary notices. Announcements of religious services. A skullcapped youth, at a corner, hands them a leaflet:

VISIT THE MUSEUM OF THE FUTURE HOLOCAUST. FOR THOU HAST CHOSEN US AMONG THE NATIONS . . .
Reject Defeatism! Let Rabbi Levine Open Your Eyes To the Dangers of the 'Peacemongers' and Compromisers. Support the Party of National Purity. Free Entry With This Message.

Yokes and Their Relation to the Unconscious (or The House of the Seven Goebbels)

All over the walls, photographs of persons of the Jewish faith persecuted for their identity. Men, women and children with starved faces, emaciated, drooping limbs. Powerful hands crudely shaving the beard of an elderly skullcapped man. Men and women in striped prison costume with gothic signs hung around their necks. Men and women hanged on gallows. Children holding their hands high, led by men with guns. Blonde square faces above uniforms, deathhead emblems and the cross. Captions add: Milwaukee. Sioux Falls. Schenectady. San Francisco. London. Paris. Amsterdam. DO NOT SAY IT CANNOT HAPPEN HERE!

Rabbi Levine rises from behind a desk, blinking his eyes at the newcomer, pulling at his neat goatee. In the road outside, children play about Hechler's box, slipping through the bearers' guard.

'Whatchagot there, Mustafa?'

'Smells like a dead dog!'

'Haven't we met somewhere before?' asked Levine.

'I do not think so,' Herzl said.

339

Halt, Neuland!!

'I predicted it,' said Herzl. 'The fall of the Jews, due to the gentiles' fear and envy. Mass destruction and cataclysm. But nobody ever listens.'

'We listened,' said Rabbi Levine quietly, 'but you didn't go far enough. Despite your moment of insight, you underestimated the magnitude of the crisis. You were shocked by Dreyfus, but it was only natural for the goy to spit out his enemy. The assimilated Jew, the Jew who pretends he is the same as all mankind. But, worse than that, you underestimated God, both in his wrath and his glory. Thus the creature that sprang from your bourgeois vision could only be a thing of clay – a Golem. A clockwork toy turned with the key of secularist ambition. Life is only the Name's to provide.'

'I always believed in the power of Faith,' said Herzl, 'but we live in the real world, after all. The world of the political struggle for survival, of competing nations and great powers.'

'My help is from the Lord,' Levine said, 'Creator of the Heavens and the Earth. Why scrabble at the doors of tinpot despots when the Greatest Power of all is with you?'

'I have never been a fanatic,' said Herzl. 'I believe in common sense and reason. God gave us these powers so we may determine our own fate, by our own volition.'

'You are advocating an individual redemption,' Levine said. 'That is a Christian, not a Jewish principle. We are redeemed as a people or not at all. All the rest is second-hand Hellenism.'

Herzl gazed at him as he sipped his tea, which a demurely coiffed and covered young girl had brought him. Herzl had drained his own gratefully in one gulp. The sound of squabbling came from downstairs. Levine rose and looked out of the window. A horde of small boys with skullcaps were dancing round the four porters and their putridinous burden.

'Rabbi Levine! Rabbi Levine! The Arabs have got a dead body in here!'

A menacing crowd of adults began forming, some carrying large sticks and bicycle chains.

'Break that box! Call the police! Kill the Arabs!' quoth the mob.

The four Assyrians grabbed their trolley and pushed their way through the crowd. 'Stop them! Don't let them get away!' people

340

cried, but the size and dourness of the guardians was too daunting. The bearers ran, trundling Hechler down Ussishkin, pursued by desperate cries. Levine turned back to question Herzl further, but his visitor had taken advantage of the mêlée to slip out down the stairs, evade the skipping children, and vanish in the hillside alleys of the Nahlaot district . . .

History Is Bunk, I

Shabetai Tsvi spiralled, soared, watched as the mob chased after the four Assyrians bearing the Reverend Hechler, flourishing their stones and cudgels, noting the civilian Volkswagen van of the Department of Apocalyptic Affairs' hit team converging on the disturbance. He looked away, as directly below him the centripetal highways across the Mediterranean Isthmus buckled, snapped and fell into the roiling waves, shedding stalled cars, buses, container trucks and trailers, upon which the waters closed. Inland, tiny figures crawled upon the parched desert towards the receding City, shedding their faded uniforms, dogtags, steel helmets, personal weapons and battle pouches as they went, their squeaking voices reaching him by dribs and drabs in the twists and turns of sandstorms:

'Fuck the war! Fuck the war!'

'Home! Home! Home!'

A vulture hovered.

'Who has the One-O-five?'

'Bore him to death with one of your monologues, Werther!'

'Just breathe out the Lebanese air, Avi!'

'Goddamit, Yasu! Who has the water bottle?'

'Wait a minute!'

'Hoy!'

'Hoy!'

'Hoy – there's somebody out there, coming towards us!'

'A figment, Yasu, a figment.'

'No, it's a Bedouin in a dirty white *jalabiyeh*.'

'Greetings, friend!'

'*Salaam aleikum!*'

'*Aleikum salaam.*'

'Has any of you a bullet broof best, brothers?'

'Ah!'

'Ah!'

'Ah!'

'You seem to have been in an accident, brother . . .'

'*Aywa*, you could put it that way . . .'

The vulture, scenting blood, swooped, beak poised for the wanderer's open, jagged wounds. The three soldiers beat the beast off, desperately whacking its head with their canteens . . .

The Interpolation of Dreams (or: The Reluctant Voyage of Sindbad the Porter)

'Zeppelin' Khalid, having parted from Blok and Adolphe, continued east towards the Old City, mulling over his brief mention of the *Zurafa's* play, which had been cancelled on its opening night: the tale of Sindbad, the porter of the poster upon the wall, who carries the City of Jerusalem on his back, making his meagre living by showing its splendours to visitors and tourists. One day, unfortunately, he put down his burden in the corner to relax with a spot of kif. But when he rose to resume his chores he found the City had been stolen, under his nose, by an unknown hand.

'And how do we show this City on the stage, smart boy?' Latif Sa'adi had asked him, when he had first proposed the concept.

'We never see it. It is already gone when the curtain rises. Our play will be the story of Sindbad's journey. First he questions all his neighbours, the local police, the kadi, the governor, the King, has anyone seen the City? But they all laugh in his face, saying: What a prize idiot, he let slip his life's blood for a little puff of kif.'

'Anti-National slander! Imperialist lies!'

'He leaves his homeland, and travels all over the world. Rumours tell him the City was taken by the order of powerful distant potentates. He travels to Washington, London, Paris, Moscow. No stone is left unturned. But at the end, he has to return to the source: the new neighbours who have moved in across the valley. Do they have the City? Or did it never exist, except in the porter's own dreams?'

342

Land O'Goshen!

The vet's clinic was in the same Jaffa Road building as Thin Avi's defunct 'Bridge Publications', which had since been replaced by a cut-price travel agency, now also closed down. The newspaper distributor Kastorak, on the second floor, however, was still present, venting his spleen to the four winds: 'Goddamn the fucking bastards!' The dwarf vendor scurried out, explaining gleefully to Blok that the office had just been raided. Plain-clothes agents, accompanied by police, had impounded all the *World of Puzzles*: new editions, back numbers, returns going back seven years. It was part, the dwarf said, of a general clamp-down on mysteries. Chortling, he bounded off down the stairs, scattering copies of the *Dishwashing Daily* and the *New Police News*. Blok proceeded, carrying Adolphe in his box, up the stairs, past the false beard macher and the writer of sex manuals for the orthodox, drawn by the smell of piss and inhuman yelps and squawks to the unmistakable waiting room of Dr Fish, Veterinary Surgeon. The lobby, despite the Crisis, was filled with anxious pet owners and their infirm beasts: dogs moping on the beige tiled floor, mice lolling on their backs in cages, growling cats, a snake sighing in its box, and a small monkey, with a heavy bandage round its head, dolefully perusing *Bul* Magazine.

'Who has the last number?' asked Blok.

The snake, languidly raising its tail, displayed a tag marked '23'. Tired, wrinkled, desperate faces turned towards the newcomer, while, from the hidden surgery, a high-pitched rapidly fading wail denoted the injection of a tranquillizing drug. Blok lifted the cardboard cover on his box. The bald, scarred, festering Adolphe looked up at him with his remaining baleful eye.

History Is Bunk, II

'On June 5, 1967,' Anwar el-Sadat told the three demobilized soldiers, 'I was woken up and told that the Israelis had attacked our forces in Sinai. I listened to Cairo Radio. It said our forces were rebulsing the invader with stubendous success. Over thirty Israeli blanes had been shot down. The desert was covered with the enemy's corpses! It was not till I reached the General Staff bunker that even I learned the terrible truth: our entire air force was destroyed. We had in fact lost the war. Still we told lies to the beoble. But they found out the truth in good time. As will yours. I shook your Brime Minister's hand and embraced him. I offered you hope, and what did I get in return? A hail of bullets from fanatics! I remember the night I landed at Lod, and later, in your famous King David Hotel – blown up by your own Brime Minister thirty-two years before! – I looked out of the window at the illuminated walls and battlements of the Ancient City of Beace! My heart leapt and my blood sang joyously. I knew I was bart of that noble vision which moved the hearts of the Brophets: Swords into blough-shares! Spears into bruning shears! Beace, the greatest blessing of God! The next day I walked through the markets of the Old City, towards al-Aqsa. Beoble could not believe I was there! Berhaps you all thought it was my ghost walking the streets! Did we ever truly exist in your eyes? No, it seems only now, when I am dead, that you see me, that you trace the footstebs of my fading voyage . . . '

Beyond the Bleasure Brincible

'This cat is dead,' said Dr Fish.

'What?' said Blok. 'What are you saying? He was alive and angry in the waiting room.'

'That's the nature of existence,' said the veterinary. 'One moment you're kicking your heels, singing *Hatikvah*. The next – pouf!'

Blok gazed at the inert ball of flesh and torn black fur in his cardboard box.

'It's in vogue, death,' said the doctor, shaking his white mane of hair. 'People are bringing me in dead poodles, parrots, tarantulas in rigor mortis. A few weeks ago I was called out to a top secret Ministry of Defence bunker. You'll never guess what they showed me there – a dead sheep. Well, with those people you never ask questions. Can you do anything for him? they said. The thing had been dead for twelve hours. Riddled with disease. Burn it, I said, don't leave a fleck abiding. We'll have to do the same for your poor moggie, I'm afraid. You'll have to leave him here with me. It's the law. There's a small crematorium for dead pets in the

344

outskirts. They keep it secret, for fear of potential analogies. It's disguised as a pitta bakery.'

Blok left the clinic empty handed, his mind in turmoil. Long buried memories again surging, bubbling to the surface: another cat and an affair of the heart long dormant . . . frisson of abandoned asylums . . . the fated peep of Original Sin through the window . . . the ripe and rotted fields of Fifties' porn . . . porcine hallucinations . . . living legends of Olde Jerusalem, the lost and found City . . . He walks, past the pillars, round Mayan Stub, up Strauss to the old Bikur Kholim hospital, down the Street of the Prophets to the Davidka Memorial and down Pines into Mekor Baruch. The sun, the sun, the quarried stone, red rooves, wrought iron balconies, faded blue iron slatted shutters, the buckled asphalt pavements . . . Shuli: I love the City. I want to live and die here. The unholy transfer of compassion from the living to the dead. The heart, torn asunder by the pushmepullyou of opposites. The constant existence on the brink of the horrible. Is the nation adjusting itself to Blok's fears, taking on the warp and weft of his soul, the genetic inheritance, the global village broken down, battlefield of faiths, rebellion and order, the headless spiritualist, a negative Pangloss, all's worst in the worst of all possible worlds, but Nevertheless . . . ! Nevertheless . . . ! travels in the oceans of the mind . . . the counter-thrusts of one's own body, the life force *v.* the death wish, again . . . but, in the wings, the ultimate crime, the mirror image of unfinal solutions . . . the terrible fear of repetition of the same stupid acts, thoughts, errors, crimes, sins of commission and omission.

Irrelevant Gods.

Back, catless, to Hageffen Street, the silence upon the unwhitewashed rooftop, the sullenness of an absent Salim . . . Waiting for Shuli's phone call. Or anyone's, in khamsin pall . . .

WE DEMAND!!

Justice, Freedom, An Immediate End to Oppression, The Rights of Man, the Right to Sleep Easily in Our Beds, An End to Helicopter Night Flights, Cessation of Guilt, Angst, Shame, the Fulfilment of All Desires, Mass Trials for Treason, Public Hanging, Stoning, Reintroduction of Impalement, a Tourniquet for

Bleeding Hearts, the Complete Destruction of the Enemy By Land Sea and Air, the Preservation of Our Traditional Way of Life, An End to 'Moral' Dilemmas, the Abolition of Doubt, Criminalize Hesitation, Instant Unity, Appeasement Out, No Fraternization, Clarity, Charity, Charisma, Cant, Claptrap, a pot for every piss, a day for every dog, a City for every slicker, Absolute Certainty, An Open Mind, Universal Happiness, Heaven on Earth, One Moment of Silence, a break, a break, for God's sake, in the looming tempest clouds . . .

Night.
Day.
Night.
Day.

The telephone rang.

It was Avi.

'Avram!' he cried. 'Whenever I return, she's not here! What the fuck is going on?'

'I don't know. I'm glad you're back, Avi. The fucking cat has died.'

'Let's meet at the traditional venue.'

'SWALLOW, DON'T CHEW, COMRADES. I'M A PAUPER. SEE THIS SHIRT. ONE MORE HIT ON THE IRONING BOARD AND IT'S THROUGH. HOW CAN I FINANCE MY DIGNITY?'

'You won't believe what it took me to get home, Avram. The effort, the time, the aggravation. The Apocalypse, it wears you down, Avram. And what do you do the morning after?'

'Just a humus and a ful for me, Ezra. And an orangeade.'

'YOU'LL GET A SMALL ONE.'

'Did you see in the newspapers? My Colonel Adashim, Young Werther, refused his orders. He refused to take the battalion into Beirut. They reduced him to the ranks, right there. Private The Sorrows of Young Werther. I've never seen a man more ecstatic. We travelled together, with Yasu too. We're going to demonstrate here in the City. I mean fuck Tel Aviv. Nobody cares there. It's here the real impact.'

'Yes.'

'Right-wing fanatics, flat earthists, creationists, Jewish nazis,

346

religious maniacs, "warriors of the temple mount", flagellators, arcanologists, gnostics, repentants, revenants, spiritualists, ghosts, gurus, geeks, freaks, supporters of the Likud government are gathering here in ever greater numbers. Haven't you noticed? there's a showdown in the air. This time they've gone too far. We have to act. It's infecting everyone. Do you know where Esther has gone to?'

'I told you I just met her in the street the other day. When Adolphe died. But I haven't seen her since then.'

'I located that Sergeant Tuvia. He told me they've all gone down south to the Negev to the "coronation" of the Dayan Ezuz. That fucking bicycle thief, can you believe it? The sergeant's going down there too, with guess who – your Shuli. Did you know that? Apparently there's a shortage of police down there, for crowd control. They expect a cast of thousands. A carmagnole while the house burns!'

'I don't know where we're going at all, Avi.'

'We're going nowhere. We've already arrived. The terminal stop. Why not? We have the technology – you should see it all in fucking action: napalm, cluster shells, phosphorus bombs. The Rockeye MK-118, the CBU-58/B. The BLU/63/B – you know what they call that one? the "Goyak" anti-personnel bomb! The SUU-30 Air Launched Free Fall Dispenser. Sounds like a candy machine, no? State of the Art, boy. Stomachs rupture, intestines spill out, bodies fill with a hundred metal fragments. Phosphorus burns the body from inside long after the initial impact. Smoke coming out of living mouths, consuming the larynx, gums, tongue. That'll teach 'em to talk out of turn! But who sees that on television? Abroad, maybe, in forgotten lands. We here are doomed to live with long shots. The long view, that's always the one to take, isn't it? How else can one survive?'

'Perhaps one shouldn't.'

'That's what I once told Karish. He blew his top. You know he got it in the right leg up there. But did it stop him? No, sir! Hobbling out of his stretcher, volunteered to pass out leaflets of the Habad Hassidim, telling the soldiers God loves only them . . . But what has this war got to do with survival? It's merely a profession turning into a hobby . . .'

'I USED TO BE A HAPPY MAN,' Ezra boomed, 'BUT

347

THEN I OPENED A RESTAURANT AND ALL SORTS OF INGRATES BEGAN EATING AWAY AT MY JOY . . .'

'I no longer exist,' said Avi. 'I feel I am just a machine programmed with emotions of anger and rage. I want to kill. This is the sum total of my pacifistic journey. Is this what we were born for? Just tell me. Is it for this shit we passed through the whole purgatory of short trousers, short rations and wellies? I don't blame you for not wanting to remember. The farce is blackened by its prologue. God, the naivety of it all, when we thought we'd be spared the corruption and double-dealing and self-loathing of our Past . . . I thought about it a lot as we trudged home, growing smaller all the time. Half way back we met a Bedouin who said he was the dead President of Egypt. OK. We gave him a tot of our water bottle, and a cigarette – he said he had lost his pipe – and we sat at the side of the road and talked about Sufism – Private Werther showed a keen interest – the need to cleanse one's soul of the impurities of human nature. To become free from desire. To possess nothing and be possessed by nothing. Well, we had already thrown most of our equipment away, and were left with just about nothing but the underwear sent to the front by concerned citizens. Werther had our travel vouchers and a sheaf of credit cards. Yasu his prized collection of Bazooka bubble gum footballers. We gave the dead President Puskàs and Chodorov and a defunct American Express. Do you think we did the right thing, Avram?'

'SWALLOW, GODDAMIT! DON'T CHEW!'

348

In the splendid space of the Temple, the sweet voices of song and music of harps rose into the air. The chords had a wonderous effect on the pilgrim Friedrich's spirit, returning him to his earlier life and to earlier days in the life of the people of Israel. All around him the worshippers sang and murmured the words of the prayers. But in his own mind rose the fine German verses of Heinrich Heine's 'Hebrew Melodies'. Before his eyes stood the Princess Sabbath, she 'who is called the Silent Princess' . . . Yes, Heine, as a real poet, felt the romance hidden in the fate of his people . . . But now Friedrich was reminded of those humiliating days in which the Jews were ashamed of everything that was Jewish . . . and these were the reasons why Judaism had reached its nadir, the '*Elend*' in the ancient German sense of the word, that is an '*Ausland*', a foreign land, dwelling place of the pariahs . . . and whoever is bereft in the '*Elend*' was a victim of fate, who, seeing no way out, burrowed deeper to hide in the '*Elend*'. And so the Jews deteriorated, by their own fault. '*Elend*', Exile, Ghetto! Different words in different tongues, with one meaning: to be an object of contempt, and to arrive, at the end of the road, at contempt for oneself . . .

Theodor Herzl, *Altneuland*

THE NEWS FROM THE BATTLEFIELD was all bad. A massacre had taken place in the refugee suburbs of Avi's besieged northern city. Nazarene forces, followers of the Lamb of Bethlehem, sent into the suburbs by our own forces, to do battle with the armed Enemy, went methodically instead through the poverty-ridden, bombed-out streets, house to house, dragging out men, women and children, cutting the throats of the boys, raping the girls, disembowelling mothers, splitting the skulls of fathers with axes before the eyes of their seed, mutilating the dead, cutting off hands, feet, breasts, genitals, crushing heads with rifle butts, tearing out the unborn child of a pregnant woman with a bayonet, scattering her intestines in the dust, machine gunning a family caught watching television, killing a paralyzed old man in a wheelchair, throwing grenades at doctors in a hospital, finishing off the patients, raping the nurses, cutting off fingers to extract gold rings, shooting everything that moved in the streets, cats, dogs, goats, horses, mules. Then they requested and received from our forces heavy bulldozers with which they toppled the houses on top of the dead and dying and dug out and filled mass graves. Nevertheless the world's press, swooping like vulture angels, recorded the blurred sight of the slain. Carcasses like meat in a scattered abattoir, bloated bodies, thick with flies, heads like split watermelons, putrid buttocks swelling through ripped trousers, the slashed soles of bare feet upturned, coagulated red-brown goo. Survivors had been taken away in trucks by the Nazarenes, and were never heard of again. Later old men took to wandering the streets of the city, fanning out in trembling fingers the sheaf of faded snapshots of sons, daughters, missing grand-children, a patrimony wiped clean.

Saladin's Fifth Dream

He continued to wander through the blossoming garden sprung up from the desert sands: landscaped bushes of rhododendrons and violets, an undulating carpet of anemones, orchids, ger-aniums, hyacinths and lilies, rows of ornamental cactii, fountains spraying golden liquid into jewelled basins, singing trees, their leaves rendering harmonies no lute or harp could match, the Talking Bird, Bulbul al-Hazar, flitting from one branch to another under a turquoise sky, and, in the shadow of the trees, seated on lush green lawns, he could recognize many of the friends of his youth, and famous Sufis and philosophers, whose names were bywords for the quest for truth and purity, Ma'aruf al-Kharki, Dhu al-Nun al-Misri, Ibn al-Farid, Habib al-Ajami, al-Marwazi and Hassan of Basra. Among them he also recognized the sainted lady Rabiah al-Adawiya who had said: 'My great love for God leaves me no room to hate Satan.' But above and beyond all these, on a bald hill crowned with a single silver tree, Saladin saw the figure of the slight golden-haired maiden of the ball of string beckoning to him firmly. He approached, and found himself, on the summit of the hill, looking down from the edge of a vast, chalk rock cliff upon the City, carved in its entirety out of a giant diamond, its spires and battlements hewn from great gems, topaz, rubies, jade, chalcedony, onyx, turquoise, lapis lazuli, glinting and glistening in the sun. He looked sideways at the lady of the string but she was unsmiling. She thrust an AK 47 Avtomat Kalashnikov into his hand with seven full clips of ammunition and, pointing towards the City, delivered a mighty kick up his backside, precipitating him willy nilly down the steep cliffside, leaping and weaving to keep his balance . . .

Minutes of the House Committee, 35 Hageffen Street (Third Day of the Jewish New Year)

In the absence of Elyakim Tolstoy of Entrance D, Flat 3, who was away on Special Duties for the third consecutive week, Kadurie, of Entrance C, took the chair again, noting the presence of old stalwarts Kimchi and Kishonski and the welcome addition of Mrs Tishbi. He wished them a Happy New Year and well over the High Holidays but noted it was a sad time for the House of Israel, beset by external tragedies and internal dissension. He expressed the heartfelt desires of all present that Unity and Peace would soon be restored. Kimchi, of Entrance C, commented this was unlikely as long as traitors and spiritual weaklings in our midst continued to impugn the government and our heroic Defence Forces and stab the Nation in the back. Kishonski, of Flat 5, Entrance C, wished to take exception at these remarks, claiming it was precisely such bigotry and blunting of moral judgement which was the root of present troubles and of the shameful horror which had overtaken the entire Jewish people. Mrs Tishbi, supporting him, said the House Committee should post a statement on its notice board condemning the refugee camp massacres and inviting further signatures. Mr Kimchi became agitated at this point and over-turned his cup of coffee. The Chairman, Kadurie, tried to smooth

351

the atmosphere, suggesting the purpose of the Committee was to deal with the more mundane aspects of the daily life of our little community, and that well-intentioned expressions of social and national import would hardly remove the accumulated litter in the front yard, or convince the Teherani's boy to tune down his video, or improve the garbage collection.

'Exactly!' Kimchi banged the table, reiterating: 'What about these Arab garbage saboteurs?!'

Totem and Tabouleh

'What a farce!' Salim whispered, sitting on his bed at his mother's home in Khalid Ibn el-Walid Street, facing the communal tapestry on the wall: the History of the Arabs – no room left for any further embroidery: a small flame of orange, in the lower left corner, had appeared in the night to represent the latest episode of the National Disaster. The central panel of the *isra*, Yarmuk and the Crusades was already pale and faded.

'How can one remain idle?'

My son, my son. In the kitchen, his mother plied the knife to chop tomatoes, green pepper, cucumbers, mint, parsley. Mixing in the rinsed burghul. Washing the lettuce in the sink. My son, my son. Your father painted the Jews' bathrooms. He just had that little piece to finish in the corner.

'I shall finish it,' Salim vowed.

Ashen silence in Zaroubi's Café. The *Zurafa* actors sit ignoring even the backgammon boards. The streets outside denuded by the sudden fall of the axe on the execution block. The searching porter, peeking in to ask his perennial question, withdrawing hurriedly, on tip toe . . .

No Vitamins, No Cornflakes

An eerie silence, too, in the main square of the Negev town of Arikha, the hundreds of tables and folding chairs removed, the gravel ground littered with ripped tablecloths, food cartons, napkins, empty brandy, gin and whisky bottles, paper plates and cups, chicken bones and spilled couscous, rotting lettuce and cabbage leaves, and no one left but Esther and Shuli, sitting on the bare concrete parapet of the Heroes' Square, surveying the echoes of the boy saint's triumph, dulled as it was by the terrible news filtering through from the north. The smell of hard liquor mingled with particles of sand wafting across the pre-dawn, under the fallen banner proclaiming: THE HEAVENS SING IN HIS HONOUR AND THE LAND IS FULL OF HIS MERCY.

'What conclusion can we draw?'

Shuli, in her mussed-up uniform, clutched, pummelled and kissed by the happy crowd as they danced the night away for the Young Savant, inheritor of his father's blessed wisdom, resplendent on a silver dais in a pure white silk robe, drunk as a lord on Napoleon brandy, flanked by the Chief Rabbi and the District Chief of Police, with Sergeant Tuvia sitting uncomfortably at the right hand of the Saint he had arrested twelve times, looking on nervously as the ecstatic worshippers, men and women, stampeded, reaching for dollar bills signed by the deceased Sage and auctioned by the town Mayor from the podium at a minimum of a hundred greens apiece:

'WE BELIEVE! WE BELIEVE! WE BELIEVE!'

Esther took Shuli's hand. A breeze ruffled the mounds of rubbish. The new Dayan Ezuz long departed in the embrace of his adoring multitudes. The prodigal son fully reclaimed with no break in the paternal chain.

'He doesn't need me any more.'

Shuli's head lying on Esther's shoulder. A police jeep puttering up under the stars, punching lazily through the sandstorm. The friendly unshaven moon face of Sergeant Tuvia: 'Jerusalem, Express?'

Hand in hand, they climbed aboard, into the back seat.

What Is To Be Done?

'The Reverend William Hechler, I presume,' said Tolstoy, addressing the scuffed, sealed black box deposited on the floor in the bargain basement of the Apocalyptic Department deep below Mittag's Café, the four Assyrians, rescued from the wrath of Rabbi Levine's followers, now firmly under lock and key. The Reverend did not answer, but the odour of putrescence oozed out beyond the safest seal. 'We can help you,' said Tolstoy. 'A trade off, your results for ours. We have cryogenic facilities. We can arrest your imminent death, until further notice. Speak up man! This is your last, your only remaining hope . . .'

Moral And Intellectual Decay Of The Bourgeoisie

– The gathering storm. The lightning sheering the bridges. All aboard who're due aboard: Meetings of Peace Committees, de-mobilized soldiers, outraged citizens, haemophiliac hearts: Avi, Amnon, Yasu and Werther, ex-Colonel Adashim in his new-found dissenting fame: 'I am not an example to anyone. I just got fucking pissed off.' Avi elected chairman of a new movement: Soldiers Opposing Slaughter – SOS . . .

All over town, concerned citizens girding their loins, preparing to make their voices heard . . .

. . . But the Prime Minister, burrowed into a wormhole in the kitchen cabinet, refusing utterly to come out, denying all knowl-edge, complicity, culpability, any stigma, blame, onus, sin. My Hands Are Clean! Rubbing them desperately against the whitewash of the wall. The cabinet in disarray, a scattered jumble of bitter herbs and sour condiments left for the cleaning lady . . .

Snip! Snip! Snip!

'Haven't I seen you somewhere before, sir? On a stamp? or a banknote?'

'I don't think so,' Herzl told the barber. 'Take the whole lot off, will you.'

'Certainly, sir. A bold move, I can tell you. Not many people have your courage. That beard must be a lifetime's investment. But sometimes it hides the personality. Karl Marx, there's one I'd like in this chair. Or Moses, or Theodor Herzl. What lies behind that great mane, eh sir? A real lion, or just a lamb, terrified of baring its naked chin? You never know. A man's a man for a' that. What can't be cured must be endured. Blood's thicker than water. I've had all sorts in my chair: sinners, saints, heroes, delinquents, cabinet ministers, religious leaders. At the end of the day it's the same dead hair that lies about on the floor. I sweep it up and throw it in the dustbin. Some people sell it, for use in wigs. Anything for an extra shekel. But true happiness lies in lack of ambition. Being content with what you have. I had Hubert Humphrey in this chair once. The Vice-President of the United States. He was polite, courteous, a real gentleman. The next day I had a hippy from one of the cafés, an upstart who was content with nothing. You cut too little, you cut too much. Leave the sideburns. Take them off. Of course, this is merely a personal opinion. Live and let live, that's my motto. If I had Yassir Arafat in this chair I'd say Yes, sir, shampoo, set, short back and sides? Another person would cut his tongue out. I believe there's enough conflict in the world. In this shop, I cut hair. Shave, shampoo, no newfangled fashions. If I may say so, sir, you look fifty years younger. Will there be anything else?'

Co-Optus Interruptus

'Keep quiet, for God's sake!' Kokashvili clapped his hand over the Messiah's mouth, muffling his mumbled protests. They had emerged into the sunlight, in the middle of the Jewish Cemetery on the Mount of Olives, two dark dots in an immense swathe of blinding white stone and marble. Above and behind them, the Intercontinental Hotel (Double Room $70–80; Breakfast alone $8). Below and before them, the walls of the City, the spires, domes of the mosques, across the Valley of Yehoshaphat, location of the Resurrection (Joel, 3, 12–14). But the dead, Moslem on one side of the valley, Jewish on the other, remained stubbornly interred. Kokashvili swore, flicking his worry beads, railing at the two weeks he and Shabetai had spent in the cellars and tunnels underneath the hill, after escaping the police dragnet thrown around the Kokashvili Leisure Centre and its ersatz Temple by the Department of Apocalyptic Affairs, subsisting on Emergency Rations among the shells of audio-animatronic Arabs stockpiled by the film mogul for his Model Village, but left to rust for lack of batteries.

'Wake up, God damn you!' Kokashvili cried, striking his fist on the tombstones.

But the Messiah shook his head.

'You blew it again,' Kokashvili told him.

355

The Messiah spread his hands.

'The ambience was wrong,' he mumbled. 'The false setting. The unfinished building. The fake altar. I should have been at the genuine pivotal point, the central hub, as it were –'

'Out there?' Kokashvili pointed towards the grand mosques, gleaming, silver and gold, in the sun. The Messiah shrugged in reluctant assent.

'All right,' Kokashvili said. 'Let's go.'

Thus saith the Lord

'FOR I WILL NO MORE PITY THE INHABITANTS OF THE LAND, BUT LO, I WILL DELIVER THEM EVERY ONE INTO HIS NEIGHBOUR'S HAND, AND INTO THE HAND OF HIS KING, AND THEY SHALL SMITE THE LAND, AND OUT OF THEIR HAND I WILL NOT DELIVER THEM . . . Zechariah, 11, 6.' The Reverend Hechler lambasted his host/captors as they carried his box out of the Department's Volkswagen van, down the sun-baked swathe of the valley, just as Kokashvili and Shabetai disappeared beyond the Lion's Gate . . . Tolstoy, Istiqlal and Co accompanied by Inspector Kandide and four constables freshly signed on the Official Secrets Act, protecting the guest's public exposure . . .

'FOR THE VIOLENCE OF LEBANON SHALL COVER THEE, AND THE SPOIL OF BEASTS, WHICH MADE THEM AFRAID, BECAUSE OF MEN'S BLOOD, AND FOR THE VIOLENCE OF THE LAND, OF THE CITY, AND OF ALL THAT DWELL THEREIN . . .'

'What does he want from us?' Kandide mumbled, holding a handkerchief over his nose.

'Humour the man,' whispered Tolstoy, 'think of the pay-off: the very Ark of the Lord, and the possible solution to the crime of the century – the assassination of Theodor Herzl . . .'

Kandide groaned, but continued down the dry dusty parched valley.

'After Mount Nebo,' Hechler rasped through his speaking tube, 'I was stumped for several decades. My expedition with Theodor and Baraq al-Zahr, under the Dome, convinced me the Ark was not there, the most obvious alternative hiding place . . . But I was sure, nevertheless, he had the key . . . and, sure enough, the figures show . . .'

They had reached the point, half way down the valley, indicated on the map Istiqlal held. 'Is there an olive tree here, its trunk shaped like a marrow?' Hechler rasped. 'I knew it! the solar axis . . . the equinoctial line from the Mount of Olives . . . but at what depth? the archaeologists had sucked all the tunnels dry . . . Gihon, Silwan, the Gethsemane Olive Grove – all useless red herrings . . . but if one draws a pentagram, base at Jerusalem, apex at Nazareth, left and right feet at Beersheba and Kerak, with the upper right side of the star transecting Jabesh-Gilead, the left Nebi Samuel, Dir Ibzi, Kfar Saba and the main coastal highway at the Lubrani Petrol Station –'

'Where do you want us to dig?' asked Kandide.

'Right here, under this very tree . . .'

WE DEMAND!

the cessation of all evil – egality, throughout the species – fraternization of all colours, races, creeds – all power to the people – sanctuaries, from the people's power – the sacred right of secession – the understanding of desire – the desire to understand – the knowledge of needs – the need of knowledge – self determination – determination of self – beauty – peace – a good night's sleep, Asargelusha!!

★

Salim took the last tissue-wrapped grenade from its shoebox and placed it in the same old holdall he had used in his abortive attempt at the Hamashbir Department Store. He sat in his room, bag on his bed, emptying his mind of all memories and drinking in the damped down sounds of the strike stricken city. The oppressed mourning their latest calvary. The oppressors, mourning the painful wrench of the mote from their eye. Magic mirror on the wall, who is the ugliest of us all? But the tapestry told him nothing. Waiting for the tick-tock of time . . .

★

Blok, back in Hageffen Street, the telephone fails to ring, ants maraud. No cat, but a lingering smell which does not seem to leave even through wide open windows. Scorched earth behind closed eyelids. That sense of time winding down. One senses it clearly in the streets: the slow motion of the Jerusalem soft shoe shuffle. Heaviness and disco-ordination of limbs. Apathetic keychain twirling. The gaze, hoovering the baked pavements, desperate to be disengaged from the fellowship of confusion. The croak of life escaping through reluctant sphincter muscles, who-ooshing through loosened nostrils. The headlines on unbought newspapers, drooping at high noon:

HOPES RISE FOR CEASE-FIRE

THE FOURTH MONTH OF THE TWO-DAY WAR

EMPIRE OF TERRORISM SMASHED

THE ENEMY'S LAST STAND

The cyclical duty of the City walk, hoping against hope for a balm the present cannot provide. So what's wrong with living in the past? Everyone else does. Setting off about the narrow contours of his Mekor Baruch lebensraum, the old streets with the resonant names: Reshit Hokhmah – the Beginning of Wisdom, Hafetz Hayim – the Desirous of Life, Sde Hemed – the Pleasant Field, Pri Hadash – New Fruit, Ha'Amarcalim – the Administrators (of the Temple). Even recklessly venturing into the ultra-orthodox quar-ter of Mea Shearim, A Hundred Gates, lair of the acid-throwing zealots, Keep Out signs and dire omens. The old low stone houses, alleys opening on to ancient courtyards of a thousand and one synagogues, seminaries, schooling houses of the pure. The writing on the wall: *Mene, mene* – you have been weighed and found wanting . . . and through, and up Salant and round the Ethiopian Church, full of Whittemoresque mysteries, iron gates, hiding gardens of cypresses and wizened black men with millen-nial cares, across the Street of the Prophets, down Rabbi Kook, past Doctor Ticho's alley, the Maskit fashion store, and the city's best public toilet. Across the sparsely populated Jaffa Road and the barely pedestrian precinct of Ben Yehuda. Many kiosks inexplicably closed.

'What sort of town is it where you can't get a decent hot dog at noon?'

Your home town, asargelusha! the City of Blok, at its dimmest.

Land of our Fathers, no less, the living tomb of our poor mothers. He sits at the almost deserted tables outside the Café Atara, ordering a Kinli orange drink, not freshly squeezed, and a toasted cheese sandwich. Remembering all those snippets he had laboured so long to disrecall: Mama Blok, preparing his school sandwiches of olive segments on margarine. Howling at the gates of the kindergarten. The pedagogic claws. Simpler times. A city divided, but somnambulant, not tossing in a demented fever. The old clothes man pushing his cart, the ringing bell of the kerosene vendor and the Sabbath crier, so that the Sabbath always smelled of petrol. The iceman dividing his blocks with an axe. Lemon and red popsicles sold from a wooden box. And yet we progressed from folly to folly! Desperate for ignorance, they gave us knowledge, cramming us chock full of memories even our grandparents had forgotten. The suppository of lost hopes. Papa and the balm of the stamp collection. Mama and her Psalms and Ecclesiastes . . . And I grew up, all agley, twisting this way and that: wars, crises and campaigns passing me by, Holocaust trials and memorials, the patrimony of corpses . . .

– Land of our Fathers, ladies and gentlemen, the living tomb of our poor mothers . . . Letting the City grow around me, taking on new stone, concrete reconstructions. Armies parading proudly down its freshly asphalted highways. Dressing me in khaki, they plucked me from home and tried to make a man out of me. The bullets with our names and addresses on them . . . the random survival of our heritage . . . new conquests and victory parades . . . who would have ever thought it? From Holocaust rags to gauleiters in a few easy moves! But I grew on, even more agley, twisting this way and that. Asylums and circumnavigations of the globe . . . But still the lost and found City in me: The Jaffa Road running up my spinal column, Kiryat Moshe in my ganglia, Mekor Baruch in the occipital lobe, Mea Shearim in my hippocampus, the old walled City in my gut . . . A cancerous growth, without a doubt, as the City bulged and swelled in its new glories to three times its former size: a magnificent mutation, with glittering knobs of glass, new towers of Gog and Magog, international conference centres, towerblocks on bald conquered hills, the multi-confessional multi-accessional reborn resurrected reunited hydra-headed paradise, with art galleries and health food restaurants and Tai-Chin studios and tennis clubs and pet stores, tourist traps of a thousand and one gew-gaws, discotheques, cinematheques, sushi bars and pizza parlours and national parks and sexual licence sauced with puritan restriction, *kulturkampf*, summer *kampf* and pure *kampf*, concert halls and hi and lo culture, the City crowned in glory, the City of poor men's dreams, the City going to the dogs, the City of dope smoking and *Kiddush* wine addiction, rock of phages, draft beer, hamburgers, seventeen flavours of Dayvilles, night vice and twenty-four-hour autobanks.

Get thee out of thy country, and from thy kindred, and from thy father's house, unto a land that I will shew thee. And I will make of thee a great nation, and I will bless them that bless thee, and curse him that curseth thee, and in thee shall all families of the earth be blessed.

Pull the other one, schmendrick.

Can't Buy Me Love, Love, Love

Repelled by his cheese sandwich, Blok walks on down the baking oven of the road, hugging the paltry shade of the shoe shops, hat shops, clothes shops, the bookshop and the barber who used to cut his hair in his childhood, sitting on the board laid across the arms of the chair, waiting for the assault of the clippers. Snip! Snip! Snip! The cutter still waiting for his next victim, while his assistant sweeps up the detritus of a great black mane. Ambling on, across Zion Square, down the Jaffa Road, the bagel kiosk, Steimatsky's, Tamar's Gifts and Souvenirs (Happy Jewish Family Cards, *tembel* hats, lurid colour pics of the new Dayan Ezuz), the wicker bag and hat shop, the alley of Mittag's Café, huddled figures dashing furtively into a jeep and off along the hot main road . . . Crossing towards the Post Office building, by Amkor frigidaires, PNM Real Estate, Spinel's Jewellery, the Golden Chicken and Au Sahara Restaurants, Abramowicz Import-Export, Tiano Plumbing and Sanitary Fittings, the Bible Society, Kravitz Furniture, then across the open junction to hug the Old City walls. The blue canopy sky – Mount of Olives ahead, down, past the Damascus Gate, Nablus Road, the Arab bus station with its coughing old wrecks loading, Salah ed-Din Street and its Post Office, Crusaders still mailing their plaintive letters home. Brushing off the accosting porter, on, past the Rockefeller Museum, once the pride of Jordan, now of Israel, the wraiths of absent friends materializing, as he walks, by his side: Yissachar and Bentov, lugging the Canon Scoopic and camera accessory boxes.

'Vitamins and cornflakes, brother! sugar coated pills of wisdom! timelessness, that's the important factor! Who cares about the future when the past has taken over the present? Everything is one seamless line of beauty and pain, order and confusion, life and death, Easter Eggs in September, Christmas all the year round, the resurrection preceding the crucifixion, imagination made material, the spiritual made bankable: it is no myth that loaves and fishes multiply by faith alone. The angry western cry: is it true? pales before the leisured pragmatism of the east's great pack of lies . . .'

And what do you think, Yissachar? It's all the same to me, Avram! Any fool can see – it's biological – the climate – *khamsin* – falafel overdose . . .

He walks on alone, rounding the corner of the walls at the Stork's Tower, the intersection plunging down the valley to Jericho, or down and up to the Mount of Olives and the Augusta Victoria Hospital. Blok turns right to edge his way along the walls through the Moslem cemetery, old gravestones scuffed by Baba Time, stopping suddenly at the sight of a group of men, by a van and jeep, midway between the Golden Gate and Gethsemane, digging feverishly under a tree, beside a large sealed black box or casket emitting a fearfully putrid smell reminiscent of Adolphe in his final hours. A man with a pistol at his hip shoos him away, but not before he recognizes Inspector Kandide, in plain clothes, among the knot of diggers. They seem to have unearthed a small, round object, holding it in the air with astonished cries which waft up to Blok on the hot air:

'Nothing here but a fucking skull, Goddammit!'

'What else would you expect to find?'

'This is no ancient artifact – there's still flesh on the bone . . .'

'Look at that neat cut through the vertebrae . . .'

'Ah, dem bones, dem dry bones . . .'

'Shut up, Istiqlal!'

'Fuck off, Tolstoy . . .'

361

'!!★★?!??★★!'

Pushed out by the police from the Valley of Yehoshaphat, Blok catches a last glimpse of the entire crew piling into their Volkswagen van and jeep, with the casket, and driving away, sirens howling in frustration. He re-enters the City through the Lions' Gate, Bab Sittna Mariam, or Saint Stephen's: the Apostle who preached the word of the Messiah nearby, and was stoned to death for his pains. Acts 7, 54–7: 'When they heard these things, they were cut to the heart, and they gnashed on him with their teeth. But he . . . said, Behold, I see the heavens opened, and the Son of man standing on the right hand of God. Then they cried out with a loud voice, and stopped their ears, and ran upon him with one accord.' One of the crowd was the young man Saul, of Tarsus, who later saw the light, they say. Down the Via Dolorosa, the cross-bearer's route, the tourist trail of the ages. The Chapel of the Flagellation. The Condemnation Chapel. *Ecce Homo*. Our Lady of the Spasm. Round the corner of the Khan el-Zeit market. So many stalls and shops closed and shuttered, in protest over more recent calvaries. Only a handful of devil-may-care stores remain open, catering to a few bewildered Mexican pilgrims dragging their own home-made wooden cross in the direction of the Holy Sepulchre, offering them plastic dolls, soup ladles, coat hangers, lightbulbs, thermos flasks, bags, toilet soap, motorcycle helmets, tennis balls, needle and thread sets, boot polish, brilliantine, shampoo, souvenir plates, mugs, eggcups, aprons imprinted with the Stations of the Cross, little brass models of the Sepulchre, el-Aqsa, the YMCA, the Windmill, the Dormition, multi-coloured candles, Tampax, towels, shaving brushes, Creme Nivea, suntan oil, mosquito oil, holy oil, Jordan River water, Eilat sand, pencils, Parker Pens, bathsalts, saltcellars, pepperpots, cruets, kettles, pots, pans, chamber pots, maps, postcards, 250 stamps of East Asia, corkscrews, mousetraps, papier-mâché masks of famous statesmen, London policeman's helmets, copper balls, and other items that would not pass through the eye of a needle. No sale. The Mexican pilgrims drag their cross onward, singing hymns to the Virgin. As their footsteps and voices fade Blok hears the distinct sounds of tumult and riot coming from the Haram. Idling, his feet turn him towards the compound, fetching up against the arch of an ornate Mameluke doorway, a great wooden gate

362

shut and barred by border police, weighed down by radios and guns.

'You can't go this way, *habibi*, there's a disturbance on the Mount.'

When is there not??

'Don't get smart with me, honey, these situations are not picnics.'

Indeed not. Blok retreats, up al-Khalidiyah, into David Street, but is then borne with the tide of the curious, left into the rebuilt Jewish Quarter, swinging by the reconsecrated synagogues, the concrete echoes of past glories – the Tree of Life, the Ruin, the Splendour of Israel – twisting to avoid the ersatz art galleries and Steimatsky's Branch and the Tourist Information Office, emerging on to the neat white-stoned terraces overlooking the vast courtyard of the Western, Wailing Wall. Puffs of white smoke rising over the wall as knots of soldiers and armed civilians close in on the Temple Mount.

'What's going on here?'

The kibitzing crowd, tourists and tourist guides, day trippers, skullcapped residents, shitkickers, mid-day bums –

'They caught a Jew in disguise trying to pray in the Mosque . . .'

'There were two of them, dressed in Arab clothes . . .'

'Anyone from your group, Yosske?'

'Nothing planned for this week, Mottke . . .'

'Maybe Levine's boys, or the Temple Faithful . . .'

'Wait a minute, something's happening out there . . .'

Elend of Hope and Glory

This is what had occurred:

Shabetai Tsvi and Kokashvili, having dressed themselves appropriately in Kokashvili's basement in standard Arab petit-bourgeois garb, old faded Harris tweed suits, grey trousers, black pointy shoes and white kefiyas, garnied with dark glasses, had joined the thin but converging stream of daily Moslem worshippers heading for the grand mosques. The guards at the Bab al-Qattanin did not even give them a glance as they floated through, up the stairs on to the broad forecourt of the Dome of the

Rock, under the great stone arches crowned with the muezzin's loudspeakers. Shabetai, recalling his long years of apostasy and Islamic dissimulation in the seventeenth century, lead Kokashvili towards the water fountains in order to perform the necessary ablutions prescribed by the Faith before prayer in accordance with the Shafi'ite tradition, pronouncing the required formula: 'In the name of Allah . . .', he first washed the palms of his hands, then rinsed his mouth, rubbing his head, then his ears, and his beard, twisting his fingers and toes sharply, putting his right foot before his left, pronouncing the act of Faith after each wash and repeating the process three times. Kokashvili, on the other hand, trying to follow, became hopelessly snarled up: he plunged his hands first thing in the basin, then put his face in it like a goat, then watered the base of his neck, then put his left foot before his right, then repeated the process five times, reducing the formula to a hopeless mumble. A nearby worshipper, noting this, whispered in the ear of a *waqf* guard, who, as the two impostors entered the hallowed space of the Mosque, shrewdly challenged them in Hebrew. Kokashvili, keeping his nerve, answered in his best, outraged Arabic, but Shabetai, true to the colours of his indecision, broke free and ran, his exit cut off, into the centre of the holy place, through the startled Faithful prostrated in the afternoon prayer, clambering over the wooden balustrade on to the Sacred Rock itself.

'ALLAH! ALLAH!'

The worshippers rose in the fever pitch of absolute scandal, their cries reverberating in the interior of the dome, bouncing off the gold, black, red surfaces, the gilded arabesques of Koran verse: 'PRAISE BE TO GOD WHO HAS NO SON OR COMPANION IN HIS GOVERNMENT, WHO REQUIRED NO HELPER TO SAVE HIM FROM DISHONOUR; HE GOVERNS HEAVEN AND EARTH, HE BRINGS TO LIFE AND CAUSES TO DIE, HE IS ALMIGHTY; TO HIM BELONGS ALL THAT IS IN HEAVEN AND EARTH, HE IS ALL-SUFFICIENT IN HIMSELF; GOD IS MY LORD AND YOUR LORD; THEREFORE SERVE HIM; THAT IS THE RIGHT PATH.'

The stained glass windows whirled above him like a massive spinning top, guards rushing up from the interior of the Well of

Souls, he slipping from their grip, rushing down the rock-hewn steps into the sacred cave. Kokashvili, meanwhile, all but disappeared in the press of bodies, feet and fists. But there he is, nevertheless, hoisted up by the multitude, borne, kicking and struggling, out into the yard of the Haram –

'ALLAHU AKBAR!'

'ALLAHU AKBAR!'

'GOD IS GREAT!'

'DEFEND THE HARAM!'

'MOSLEM RIOT! MOSLEM RIOT!'

Sirens blast through the City. Tear gas clouds billow whitely in the blue sky. The crack, crack, crack, of fired canisters. Shops emptying, bunkers filling, panicked tourists, Christians melting into brickwork, Jews arming themselves with whatever weapons come to hand: sticks, stones, rifles, submachine guns, grenade launchers, 105s, mortars:

'BLOOD IS BLOOD! FLESH IS FLESH! WHO IS FOR THE LORD, TO ME!'

Blok looks up to see Rabbi Levine, above the throng, perched on the cupola of a newly rebuilt seminary, arms outstretched and beseeching:

'I TOLD THEM WHAT THEY ALL KNEW IN THEIR HEARTS! I SAID OPENLY WHAT THEY ALL THOUGHT IN SECRET! But did they listen to me? No, they never do, until their pants are on fire!' And he cried out in wrath: 'WHICH SIDE ARE YOU ON NOW, BLEEDING HEARTS, PEACE PISSERS, DEFILERS OF YOUR ANCESTORS' GRAVES?!'

Ten Eyes For an Eye! A Thousand Teeth For a Tooth! The outraged worshippers pour out under the golden dome, carrying high the fat, struggling mound of Adir Kokashvili, his fake robes hanging from him in tatters. The mob hoists the battered mogul by a pulley, up the Haram side of the Wailing Wall, dropping him like a sack of stones down the other, his voice spitting loud defiance:

'KOK MOCK ROCK SHOCK! INDIE ENDIE TRENDY 750G!'

Whack! his bones hit the crazy paving.

'MOSLEM RIOT! MOSLEM RIOT!'

Blok runs back into the bazaars. At the turnoff to El-Wad Street a hand grips his elbow. 'Zeppelin' Khalid, dragging him into a café in the wall. The fatigued and worried faces of one-time comrades: Salah the Nose, Yassir Not Arafat, Ali Fitzpatrick, Rasha and Mouna Elias.

'Get out of the way, Ibrahim!'

Doors shut, windows shuttered, bolted. Outside, clubs, planks, broken bottles, plenty of gnashing of teeth . . . Sindbad the Porter disappears under the welter of stomping feet, carried off by ululating seamstresses. Across the valley, Saladin's forces advance, armour clashing, speartips glinting, the diminutive Kurd's eyes flashing with a terrible, exclusive desire:

'BLOOD IS BLOOD! FLESH IS FLESH!'

Which side are you on, schmendrick?! Do not confuse the cohorts of the faithful with the phalanges of Pharaoh!

A THOUSAND EYES FOR AN EYE! A MILLION TEETH FOR A TOOTH!

'Has anyone got a bullet broof best?'

Salim, snapping out of meditation in his room, hearing the welling cries from the City, grabs his lethal holdall and runs out –

– 'Do you hear anything?' Shuli asks Esther.

They prick their ears out of the windows of the Bak'a apartment. The wind has veered a little. Esther shakes her head. 'Nothing that can be worth hearing.' They return to each other's arms, softly caressing, exploring new worlds of subterfuge and salvation –

– A spreading pool of glop oozing out of the opened reinforced steel door of the cryogenic capsule. Tolstoy, Istiqlal, Lermontov and Rashi gazing equally aghast at the melted mess on the floor, eyeballs rolling loose into corners, fallen teeth rattling on bare concrete. Hechler's empty box standing, unhinged, a sad memento at their side.

'How the hell did this happen?'

'Another power failure. Both auxiliary generators failed to trip. The backup system is in repair . . .'

'The fuck . . . we'll never know now . . . the Herzl murder, the Ark . . . the elixir of life . . . Goddamn fools . . .'

'But does anyone need to find this out?'

'Did they ever burn that fucking sheep's carcase?'

'Shit. That's possible . . . No one will know . . .'

'Until AD 2080 . . . unless the press . . . traitors within . . .'

Visual display units all round them bleeped and buzzed, tinkled, chimed, clicked and moaned.

– While Kandide, in the basement of the Russian Compound, watched impatiently as figures in white coats tried to match the disinterred Valley of Yehoshaphat head with the preserved body from Ein Karem.

'Difficult to tell . . . spectrograph analysis . . . missing fragments . . . the crushed hyoid bone . . .' Murmurs merging with the air conditioning –

'Can't anyone identify a fucking dead body?!'

The tinny laughter of bluebottle flies . . .

– Shabetai Tsvi, cornered in the Well of Souls below the Rock of Moriah, dashes between the altars of David and Solomon, Abraham and Elijah. The guards, having cut off the exit, approach him now with long staves. He tears off the robes of Kokashvili Leisure Corporation's Wardrobe Department. Standing, naked, on the balls of his feet, he begins to swivel in place, pirouetting faster and faster, becoming a blur which the guards watch sombrely as it disappears through the solid rock floor. They extract from a wall cupboard several small brooms, and wipe the dust under the carpets.

'What'd'you think, Khalid? Is it safe for Avram to come out?'

'The fracas seems to have died down, so far . . .'

'Stay, Ibrahim, have another few cups of coffee . . .'

'No thanks, maybe another time . . .'

'*Inshallah* . . .'

'*Inshallah* . . .'

'*Inshallah* . . .'

– Below the floor Shabetai twists silently, floating past the assembled praying dead, the vast spit turning the roast Leviathan, the stockpile of armaments of all ages, the vacant cavern, the

367

vermin cave, finally entering the torchlit gaming hall and taking his place at the backgammon table.

'Welcome,' says the Sheikh al-Islam. 'Will you take the black or the white?'

The demonstration of soldiers against the slaughter wends its way through the New City. Ten thousand strong in the cool snap of evening, a headless snake with sheathed fangs, each separate scale carrying a lighted candle, a banner, a cardboard placard of outraged convictions:

'DOWN WITH THE GOVERNMENT OF SHAME!'
'I AM MY BROTHER'S KEEPER!'
'MINISTERS OF THE BLUNDER – RESIGN!'

From the mouth of the Independence Park, up Hillel Street, past the Gallery Café, the Chinese Restaurant, the Ron, Orgil and Orna Cinemas, the El Al Office, the Promised Land Travel Agency, round the corner into King George, with a reproachful side glance to the Ta'amon Café, past the old Parliament building turned Tourist Information Centre, the Yeshurun Synagogue, the Jewish Agency compound, the Chief Rabbinate Building, the Supersol and Plaza Hotel, turning right at France Square towards Ramban Street. Phalanxes of the young, squads of the old, demobilized soldiers, soldiers in service, peace women, wives and mothers against the war, bereaved parents against bereavement, civil servants against incivility, war cripples against crippledom, pensioners for survival into old age, ex-heroin addicts against addiction, ex-mental patients against insanity, concentration camp survivors against new final solutions, believers against the ultimate heresy, slum-dwellers against the extermination of slum-dwellers, infants against infanticide.

But the obvious does not go unchallenged: on either side of the snake, small groups of counter-demonstrators, stalwarts of the

Party of National Purity, feebly held back by police, jeer and spit at the column, darting in and out to grab placards, tearing and smashing them underfoot:

'DEATH TO TRAITORS! RENEGADES AND APOSTATES OUT!'

Salim/Omar joined this company. Merging his identities of actor, whitewasher and terrorist, he slipped a skullcap on his head and now runs with the zealots, hugging his lethal blue holdall:

'LIBERTINES! HELLENISTS! SONS OF WHORES! PARRICIDES! ENEMIES OF GOD! FALSE PROPHETS!'

Consumed by a fury which fills every pore, he chafes – how dare these murderers of his own people march in inculpation of their own monstrous acts? What right have they to censure the vile crimes their very presence here made inevitable? Who are they to speak for the victims, the torn, the mutilated, the dispossessed by their hand? The putrid odour of liberal guilt, hypocrisy and double dealing rises as an incense in his nostrils. The crocodile tears burn him like acid. He cries out:

'FALSE WITNESSES TO THE GALLOWS!'

Down Ramban, past the Isaac Wolfson Buildings, into the cool breeze, under the open stars of the Ruppin Road's valley. The smell of the glades of pine which stand in the night between the criers and the Knesset Parliament building. The soothsayers' rabble at *iftecha de'karta*, shadows shimmering in the wavy candlelight – an almost negroid Arab, in a white *jalabiyeh*, spotted red, smoking an old brier pipe, a tall heavy-set man in a nineteenth-century frock coat, uneasily fingering newly shorn chin stubble, a man in ragged shorts and a torn T-shirt who seems to carry no head, leading weaving shapes and vapours in the jingle-jangle evening of an old defunct familiarity: Maccabees and Macedonians against the Massacre, Crusaders against the Crusade, Greeks against Greed and Genocide, Persians against Purges and Pogroms, Medes and Molochs against Murder, Byzantines against Bad Business, Ashtoreth against Assassination, Tammuz against Tammany Hall. But in the forefront of the march Salim, racing with the mob, lights his eyes on clearer recognitions: Blok, the complaining tenant under the whitewash, Thin Avi, the would-be-bridge-builder, arms linked with a knot of young men of solemn mien – Yasu, Amnon, Private né-Colonel The Sorrows of

Young Werther – while, a way behind them, Shuli and Esther, meeting on the barricades, nevertheless, with pails of sand to pour on blood and fire.

'WE DEMAND AN IMMEDIATE COMMITTEE OF INQUIRY! WE DEMAND THE RESIGNATION OF ALL THOSE RESPONSIBLE! WE DEMAND AN END TO THE WAR TEARING OUR NATION APART! WE DEMAND, WE DEMAND, WE DEMAND –'

'Look out!'

A grenade comes sailing over the crowd. Floating out from behind police barriers, describing a lazy, tangential curve in the soft lullaby of the breeze, tumbling gracefully as it proceeds, over the convocation, over the tousled, dark, grey, white, bald, covered heads, towards the front line, twirling unerringly to land and roll forward towards the feet of Avi and Blok.

'GRENADE!' Avi shouts, but remains in place, frozen, with Werther, Yasu and Amnon, poised against the Knesset gate.

Blok throws himself on the grenade. Curling himself into a foetal position. Clasping it to his belly.

Time stands still, clicking its worry beads.

The grenade fails to explode.

OUTREMERE

If I were only a peeled grapefruit,
If I were only a peeled grapefruit,
A pretty girl would eat me up
If I were only a peeled grapefruit.

Commercial jingle

Rolling fields of corn, beet, alfalfa stretching as far as the eye can see, towards a line of tall eucalyptus, hiding the lower coastal highway. A tractor buzzing lazily across brown virgin furrows. Neat white-painted two-storey houses separated by patches of green. Birdsong and water sprinklers on the lawn. An old woman with a watering can at a flower bed. An old man in a wheelchair.

'Hell on earth,' said Baruch. 'The soil. It's for worms. Caterpillars, beetles and snails. God knows I'll be with them soon enough.'

'I'm leaving, Papa,' Blok told him, straightening an askew pillow. 'I bought a one-year open return ticket. I shall throw away the return on take off.'

'Who can blame you, Avremel?' said Baruch. 'Certainly not me.'

Rosa Blok, wearing heavy wooden sandals, strode determinedly across the undergrowth, bearing her big tin can.

'Shouldn't you be out of the sun, Baruch?'

'No,' he said. 'The sun boils my brains, and makes me less aware of my fate.'

She strode into the house to commiserate with Aunt Pashtida, who was composing a letter to the President of Paraguay concerning his scandalous protection of the Nazi war criminal Josef Mengele.

'There was no choice,' sighed Baruch. 'No legs, on the fourth floor. And look what a lease of life it has given your mother. Twenty years in bed with the Book of Psalms and suddenly – oompah! I won't have to bury her after all. She can wield the shovel for me.'

'Do you want me to stay, Papa?' asked Blok.

'Go,' said Baruch. 'Make Life, not Death. I'll hang on somehow here, melting in the pot. Go, unmelt. Make something of yourself. I understand the bind.'

Indeed. The impossible emergence of Blok the hero on the front pages of the daily press. EX-MENTAL PATIENT SAVES FRIENDS. Pursuit by microphones and cameras. 'What did you think of when you threw yourself upon the bomb?' 'Mainly the unpaid water bill.' The stunned and unavoidably reproachful look of Avi, robbed of his own birthright.

'What made you do that, Avram, for God's sake?' No God, no sake at all.

'It just seemed to happen. But I did think: What an absurd end.'

And Yissachar had telephoned, saying: 'That was definitely biological.'

'Why, Avremel?' Baruch, in a moment of privacy.

'I knew Avi would jump on the fucking thing,' said Blok, 'to expiate his guilt, or sins, God knows, all the baggage he carries on his back, invisible old men of the sea . . . I thought, better me than him. What's the point? He believes in something. What can I say? The farce of my life: a useless hibernation, a failed escape, two girl friends who ended up – the hell with that. What would Mama say? – there's plenty more fish in the sea.'

'Smelly things, fish,' said Baruch. 'But women . . .' he gave a deep sigh. 'Tell me, Avremel, do you blame me, do you hold me to task, for taking you, albeit in your mother's womb, all the way across the sea to this country of lunatics and feinschmeckers?'

'No, Papa. You had no choice.'

'I suppose we could have stuck it in Hungary. Would you have wanted to be a Hungarian, Avram? Sachertorte and goulash? The dome of the Buda Castle, the oak trees of Margaret Island, the Danube bridges in the sun . . . There are beautiful women in Budapest, Avram. But in the end I married your mother.'

'That's life, Papa,' said Blok. 'Why should I blame you for anything? We're all simply moved by circumstances.'

'Don't get me wrong,' said Baruch. 'She was a striking girl in her day. But it was like marrying into your own family. Do you understand that? I feel that I've been committing incest for the last forty-four years.'

Have we not all? Later, over the dinner table, attempting to disengage from Aunt Pashtida's vegetarian mushroom pie (Baruch: 'I can't eat this swill.'), Rosa, inclining her grey thatch towards her only begotten son: 'Not that I want to stop you, Avremel, but are you sure this is the right time? Just when things seem to be getting a little better?' She did not repeat her cousin Nachman R.'s offer to arrange for Blok to be returned to the roster of Reserve soldiers cleared for duty, but it hung in the air, a cloak of acceptability ready to descend.

'I don't know, Mama. But I got paid a lump sum by Yissachar for reading all those scripts. I might as well use it, and things are still a little tense around here.'

'It's the global village,' said Aunt Pashtida. 'When everything's the same, what's the difference?'

The cheque had come in the mail. Yissachar had written: Cash it now. I've just come from Kokashvili's bedside; the man is spewing new ideas. Lying there in quadruple traction, limbs in gibbs and stapled bones, surrounded by family and attorneys, arranging the sale of the great Temple set to a West German TV series, the interrupted Leisure Centre to a Baptist Group for a Holy Land Theme Park, the shells of the animatronic robots to a Palestinian entrepreneur, a deal frowned on by State Security, but he does not seem to care. 'Money has no colour, brothers.' Banished, the mediums, rabbis, saints, kabbalists and mystic seers. I have been instructed to budget for a whole new series, said Yissachar, of old-style Kokashvili productions: *The Singing Beggar*, *The Dancing Night Nurses*, *The Little Soldier Who Lives Down the Road*. Comedies, snarls the broken-backed Georgian, that's what people will pay to see . . .

Make 'em laugh. Make 'em cry. The *Zurafa's* revamped Sindbad production, adapted to national needs, finally had its one and only performance, the press reported. The déjà vu of police swooping to stop the show and close the hall. A fracas, a few arrests, tin mugs against the walls of the Russian Compound cells. And nevertheless, she revolves. Shuli, in plain clothes, having decided not to quit the force, beginning a new course of forensics. 'It's liberating, to work only with science,' she told Esther, 'and take the passion out of it all.'

'That would be very nice,' said Esther. She had informed Blok of the curiously flat resolution to the mystery of Armand's murder: confession, by the Hairy Beast of Ein Karem, caught resuming his old compulsion of laying his hirsute corpus by sleeping lone ladies, only to be knocked flat and secured by his last victim, who ran a ju-jitsu class. The Beast was a delivery van driver. 'Armand had seen him returning from one of his jaunts, so he killed him,' said Esther. 'He hid the head in the Silwan valley, but that, too, was found by chance a little while ago, though they weren't sure of its identity . . . and all those elaborate theories . . .'

She had to meet Blok face to face at least once more – smoothing negotiations with her aunt, Blok's landlady, as he gave up his apartment: 'Well, so what's wrong with the place? You weren't happy here? We all have to make sacrifices. At least you could have tidied up a little. Well, I see you've swept the floors. But I don't remember, was this chairleg broken? I'm sure it was all right. You still have the ironing board, the mops and the brooms? There's a strange smell in here, I have to tell you, almost like a dead cat or something. I hope you haven't been keeping animals here. They leave their traces years afterwards. Are you all right with the House Committee? You know I haven't asked or meddled. Have you seen a trace of me in three years? That's the sort of landlady I am. I like to provide a home, not a prison. And how have you been, Estherke?'

The mute glances round the back of the wiry bustling auntie. The wary silence, contrapunted with short quivering chords of small talk. And how's Shuli? Shuli's fine, we get on well together, it's nice to be a little free of aggressions . . . yes, the forensic course is almost finished . . . Will she spend all her time with corpses? No, you're mixed up with pathology, Avram. She will only be dealing with trivia, drops of blood, fluff from trouser cuffs, bits of hair, dust, dandruff. Prima materia. Ashes to ashes. And Avi? We haven't spoken for a long time. He spends all his energies with his group, you know, the Warriors For Peace, picketing government rallies, confronting and fighting Rabbi Levine in the streets. They have a new slogan: Peace Is Not For Pacifists. The Dayan Ezuz? I read they found him a Moroccan heiress. They're having the wedding at the grand mausoleum they're building in Arikha for his father. Did you ever meet the old man, Avram? He was a character. He read my future. He knew the men in my life would recede from me. It's just the way things happen, Avram.

There is a flame-red sunset, e'en out of the Hageffen Street window. The women returning from the market with shopping bags. The men with beards and hats and sidecurls. Mrs Almoshnino preparing supper three rooms deep in Entrance B. 'Elik, stop doing that. What do you think, we're Arabs here?' No sign of Salim/Omar, waiting somewhere, or, perhaps, over the border in Jordan, joining hands with Lena Khalili? a pact of bloody return from the grey of exile, a true '*Elend*' of hope and glory . . .

Tolstoy hoves into view, treading wearily, with his half empty bag of sandwiches. Bearing his lopsided sense of failure, the eternity of futile searches. He glances up, glimpsing Blok at the window of Entrance A, Flat 8. Shaking a metaphorical fist. You get away scot free, bastard! (While rumour has it: the four Assyrians, Shangalay, Charapinsk, Yashmak and Barud, had been recruited by the Apocalyptic Department, sent off as a field team into the depths of the Soviet Caucasus, in search of –)

Go, Avram, Go. The House Committee Chairman, Kadurie, called, helping him carry his two suitcases down the path to the taxi for the airport.

'Is this all you have?'

'Who needs more?'

'A wandering Jew, Mister Blok, you may be right. We carry the world with us.

'I'll try to clean the cat smell out!' he cried to Blok as the service taxi accelerated, round the corner of Hageffen Street into Haturim, on its way to pick up the rest of its allotted passengers from locations round the town. Two rucksack-laden youths from Ramot Eshkol. Two returning tourists from the Plaza Sheraton. A nut-brown stewardess from the Holyland Hotel, an old orthodox man from Bayit Vegan. Last time around the City, the hills, the terraces, the quarried stone. Posters of Rabbi Levine on lampposts, billboards, pillboxes, the gates of schools. Visit the Museum of the Future Holocaust. The Inevitable CAN Be Avoided.

'. . . That window, I daresay you could have fixed it, it's been stiff for fifteen years . . . I'm sure that crack in the bathtub wasn't

379

there, but what can't be helped can't be helped . . . in the old days we had to make do with much less . . . people take so much for granted now . . . but there's no point in complaining . . .'

'. . . I often thought, Avremel, in these last years, as I gallop towards the worms, what was the point? there's a cliché . . . and – there's no point – another cliché. The will of God – well, I don't believe that . . . succouring the victims of oppression . . . well, we pushed it on to someone else, some say, and we're not so free ourselves . . . In the end we make of ourselves what we can . . . only if I'm honest, I didn't really do that . . . except for the stamps, and look – I've burnt all those, see that funny pile of ash in the garden: that's twenty years of philately, Avremel, poof! It goes so fucking easy . . . it doesn't matter a jot here, among the cow pats, in this fake pioneers' dream . . . so I made your mother happy, with an act of destruction . . . at last, she thinks, Baruch's a man . . .'

Make something of yourself, Avremel.

The humid heat of the coastal plain hits him. The Tel Aviv–Lod Intersection. Triple carriageways and flyovers. The tail of a plane in the distance.

The previous week's swan song from Yissachar, in the farewell air-conditioning of the Tel Aviv plush flat. Bentov's footsteps clomping above, the scrape of the dragging of his tripod for a resumed still life frame. 'He has got himself a set of macrolenses now, Avram. He is into microscopic close ups. Cigarette ash on floors, carpets, tracking shots of bugs, ants. The grain in wooden cupboards, wardrobes. Mothballs rolling down sleeves. Myself, I'm getting back into money. Cash, consumer goods, bonds. This past year was a dead loss, Avram. The ideologues fucked us all up. But it's a mere stumble in the Long March. Normal transmission will resume . . . But good luck to you, old friend, it's a far far better thing that you do, et cetera . . . Which airline are you flying? M—m Charter? There's one thing you must keep in mind . . .'

And Blok remembered this final word of advice, repeated out of the window of the fourteenth floor in a desperate cry, recalling it as he strapped in to the battered, cramped seat of the charter airliner bearing him out, out, out, the single-choice menu open upon his knees, as the orthodox passengers quibbled feistily over the purity of the glatt kosher meal, the shout, cast over the sweaty streets:

'WHATEVER YOU DO, DON'T EAT THE FISH!'

The aircraft rolled, rumbled, thundered, pawing the ground, leaping forward. It left the ground, banked, thrust higher, crossed the thin line of the coast, the soft lapping Mediterranean waves, entering an autumnal fog.

'M—m Airlines flight 016 welcomes you aboard. Our staff will now demonstrate the emergency procedures. We hope you have a pleasant trip.'

He sank back in the seat, grateful for the pinion of the fastened safety belt. He closed his eyes, remembering, for no particular reason, the words of his ex-neighbour, the merchant seaman Sirkin, who had brought an ape to the promised land:

'I tell you, if I had not seen it with my own eyes, heard what I heard with my own ears, experienced what I know I experienced, dreamed what I knew were true dreams, there is no way I would have believed one fucking word of the entire megillah.'